Copyright © Lojze Kovačič, 1984-85
Copyright © Ksaverija Kogovšek, Darko Kovačič, Janko Kovačič, and Beletrina Academic
Press, published in arrangement with Michael Gaeb Literary Agency

Originally published as *Prišleki II* by Slovenska matica, 1984

English language translation © Michael Biggins, 2020

First Archipelago Books Edition, 2020

Library of Congress Cataloging-in-Publication Data
available upon request.

Archipelago Books
232 3rd Street #A111
Brooklyn, NY 11215
www.archipelagobooks.org

Distributed by Penguin Random House
www.penguinrandomhouse.com

Cover art: Photograph R 49 Bild-1432, Bundesarchiv (Federal Archives of Germany).

This book was published with the support of Trubar Foundation
at the Slovene Writers' Association, Ljubljana, Slovenia.

This work was made possible by the New York State Council on the Arts
with the support of Governor Andrew M. Cuomo and the New York State Legislature.

Archipelago Books also gratefully acknowledges the generous support
from Lannan Foundation, the Carl Lesnor Family Foundation,
and the New York City Department of Cultural Affairs.

PRINTED IN THE UNITED STATES OF AMERICA

Lojze Kovačič

NEWCOMERS

BOOK TWO

Translated from the Slovenian by Michael Biggins

archipelago books

NEWCOMERS

THE ITALIAN SOLDIERS would cook spaghetti and vegetable soup on mess vehicles that were parked in the courtyard of the casino. They doled some of it out to kids...Karel, Ivan, Andrej and I would run there with canisters...We would wait in the entryway next to the Rio Café until the soldiers in the courtyard had eaten their fill. Then the cook would call out that we could approach one of the kettles on the high flatbeds. The ladles they used were as big as helmets: our gallon containers had never held so much spaghetti and tomato sauce, or rice with big chunks of meat...Now, in addition to breakfast, at which we crumbled into our coffee white melba toast from the crates we'd brought home, we could also look forward to hearty and truly filling main meals at our table...Then the Ninth Army Corps of the Ljubljana Region issued a decree that by a certain date all inhabitants had to return any weapons, clothing or foodstuffs that they'd looted from the barracks of the former Yugoslav Army. Anyone failing to do so who was found to have such items in their possession after the two-week grace period had passed would be punished: 1; 2; 3...Vati and I hid the crates as best we could, under some rags and old clothes... No, we weren't going to give up that glorious toast at any cost, not even under threat of the death penalty...Sadly I was no longer able to take it with me onto the street because there were spies everywhere, and we couldn't let anyone, not even the most innocent person, know that we had government-issued supplies at home.

At that time, they began using machines to cut down the gigantic bronze statue of King Aleksandar that was surrounded by a railing in the Star Park ... It had been barely a few months since the formal unveiling, which the young King Petar II had attended wearing the uniform of an air force lieutenant ... Before that, our whole school had gone to watch them use pulleys to hoist parts of the monument onto its high marble cube of a pedestal ... an enormous boot in a stirrup ... the muscular hindquarters of the horse ... the king's gloved hand holding the reins ... half of his head with a pince-nez and that narrow hat. Now all of that bronze lay around in scales of varying sizes or dropped onto the sand ...

I would go with Karel and Ivan to collect thorny-husked wild chestnuts off the roofs of the butchers' sheds, which were also about to be demolished. Beyond the barracks, the tall columns and the denticulated roof of the new market were already going up, reaching from the Dragon Bridge to the Triple Bridge ... From the river, its facade looked like a synagogue ... The plans for it were by the same white-bearded, little man who had designed the chapels and a temple in the grove of the dead at Žale Cemetery ... From the barracks to the fence posts of the new market, we could see Italian soldiers in the company of young women. There were market vendors, housemaids, salesgirls, all sorts of them ... We crept to the edge of the flat roof in order to see ... They would be hugging and kissing. Some of the girls would be pressing those dark, wavy haircuts to their breasts, while others would be trying to fend them off, so that the soldiers had to pick up the girls' arms and put them around their necks ... I felt sorry for the poor girls, but not all of them were equally deserving of pity…Once we caught one sitting on the seat of a bicycle that was leaning against a fence, with an Italian soldier standing on a block of wood in front of her…Ivan practically burst out laughing. Karel and I had to stifle him with our hands…The girl on the bicycle was still pretty young, blonde, wearing a blue apron – she was probably from one of the fruit vending stands in the market…She had her legs lifted up. She had thighs like some statue, like columns, hair on her ass and fur up front all the way to her navel   The fur opened up…like a mailman's pouch…Ivan couldn't stifle his laughter. Idiot! The Italian glanced up…He had his trousers bunched at his feet like a basket…"*Avanti!*" he roared…and he grabbed onto his red grenade…We jumped to our feet and ran over the rooftops until we reached the Dragon Bridge…Somebody whistled to us. It was some other soldier who was walking between the sheds and signaling something to us…"Hey!" he shouted. He pointed to a barrack and made that gesture…Poking the index finger of his right hand into the gap formed by the thumb and index finger of his left… That meant fucking. Gestures like that didn't suit grown-ups at all. He pointed toward the barrack again, and we nodded. He turned around, took one step, and then, as if suddenly realizing something, turned back around. "*Arrividerci!*" we waved at him…Although these weren't real soldiers in any sense of the word…more like pranksters in their baggy, comedic uniforms…you still had to take them seriously, if only on account of the grenades they carried and their hot temper, much less so because of the carbines, which were more suited to cavalry than foot soldiers.

Behind every bush on Golovec Hill, beneath the parapets of the castle, in all the entryways, someone was making out with somebody. The Unity Cinema showed movies from ten in the morning till eight at night…two at a time, lasting four hours…If you got there halfway through the first one, you could watch it to the end, then see the second film straight through, and finally the first half of the other…and then you could go. The Italians sat in the crowded theater with whole bevies of women. They hugged and made out…various voices, smacking sounds, the rustle and zip of clothes emanated from the shadowy groping couples while the movie was showing…In some of the second-tier boxes, which were always the first to sell out, not a single head showed over the railing. That's where the NCOs were rumored to make love to women right on the seats…Somewhere toward the middle of the first or second film, when none of those ticket-taking men in their blue uniforms with the silver trim were left standing by the velvet cord in the lobby…just the cashier, who was knitting in her ticket booth…we hurried out and crept up the stairs to the balcony level. We opened the doors, then shut them again…We would be a bit tense, as though any instant we might witness a murder. Then we pulled the velvet curtain aside and looked…The gray glow from the screen and the red bulbs over the exits were the only illumination…Between the balcony railing and the wall of the theater there was one dark figure lying on top of another, all the way back. They were wheezing and sniffling, not at all like the actors up on the screen…Through the dark, somewhere in the middle, there was some fuss underway…When our eyes adjusted to the darkness, someone was standing on his knees on a seat, showing his luminous rear end, cleft down the middle…or he may just have been feeling sick. There was something in front of him…a heap of outer garments or actually a woman, on her back, naked?…"*Maledetta puttana!*" he said…He shook the dark heap like a pear tree. It was a showdown…or maybe a murder…Amid all the commotion several of them went running out…If that wasn't just a pile of coats on the seats…it was some poor woman…unless she hadn't resisted or simply didn't care, like Andrej's Marjana back on Jail Street…We were as quiet as mice…We went back to the main level, as if we were going to watch the movie. We didn't want to be present if someone was about to get killed or strangled…But from the auditorium there were other places we could go. Up steps that ran alongside the wall and through a door onto the stage…behind the big screen and the curtain…The images of the actors struck through the screen, and the subtitles ran backward, from right to left…It was such a dark, cavernous place that we felt like dwarves…There were chairs, tables and pictures in big frames leaned up against the walls…Occasionally we could make out couples there in the murk…one or more…They would be moving at the foot of the high curtains that covered the back wall…invisible hammers striking them from above…We kept together, as if the three of us were a couple…They panted and moaned and sometimes squealed, which you could hear through the words the actors spoke in the movie, through explosions from the guns of Navarone, through the music or birds twittering on mountain trails…We could also see them going out…two shadows, one after the other…together or separate again…Sometimes nobody was there. The floor was smooth and slippery...Little chocolate wrappers were strewn all around, little Camelia paper handtowels, balloons, white and soggy rubbers which, if you stepped on them, would squirt out that stuff that we men had in our scrotums and that babies came from...It smelled bafflingly like orangutans and fish. What was with that, why sardines and monkeys, of all things?...The floorboards were so slick with slime that you would slip on the little balloons...Behind the high curtain next to the wall, there was a door that led out to a courtyard...but there was no way out of the courtyard. You couldn't climb over the tall iron fence on the left, where there were grave markers lying around on the other side, because the stone cutters would catch you...On the right, behind a wooden fence, was a printing shop and the Railwayman's Gym, which had boxing rings and parallel bars in its courtyard. We had to go back into the auditorium and make sure that none of the uniformed ushers caught us...Did they or didn't they know about the mysterious things that the soldiers and girls were secretly doing in the balconies and on the stage behind the screen?

GISELA'S LEG HAD BEGUN SWELLING at the hip...maybe from a miserable fall she'd had when she slipped off the wide plank over the hole meant for a bathtub?...Her hip swelled up like a balloon...She had to stay lying down, because she couldn't stand on that leg...The doctor came and prescribed cold compresses...The swelling didn't subside. It paralyzed the entire limb...The heart and soul of our family!...Clairi's nerves were shot, and mother got so depressed she forgot to yell at me. Even Vati was so overcome that he would go over to the corner where we'd made up a bed for Gisela... She lay there, playing with her African dolly... That figurine had never been a proper baby doll. The dark paint obliterated any trace of a facial expression and the hoops, earrings and wire coils around her neck made her a grown-up... I made her a new doll out of rags, some furniture to go with it and all kinds of other things... a little man out of chestnuts... a paper movie theater... and various cut-out games she could amuse herself with whenever I wasn't home... The swelling continued to grow. We had to take her to see a doctor. The old wagon was too small for her now. We used the Hamman's handcart to take her to the hospital near St. Peter's Church... The doctor was a nice blonde lady, Dr. Zora, who spoke excellent German. No longer dependent on my faulty transla-tions, mother and Clairi were able to go over Gisela's condition with her thoroughly, and I didn't have to worry about blurting out some-thing that might actually harm her. They sent her to get X-rayed... then they drained the swelling... and then they put her leg in a plaster cast all the way past the hip, up to her waist. Every four weeks she had to come back to get the swelling drained again, and every two months to get a new cast. She wasn't allowed to walk on that leg... The hospital recommended a flat wagon where she could lie stretched out and motionless. There was no wagon like that to be found anywhere in Ljubljana, not in the second-hand stores and not by posting a want ad... We would carry Gisela outside on our outstretched arms – Clairi, mother and I – and set her down on some pillows on the embankment, on a bench in the Star Park or in Tivoli... She didn't complain. The only time she cried had been when she fell off that oak plank...

My school days at Graben came to a close. I barely managed to pass. With grades like that, a better future for me was out of the question... My parents enrolled me in the trade school in Prule so I could learn shopkeeping, commerce or maybe some trade. *"Bubi muß eine kaufmannische Bahn einschlagen,"** mother said. The kids who went to the school in Prule were ones who had decided to become merchants or craftsmen or were themselves the sons of tradespeople, locksmiths, mechanics or semi-peasants from Two Emperors' Road or Žabjak... brawlers and kids who were too clever by half... If I thought about my life much, it made me depressed... Two years in the hospital and then a sanitarium in Switzerland on account of my lungs... first grade in Basel, which I then had to repeat in Cegelnica... third grade, which I failed... *"Der Bubi hat überhaupt kein Köpfchen oder keine Ambition für das Studium oder eine höhere Laufbahn,"*** is what mother said. I was a pitiful blockhead. The world would have been better off without me... If only I could have killed myself like that fourteen-year-old Gregor from Slovenj Gradec, who got written about in the papers for having hanged himself in some abandoned shepherd's hut after he got bad grades and didn't dare show them to his father. If only I had the guts do something like that!

ONE DAY, I TOOK GISELA WITH ME to the Triple Bridge, where I was going to join Ivan and Karel in throwing pebbles at the fish... I

*We need to get Bubi on track to become a businessman.
**Bubi has no head at all or at least no ambition for book-learning and a better life.

set her down on a patch of fine grass by the steps where no one would bother her. As the water level had lowered, a small sandbank had formed at the foot of a ladder leading down from the embankment... This was practically tailor-made for us, allowing us to spot the fish through the algae and then hit them dead on, though they escaped from us anyway. The fish were common bleaks, long and translucent, like laboratory distilling flasks...and good eating, except that they stank of stagnant water and putrid scum...Instead of them, we hauled onto the gravel empty army canteens, rusty cartridge clips, rifle bolts, big boxes for bullets, and warped pieces of cardboard. I was trying to start a fire with the cardboard when Ivan began shoving me and pointing upward. Tatjana was standing on the steps above Gisela. She was still making the rounds on our embankment as she had before the war broke out. She stood by the wall, which also bulged out at that point, leaning her straw-colored head over the water...I squinted as though from the glare, but still our eyes met...So instead I started looking around, because my face felt like it was on fire...Karel and Ivan kept shoving me from either side. "Go on! Call out to her!" All I needed to do was holler or wave a hand, but I couldn't. Besides, there was some man in a black hat standing up there, looking across the river at the Mayer Building...Out of the corner of my eye, I noticed the head up above withdraw from the edge of the wall..."She told Franci that she'd like to be your girlfriend," Ivan said. Franci, the eternal delivery boy?..."Venn?"...Back when they were both still delivering newspapers door to door?..."Recently"...A streetcar rumbled across the bridge...When I turned to look back at the wall, there was a gaping empty space up at the top. Too late, too late. Angry at myself, I climbed up the ladder and then dashed up the steps past Gisela. I caught sight of her in the distance...near the Black Cat Café, the shadow of her red dress. "Dit she really say zat?" I asked greedily. It was shameful to ask something like that. It betrayed a perverse desire to do something like the grown-ups, walking down the sidewalk in their big polka-dotted shoes or spiky pumps..."Yes, she did...three times," Ivan said. "Before she was going with Sandy, and now she wants to go with you. She said that to Franci and Firant." He was grinning with every crease of his face, like a cracked platter...My eyes were hurting. "Tit you hear zat, too?" I turned to Karel...This was important now, what he was about to tell me...I looked him straight in the face and that wet hank of hair that stuck to his forehead..."No," he shook his head. I looked into Ivan's bulging eyes as I tried to calm down...I should have called out to her or at least waved. I was furious with myself. The worst thing is when it's your own fault...That night, I thought of her again. She appeared over my headboard, like a kind soul that my own indecisiveness had driven away...

At one point during those days, I got caught up in a round of that stupid game "Daddy, what time is it?" on account of Tončka and that posh friend of hers from Fish Street. They designated me Daddy. I took up my position at the door to the warehouse...while all of the others, except Karel and Gisela, who was lying on the cart, lined up down the sidewalk and started asking me questions...I was supposed to answer them: "three elephant steps, five insect steps, two puppy steps, six bunny steps"...as they advanced two, three, a half, a quarter of a step at

· 12

a time...depending on what time I gave them...The first one to reach me would replace me as Daddy...During the game somebody noticed Tatjana...and, when I caught sight of her red dress, I swore I was going to talk to her this time...Ivan was just in the process of asking me the time when she appeared around the corner of the Black Cat Café, which was crowded with *bersaglieri*. I looked at the ground and didn't look up until she reached the last tree...My God, how my voice worked like a bellows...and burst like a bomb at the same time..."Tatjana, vie ton't you choin our kame?"...Tatjana turned around...To my great relief I could see she was red all the way up to her forehead...Ivan jumped in, stalwart that he was. "Come on!" He pushed the line back, reorganizing it...Tatjana immediately joined at the end...She fidgeted with her hands, because she was the newcomer, and kept turning her head to each side. Tončka fell quiet, while the others leaned forward to get a good look at her..."Your turn to ask," Ivan said. My God, she was gleaming into my eyes like a diamond. "Daddy, what time is it?" she blurted out at last. She had a slightly husky voice..."Four," I hollered, but quite decently. Others asked, too. I didn't hear all of them. While wanting to be fair, I wound up being anything but...All five of them gradually drew closer, while maintaining their orderly line...they were right in front of me when I dealt Tatjana "five insect steps"...She came right up close, her belly brushing against me. My head practically exploded...What now? Just "two mousy steps," and she would be at the door. I had seen lots of movies and now they came to my rescue. I put my hands up...with the cruelest scene from *The Indian Tomb* in mind...I took her by the shoulders and pulled her by the fabric of her cheap dress toward me...while just at that moment a window above me opened, and the shaven head of a young man jutted out. I let go of her shoulders and then the whole line circled around us and began jumping up and down...Firant, Ivan, Marko. "Long live the bride and groom!"..."Long live the bride and groom!"...I couldn't see, I was so completely beside myself...Tatjana grinned bashfully... The rest of them cheered...Gisela clapped, although she couldn't see what was happening from where she sat...When Tatjana assumed a place beside me, I stepped away from the door. Ivan, Franci and Marko climbed up onto the wall. All of them except Tončka laughed, waved, and dangled their legs...The young man up above put on a cap and disappeared back into his room. Thank god!...Firant, Ivan and Marko were breaking off willow branches, throwing them onto the pavement and shouting, "Hosanna to the bride and groom! Hosanna to the bride and groom!" All the others joined in with them, even Karel, just not Tončka or Gisela...Ivan even pushed us out into the street, where we had to walk over the branches and leaves...It was like the arrival of Jesus in Jerusalem at Easter...I didn't know which way was up... Tatjana's pale, creased lips were smiling ever so slightly...her hair gleamed like a sunflower and her eyes were a murky blue. I thought I was going to have to swallow the whole street, dust and gravel included, before we would even get to Cobblers' Bridge...There, on no man's land, I would quickly bid her adieu, and each of us would go our own way...That snow-white bridge with its columns and lanterns! "Oafer zehr, tomorrow mawnink at ten." I pointed toward Breg, where the benches and bomb shelter were...Tatjana looked me straight in the face…I squeezed my eyelids shut to stop the magic…Scoot! I thought to myself, hoping that would hurry her on. Tatjana crossed the bridge, while my jokester friends kept shouting and scattering sand on the bridge and into the water…I had to get away from there fast…Outside the Albanian laundry on Jail Street, I leaned on a rail that ran along the storefront: I needed five minutes without any witnesses before I went to get Gisela…I'd never thought there could be so many things going on in my head. At first I saw everything red, until I recalled that Tatjana's dress had been brown, yet even then everything kept showing as red…like a blood-drenched cloud…Then her eyes came floating into view, outsized, gigantic, convex. Their pale irises and watery whites…Her lips had some kind of crease down the middle…Her locks of blond hair cascading downward but then turning up at the end…Her dress, which breathed…Her hands, her fingers like sunbeams, the half moons of her nails…She went flying over the wall…heading uphill past the Kantz Drugstore…past the red library and the pavilion. She kept flying into the depths of the sky…soaring over the wheat fields of Nove Jarše, over meadows that were full of people, as if for an air show…I hurried after her, following her trail… in the clearings between the clouds…with a bag full of money stolen from all of the banks…It was getting toward evening, with a black cloud floating over the Sava…In front of an altar, countless candles were lit…canons and a bishop wearing at least twenty chasubles were marrying us, and the bishop had just put a little crown on her head… The White Prince emerged from his chapel…Then cooks and bakers came running in from all sides carrying huge platters…Fried chickens, veal roulades, fish, whole whales…green cakes, blue cakes, lemon cakes…Heraldic lamps were lit in the garden as candle-lit ornaments floated down the river…Liliputians from Polynesia strewed jewels all over the glass roof covering the veranda…amethysts, which made our surroundings violet, and topazes, which turned the people yellow. Tyrševa Street echoed with joyous shouts of "Hosanna! The bride and groom! Hosanna!"…At a barrier, the Holy Cross streetcar was crushing a crowd from the front, while near the post office the Rakovnik streetcar nudged at it from behind…The crowd drove us upward, like windmills, toward Basel…

This went on for a long time, all the way until morning…I felt weak from no sleep. I washed up out of the bucket, brushed my teeth and combed my hair, but still my head didn't stop aching…I put a toy cork pistol into my pocket…Ivan and Karel were still asleep. I paced back and forth outside their open window with its iron crosses…The rooster was already up and strutting around their room. I tried scaring it with my hands, to get it to crow or jump on their bed and wake them up…What a day! Every object had its own, completely independent body. The bridge. A wall. Some trees. A cart. The sign over a business. One huge agglomeration of independent bodies. I would never have dared to cross over the bridge by myself…

Finally, Ivan and Karel came plodding out of their storefront… "Let's kow," I said…Franci came running from the pub carrying his delivery bag for the *Morning*, shouting, "Wait for me! Wait for me!"… Did we really have to take him along, too? Wouldn't that make too many of us, mortify Tatjana and cause her to run? There was a blue sweater out squirming on Cobblers' Bridge. Firant! He was hopping over the columns and then bent down to look back at us through his outstretched legs...So he was out on the prowl early, too! "Let's kow," my hand pointed the way ahead, all on its own...We climbed up on the shelter...My heart was pounding under my shirt, causing my chest to throb visibly. So that was it!...The four of them sat down on the railing and looked at me like some sort of champion...They lay stomach down on the patch of grass, clasping each other's ankles to form a merry-go-round...Then they tried doing somersaults... At last we caught sight of Tatjana outside the Knight's Restaurant... and everything else around us on Breg became inconsequential. She was carrying a basket in one hand and had her little brother in tow with the other. With her was another girl wearing a plain yellow dress with white sleeves...I went toward Tatjana...with the whole phalanx marching behind me, grinning..."Hi," I raised my hand like the goddess on the lira...Tatjana blushed and her friend laughed out loud...perhaps she was older or perhaps just taller than her. "Vehr are you koink?"..."To Kham's Bakery for bread." "Shall ve ko tokezer?" "Sure," she said. All of us turned toward the House of Furniture on Jewish Street. Both girls looked back, and the other one in yellow emitted an abrupt but calm laugh...very sweet, very restrained. The whole squad made its way behind me, while I walked two or three paces behind the two girls...I didn't know if I was supposed to walk abreast of Tatjana or if I should walk with the boys...so here I was, in the middle, between the two girls laughing ahead and the guys grinning behind, walking stupidly, like a cow with a saddle...

Tatjana's gait was kind of strange…She would fling one foot to the side, as though her ankles were injured or her heels had been smashed. I hoped it wasn't as bad as what Gisela had. But with each step her calves shook mightily…At the top of the hill, she went into the store with her friend and her little brother…We stayed outside. This was a transitional stairway, a thundering space where you could hear every sound, even if all you did was stamp your bare feet on the ground… Although Kham didn't have anything in his display windows anymore, the place still smelled strongly of the hams, cheeses, spices and choc-olate that were there months before. I got my pistol ready, and when Tatjana reappeared, I shouted "All hail!" and fired it. That was a bang! It lit up the stairway, knocked down a column, and at that instant, on the other side of the street in front of the Prinčič Store, we saw an Italian drop to the ground and look for cover behind a wall. That wasn't a bang, it was a thunderbolt!…Tatjana laughed, while a patrol of *carabinieri* was already running our way from the Star Park and a couple of *bersaglieri* in helmets dashed down the street…We set out at a sprint. I ran after Tatjana, her brother, the other girl, my friends…We hid in a gigantic entryway on Gosposka Street across from the university and kept on the lookout…Nothing happened… Tatjana got ready to head home with her brother. "Two o'clock at the shelter!" she said. "I'll bring a blanket." I couldn't believe my ears…"You're koink to prink…a planket?"…I thought she was about to slap me in the face…"I'll bring a blanket from home," she said. She and her brother ran off toward the library…She really did limp a little…

MUSIC ENGULFED MY HEAD...it was inside my head, in my chest...I had no idea where to go or stay in order to get away from it. It experimented with a hundred-thousand different sounds inside me...a hellish clamor. I was incapable of describing what I'd done just a minute before...Was I quicker than it or not?...I went down to the river, then came back up and stood on the walkway. The trees on the side of castle hill behind Hamman's Laundry swayed, green and innocent, although they were hundreds of years older than me. The trees next to the warehouse were a lot younger...If I tried to imagine what might happen that afternoon, everything got ripped to shreds in my head...I could guess...It would probably be like the far side of the market, during shows at the Unity, or behind the bushes on Golovec Hill. My God!...I asked Karel to go with me...and at the same time prayed that he wouldn't. And then, two seconds later, that he would... I had already seen girls' pee-pees...Anica's, Adrijana's, the Gypsy girl's on Bohorič Street, Gisela's...that tender, downy bulge with the red slit down the middle...a cute little smile, so forthright!...On the far side of the market I'd also seen that frightening mail pouch propped up on a bicycle seat and covered with bristles all the way up to the navel. What was it like when it got inflamed with love? Red? Yellow? Did it sting?...The music took no heed of my thoughts...it tripped them, threw them down on the floor, so that they rolled all around...That music! All those sounds...from a piccolo to the booming of waves! I ran outside with that whole orchestra in my head...people must have been able to hear it...and indeed, they were standing still! They were listening...Here it comes! Any instant, I was going to discover the mystery of mysteries...the meaning of everything!...*ka-slam*! And again everything was rolling around on the floor in my head...I sat down on the wall and waited for Karel and Ivan to come...and for the clock on the Franciscan Church to strike two...I could have ripped out both clock hands and broken them over my knee, it dawdled so much...All of the clocks on the churches and City Hall either rang after each other or all at once, so that I never got the time right... I ran to look at St. Jacob's Church...it was pretty far away, in a different neighborhood...self-sufficient, independent of anything else, it could show the right time dispassionately...then I ran back to the cart... There was quite a crowd on City Square...I noticed their big shoes, their waxed hats with polka dots, their neckties, their painted lips... all that grown-up maturity, all that rancid old age...Oh, just give me a minute and I would catch up with them...pass them...wipe all of them out at the finish line!...I wouldn't have to become old, wrinkly and stupid...Now and then the music subsided, like a train in the distance. Then there were both of the gussied-up clock hands amid the Roman numerals. 1:55...Now I was really dead...

As ivan and i were crossing the bridge, I just closed my eyes...Ivan was talking about Tatjana. "She's totally gone over you," he wheezed through his broad, blunt nose...I could see her face before me, smiling at me, as she had that morning outside Kham's...Instead of Karel, Franci came running toward the shelter..."Beat it!" Ivan swung at him with a branch. "Beat it, snitch!"..."You're not koink to fight!" I shouted so loudly that I went deaf. I needed to calm down!

"If that creep is coming, I'm going home," Ivan roared...I ran after him and took him by the arm. "No, please, stay viss me!"...Although I had become used to walking barefoot, I still kept kicking at stones... O, how tired I was. I sat down on the vent of an airshaft. I closed my eyes. I couldn't go on..."Bubi's going to have a girlfriend now," I heard Ivan saying behind me..."All chiefs do. Why shouldn't he?" Franci said...Ass kisser!...If only I had just a little more courage...the tiniest bit, so that I didn't care...Finally the red dress appeared outside the Knight's Restaurant...Tatjana...When she reached the bakery, I ran out to meet her. She was smiling a bit in the distance, I could see that, and it gave me strength...She really was carrying a rolled-up blanket under one arm, and that made me feel elated again...When I reached her, she suddenly scowled...lips compressed, eyes harsh. "Why did you bring those two creeps with you?" she asked angrily...My arms hung uselessly at my sides...the charm had almost been squashed... I had done something stupid. "Zey're chust out for a valk," I said voicelessly...As though moving my lips while reading...I was seized with despair...If only she were Gisela, so that I'd have at least some sense of how to treat her..."They're not going with us!" she said again... How was I supposed to get rid of them?...They were standing just a couple of paces behind us. If only they could figure it out on their own...But no, Franci was looking at Ivan, who – stupider yet – was gaping at the corner of the House of Furniture. If only something would sweep them off the street, or if Tatjana and I could just take off into the sky...It was unbearable for me on the ground here. There was no place anymore where I could just be!...I was digging at the dirt with my big toe…it was gray, but shone white…amazingly, I was unable to think…"Zo vehr ahr you sinkink off koink?"…Thank god for that question, which saved me! She smiled almost from ear to ear. "Mirje."…"Mirje? I voot razzer kow to Tiffoli or ze kessel or Kolovec"… The words were as big as mountains…"No, I took Jurij there after the store. There aren't any people, no houses"…My head was ringing… with all kinds of noises and sounds…"How olt is your prozer?" She laughed as she had outside Kham's…"What are you thinking…he's just my half-brother…and he's three years old"…"Let's kow," I said voicelessly, again as if reading and moving my lips…

The walls shook as a car drove by in reverse…My feet spun around so fast that I limped the first few steps. But it was worse in my head and my chest…Everything pounded and rang…like a pipe organ!… and I added everything to it myself…flesh, bones, spirit, breath… What if I was about to have a seizure or come down with pneumonia again?…Outside the bookbinder's on the corner, Tatjana turned around. "I'm going to walk across New Square alone, so that mother doesn't see me. I'll wait for you on Roman Street."…I lingered outside the display window…That was good, because everything had come to a pause…I stood there for a long time, until she got a long way ahead, until she vanished around the corner of the Academy, until she'd been gone for quite a while…then I also set out…and both of those squirts followed suit…Near the red library I saw her again just as she was turning around a corner past the shoe shop…the red wall that had little crags jutting out of it, stretching out to infinity…I next caught sight of Tatjana outside a grocery store…The crowns of sparse trees loomed up over the Cloisters, where the stinking urinal burbled with cool, clear water... It wasn't until the "Accordion" that I saw her again... she was standing outside the store, waiting for me...

Now we were amid the wide sidewalks of Roman Street, which had people walking down it and cars racing past, and which had the new school dispensary at its far end... My God! How awful it was to walk with a girl that you liked!... My arm grazed against hers as we walked, but she just kept looking ahead. Both of the little buffoons were making their way behind us, shoulder to shoulder like a couple of sotted *gendarmes*... Tatjana took my hand in hers... which was slender and white... neither hot nor sweaty, only the pads at the tips of her fingers were pink... five long, pink fingers... It was awkward when a grown-up man appeared on the sidewalk, then some woman... When an Italian in his baggy uniform came toward us, I didn't pay him the slightest attention... The Italians were as artless as children... they laughed more in embarrassment and more out of fear than the most timid child... Just as we were about to cross a side street, Tatjana reached down for my blue shorts and squeezed my balls... The bells started ringing ever so gently... She smiled when I looked at her, and suddenly it occurred to me: I've got a girl now, whom I can touch, too... not just some vision floating in the air... What's more, now we belonged to each other, like a prince and princess... her to me and me to her – two in possession of both... and she was immeasurably braver than I was... On the far side of the street, as we both simultaneously lifted a foot onto the sidewalk, she grabbed me even harder by my pee-pee... I quickly put my hand over her skirt... trying to cover that mound, but it was too far away, there was too much air under the fabric…and then some lady wearing a black hat came toward us, which made me give up…My hair stood all on end as that bell rang in my head…Not, of course, in the middle of the desert of Roman Street, but in some hiding place, amid the leaves of a dense shrub, once we were alone, we were going to undress and do all the things that were now dancing before my eyes like red oranges. She was impatient, too…I could sense it from the way she swung her arms…Those two, hugging the fence but still following us, were grinning…a little afraid, bewildered, a bit glassy-eyed…When she took off her dress…I could already see her naked, as white – no – as yellow as butter…Below her belly I was going to see what I had never seen, ever…in my mind's eye I had to paste a pink apricot there with a crease down the middle…As we walked across the sand, she leaned her head toward me, pressing it to my shoulder. Was it true that I had a girl who was giving herself to me the way, so far, I'd only submitted to myself?…Was it true that now…long before the future arrived…I was going to have the most wonderful creature that existed on earth…a woman? Was the sort of bliss that I'd known only in dreams even possible in real life?

We crossed the main street, far from the dispensary, in order not to run into any fellow schoolkids who might just then be coming from the doctor's…Mirje was just on the other side of the tall building of the Technical School now…A great big grassy space enclosed by a wall, overgrown with ivy, and, outside the wall, a hummock with a bench, on which two lovers, a boy and a girl, were sitting…On the other side, next to a dense bean patch, there was something else:

a wide, level wall with arches…"That over there…I'd forgotten about…Those are the ruins of an old Roman house that they've excavated"…It really did look like the wall had once been part of a house. Although it was impossible to imagine how they had lived here…how ancient Romans in their white togas could have entered and walked around the house and felt as at home here in Mirje as they did in Rome…The ground under the arches was all dirt, but full of trash, cigarette butts and matches. It was a good hiding place, except that some fat woman was weeding the bean patch next door…I looked at the arch facing the wall and the bench with the two lovers. "I'fe kott an itea!" I said…We would use the blanket to cover that side, keeping it in place with stones up top and down below, I explained. Then we could be in the arch like a tent…Tatjana nodded…I unfolded the blanket, which had red fabric flowers sewn into it. It reached to the grass, and Ivan and Franci gathered stones we could use to secure it…First, I told Tatjana, we're going to play house, so the old lady over there in the bean patch doesn't suspect anything. "You're koink to cook ant zen you're koink to call all sree off us to tinner"…"I'm only cooking for you and me," Tatjana said firmly…She darted over to the wall and snatched a few leaves of lettuce that were hanging over the edge…The fat lady looked out from behind her beanpoles and began shrieking, her face flushed red, "You miserable brat! Thief!"…No one paid her any attention, although it was annoying, because she kept glaring at us from her bean patch…Tatjana poured sand and blades of grass, which were supposed to be soup and meat, onto the leaves of lettuce, which stood in for plates. We did some "work" around the house, and here

I noticed those "burning coals," red flowers with a black center, and the blue and orange "tousled ladies," as the Frenchman's wife in Jarše used to call them...Ivan and Franci helped the owner as day laborers, until Tatjana called us in to dinner...We climbed up on the wall where she was perched in such a way that you could see all the way up to her yellow panties...We made appreciative *yum* noises and smacked our lips, then Tatjana fixed us dessert, which was cakes made out of dirt that we ate by flinging them off the wall...Soon we got tired of this stupid game, out of which we got nothing aside from blunting the attention of the old market lady and the young couple on the bench...

Finally the old lady left her bean patch..."Shall vee ket town zehr now?" I asked, as red as a lobster..."Wait just a little bit longer, till we can't hear her anymore," Tatjana said...Finally it became quiet... I climbed down under the arch and crouched down next to the blanket. I could see the path through a tiny hole...and the bench with the young couple through another one near the top. Ivan and Franci were dawdling outside...now they felt really embarrassed...I called them in. Ivan took a seat next to me. He had the same glazed look and red face as before...Franci could barely breathe through his stopped-up nose for all the excitement...Tatjana came down off the wall – *pffft* – like a gymnast, and when she came in, she had to bend down because the arch was too low...There were way too many of us inside now... Franci lay half outside in the sun...Tatjana was really brave! But also rather mean...angry. "You two get out!" she ordered..."Only Bubi is my boyfriend!" "Pleasse, Tatjana, ton't," I said. "Come on, Tatjana, please," Ivan pleaded. Tatjana, crouched down, crept over

toward me. "Vat now?" I blurted. "Off with your shorts," she said…
She remained crouching but managed to get hers off…they were
swim shorts…as though she were about to go to the toilet. Then
she got on her knees. She lifted her dress, exposing her belly, which
was white and not very big…The other two were as quiet as mice…
I didn't want to look there, but still…there was nothing to see…her
belly button…was that thing that was way down between her thighs
and looked like a slug her pee-pee? Maybe she didn't have anything
and that's why she was the way she was…But that wasn't possible…
Oh, Tatjana had to know lots more than all three of us put together.
She paid no attention to either of them…and went straight for me.
"Take your shorts off and stretch out your legs," she said. I won't do
it…Ivan and Franci had already pulled their shorts down to their
thighs. Their pee-pees were dangling…both identical…like two
white bread croissants…Undressing in front of a girl was like subor-
dinating yourself to her. I wasn't going to obey anybody. They could
beg me or order me, it didn't matter. I wasn't letting anyone get the
better of me. And if she was going to try to force me, I'd wallop her
so hard she'd see stars…Yet out on the embankment we'd show each
other our penises in our undershorts, those ludicrous little sausages
with the buttonhole in the middle…But this here was different…It
would have been best if everything could have stayed the way it was
before, on the wall, or on Roman Street…or, best of all, as it was
that morning outside Kham's or the day before on the far side of
the Ljubljanica.

When I opened my eyes, I saw a bare little protruding belly…

Beneath it was something like a rude facial expression...a barely healed wound. It was painful and unattractive...that was the worst of it for me. She held her skirt up to her chin and looked straight at me with those wide-set eyes..."Come on, Bubi, take them off," she said, pointing down..."I vill...You chust kow see zem first, ant I'll take zem off." I pushed her an ankle's width toward Ivan. I couldn't bear to look at her for another second...Then something slammed into the blanket...I felt frightened and relieved all at once that someone might be on the other side...maybe the guard of the Roman wall...I'll shout out "Alarm!"...Sadly, it was only the wind...I told myself that somebody was bound to come...I'll make it look like I've taken my shorts off...Just like in the middle of the night, when, half-awake, I'd try to get the down comforter off me if it was too hot...I kept reaching my hand down for a belt and buttons that it never found... Tatjana had obligingly sat down on Ivan, thank god...on his belly, square on his pee-pee...His face became as taut as an athlete's, and his legs straightened out like sticks...Tatjana rocked back and forth and up and down, as though she were on a teeter-totter, the whole time looking over at me and practically eating her hair as it flopped into her face...How incredibly stupid this was, all of it! The way Ivan was slapping the arch with his gasps...he was practically frothing at the mouth, while the arch mimicked him with the most ridiculous sounds...So this was supposed to be fucking – the ultimate mystery between a man and a woman? The most boring gym exercise in the world would be preferable. There was nothing interesting about this at all...I couldn't watch them any longer, so I looked out through the

· 28

hole at the bench and the wall, which was engulfed in a whole forest of ivy and looked very beautiful. "He's had enough," Franci complained, grabbing her by the elbow. "Now it's my turn, Tatjana, he's had too much." She stood up and stumbled off of Ivan's belly. She sat down on the paperboy, and I could hear him gasping, as though he were blowing into a hot water bottle... "You've had enough now, too," Tatjana said and got up. Franci clung to her elbow, attempting to get her to stay, but she gave him such a whack that it popped. "Stupid snot-eater," she said...

She came back to the blanket where the wall was lowest. "Now you have to, Bubi." Her face brightened when she saw that I was partly undressed... I squeezed my eyes shut. She sat down on me. She used her little slice of dried mango to push my pee-pee up toward my navel, like they did at the doctor's. She bent forward and planted a big kiss right next to my mouth... I took hold of her by the hips at belly level... and my hands slid, her skin was so soft. Then I put a hand on her shoulder and shoved her and her belly back up onto her feet... I felt like kicking her, but this was a girl... "What's wrong?"... "Not now," I said. "Lader." "But what's the problem? You're my boyfriend. Lie back down," she said angrily and slightly depressed... "But vat if zompoty ketches oss?" I said... I would have preferred to run... but if that wasn't to be, then I could at least hug her... just someplace else, where it was safe. Tatjana dropped her skirt and picked up her swim shorts... "If you don't like it, I'm going home. But those two aren't getting any more either," she said, like a grown woman... Ivan, who had been waiting impatiently for her to come back to him, started pleading with me...and even Franci was clearly upset. They were frustrated by my obstinacy..."Come on. Please..." Ivan said. "She's your girl..." He'd always been pale, but now he was yellow. I felt ashamed for him..."Not here. You ant Franci maype, put not me..." "If you go, they're not getting anything." Tatjana tugged at the blanket to release it from the stones pinioning it at the top...Ivan suddenly drew his head in and began pulling his shorts back on. "If you don't want to, then you and I are quits..." This sent me into a panic, and I started to sweat...I had to do something...think of something..."All right, you know vat?...Let's blay grusaters..." That got them interested. That worked on all three...I made the most of the opening and began to tell them a story..."Ve're knights in a gastle who haff fallen azleep. Zen comes Tatjana, who's a zpy, ant she vorces oss to..." and so I went on...We were alone in Palestine...in a small fortress...the last crusaders...the infidels had already tried everything to capture us...but in vain...they were helpless against us, three of the most valiant knights ever. But they were determined to take us alive, or else they would learn nothing about important plans for an attack on Jerusalem. All around they had deployed whole legions of barbarians, fire catapults had destroyed a good part of the fortress and elephants with upraised tusks had crashed through our penultimate line of defense. The town was as good as deserted. The White Prince and his two best friends, crusaders tempered in the fire of battle, had finally fallen asleep in exhaustion. They had food, water, horses and even a chapel where they would go pray... They had all the supplies they needed. They just couldn't escape...And disaster was lying in wait on the pier. What would they do?... They were all ears. This kind of plot appealed to them, the bloodier and more fraught, the better... I didn't want to break the spell. We were all primed for this, myself included. Tatjana was standing next to me. I lifted her skirt... shoved my head under it, followed her legs up and grazed my lips over her belly, which was sheathed in her swimsuit. For the minute I spent with my head under that pink veil, separated from the Roman house and those two, it was as though I was alone... The fear and revulsion, all that silliness, vanished... Tatjana pushed me gently away... completely entranced. "He'll be the knight, a count, because I'll come to him first. You two are his soldiers, his shield bearers"... I ran outside... Without opening my eyes, I lay down with my head propped against the wall and started to snore... the other two immediately followed my lead. The game had begun. Bent over, Tatjana furtively crept in on tip-toe like a regular Mata Hari or the bloody Muslim Wanda, who as a girl had been kidnapped but was now discovered to be a princess... she came from outside, past our snorting horses... over the drawbridge, taking care not to make the slightest sound... or run into the blazing torches jutting from the wall... she carefully picked her way over the legs of both shield bearers, so as not to wake them... and made sure not to bump into the shields, swords and pikes, or the overturned wine cups... she paused at the wall for a moment, then dashed into the bedchamber, tucked up her skirt and fell onto the prince, who, exhausted, was sleeping on a bearskin next to the fireplace... Now, as she played the game, Tatjana had a wild, vacant look on her face. I liked it…but I didn't bother to lift my eyelids to see her…I lifted her hands from the floor toward my ears, to get her to take hold of them like a bridle near the horse's mane…She gave me a big kiss on the mouth, and her hair tickled. I didn't open my eyes. I just wanted everything to be like it was before, under the blanket…I could feel my pee-pee pressing against two little pads that were warm in the middle but cool on the outside, but no less impassioned and submissive with love…maybe even more carried away than she was, because of the distance. I didn't dare open my eyes or the whole spell would be broken…I wanted her to laugh like those drunken women at the Harbor Tavern…with their abundant breasts and hips…I'd looked at pictures and witnessed whole scenes taking place on carts on the far side of the market and in the Unity Movie Theater…Laugh, I said, but not out loud…Sing bawdy songs!…Be as sweet as cream!… Go fast!…I didn't blurt a word of it…just opened my eyes the tiniest bit…saw her wide fish eyes through her hair…she was a regular castle strumpet. Suddenly, I felt a terrible pain in the small of my back… I jumped to my feet and saw everything before me, under the arch. I picked up my trousers…Now it was the shield bearers' turn…

I sat on the wall until each of them crawled out fully dressed… Ivan and Franci had to go home right away…one of them to scrub floors, the other to deliver newspapers…Tatjana and I rolled up the blanket, threw the stones off the ledge and went back along Roman Street. It wasn't until we reached the Cloisters, where we sat under the magnificent trees and I put my arm around her waist, that I suddenly got the full sense of it: I had a girlfriend now!…This was something so new and so terribly alive that I couldn't compare it to anyone or anything else...not to a tank, not to food, not to the war and not to the movies...There wasn't a thing in the world that could substitute for Tatjana.

FROM THEN ON, SHE CAME BY the house every day with her canvas newspaper bag slung over her shoulder. I would wave to her from the window carefully, so that mother, Vati or Clairi didn't see, then run downstairs and out of the house toward Jail Street...Now, since the German army had invaded Russia, Mrs. Hamman had ordered the flag to be hung from the ledge once again...of all the windows in the neighborhood, ours with its black hooked cross in the white circle was once more the darkest and most deadly by far...I had quit attending Hitler Youth events. Fischer's son tried to stop me on the street...he was wearing the plush cape of a group leader. "*Warum kommst du nicht mehr zu unseren Übungen?*"* "*Ich muß dem Vati helfen und mein kleines Schwesterchen ausführen...,*"** I called back to him as I kept walking. Tatjana was waiting for me on Jail Street, next to the fruit stand. I put one of the delivery bags over my shoulder, and we went to deliver papers to the houses on Gosposka and Salender Streets and on Napoleon and New Squares. Here on Gosposka the buildings were huge, with numerous passages, balconies, arches, hidden nooks and courtyards somber or sunlit...We shoved the newspapers into slits,

*Why don't you come to our drills anymore?
**I have to help my father and take my little sister out on walks.

under wooden and metal doors, behind door handles, into mailboxes hanging lopsided on walls... I saw all kinds of people... a man with a red head and a white scalp, as though he'd fallen face-first into nettles; women old, young and very refined; dentists in gold spectacles who had their offices in their house... dogs, cats, canaries, guinea pigs, rats, beautiful carpets... We heard shouts, blows and arguments that echoed outside for nearly five houses in every direction... I saw a man on a balcony swinging an armchair like a battle axe and a woman defending herself with a log as though it were a sword... Some windows were lifeless, while others poured forth music, a record player, a violin... I developed a power, a miraculous power, the ability to recognize the world's resemblance to home. There was no bottom to anything... We went from the cellar way down below to the attic up at the top. When I thought we'd come to the end, there were suddenly new lamentations and moans that I'd never heard or understood before... Tatjana and I would squeeze and grab at each other's crotch between pillars, on stairways and walkways, in dark corners... I would unfasten my fly, and she would drop her thick panties, and we would mate standing, like the Italian soldiers behind the butchers' shops along the perimeter of the new market... The feelings of pleasure were unbearable and painful in a previously unfamiliar way... Sometimes Tatjana would climb up on a stair railing, like the girls on their bicycle handles... I kissed her white slit gently and fearfully, like the cross in church on Easter... She pushed my face into her lap and leaned her head forward so that her hair engulfed me, and I was hidden from my own view...

We embraced and caressed one another at least three times in each building, which put a cramp in my arm. The juice came out of my pee-pee as though I were afflicted, making a sticky mess of my trousers and her skirt. We tried to rub the greasy spots out with stucco dust and saltpeter. We came out of every building as rumpled as though we'd just climbed out of bed still half-asleep. It took us an age to deliver the papers... There was a catacomb under the street outside a furrier's shop... We slid through the iron bars of the locked gate and went down the gracefully arched staircase... Those catacombs had been built by the same man who had built the red library, Žale Cemetery and the new marketplace. Patties of old shit lay strewn over the pavement, and on the walls there were drawings of hearts, pussies and dicks resembling fish, snails and geese, and inscriptions like "Cunt and prick make little Dick"... Tatjana told me to lie down on her. She lay down on the cleanest patch of pavement between two columns and spread her pale legs wide. I gasped and sweated, but my pee-pee refused to go into the crease of that soft eraser, with at most just the tip coming close... And when it disgorged its thick slime, it felt as though all the marrow were being sucked out of my spine, and my face twisted into such contortions that I feared it might never come unstuck... Then we went out or sat on the edge of the catacombs, right at the edge of the water... One day, she said, we'll be lying on stacks of money and be able to afford whatever we want... clothes, white motorcars, old castles... One day, after she and her mother collected the subscription money for the paper from house to house,

Tatjana brought both canvas satchels tied up like bags and full of lire and centesimi to the bench under the trees at the Cloisters. She told me to sit down on one of them. We sat side by side, each on his own satchel, without anyone knowing just what we were sitting on... The coins were as hard as a chain, although barely worth as much. If you sit with your fiancé on money, her mother had predicted, and you hold each other by the hand, you'll both get your wishes fulfilled... We sat on our untold wealth, and so unusual was this sensation that I could feel the square closing in on me from three sides – the long one in front and the two shorter ones on the sides – the monument to Napoleon next to the library on the right and the butcher's shop and grocery store on the left. I blanched and felt a shiver of cold under my suntanned skin. Something like a mixture of hilarity and terror took hold of me. We clasped each other by the hands. We wished that we could to go to America and become movie stars in Hollywood, those were our wishes. As soon as we spoke them, I stood up to shake off the strange feeling and the images of the square in front of me... Since I'd been going with Tatjana, I'd been living in an unusual time... sort of a dirty period of life. Not that I was ashamed, but I had something like a sense of loss, of mourning for the self I had been up until then... Tatjana wasn't a real woman, she was just a snot-nosed kid like myself. The only things about her that were womanly were her long hair and the fact that she wore a skirt. Her interest in me made me increasingly apprehensive and, over time, I stopped feeling any pleasure when I was with her... I ate apples and drank cold water, as Father Chrysostomos had advised us to do whenever we felt the desire to defile ourselves or sin with the opposite sex...It got to the point where, if I saw Tatjana out on Town Square or standing down in front of Zos's shop with her delivery bags, I often steered clear of the window altogether...

At home in the workshop, all they talked about was moving back to Germany...To Neunkirchen, possibly, or Saarbrücken, Saarlouis, where mother's relatives lived, if they were still living at all. I refused to accept this, much less buy into it, because I didn't want to leave this place. Barely would we start talking about it than I began to feel nauseous...They would suggest other towns where we might live. *"Die Hamman hat uns eine neue Adresse gegeben...ein gewisser Dr. Heinz Kreuzhacke in Kospis bei Hessen...wo wir die erste Zeit unsere Unterkunft bekommen könnten."** My head started to spin...strange black spots multiplied in the corners, and a welter of sounds hissed in my ears at the same time...*"Ich gehe nicht!"*** I stomped on the floor. *"Ich gehe nicht von hier weg!"* *"Du bist noch jung, Bubi, du wirst dich schnell angewöhnen!"**** *"Nein, nein, nein!"*...I had an attack, I writhed on the floor, the ceiling exploded above me, the floor gave way, I ran out of breath...this was my other mode of existence, which worried no one but me...I saw Germany as a gigantic, black, marble block filled

*Mrs. Hamman has given us the address of a friend...a Dr. Heinz Kreuzhacke in Kospis near Hessen...where we can stay when we first get there.

**I'm not going. I am not leaving this place.

***You're still young, Bubi. You'll adjust.

with Hitler Youth brats with whom I would have to stand at attention, striking some drum. If only my buddies Karel and Ivan could go with me... I wasn't budging an inch from this place. I wanted them to leave me alone, once and for all... I tried to shake off the thought of moving. I found a thousand reasons not to move to Germany. First, because I was going to school here and soon Gisela would, too. Second, Vati had his rabbit farm, and he couldn't very well just turn it over to anyone. The hutches were all built, and the little critters were prospering... There were a thousand other reasons that would keep us from leaving. No, it was impossible for us to move...

One afternoon, Vati and I set out by train to Uncle Rudi's place in Polica for the very purpose of checking up on the farm... Rumor had it that former soldiers of the Yugoslav Army were roaming the forests and inciting the locals to resist – they were essentially bandits, robbing and attacking the peasants... Vati and I had to walk through a forest to get to uncle's house, then go through it again in the dark on the way home... Vati brought along his sturdiest black shears for leather. They were made of pure steel and weighed five pounds at least. I would have put on my bayonet if I thought it were safe for my parents to know I had one... Vati put the shears in a bag, which he clasped in his arms the whole time... At uncle's place in Polica, there were about twenty of our rabbit hutches on stakes dotting a hillock off to the side of the farm... In every box there were two or three each of several breeds of rabbit... striped, argentes, grays, angoras with brown heads and ears... Through the wire mesh I could see them twitching their whiskers above their incisors... I was proud they were ours... if they really were ours...

While we were walking back through the forest toward a tall ridge, we heard some noise in a ravine. We dropped to the ground. Vati took out the shears and set them down on the ground with the blades open and pointing ahead of him. When the noise subsided, we slid down through the ferns to where some black and silver trees stood in a ring in the dark... Then we found our way back onto the path, which was lit by the early evening moon. We were carrying some foodstuffs back with us in a suitcase... People on the train also had food... bags of potatoes, lard, meat and flour. It was even more packed than before the war. Not only did we have to sit on the floor, some people sat on the bumpers between cars, with children sitting up on the luggage racks. People were playing button boxes and singing. The whole train sang. In spite of the war, people's faces were ruddy and kind... they were having friendly conversations... offering each other food in spite of rationing... apologizing to each other, then singing again... Again I got the feeling I was one of them...

One day, Tatjana wanted to go fishing under the Triple Bridge with the three of us... When I took off all my clothes down to my swim trunks, she became determined to try on my blue shorts... and then started prancing around in them like some newly minted boy. She began playing some dangerous game of gymnastics, grabbing onto stone steps that led from the toilet under the bridge up to the sidewalk... and dangling under the arch of the bridge at least twelve to fifteen feet over the water... It wasn't until I yelled at her to be careful that she came back toward the embankment, then jumped straight down onto the gravel... One day we headed out to Trnovo through City

Commons to take on the Trnovans and swipe some of the fruit from their territory...We set up a tent using two blankets. Slightly farther along, by the water, some Trnovo kids were kicking a ball back and forth. We brought along some gutter ends, tucked under our shirts like big fountain pens, and my bayonet. We stripped naked inside the tent and started monkeying around. Even Firant was there. Tatjana was mesmerized by risk. In the dark, our pee-pees swelled up like sponges...and Tatjana sat down on each one...Again she wanted to put on my blue shorts. When she had them on, she started cavorting outside the tent and provoking the soccer players down by the canal... Suddenly they'd had enough of us...In the midst of their game, they assembled in battle formation and started running toward us, shouting "Hurrah!"...At the last instant we snatched up the blankets and our clothes...I went running in my swim trunks, with Tatjana's dress over my shoulder and my bayonet in hand...

All of this was starting to bore me...things couldn't go on like that much longer...We had to come up with something new and amazing...I remembered the theater we had once thought about setting up in that high-ceilinged red room of ours, where the plaster was peeling off the walls...We needed wood for a stage, fabric for the curtains, costumes, some scenery and props...What would we perform? Old-fashioned romantic plays. Jousting tournaments. Robinson Crusoe. Gangsters of New York and Chicago...We went to construction sites in remote streets and through every courtyard...We would set our sights on a particular board or beam...and no sooner would the watchman turn his back...than – *fsshhht* – we whisked the board out of a woodpile or several clamps from a big stack of fasteners, because we needed those, too...Sometimes Tatjana would go engage the guard in conversation...boy, was she good at that, though I have no idea how she did it, but, like all adults, the old men in their booths were terribly childish and rotten, like the dirt all around, mixed with piss and cement. While she served as a decoy, we were free to lift battens, nails, trowels...At one building site, we discovered a whole hayrack's worth of gunny sacks. We used these for our curtains and stage costumes...We stole them gradually, a few per day, over lunch or late in the afternoon, when the masons headed to the trough to wash up and head home...We also needed set decorations...a variety of pillars, chairs, park ornaments, jail bars, bushes, and trees for our fields and castles...We ripped out whole bushes and pine trees, complete with their root systems and sod...Soon the room was crammed full of junk halfway up to the ceiling...with beetles, lice, and ladybugs still clinging to the plants...We got together every morning, all except for Firant...We hammered a stage together and practiced a variety of scenes. Tatjana would be a wicked queen in one of them, a spy in the next or the Maid of Orléans in another. Tončka would play Bernadette opposite Franci, who played her little brother, as the Virgin Mary appeared to them first in Lourdes, then Fatima...We would try to roll everything up into a single play...Robinson Crusoe, gangsters, knights, an operetta or a musical comedy with dance numbers. We were constantly rehearsing and expanding our repertory..."The terrible monster that hides in the heart of the forest...In the background are castles with towers and zig-zagging battlements...down below is the sea, distantly thundering…A guard in a watchtower, his eyes bulging in terror of being hanged…Still farther up, above the *Swamp of Lost Souls*, atop the castle keep, flutters a flag bearing the king's coat of arms, a dismembered snake with blood gushing out of its neck. Traitor, beware! The White Prince will atone for his sins…" I drew up posters and tickets…But it never came off…Besides, Mrs. Hamman had told Mother that she was going to rent our room to some mason and his son, because she was planning to renovate the building…Our efforts stalled. We didn't have a proper script, and we had no experience. All of our scenes came from movies, fairy tales or the catechism…The guys started claiming their stuff and taking it home…Ivan and Karel their women's hats, others their suits, or their parasols, fans and lace… One day, we started selling the gunny sacks to some pawnbroker who lived toward the back of a courtyard on St. Peter's Embankment… With the lire we got for them, we bought some soda pop and went to see *Frankenstein* at the Unity…we used the boards and struts for heating fuel at home.

Around that time I started avoiding Tatjana as much as possible. Now and then I'd go with Andrej, his half-sister Neva and their mother to the movies…One day we went to see a musical that was showing in the new movie theater. After the show, we still had three hours until curfew. We found a bench in the Star Park to sit on, because it was still light. We talked about the movie, and Andrej's mother started to hum one of the arias from it…She seemed as small as a teenager, sitting there on the bench, yet her legs were as hairy as a spider's. But she sang wonderfully, with feeling. She would fall in love with practically every movie star…which wasn't hard, since up on the screen they were five times bigger and more ambitious than ordinary people… She even collected photos of movie stars, as though she were still a young girl…Neva, sitting next to me, made fun of her for that…The relationship between Andrej and Neva was strangest of all. Because she was from another father, now and then Andrej would go after her, lift her skirt or reach under her blouse. Sometimes they'd go rolling around on both beds, wheezing and squealing like a whole blacksmith's shop. She was a strong but delicate girl with light gray eyes like her mother's…amid all the wrestling her backside would show through her skirt as taut as an apple and, contained in the soft baskets of her bra, her big breasts would shake…A real woman, with all the hidden, mysterious landscape of prominences and hollows under her dress that entailed. Not like Tatjana, who was as skinny and square-edged as a toothpick…She put her warm hand on mine, which was clutching the bench…even though she was already eighteen years old! I thought I was going to pass out. Oh, if only I could have had her as my girlfriend!…

One afternoon after a pouring rain, as the fruit vendors were packing their wares up and starting to head home, I went to the market to gather anything edible they'd left behind…here and there you could find a half-decent apple or a head of cabbage that wasn't completely rotten…when I suddenly ran into Tatjana, who was out with Karel and Ivan…I had just reached the bookstore, when both Prinčičes, with Tatjana sandwiched between them, appeared from behind a kiosk covered with posters. Tatjana had a curly-coated dog on a leash and was wearing rubber galoshes. I didn't know where to hide, so I tried to make a beeline for the other side of the street, toward Meinel's store...But Karel was already crossing the roadway in my direction... "Tatjana's calling you!" he said..."Let her! I'm not koink out viss her anymore!" Karel looked at me harshly, reproachfully, angrily..."Listen, if you don't, then I'm not going to be your friend anymore. And don't you dare show your face on the other side of the river..." I crossed the street resolutely in Tatjana's direction..."Vot iss it?" I asked. Tatjana turned her unbearable white face toward me and looked at me with those watery fish eyes. "You're my boyfriend, but you don't go out with me anymore..." "I chust ton't feel like it," I told her truthfully...and suddenly felt relieved. Then Ivan said, "You're going to go out with her, or else Karel and I are going to stop being your friends."... "Let's ko ofer zehr!" I pointed in the direction of the butchers' shacks and instantly both of them became friendly again...We walked across the square...We went up to one of the shacks that was open, the one where I had once tried to spend the night when it came to light that I'd borrowed money from the tobacconist...The shack had a counter covered with a sheet of tin, with nothing underneath, and next to it an enormous butcher's block nailed to the floor. "Zehr, on ze floor" I said, although that's where it stank most of raw meat. We lay down on the greasy floor under the counter, though our legs still jutted way out, especially those two bean poles'. "Zem first," I said to Tatjana. "No, you first, you're my boyfriend." She took off her snow boots, which were actually her mother's. I helped pull them off and almost couldn't suppress a shriek when I noticed that her foot, the left one, had its toes and nails all fused together in what looked like a lump. "Tit you haff some agzident?" I asked. "No, it's been like that since I was born," she said. Was it possible that we'd been close for so long, yet I'd known her so little that I'd never noticed till now...? I pulled my trousers down to my knees, and Tatjana sat down on me. Ivan did guard duty outside and minded the dog. Karel lay next to me and watched. After a few minutes, I told Tatjana to stop, and Karel rolled over into my place under the counter... Ivan came in... I watched for a few seconds, then tied the dog's leash to the paneling, crouched down and slipped out the door.... And I ran as if my hair were on fire... At the bookstore, I didn't know which way to turn. I ran into people, bumping into old women who were just then crowding into the side door of the cathedral... I found a place to stand at the first altar to the right of the main one, where a silent mass was taking place. This was a good hiding place... The painting possibly depicted the Mother of God with baby Jesus, but it was hard to make out the figures on the darkened canvas... it could also have been Saint Anne or Elisabeth with her child at christening... A few people were standing around looking upward... I didn't know how I was supposed to act... At random, I cast around for some words from the venerable and uplifting parts of the rosary... When I found the sentences, I frightened myself by saying them so loudly that I could hear my own excited voice, and a devout young girl turned around and stared at me... So I began just moving my lips like the others... These were the words from prayers I'd never understood, but which undoubtedly reached that place way up high where they were understood... The church was good protection against those three. Never in a million years would it have occurred to them to look for me here, and even I wasn't quite sure where I was...

This is when Gisela got something new from the orthopedic doctor...a high boot that laced all the way up to the hip, with an artificial pelvis made of hard pigskin reinforced with steel rods. She could walk, but not much. I would take her in the wagon to Tivoli, where there were nicely mown lawns and dense flowering shrubs and where she could rest, dip her leg in a pond or play in the sand. Best of all she liked the black elder bushes that grew behind Cekin Castle. She would have liked to have a dog to play with, but our parents wouldn't permit it. Or a kitten...Vati had a number of black cat furs...which he'd got from the Italian soldiers, who liked to eat cat meat...but he wouldn't stand for any live animals in the house. So all that was left to us was other kids' dogs and cats...Those cat-eating soldiers had been directed to us by Sergeant Mitić. Now he was a civilian, not in the least reminiscent of a non-commissioned officer, more like a typical peasant lad. He worked for the Italians and was getting ready to become a sergeant again in some sort of Slovene legion that was being established...He and Vati would still look at the maps in the newspapers and my atlas...The German army was advancing in the shape of antlers in three directions: toward Leningrad, Moscow, and Ukraine...The Red Army had lost two and a half million men, 22,000 cannons, 18,000 tanks, 14,000 airplanes...Lots of planes had been destroyed on the ground. Even the whole Cossack cavalry had bit the dust...The newspapers had lots of photos...of people, women and children in folk costumes carrying flowers and bread out to welcome some German soldiers who had arrived in their village on motorcycles, all caked in mud…"All of Russia is going to rise up with Hitler against Stalin," Sergeant Mitić predicted…There were also aerial photos of the USSR. All of Moscow was covered with camouflage, draped in huge stage curtains that had forests and villages painted on them… The main squares were painted over to give the impression of a rural landscape…It was nice to look at, like a circus backdrop, but it was childish…Where there should have been rooftops jutting up, the sides of painted houses sprawling over the tarps looked with their facades straight up into the cockpits…That couldn't have fooled any pilot.

REPAIRS ON THE HAMMANS' HOUSE got underway…Masonry scaffolding surrounded it on all sides. Mrs. Hamman wanted to renovate everything, because she was planning to sell the house before moving to Germany…The scaffolds, ropes, burlap and construction workers began casting new kinds of shadows and light into our big room. Now, because of the way the light broke, I could see on the wall the silhouettes of people outside getting perceptibly smaller as they passed by on the street, then suddenly vanishing as they moved on, only to be replaced by the shadows of others. It was easy to make out the men from the women, the ones wearing hats from the ones without them…Now I could easily climb out the window and up, or down, to street level, thanks to the network of posts and boards… Vati, mother and Clairi talked more and more often about moving to Germany. And if that didn't happen before Mrs. Hamman sold the house, we would have to find another apartment for the time we had left until we could leave...I was on pins and needles, as distant and nearby things got all mixed up...Sometimes City Square, the dressmaking shop, both Karel and Ivan, and everything else became distant, while the Germany I knew from pictures, with its big cities, blackened monuments and palaces showing their stair-shaped rooflines to the narrow lanes and squares, seemed right close by...And then vice versa again...Nobody asked me anything...I expected some hand to appear that was going to fling me out of all this...I cranked the little handle to open the Hammans' storefront awning, but the framework got blocked by the scaffolding just a few inches out. I pounded my chest, but my hands were like some sort of tools striking against my sweater, which was all too familiar. If I looked at myself in a mirror, I could believe it was somebody else...I saw a new journey ahead of me, with train tracks vanishing into a tunnel...I would be vanishing, too...

I still had no real friends among my schoolmates in Prule...so I would wind up passing the time in the old dressmaker's shop. At least it was warm. I would sit on the floor next to their big metal stove, between Ivan and Karel, and help wind ribbons for hats onto tubes. They didn't try to sweeten the pill, as mother had the habit of saying about Germans. Nor did they try to trick me...Now and then, their mother would offer me a cup of hot water with dried pear slices floating in it...sometimes a slice of baked macaroni and walnuts...Cvetka sat on her bench opposite Ivka, her breasts pressing up against the table. She was well fed and all curves, causing her apron to bulge...She would crush walnuts by smashing them with her fist...which came crashing down from on high in a powerful swoop, causing the furniture to shake. Such a powerful woman. But she was too much like Ivan... She and Ivka just sewed, while their mother mostly supervised them and looked after the fabrics and the store, where they had just three different models displayed in the cases. There were hardly any customers... Ivka was working on a hat crown made out of two layers of fabric, which was complicated work... As she bent over, her eyelashes concealed the fierce look in her eyes. Her hair drooped limply to the left and right from her middle part, away from her triangular face, and only showed some body at the nape of her neck, where it formed a wreath of tiny curls stretching from ear to ear... She didn't say much, except for what was really essential, and even that came out in short, choppy bursts. I took great care not to get too close to her...

One day when she and I were alone, she stood in front of the mirror for trying on hats and started combing her hair. She looked at herself in the mirror just as fiercely as she looked at others, taking no pity on herself. "I'd like to have a fur stole and hat for this winter. Even rabbit fur would do," she said, out of the blue. I got up... What she had said could have been addressed to me, since there was nobody else in the workshop... This was an opportunity, it suddenly struck me, to finally make contact, the thought of which made me quite dizzy... "Maype I can help you," I said. "Fahzer has lots off nice rappit furs."... At that instant, I knew I was going to steal them from him... from the same supply that he got from the farm and kept stored in boxes... I knew that, if she showed even the slightest interest, I was going to swipe them for her, even if it meant running the gauntlet... There was silence... That was understandable, since this was the first time I'd ever talked to her...She stepped back from the mirror and stared at me fixedly...perhaps just a shade more gently, I thought, than she'd been looking at herself in the mirror...I had to turn away to avoid getting lost in her eyes, which drew me in, as if they were going to swallow me whole...But even then, facing away from her, it was almost the same...her dark checkered dress was an inseparable part of her body...She never wore light-colored blouses, and yet the contours of her beautiful breasts showed through the coarse fabric. And her sleeveless smock...how elegantly it suited her slim figure..."Vell, you know," I said in an effort to break the spell. "Ve haff lots off zem. Rappit furs and ozzer kints." For the very first time I felt something like pride that we had a fur shop at home, and a magnificent feeling that all that disgusting junk could be useful to someone..."Are you thinking, from home?" she said drily. She leaned back up against the table, crossing her arms as though she were engaged in a serious conversation with me..."Yes," I nodded..."How many would I need for a collar, a hat and maybe a muff?" she asked. "Maype fife peek vons," I hazarded. "Putt vaht color voult you vant?"..."Oh!" She knitted her brow, causing a tiny triangular wrinkle to form between her eyes...that's where I most would have liked to kiss her..."Gray would go best with my black coat..." "Ve'fe kot lots off zem. Russian rappit furs. I'll prink zem tomorrow..." I turned around, hoping to leave now, fast, right away..."But how much will they cost?" she asked...She'd caught me! I was wanting to give them to her as a gift...But this was a dilemma... If I didn't give her a price on the spot, she would immediately suspect that I was planning to swipe the furs instead of getting them from

Vati. "Two lire each," I blurted. But that wasn't enough to get the smallest unit of fur, the size of two hands…"If your father lets you have them, bring them on over," she said…"I vill tomorrow," I exclaimed…I had to get out of there fast…the curtain stirred and Cvetka came in from the kitchen. I bounded headfirst out of their store…My head felt like a beehive. I sat down next to the cart…What I'd done in their store just now was sheer, self-aggrandizing rubbish… But I didn't want to have to renege on my promise. Stealing furs from Vati was nothing…it was like chopping down a sapling in a dense forest…Going back on my word would be far worse villainy…But how was I going to pull this off without anyone noticing? I couldn't do it all by myself…Vati kept close watch on all of his boxes, rags, furs, scraps of fur…Karel and Ivan were going to have to help me, or there was no way of making it happen. I just had to make sure they didn't know what it was for…There were some women who rented rooms over the Black Cat Café and had surrounded their windows with wardrobes. Now and then, soldiers and officers would appear between the wardrobes…and once even someone with a colonel's ribbon on his cap…The wardrobes reminded me of builders' scaffolding. If one of the Prinčičes sat on a board under our window and the other one stood outside the store, I could hand the first one a package, then he could toss it to the other down on the street…I could tell them, let's say, that I had to get something that my parents would never let me take out of the house…When Ivan and Karel found me by the cart, they were at first surprised…then they started to grin. Had they figured it out? I suddenly felt so hot that I could easily have stepped into the loo to strip myself naked…"You haff to come ziss afternoon, vissout fail," I ordered them. "Iffan, you stant outzite ze store, ant Karel vill pee unter ze vindow venn I srow out ze peckach."…Ivan rebelled. "Why can't I be the one under the window?"…"Oh come on, you can't climb," Karel said. "How are you going to shimmy up that pole?"…"Liar! You want to have everything for yourself!"…And then they were all over each other…for the first time since I'd known them…They grabbed each other by the ears…spun each other around…tried to trip each other…fell under the cart and began rolling around until it was almost incestuous…The bell over the front door jingled. "Inside, you two! Start scrubbing the floors!"…The old dressmaker grabbed the two by their suspenders and yanked them into the store…No injuries were incurred. A minute later they were back on the street, still a little worked up, but reconciled…"Hey, listen…" Karel began. "Vat? Aren't you comink ziss afternoon?"…"Are you getting any money for this?" Ivan asked. I breathed a sigh of relief. "Ve'll split ze money betveen us." This instantly put them both in a better mood…That evening…whenever Vati stepped out of the room…I searched through the boxes in the corner to find gray rabbit furs…At intervals I managed to wrap three up in one newspaper and two more in another and shoved the packages in amongst the stack of wood for the fireplace. After lunch the next day, as Vati rolled his smock up into a pillow and lay down on his work table, Karel was already waiting outside our house. The builders had gone, and Karel climbed up one of the poles to take a seat on the plank under our window. In the display window of Zos's across the street, I could see

a reflection of Ivan standing outside the door to Hamman's store...
I went on tip-toe to the stack of firewood and tossed the first package
to Karel. The newsprint rustled slightly, causing Vati to open his eyes
and sit up..."*Was ist? Was ist los?*"*..."Nosink, nosink!"...I stood by
the window with no idea how to react...Then a woodfired truck, one
of those mastodons, came to my rescue...right outside our house it
started to backfire, sending up tons of smoke and steam..."Zere's peen
an agzident!" I shouted...Vati had to race around two tables to get to
the window...and the fact that by fooling him I forced him to run
was the most ignominious part of this whole heist...As I ran past the
boxes and went flying through the vestibule out onto the veranda, Vati
shouted, "*Wo gehst du hin? Paß auf!*"**...Karel and Ivan caught up with
me on Locksmith Street. Ivan unwrapped the package. "They're
beautiful..." I looked at them as though I were seeing them for the
first time, the gray shimmering fur transitioning to deep blue. It wasn't
at all like when you plucked something out of the grass or pulled it
out of the water and the thing in the vase or on the table was uglier
than where it had been before, in the field or underwater...the furs
were more magnificent than they'd been in their boxes, I couldn't
compare them to anything...I folded them up nicely, one on top of
the other, with sheets of newspaper between them, as if getting them
ready for a proper sale, and then wrapped them up in an elegant package...It felt like the story of the shepherd who accomplishes the task

* What is it? What's happened?
**Where are you going? Be careful!

he's been given and then heads to the castle, where his princess awaits him…The workshop at the back of their store was dark and uninviting. Ivka was standing by the table threading a needle. She looked up when she noticed I was bringing a package…"Have you brought them?" she said, almost with an air of surprise, which I expected. "Thank you, Bubi.".…This was the first time she'd ever addressed me by name, and she looked at me as if at a courier who was bringing her good news from afar…She unwrapped the package and took it over to the display window. She blew on the fur and tugged at it. But the pelts were sound and the fur held firmly onto the hide. She knew a thing or two about the fur business…"I have to hide them away so mother doesn't get them…" She opened the table drawer and patted me on the wrist. This sent a shudder through me, and my arm froze and turned blue as if jolted with electricity. "We agreed you'd sell me these for two lire apiece, right?"…Karel and Ivan, who had been fidgeting in the showroom, suddenly grew still. Ivka reached into the table drawer and counted out ten lire in paper and coins. "Of course," I forced myself to reply…I thought the light bulb hanging from the ceiling might blow out from all the accumulated energy after killing me with its radiance…"Who coult ask for anysink more?"…Who could ask for anything more? It was a good phrase. It wiped out my intensity… brushing in the dark against some other meanings, secrets, words and phrases…it attested to my maturity and my coldblooded determination not to be frightened by the spotlights and police who were about to come crashing through the display window any instant…There were a lot of phrases like that…blow in my ear…as snug as a bug…man proposes, God disposes…the early bird catches the worm…Ivka put one of the furs on her head and another on her shoulder…"Wide collars are in now, aren't they?" she asked me…"Yes, vide vuns viss blunt tips," I said, happy to have an authoritative response. "Where do you think I could get some silk and backing material for cheap?"…"Next to ze Franciscan church," I blurted out. "Fahzer puys his zilk and yarn cheap zere from Mr. Rutolf."…Oh, what had got into me to blurt out where Vati got his material? He'd hammered this into me a million times at least. At Napotnik's, a bald gentleman named Mr. Rudolf sold backing material, yarn, silk and canvas out of a special box under the counter that was his own property. If all the clothes makers in town went there and bought what Rudolf sold for next to nothing, then pretty soon his whole supply would be gone…"Do you want to make a hat for yourself? A Russian one?…Like this or like this?"…She raised her hand higher and then lower over her head…Her hands were smooth…right up close…her fingers like rays of sunlight…I grew soft and didn't want to get mixed up in anything anymore, that's what I kept telling myself, and that's why I kept my hands behind my back, and yet…I took hold of her wrist and lifted her hand up over her head. Those were high hats, Vati's so-called version of the Siberian *ushanka*. "Like ziss!"…"Yes, that would be nice," she said, freeing herself from my grip…She seemed to be satisfied…"Do you think there will be enough furs?"…"Of course, zey're peek," I said voicelessly…"In two months it will be winter. I need to make myself a hat, muff and collar by then."…She brushed the gray silken sheen with her hand…"If you haff anysink left ofer, you can make etches for your pockets," I said, putting my hand on the fur not far from hers. She pulled it away and I drew my hand back…"You're koink to pee varm ziss vinter…" Karel and Ivan were pacing impatiently in the store…"Fine, now why don't you go to the movies. You're a rich man, after all…" Her bright, motionless eyes twitched slightly… that meant I was dismissed…

We went to a pastry shop and then to the movies. After the show, I had a few centesimi left in my pocket. I sat beside the wall for a long time once the two of them headed home for bed and didn't go home myself until just before curfew. I knew I was going to catch it for this, that sparks were going to fly, and also that they might even call the police. They were prepared to do anything for the sake of a piece of fur…even summon heaven and hell onto earth. I could already hear mother…"*Was haben wir nur verbrochen, daß wir ein solches Geschmeiß auf die Welt gesetzt haben?*"*…Now that they couldn't get rid of me anymore, they were really in a fix…I could see light through the waxed paper. I stayed out on the veranda. I hopped around a bit this way and that… one, two, hop!…as far as the pole, to get my muscles ready for the blows, I tautened my skin. Mother came out through the arch of the door. Even in the dark I could tell she was red in the face. "*Was machst du denn da draußen?*"** She was worried where I was roaming around after curfew…nothing more. Vati was also still clueless, he was snoring away on the table with his whistling lungs and a fur hat on his head…I

*What did we ever do to deserve such misbegotten offspring?
**What are you up to out here?

undressed by the window. Woe betide you on the day they discover that five Russian rabbit furs are missing from that welter of stinking hides. On that day you'll envy a horse, a stone in the street…Until then, my only hope was to avoid provoking my folks in any way. To obey every order…I couldn't soften the blows of the fate that awaited me, this much I knew – I might as well have counted on a miracle…I could practice patience and restraint, and get as ready as possible for the nightmare that was bound to unfold one of these nights and deprive the whole house of sleep…

Everything remained peaceful for two weeks…In the Prinčičes' workshop, Ivka had all of the pelts spread out on the table…trimmed and half-assembled with stitching…I thought that was better than seeing them whole…She was making an ensemble to suit her own taste…Her mother, the old dressmaker…did she or didn't she know where her daughter had got them?…would stand at the table, diminutive, black-clad, with Ivka undaunted, cutting and stitching right there in front of her. Once again, she was remote and kept to herself…after initially rejoicing at the beautiful furs she became as stuck up as ever. Her eyes grew as fierce and chilly as before… During the first few days, I tried to bring her some patterns so her work would be easier. She refused them. "No," she said, throwing me a brief glance…She spent the whole day, morning and afternoon, cutting and stitching the pelts. As she stood at the work table, the black puffs at the shoulders of her smock would graze against her face, without her seeming to notice or derive any pleasure from it, when it was precisely those pleats that made her more attractive. To be on the safe side, I took a seat somewhere near the stove, in case she needed me... For advice, to try something on, for whatever purpose, to run to the store for a spool of thread, to bring her this or that... She didn't even lift her head or look my direction... She couldn't even spare me a word... I paced back and forth... her white hands held firmly onto the shears... which cut expertly and forcefully into the pelts... Her mystery was impenetrable... I was thin air for her, she didn't like me, she despised me... I could feel that on my skin and in my hair... That's why for several days in a row I started calling to Karel and Ivan through their window again. I suspected that Ivka probably knew how I'd come by the pelts... maybe Karel and Ivan had blabbed to her, although I didn't believe that guys would reveal a secret to girls... Something was different... they didn't trust me anymore. I entered their workshop and said hi... They were all sitting around the worktable, and not one of them looked up. They couldn't leave me by myself anymore, either... if I happened to be alone by the stove for a minute, suddenly one of them would have something to do in the workshop, albeit trivial... I was a thief and thus capable of anything... I understood that... still, when I felt cornered I could burst into tears. I took to staying outside so they wouldn't have to worry with me in the store... Karel and Ivan came clomping out on their long legs... just for a minute, all bundled up for the cold in their woolen caps, which were tied under their chins... they talked with me for a while, then they went back in the door to their store... Things weren't all that terrible, although I was afraid they were going to have to drop me as a friend now... that the old dressmaker might suddenly ban me from the embankment…that my parents might suddenly discover the theft…

It snowed, contributing to a severe winter…When I got back home, mother and Vati were standing in the midst of boxes that had been flung all over the room…"*Bubi, komm her!*"…and I could tell from the sound of their voices and the way they looked toward the door that the jig was up…"*Hast du einige graue Hasenpelze vielleicht wo versteckt?*"* mother asked. They could probably tell from my face it was far worse than that…"*Du Lümmel, hast du sie vielleicht sogar gestohlen und verkauft?!*"**…That must have been what was written on my face…I watched what followed in rapt attention, as one watches a gathering storm…Vati turned away…an instant later he was stammering and shaking…flinging some tongs, scissors, a whetstone aside as he looked for a bamboo rod on the table…Mother pried the rod out of his hand…he would have whipped me too gently…I quickly retreated to the corner next to the window, because the people outside could see and hear her, so the blows would be milder and her shrieking subdued…But no, it was the other way around…mother turned into a hurricane…The yellow rod with its green knuckles turned into a darting rattlesnake…*Zzzap! Buh-dum. Clack, clack. Eeyaaah!*…The rod bit into my cheeks…my hands…my knees…straight across my open mouth…The torturers of the dark ages would have hidden their

* Have you maybe hidden some gray rabbit furs somewhere?
**You lout, don't tell me you actually stole them and sold them?!

faces in shame in her presence. The rod writhed like an eel…while mother screamed curses and oaths…*"Sag, Dieb! Wo hast du die Pelzen hingetragen?"*…*"Elendes Kind, du wirst in dem Kerker enden…Luder! Mistfink! Uns auszuplundern!…Widerlicher Bengel!"**…Her face changed colors from red to yellow to blue…*"Jede Stunde werde ich dich verprügeln, bis du es sagst!"***…I didn't blab, I didn't cry…I got thrashed all over my body, down to the bone…with blood and bruises like zippers, swellings as though I'd been raked with nails…my gums bled and my tongue swelled up like a sausage…but none of that mattered. What mattered was…what?…mother went into the kitchen and Clairi knelt down beside me. *"Sag es, Bubi,…war es der Karel und Ivan…oder ein Mädel?…Sag es, dann gehen wir beide zu ihr…"**** I shook my head and kept shaking it…Gisela knelt down on her healthy knee and cried as though I were dying. "Tell them you didn't do anything," she begged me. I wanted to hug her and cry. She was the only one of them I could have confessed to. What mattered…and mattered most of all…was that whatever I'd done in this world, it was always in vain…Clairi and mother were making a big racket with pots and pans in the kitchen. Vati and I were left alone in the main room…He was putting his smock on…His crooked arms had trouble fitting into the sleeves, and then

---

*Speak up, thief! What did you do with the furs?…Wretched child, you'll end up in prison…you good-for-nothing! Bastard! Stealing from your own family!…Filthy rotter!

**I'll beat you every hour until you talk!

***Tell us, Bubi…Was it Karel and Ivan…or a girl?…Tell us, then you and I will go see her.

the smock refused to sit flat on his back... He took a seat, and when he
set a piece of fur in his lap, it slipped off onto the floor. Then his thread
broke, and his needle got bent... and he hurled the iron at the door
under the window... He couldn't work. He buried his head in his hands
and was motionless. His chair creaked. When I looked his way again a
minute later, he was still hunched over, with his head on the table. I got
up, I couldn't hear him breathing anymore and I was seized with
panic... "I sold the furs to the dressmaker," I told him. He raised his
head. So he wasn't dead!... After that, everything happened so fast...
Mother and Clairi ran down to the police station, and Vati took me by
the shoulder. As we walked across the streetcar rails on City Square,
I realized that what I had done was as final and definite as treason
or war... I didn't even have enough strength to open the door to the
store... A table in the middle, two chairs, a picture of the Angelus on
the wall... They were all sitting here... the old woman, Ivka, Cvetka,
Karel, Ivan... they were sitting in their workshop, as though unaware
of a thing... standing off to the side was a stout man wearing a leather
jacket, a cop... Could a stranger be the arbiter of my doom?... Ivka
had her hands on a piece of cut and stitched fur. She looked at Vati
and the policeman with her light blue eyes, as though neither of them
were actually present. The policeman was jotting things down in his
notebook... name, date and place of birth; me thirteen, Ivan fifteen,
Karel thirteen and a half... there was no hope for me or anyone else
here... everything had come crashing down... Karel and Ivan were
perched by the stove with their arms hugging their knees and staring
at the floor... It couldn't have been any different. Then the policeman

began his interrogation...each of his questions was left hanging in mid-air like a blood-sucking spider..."How many pelts did you bring here?"..."Five."...Ivka calmly turned toward him, "He's lying, the brat," she said harshly, as ever. My face...mouth, eyes...were nailed shut with boards over them..."Me?"..."He's lying! He brought two. Anyone can confirm that!"...The old dressmaker jumped to her feet..."He's lying! He's trying to hang the whole dirty business on others, the rotter!"...I felt relieved...finally she actually hated me. "Quiet!" the policeman said. "Did anyone help you steal the pelts?"... I shook my head..."Ivka, did you know that the boy had stolen the pelts?" "Not at all..." Her eyes were so close to everyone, and they didn't waver once in their sockets, that we all believed her..."You can take these pieces here on the table back home," the cop said. Vati brushed them all off the table with his arm. "You can keep them!" Karel and Ivan didn't look up once...Vati slammed the door so hard that the doorbell exploded. Outside, a watery snow was falling...fresh air and occasional snowflakes helped cool my head...

T HAT WAS A CRUEL BLOW...For days and days, I didn't show my face anywhere. I refused to eat and had no appetite, for that matter. But they forced me. I would have liked to starve down to a reed...and just blow away. I went to school and did everything assigned to me. I soaked pelts. Stretched them out. Nailed them to boards. Softened bloody, uncured leather with my fingers. Scrubbed the floors. Straightened up the workshop. Studied to the point of exhaustion. I didn't like people touching me, for fear they would shake everything out of me.

Most of all, I didn't want to talk to anyone anymore. Share my cares with anyone. Not even myself... Everything I did was still not enough. I could sense the devil inside me... for days on end, he kept prancing before me like the knight on a chess board... and whenever he was removed from the board, he would rise up again to pull some new trick on me... Vati lost a lot of weight... He began talking to himself. At the wall. There was no way to comfort him. Had he gone crazy?... My future looked grim... From the bridge I would see Karel, Ivan, Franci, Marko, Firant and Andrej in the distance... Once I went to the door of the warehouse, as I'd done a good year before... The next time I went there, Ivan and Karel showed up... We hung out for a while, talking, as though we'd just met each other...

Then came the worst news in a long time... the rabbit farm had been destroyed, Uncle Rudi informed us from Polica... all the animals had either been stolen or slaughtered... it was the Gypsies' doing, or whoever it was roaming the forests. We took the train down to Grosuplje, then trudged to Polica through the new-fallen snow. Just in case, Vati brought along his shears, and I brought my knife... In Polica, all the hutches had been smashed, the wire doors hung off their hinges, and the padlocks were left twisted and dangling... There wasn't a single rabbit hutch that still had a rabbit in it... except for two of them, where carcasses lay in a furrow of leaves... all that was left in the rest was just a little cold fodder, bark and manure... *"Was, wenn das der Onkel selbst gemacht hat?"** mother said. She had nothing but

*What if uncle did this himself?

bad experiences with people and didn't trust anyone. This now was a reverse magnification of my own guilt... I didn't dare look anyone in the eye... "The hutches were too far from the house," Uncle Rudi said. "Otherwise, we would have heard something."... Vati was beside himself... all the money from Switzerland that he'd invested in this effort was gone... He sat down in the snow, unable to believe his eyes... "Maybe, Lojze, they knew that you support the Germans," Uncle Rudi told him. "Apparently these forest bands are Reds fighting against the Italians and Germans."... We went back home, but this time without any food.

In December, Mrs. Hamman informed us that we needed to move out, because one of the owners of her building wanted to move into our apartment... She had found a two-room attic apartment for us on Old Square, in the Salaznik house, which had a café on the ground floor. At one time, bakers and confectioners had worked in the attic, so it had good ventilation for a stove, and there were shelves built into the walls... We went to have a look at it... The building was older than the Hammans', and its windows were blackened. It even had a sundial on its facade... The entryway to the courtyard was paved with round, gravel-like stones, and it smelled of ants, dirt and mice... there were wide steps that led upstairs in three flights. The stairway was flanked by olive-green columns with capitals, and between the columns there were wrought-iron bars to the ceiling, shaped into vines with clusters of grapes and birds pecking at them. In the light of the staircase, the bars cast such silhouettes on the galleries, corridors and painted stone plinths that in combination they gave the impression we were inside a palace or castle…On each floor, a dimly lit corridor extended into the very bright gallery of the building's side wing, with multiple windows and a stone-tiled floor…The stairs from the third floor led up to the attic, instead of the fourth floor…on one side there was a vast attic space with round, grilled windows, and across from it, at the top of the gallery, was the door to the two-room attic apartment…The rooms were tiny…At the peak of its ceiling, the apartment had a tall, almost industrial chimney in metal cross braces, because at one time bakers had produced their confections in both rooms. From both windows, you could see the side wing of our building and the one next door, with the paved courtyard way down below. On the far side of a one-story building in the courtyard there was a garden. The garden extended alongside a long, stuccoed wall, beyond which there were steps leading up to the castle. The first house on the far side of the wall was yellow and had a terrace. Above it, there was a triangular gray house that had goats bleating in the grass around it, and above that, through the trees, you could see the brown castle tower, blocky, with its notched ramparts on top and white, handless clock face on the side.

IN THE FIRST ROOM, which was to become the workshop, there was a big ceramic stove. At a used furniture store, mother and Vati bought a chest of drawers, an old counter and a big, expandable table that Vati would sleep on. I screwed an aluminum clothes rack that we'd brought with us from Basel into the doorframe…and hung a mirror on the wall…In the other room, which due to the baker's shelves was as narrow as a hallway, we set up the iron bedframe for the women, which we'd acquired in a second-hand store in exchange for two hammocks. Behind it, we set up the kitchen table, which was where I slept. There wasn't enough money left over for a range. We cooked food on a round burner with a single flame or on the other side of the baker's shelves on a single, small hot plate...We were able to stow most of our stuff in the chest of drawers, and what few clothes we could afford got hung up on clothes racks and some nails...So, this was to be our new home! We could hear every sound in the house because the attic walls were so thin...the doorbells, steps up the stairs, the plumbing, some canary singing, shouts and songs from the assembly hall of the German organization, drunks in the café...Otherwise, the house was quiet...The most unpleasant thing about it was when there was a storm...thunder would rumble over the roof right at the top of the tall chimney...water would come gushing in torrents down the roofing tiles, soaking the wall and carrying off any rock salt, and splashing the metal under our windows like a hundred fire hoses...Every lightning strike in the ravine between us and the castle was deafening, as if it had struck in our attic...The single-pane windows...in both the first and second rooms...would shake like the dickens. Then it would get quiet again, as the storm gave way to a huge kingdom of fog that was thicker than down by the Krka...Everything was enchanted...another world... Three feet away from the house you couldn't see anything...We were stuck in a cloud that would spread through our rooms like it used to do in Cegelnica...The sounds from the street found their way up to us, filling the whole apartment...especially the sounds from the trolley stop in front of the house. It seemed like the trolley drove right up to our front door. I could hear it rumbling and ringing behind the wall next to the dresser, inside the table drawer, behind the stove, inside the stove, as though it were driving upstairs to our apartment...A hail of hallucinations, both visual and auditory. We had to quickly turn on the lights, and Vati his copper flashlight...if we wanted to be able to see each other instead of colliding in the fog.

ONE CORNER OF THE BUILDING still stood on Old Square, while the other, which bent uphill along with the street, was planted on Upper Square...The café downstairs was always crowded, in spite of the war. It was frequented by peddlers from Dalmatia with their shoulder bags...students with drawing boards and lecture notes...a clatch of older ladies wearing hats and necklaces and older gentlemen with their cigarette holders...Some played chess at small tables by the green-curtained windows...others read newspapers stuck onto rods...still others played pool at two tables that stood in the middle. The entryway led past the door to the café's kitchen into a courtyard where its toilets and wood stacks were located...The assembly hall of the German organization that I had once visited was on the second floor...It was always emitting noise, the clatter of plates and utensils, singing...Across from it, off the hallway with the bars on one side, was where short, white-haired Mr. Salaznik lived with his beautiful wife and their only child...In the corner of that hallway an ugly little old lady, a housecleaner who was always dressed in black, lived with her daughter and son-in-law. A window of their apartment that looked out onto the staircase was right over the staircase light timer. Every now and then, the cleaning lady's daughter would appear in that window... a young blonde with dark eyes and red lips. It was like she was appearing on an altar, and because she was always wearing something colorful or terry-cloth, I imagined that there had to be either a bathroom or a pantry on the other side of the window... On the second floor, the hallway of the side wing was bright and airy. It led straight out into the garden. Behind the last door, a relative of the café owner named Praček, a cook and custodian, lived in a two-room apartment. Kind of a slovenly guy, as short as Salaznik and gray-haired like him so you could confuse the two at a distance... A bunch of women lived on the third floor, right above the German organization. All of them getting on in years and resembling each other... with coal-dark eyes, cartilaginous noses and tiny mouths. A short, pale fellow who wore a black suit with a satin collar was married to one of them. He had been a judge in Celje but was expelled by the Germans... Straight across from them was the glass door to a big apartment that was home to two sub-tenants who were twins, one of them an actor and the other a bookseller. The lady of the house, a fat old woman, was a fruit vendor at the market who had two adult sons, one a student and the other a greengrocer, in whom, to my horror, I recognized the lanky, big-footed vendor who had once chased me across the market, thinking that I'd swiped a dinar from him... The third-floor hallway of the side wing of the building was as brightly lit as the hallway on the second floor, except that it was crammed full of wardrobes, cabinets and crates. This is where our shared toilet and running water were located. An older, ruddy-cheeked waitress from the café, Miss Ana, lived in one of the rooms by the toilet. A few wardrobes farther down, near the washbasin at the start of the hallway, was where the Hirol family lived. The father or step-father was a stocky, swarthy, hirsute man from somewhere down south, half Serb, half Turk, if not an outright Muslim. He had a skinny little lady for a wife and a beautiful step-daughter named Fani...

I ran into Fani almost every day when I went with a pan to the sink next to their apartment. She would come out and look quite fetching in her little apron. She'd smile and wish me a good day. She'd load coal and kindling from one of the crates into her bucket...or wait for me to fill my pan before she ran water into a bowl. I had never before seen such blue, almost purple eyes...they were like some rare species of cultivated flower. And her hair...not black, but brown and very long. Her skin wasn't white but more of a brownish bronze, and the finely etched eyebrows reminiscent of my cousin Stanka's were like two birds flying in the distance...Whenever I had to wait behind her while she finished drawing water, everything about her would get absorbed by my skin, my hair. But I didn't succumb to temptation...I knew what could come of it, and I didn't want any more entanglements... Sometimes I ran into her when she went out or came back home clutching some sheet music to her chest and wearing a little hat on her head, instead of the broad-rimmed style that was then in fashion. She sang in some choir and was studying to become a saleswoman. Now and then, she would give Gisela a pat on the head...as indeed who wouldn't?...I was very careful not to make a sound when I took the key to the faucet out of its little cabinet, then filled my pan or bucket quietly, with the stream running along the inside of the container. If I spilled any, I would wipe it up with a rag or my sleeve, so that the tile floor dried as soon as possible...oh, I was not going to have a repeat of those nerve-wracking burlesques from Bohorič Street...Every now and then, I could hear her singing...in a low voice. They were some sort of musical exercises...sung almost in a murmur. One of those melancholy ballads. I couldn't make out the words. I waited for her to finish it...Sometimes her mother would come out...a short, blocky woman with a long, doleful face and hair that was wound up in a bun on the slenderest part of her head...Hirol, her father or step-father, an invalid with a wooden leg, was a short, swarthy man with a broad, light brown face and wild hair. His eyebrows were as pronounced as his mustache, and he had tiny eyes...like two brown screwheads. He seemed nice, too, but his red-mouthed smile under his whiskers...it was unctuously threatening, like an animal rictus. I was a little afraid of him. Was he really a Turk or a Muslim who prayed to Allah? I didn't like pale-faced, blue-eyed blond people...they reminded me too much of angels determined to live on earth at all costs...And I couldn't stand swarthy men with oily, hairy, dark skin...They reminded me of barbarians from Baghdad...bushy genitals of some sort, and hairy backsides...

For christmas, Fani took Gisela and me to the opera for a performance of *Snow White*. It was the first time I'd been to a proper theater...I'd never seen that environment before. It was like being in a cathedral, only with more light. The tiers of balconies...all the way up to the ceiling...the white, bulging loges like cells of a beehive with gilt ornamentation. And the gigantic crowns of the chandeliers suspended in air...But most of all the silence...the blue-clad ushers who attentively, almost delicately led you to the row where your seat was, totally unlike the ushers at the Unity Cinema...The gigantic, iron-ribbed main curtain that went up silently all the way to the top, where two grimacing masks looked down on the audience...Behind the main curtain there was another curtain...decorated with fairies clad in Roman togas, sitting around in a landscape of big, blocky rocks and white pillars and reaching their arms up toward a red pastel sky, while in their midst a snake coiled through the dust at their feet... Behind that one, there was yet another curtain of red velvet edged in gold cord that parted from the top onto the scene of that other life that was going to play out down below...We were seated at the far end of the first row...The electric candles in the chandeliers gradually dimmed and went out...Just let there not be a siren or an aerial bombardment...Fani's arms shone white on the armrests and my shoulder just barely grazed against her muslin blouse...I had to be careful...my imagination was beginning to get carried away, and our presence in this auditorium was like a dream. I'd never experienced anything like it in three dimensions before...this dazzlingly illuminated, unearthly Snow White in a threatening artificial forest whose treetops reached to the ceiling...a procession of dwarves wearing scarlet caps and little boots with pompoms at the toe...this music and the perfect singing...the flashes of light when the old queen interrogated her mirror...the thunder, as though, under some bell jar of fairy tale geography, the people up on stage were actually experiencing a storm.

Then there was the refined tone of the dialog...the furious shouts that you couldn't get mad at...And all the mutations of light on Fani's and Gisela's faces...the pink twilight, the green light filtered through the trees, then the flashes of the thunderstorm, followed by the harsh blond light of the sun...The prince, the fanfares, the courtly attire...the scarlet, green, pomegranate red of his ruby-encrusted armor...Intermission...lights...the velvet and balconies once again. Fani offered me a chocolate...but I couldn't because I felt too hurt inside and jealous that we hadn't been able to carry off anything like this in the red room of our old apartment, because it required so many people and things...The adults around us were eating some sort of black cookies, apparently used to mixing extreme emotional engagement with the act of stuffing their faces...The show over, I suddenly found myself outside again, as though the wind had carried me past the box office and set me under the naked stone figures looking down from the building's facade onto the thickly clad people coming out of the theater...Back to reality!

Fani and her parents had a nice apartment...consisting of two rooms and a kitchen. The kitchen table, which stood next to the window, had a nice tablecloth on it, beneath which there was an oilcloth decorated with three-masted ships. There was a black, boxy radio on top of the sideboard...you could listen to music or news on it till you were bored stiff...next to it there was a glass bell jar with a potpourri of bread crusts and crumbs...Her parents' bedroom had down comforters in lace duvets and a picture of Noah's ark bobbing over a stormy sea with gigantic, frothy waves on all sides – sort of like what we experienced in our attic apartment during a storm…Fani's bedroom was tiny. I only got to see it for a second. A round mirror, hairbrushes, a little stringed tambura hanging on the wall, a woven carpet with kittens in the design, pictures of movie stars…Claudette Colbert, the formidable Bette Davis, Errol Flynn dressed up as the King of England…Fani gave Gisela a new hair style. "You're so much prettier this way." Gisela checked herself in the mirror and nodded. "One day, I'll be a very important lady." This caused Fani and her mother to laugh. "And what are you going to be when you grow up?" There was so much kindheartedness in Fani's voice…if only she didn't have the habit of pursing her mouth, as though she had a harelip. "A singer," Gisela said. She leaned against the table and looked up at the ceiling with her big eyes, as brown as chocolate pralines. "Now she looks like a little Virgin Mary," Fani's mother said. Fani looked at Gisela and smiled. She herself sang in the choir of the Music Academy on the other side of the Ljubljanica, in the same big building that had statues of composers out in front of it. "Let's sing something, Gisela!" And they started to sing "The Orphan." Her mother sat by their brick stove, singing along. What magic passed over Fani's face at that moment! Her nose twitched and her cheeks and lips protruded, all of which made me a little crazy. It was magical, and it frightened me…How do you train a voice like that? With practice, practice and more practice. I was hearing an angel sing and was unable to move. At her slightest smile, waves would radiate magic. Obviously, I didn't dare look at her but stared at the table instead. Even her hair when she shook her head to give conductor's signals to Gisela…was nothing but brilliance and smiles.

Damn it! She had become a *vila*, a regular water sprite. The left corner of her mouth...despite the compulsive way she kept compressing her lips...was extraordinarily beautiful and special, and I could have just eaten it. "Why don't you sing along with us?" she asked. "What songs do you know?" Sing, o ye mountains...But I resisted her charm. She got up and went to her room for a song book. Her hips...almost like a real woman's...enchanted me. She had a beautiful ass, not just a marvelous face. Two firm, compact little hemispheres, neither too big nor too small, all nicely packaged by her skirt in a regular festival of muscles. It was pure heaven, made to order for me. I had to hold onto my thing with both hands in my pockets in order to keep it still. But I kept the temptation to myself...Sometimes she also sang with her step-father Hirol, who would accompany her on a small, banged-up accordion, and on those occasions I could hear her muffled voice. Just in general, there was a lot of singing that went on in that house: the old market vendor's whole family...the actor...the drunks in the Salaznik café...and the ones in the German organization...the company that got together on Saturdays on the balcony of the house next door... even Vati would join in, imitating, by turns, the various drums and trumpets of a brass band...Fani also sang in the cathedral choir. Once she invited me to go with her up to the choir loft. There, beneath the organ pipes in their gigantic case, in the semi-dark of candles and glass cabinet doors, she was even more beautiful than outside...Her profile took my breath away...I can still see it today. Years have passed, and yet here she is, still standing physically in front of me...Draped over her shoulders, her silken choir robe traced her lines and curves, enhancing the contours of her flesh in such a wonderful way that the sheer sweetness of it all made it agonizing to look at her...In my enchantment, I practically passed out, while the choir kept punching away with its psalms at the pillars...

One day, Fani came running home, clearly upset...I was just then filling a pan with water. She closed the apartment door quickly, without responding to my greeting, which put me completely off balance... Then she pushed the door open again. "Bubi...help me!" She was holding a piece of paper. "Some Italian has been following me...all day... ever since I stopped by the store. I can't get rid of him. He's waiting outside for me to come back, but I won't go. I'm terrified. Take him this note."...All of this was mumbled. I ran downstairs as fast as I could. What a mess!...It was true: there, standing in his boat-sized shoes on the uneven round cobblestones of the arched entryway to our building, was a Fascist – an *Ardito*, no less, wearing the uniform of an alpine gunnery brigade, complete with fez and pompom, a black shirt and black ribbons...Smooth shaven, with a neat little mustache...I gave him the note...he grabbed it from me and read it. *Whoosh!* he bent forward, tears streaming from his dark eyes..."*Prego, prego!* Fani!" he begged, clasping his hands in my direction...Did he think I was her brother?... Tears kept streaming down his cheeks, and he kept begging. Was this for real or what?...You couldn't count all the Italians who would chat up women on the street, go running after them, shout, implore, clutch at their hearts, sing...and then lay every single one that came within range of their zippers...It was embarrassing. This was a grown man. I felt like punching him, his incessant sobbing made me so nervous. I wanted to knock some sense into him, sober him up. "*Mio!*" I said, pointing at the dagger he wore sheathed at his waist. If he wanted me to go get Fani, he had to give it to me. He nodded and sniffled…"*Prego, prego, signorina* Fani!" Anyway, he was a Fascist, so, like it or not, sort of an ally of mine. I ran back upstairs. "The Italian won't leave," I said. "He wants to see you." Fani went white as a sheet… She began running around their kitchen…came back to the door… put on a jacket. "Come with me." I went with her and stood between the two of them. "*Prego*, Fani!" He was asking her out. Fani laughed, shaking her head. "No, no, no." She was pretending to be uncontrollable, and I didn't like it. He kept begging her, trying to convince her…with a fast-paced but long, involved speech. It was quite the show!…Stan and Ollie, Hans Moser and Fernandel all rolled up into one. "*Morto!*" He pulled the dagger out of the sheath with its little gutter for blood and held it up to his neck. Fani laughed…fearfully…I had to guffaw. "*Prego* Fani…*io Rusia*," he said gravely. They were sending him to Russia, the eastern front, and, more than anything in the world, he wanted to meet with her before his departure. Everything became silly and serious at the same time. "*Eia, eia, alala!*" he repeated the battle cry of the Arditi. "*Rusia!*"…Suddenly Fani reconsidered…She agreed to see him the next day…They would meet in the street over there…I was beside myself…I reached my hand out toward the *Ardito*…Give me the dagger. "*Domani! Domani!*" he answered indifferently. So the whole thing was a ruse to extort a date with her. Fani smiled but was shaking nervously. "Now he knows where I live," she said…"You can always leave through the café." But that was only a few paces away from the courtyard entrance. Despite the risk, it was the only way out. I didn't feel bad for her...but all I had to do was imagine Clairi in her place and I got it...

W INTER THAT YEAR WASN'T BAD just at the Russian front, but here, too...In Leningrad, three to four thousand people died of hunger each day..."Order number 45 of the Supreme Commander of the German Armed Forces Adolf Hitler: The objective of the sixth army is Stalingrad and the Caucasus" was what the newspaper said... The streetcar with its plow was just barely able to move through the high walls of snow on both sides of Old Square...overnight the Italian soldiers occupying St. Jacob's School created two super-naturally huge caricatured statues out of snow, which they doused with water to get them to freeze: a mustachioed Stalin and a cigar-chomping Churchill...One morning there they stood perfectly sculpted at the street corners like towering guards on each side of the square, one all bristles, the other all wrinkles, both glowering down at the streetcars, buildings and people passing beneath their heads, which loomed twenty feet up in the air...Sadly it was time for us to go, to leave everything...to travel to Germany. In a big envelope that came in the mail, there were five cards marked "*Besondere Umsiedlungskommis-sion*"* and confirmation of an appointment for a medical examination, a blood test and an analysis of our mental capacity. Those tests were supposed to take place in the medical train of the Special Resettlement

*Special Resettlement Commission

Commission that visited all the cities of occupied Europe...and now the train had arrived in Slovenia from Minsk and was standing on a sidetrack way outside of town, near Šentvid...On the day we were scheduled for our exams, everybody with last names beginning with J, K, and L was supposed to report...

We had to heat up a lot of water so we could all bathe...a full kettle on the stove for each one, plus a panful on the hotplate. We had to get up at three if we wanted to be ready by six, because all we had for our baths was a bucket and the tin bathtub. We carried the dirty water downstairs to dump in the toilet, then drew fresh water, and while one person was bathing, another was waiting for his water to boil... Mother was nervous, Vati smiled and trembled, Gisela twice fell asleep sitting in a chair...We had out and out travel fever...*"Schau weg!"* * Clairi shouted at me amid laughter while, naked, she bathed herself out of a bucket next to the stove in the workroom, where it was warmest...In my opinion she had a really nice body...Vati's freshly-pressed patched shirt was too big for me...I had to pull the sleeves up at the shoulders and put on rubber bands so the cuffs wouldn't go flapping a foot past the sleeves of my sweater...Since it was cold, I put Clairi's long jacket on over the sweater, because Vati was wearing the sport coat that I used for school during the week...We were the only ones out on the soundless street, walking between the walls of snow and rows of dark buildings...this was the blackest night I could remember... Inside, the streetcar windows had frost on them that bit into your

*Look away!

nostrils. We rode a long way, to the last stop where the streetcar turned around... Then we had to walk on an icy sidewalk past a settlement consisting of numerous whitewashed workers' houses amid lots of trees, where some light shone through a pink curtain onto a frozen garden bed... I felt we ought to be sneaking past these people or at least walking far away from their houses, because what we were planning to do was nothing short of treason... Gisela had it hardest of all, since her orthopedic shoes made walking on the frozen pavement like wearing skates... The cold literally gnawed away at our heads. We were about to go traveling again, we were going to take a train to someplace far away... to Germany, maybe even Berlin... bathed in spotlights, the imposing columns of the Reichstag, with the thick, heavy silk of the national flag at its top... now that I had just barely gotten used to living in Slovenia...

We saw the train on the far side of a lowered railroad barrier. It was a long composition, with no locomotive up front or in back. With long cars and whitewashed roofs that had ventilators, as though there were tennis courts on board... It stood on a track bed that ran through fields of stubble... Some people were already standing alongside it, looking like shadows, and there were some automobiles, even some horse hitches... We trudged up a path that wound through the stubble up to the track... Several limousines were parked at the head of the train, among which we could see several well-dressed people standing around and a cluster of German officers in their forage caps and leather coats with fur collars turned up... At the other end, there were some wagons and a bit of a crowd, some figures wearing fur hats and resembling shadows crowded around the door to one of the train cars. Where were the beginning and end of the train? Without an engine and in the dark you couldn't tell... Some people were also standing around behind horse-drawn wagons, where they were protected from the wind. Others were still arriving on foot, coming around the barrier at the end, through the stubble and up to the track, and at the front, from behind the cars... women in kerchiefs and shaggy overcoats arriving late, men in three-quarter-length fur coats, children... Where were they going? People kept springing up out of the snowy gloom... heads hunched between shoulders, arms shoved ramrod straight into pockets... *"Gehen wir da entlang,"* * mother said, her face bright red and stiff from the cold... Ashes of coal cinders were strewn over the frozen path. We walked past one wagon, then another... both of them a yellowish brown, lacquered, their sideboards decorated with pictures of rosemary sprigs and carnations. Two horses covered with blankets were eating hay... The train cars were long and high. Their doors were much wider than the doors of ordinary train cars, with round portholes in them. The windows were curtained with something resembling velvet... The farther away we got from the "forward" cars, the more shabbily the people were dressed, until toward the end there were just laborers, peddlers and peasants wearing little more than jackets and scarves against the winter cold... Their heads bunched together like clusters of black grapes around the wide steps of the train cars looming up high over the track bed... Not a single pair of eyes was peeking out

---

*Let's go down that way.

from inside, either that or they were still snoozing…*"Wann fangen die Ärzte an?"** mother asked a non-descript bunch…An older man with a dormouse fur cap and a strange shadow over his face appeared…*"Schnell…ich kann niks gut deutsch reden."***…"Right," Vati asked, switching languages, "when do you think the doctors will start the examinations?" The man practically bent in two from bowing, as though Vati were some sort of distinguished gentleman…"Fairly soon, sir, I believe," he began stammering. "On the summons, it says it begins at seven, and it's almost eight now…But the ladies and gentlemen up there at the front have become quite impatient, so I think it's going to start right away…" A worn out looking woman approached, possibly his wife, and a boy my age wearing what could have passed for a shepherd's hat. Behind the car several girls were jumping up and down to keep themselves warm, and giggling…*"Wir müssen uns dort vorne erkündigen,"*** mother said…Some people, perhaps even the majority, were huddled in the shelter from the wind that the train's wheels afforded…We slowly went back…when suddenly, on the other side of the buffers at the end of the car, who did I see? The Jaklič brothers with their mother and father…both skinny redheads wearing woolen caps…I remembered the Balohs, the Frenchman's boys, Enrico…where were they now?…The Jakličes saw me and quickly averted their eyes, which in the midst of their freckled

*When do the doctors begin?

**Fast. I no speak good German.

***We need to go up to the front and find out what's going on.

faces were as blue as porcelain…From one car to the next, the assembled company grew more colorful, better dressed, and I saw more and more fur coats, boots, gold-plated cigarette cases and fine scarves, with more and more hand-shaking, kissing of cheeks, good manners…*"Schau…der Baron Loretto!"** Clairi said excitedly at one point… Amid a group of animated young girls dressed in dirndls under their overcoats, a lithe, roughly sixty-year-old man was standing…he wore a camel hair coat and had steel-gray hair and firmly etched features on a fresh, well-rested face…He was telling some silly story and keeping the beat with his big, gloved hand, so that at every pause, when he fell silent, the girls burst out laughing…Clairi stood transfixed, and Vati lifted his hat, as though they'd surprised him…The baron gave him a spry salute, lifting a hand to his beaver fur hat. *"Ein schöner Wintertag, Meister!"*** What a clown…Clairi looked back, her face flushed red. *"Das sage ich dir, Bubi, wenn ich so einen Mann hätte…"*** And so on…But in the meantime there was something else…a beautiful day was dawning…the red sun rising through the clouds over the stubble…still small and pink as an orange. The cold didn't pinch at our noses and ears anymore…And then who should show up at a bound from behind the train of locked cars…wearing a lined raincoat, a checkered scarf, and a hunting hat?…None other than Mrs. Gmeiner's boyfriend from Nove Jarše himself…the banker with the

*Look over there, that's Baron Lorette!

**A fine winter's day, Master Kovačič

***I'm telling you, Bubi, if I had a husband like that…

elegant mustache and signet ring. When he saw us, his face elongated with joy…he ran toward Vati, Mother, Clairi, and Gisela with outstretched arms…"Now this is a surprise! *Das ist eine Überraschung!*" They shook hands, laughed, talked loudly…grown-ups! "*Wo ist jetzt die Frau Gmeiner?*" Mother inquired. Everyone drew close. She had gone. "*Schon abgereist! Nach Kreutzbach! Auch beide Söhne. Jetzt nach ein paar Tagen fahre ich nach.*"[*] The banker was wearing padded gloves with loose stitches that emanated a powerful scent…"*Heute,*" he said seriously, "*geht es um eines: wer wird Reichsdeutscher werden und wer Volksdeutscher bleiben…*"[**] He nodded with the edge of his hunting hat toward the ones at the end of the train…"*Die werden…*at least I suspect…become *nur Volksdeutsche und mancher von jenen auch,*"[***] and he aimed his hat toward the ones at the front…So this was a selection process for determining who was an ordinary German and who was a special one…Those ones there, who were just now emerging from behind the train cars out into the sun in their kerchiefs, their shawls, their knee-length fur coats and jackets, the children…as you could judge from their appearance, these were all going to remain ordinary Germans, just like us…What was their point in distinguishing between rocks and minerals?…Were the *Reichsdeutsche* going to live a better

---

[*]Gone already! To Kreutzbach! With both of her sons. In a couple of days I'll join them.

[**]Today there's just one issue at stake: who gets designated a homeland German and who has to make do with being a colonial German.

[***]Those folks…at least I suspect, will be designated just colonial Germans, and most of those others, too.

life than the *Volksdeutsche*? And how were they going to judge that some were better than others? By their clothes, their manners, such as they had?...Cars began driving up...black limousines with white-wall tires, convertibles with canvas roofs, and people got out of them. Look there, see that woman in the white hat and black earrings, smoking from a cigarette holder, whom everyone called "*Weihnachtsbaum*" – Christmas tree – because she was always draped with necklaces and bracelets? And there, see that little old gray-haired man who always wears a cape and a black velvet hat and is constantly shaking...and the woman I saw at Mrs. Hamman's wearing the lemon-yellow and sky-blue morning gown that she bought in Lisbon...And then somebody else arrived...stepping out of the train or a limousine. A fat little man in a gray suit, with his trousers tucked into his boots and a swastika on his sleeve...President von Wertbach...Everyone greeted him from a distance...respectfully, some raising their arms and saying "*Heil*"... "*Platz! Platz!*"* ...As well fed as though he had eight ration cards, at least...I could have decked a pudgy guy like him, strutting around in his red crocodile coat and his oversized boots, with the slightest of knockout punches..."*Gehen wir dorthin, zurück,*"** Vati pointed. He was tired of it all...he wasn't used to big events, crowds, excitement outdoors...

At the end of the train, where people were insistently pushing

*Make way, make way!

**Let's go back that way.

up against the locked doors of the car, there was such a big crowd that the way back was blocked. And this was the day when just last names beginning in J, K, and L were being considered...my God!... Some people were showing some things to each other...they were old photographs..."This was my father when he was an Austrian corporal," somebody said. It was a brown photograph that he'd pulled out of a billfold stuffed full of photographs...A corporal decked out in his lanyards. Others were also looking at something, some German certificate or diploma with some sort of distinction or seal on a ribbon... Even here the sheer density of the crowd made it impossible to study the thing..."Did you find out when the examinations start?" Vati's acquaintance in the dormouse fur reappeared, his face a strange, green kohlrabi color...Others also approached. To ask Vati for information? That was a joke! "I think," he squinted in his confusion, "it's going to be soon..." The door to the train car banged open...if the people crowding the steps up to it hadn't jumped back, it would have thrown them into the crowd. An SA trooper came out of the car holding a metal container of ashes. He came to a stop on the steps. "*Platz!*"*...People parted to form a pathway for him...some of them stopped him to ask when things would get going..."*Bald, bald!*"** he nodded back to them solicitously...The ones closest to the door were looking inside and nodding entranced...What on earth was inside?...In the meantime the soldier came back and slammed the door shut behind him again...

*Make way!
**Soon, soon!

The crowd resumed its position, pressed up against it…people began putting away their photos and documents…"Hey! Ruhe! Take it easy!" somebody suddenly called out…A kid was wailing somewhere…All heads turned to look down the track…even the ones toward the front. There, alongside the path, two boys were wrestling in the snow. One of them was flat on the ground, while the other, all covered with clumps of ice and snow, was practically on top of him…next to them was a blanket…wasn't that the kid in the shepherd's hat?…I wanted to go see. But mother held me back, "Bubi!"…"Sweet mother of God, he's ours!" the wife of the man in the dormouse fur cap shrieked. Her husband went flying as though he'd been wound up…his face going from kohlrabi ivory to a furious, bright red…He grabbed his son and stood him on the path…then he picked up the littler boy… nicely dressed, with a Davey Crockett coonskin cap…He was about to go at him, when some lady took hold of the boy from behind. "*Holger, was ist geschehen?*"*…The boy practically shrieked in fury, "*Dieses slowenische Schwein…angestoßen!*"**…Oh, for God's sake, what was this now?…It didn't sound any good…The one with the shock of hair, the brunet…stood there, also shuddering in fury…"I was just paying you back!"…He couldn't speak, for all the spit in his mouth…So they called each other names, one accusing the other of being a Slovene or a German pig. Davey Crockett lashed out again, under the lady's – his mother's – protection…pointing his finger at the other the way

*Tell me what happened, Holger.
**This Slovene pig…kicked me.

teacher's pets do at school. *"Das ist er, der mich jedes Mal nach der Schule vermöbelt hat…"* *"Was?"* the lady exclaimed in shock. Some people started to laugh, while others grumbled about the insult…but then suddenly the whole thing took a turn…"I'm koink to take all ze appropriate meashures," the lady exclaimed in a threatening voice. "You can pea shuah of zat!" She had to screw her face up the way I did when I spoke Slovene. "People like zat aren't vorzy off peaing rezettlet into ze Reich!" The crowd that had been facing the train car turned to face the boy and his father…they wanted to see what was going to happen to them…The lady took her little boy by the hand and headed off toward the front of the train…the boy, not content with the outcome, kept lagging behind and had to be dragged…The crowd around the front cars welcomed them…gathered around them…The lady spoke to them, waving her hand and pointing back at the crowd at the rear. You could see the anger appear on their faces…they turned indignantly to face the people back here…Things didn't look good…They glared at the boy and his father as though intending to skin them alive…All the busy bodies back where we were hastily dispersed and retreated, extracting themselves from the quagmire, from any connection to the father and son…I knew exactly how shepherd's hat felt, now that he had no options for beating it, for just disappearing…The anger at both ends of the train was equally distributed now…the ones at our end were even more worked up, because they'd been dragged into the dispute out of nowhere…and they began to voice threats…Now was the

*That's the guy who always beats me up after school!

time to do something to help the boy and his father…"*Komm!*" I said to mother, who was still holding me fast, but she didn't move…Then the wife went flying like an arrow out of the crowd and grabbed hold of her son. "March!" He refused to budge…People started to grumble and threaten…"Put the little bastard over your knee!" somebody bawled…"Do as you're told! Do as you're told!" a bunch of little girls shouted, small-minded little piglets…"March…take him, will you?" the wife said to her husband. The father took hold of the boy from the other side…They dragged him to apologize to the lady at the far end of the train. Abuse, curses and jeers followed them all the way there… The other boy's mother clearly had the final word there…I could sense that the boy was being forced to apologize to the lady. His mother grabbed him by the ear and talked to him angrily…undoubtedly she was telling him what to say – that's what mine would have done…He lowered his head and presumably rattled off quickly whatever she told him to say…everyone around us got quiet, as though they were trying to listen, and some of them actually heard…Finally, Davey Crockett's mommy magnanimously offered the woman her hand in a sign of reconciliation…As they returned to the back, people parted before them, as if they carried the plague…now both of them, dormouse hat and his wife, were marked people on account of this brat…you could see they would have liked to be rid of him just as much as everyone else…They stood some distance apart from the others, without the latter taking their eyes off them for a moment…For the time being, they could be apart, but what would happen when they were forced into close quarters with others who would have nothing kind to say to her? What would it be like for them in the train, in front of the commission?...

The door of the next-to-last train car opened...People crowded around head-to-head, leg-to-leg...but a soldier wearing an orderly's smock, using gestures and mimicry, instructed them to enter one at a time, in orderly fashion...The doorway was wide, and the steps up were high...When I lifted Gisela up after mother, there was a pop, and one of my cuffs went flopping treacherously out of the left sleeve of my sweater...There was an incredible crowd up top...People were more crowded there than outside. But what a train car!...Like some real big shot's office, all finished in polished hardwood, with a red carpet on the floor and velvet curtains on the windows...And so warm that my nose started to drip. Lots of hubbub and noise...People were asking questions over everyone else's heads and answering from the row up front or the row at the back...they weren't being selfish, some of the answers came from completely different people than the ones who'd been asked...The ones up front must have been office workers...sometimes I caught sight of a desk...then a phone...then the blond head of a female employee...There was a whole row of them sitting there, all dressed in gray, elegant, pink-fleshed and blonde, their eyebrows and lashes made up blue...Amid the crush, everyone suddenly fell silent. "*Name und Vorname?*"* you could hear a voice saying

*Name, last name first?

up front. A veritable music of language! And such pronunciation! Like on the radio or in the movies…A forceful male voice answered… *"Beruf?"*[*]…*"Spengler"*[**]…*"Nationalität?"*[***]…A silence ensued at the front tables as the man failed to answer…people were craning their necks…*"Nationalität?"* the beauty repeated impatiently…*"Slowene,"* came the shame-faced reply, which was heard by everyone and provoked even more grumbling…The office workers accepted people's cards and papers…They were really attractive. But each of them had a little round painted pin with a swastika affixed to her blouse. That detail absolutely clashed with their physical beauty, their skin, their voices and hair styles, their slender fingers…it was as though they were wearing a piece of a military uniform…Now the line was moving toward the desk more quickly…until the first, second, and third steps were up…Mother took all the papers out of Vati's pockets, because he was clumsy, then she collected the ones out of Clairi's purse and her own…A whole stack of papers…to think what we could have gotten for those! IDs, birth certificates, baptismal certificates, receipts, statements…it was awful how many papers people needed to live…and on top of that they were all crumpled and yellowed with age, handled hundreds of times, so that they had black creases and spots…The young beauty took them and held them under a powerful light where they looked even more pathetic…She copied them out, first by hand,

[*]Occupation?
[**]Plumber.
[***]Nationality?

then by typewriter... She was wearing black trousers and had harsh lines around her mouth... somehow those two details went with her pin... Behind her, a stove was puffing away, and I began to nod off, almost falling asleep... I saw the peach fuzz on the young woman's chin and a flurry of coats all around me, as though they were coming from another world... Suddenly Vati got up... He asked the young office worker what steps remained ahead of us on the train... perhaps merely because she projected such a harsh, inaccessible personality. But she barely glanced at him, at Vati, whom our female customers were always sidling up to, because he struck them as being "so attractive and interesting." "*Das werden Sie nach und nach noch alles erfahren*,"* she said coldly. "*Der Nächste, bitte...*"**

We waited in a dark room at a door that was covered with a heavy, motionless curtain. The curtain opened, and a soldier appeared sitting in the gangway between the two cars, stamping people's papers. Each person took blue, red and green copies... almost transparent... were they that bad because of the war or were they intentionally so thin? That wasn't clear... The next car had a long corridor that was all metal and glass... The winter sun shone over the snow-covered stubble into the car, motionless and boring as only nature can be in the presence of exquisite machines. This car had something like compartments, but they were different from the kind regular trains had. More like cabins with finely crafted oak doors and handles, upholstered in brown

*You'll find all of that out in due time.

**Next, please.

leather…The women went on to the next car, while the men had to stay here. We were separated from mother, Clairi and Gisela…Then even Vati and I had to part. A strange little lady who had hips almost down to her knees sent him and two other men through one door, while I had to go through another…I entered a small room with leather-upholstered chairs and curtains…There were several boys there already. Both Jakličes were seated in the corner, while a boy in a green sweater perched by the door, propping his blond head up in his hands. There were two more just behind him with their backs pressed to the upholstered wall…There were no windows and a harsh arc lamp lit the room…I didn't know if I should talk to the Jakličes or not. It was like being in the waiting room of the dispensary at school or in a priest's office, but then again it was different. The other boys were sitting as though they'd been cemented down and kept swallowing their saliva, as if waiting to be questioned at school. The little kid in the green sweater was probably still of an age to be playing with blocks. The other two were older, perhaps a grade behind me, and I knew the Jakličes like the inside of my pocket. Not one of them spoke, they were so nervous. But the small chairs we were sitting on were nice…gold rivets fastened the leather seats onto black legs resembling a piano stool…There was a poster up on the wall with something written on it. I read it, then tried to translate it into Slovene…"The Aryan is a born leader and conqueror – *Miss Anna Sulke, advisor for education.*" This was some tribal thing, that much I got…Then a deep male voice called the little boy…Adalbert Lißlinger, or something like that, was his name…

He fumbled with the curtain until he managed to find the handle behind it...He hadn't come back by the time the invisible voice called my name ten minutes later...This was now a different department or compartment. Sort of like a teacher's office at school...with books and charts and pictures of animals on the walls. A gentleman wearing a black suit and glasses with a gold swastika pinned to his lapel was sitting behind a desk. Thin, even gaunt, and resembling a teacher, with a narrow necktie and a black wart on his nose..."*Setz dich!*"* I sat down across from him. His voice wasn't at all hostile. "*Antworte, wann und wo du geboren bist!*"**...He wasn't unpleasant. I didn't answer him in Swiss German but in mother's textbook variety of the language..."*Sehr gut...Antworte mir: wieviel beträgt die Entfernung zwischen Sonne, Mond und Erde?*"***...I didn't completely trust what I'd learned...He helped me out and confirmed the exact distance in kilometers. That confused me..."*Jetzt eine Frage über Jahreszeiten. Was ist bezeichnend für die vier Zeitabschnitte? Winter?*"****...Here I was better off...but I only mumbled approximate answers...The gentleman finished them for me... Up until now he hadn't been too demanding...He shoved a piece of paper and a nice pencil in front of me. "*Diktat!...schreibe: Auf meinem*

*Sit down.

**Tell me when and where you were born.

***Now tell me, what is the combined distance between the sun, the earth and the moon?

****And now a question about the seasons. What is typical of each of the four quarters? Winter?

Fenster stehen 24 Blumentöpfe mit Bäumchensaamen."* I got confused, and, instead of writing out twenty-four, I used the number. He corrected me. *"Genügend...Rechenaufgabe: In einem Monat verbrauchte ein Mann zwanzig Zentner Kohle und zehn Bricketts. Wieviel verbrauchte der Mann in vier Monaten?"*** I took a long time to answer that one because I hadn't heard the whole question and was too embarrassed to ask him to repeat it...now he got cross with me, and I could feel the chill wafting out of his eyes..."*Was möchtest du werden, wenn du groß wirst?*"*** he asked sternly. *"Ich will eine kaufmannische Laufbahn einschlagen,"**** I answered cravenly..."*Kaufmann sein ist schwer, mein Junge,"*****...he pierced me with his eyes..."*Man muß guten Willen, Eifer und Intelligenz an den Tag legen...Nun, jetzt gehe zu dieser Tür hinaus. Heil!"******...He raised his arm in greeting without looking at me...I returned the greeting with my right arm. Then out! Whew, had I ever blown it...Now those two others and the Jakličes would be up.

*Now a dictation: write the following, "There are 24 flower pots on my window sill, each with seeds of little trees."

**That will do. Now for some arithmetic: a man used twenty pounds of coal and ten briquets in one month. How many did the man use in four months?

***What do you want to become when you grow up?

****I plan to become a businessman.

*****A business career is tough, my boy.

******You have to show good will, diligence and intelligence...Now go out through this door. Heil!

N ow i was back in the same corridor I had been in before, except that nobody else was there... I felt awful... as though somebody had unscrewed my head and realized I was an idiot and then poured medicine on my tongue... The door at the end of the car opened and that stern little lady gestured for me to approach her... she led me through the next car, which was almost white, except for the floor. There were women standing around here... I thought for a second that I recognized mother's red face through the window of a door left ajar. She was dressed in just her slip... I picked up the scent of medicine and disinfectant... we went through a curtain and passed into a small room painted gray... "*Ausziehen und warten!*"* the lady said. She pulled the curtain closed behind her... Vati was sitting in the compartment in his underwear... he just nodded to me... Three other men were also there... A skinny old man, bald with a white mustache, wearing long johns and pale as a sheet... Next to him a fat, ruddy-cheeked man with fringe-like gray hair, also in his underwear but wearing a green hat and a hunting jacket draped over his shoulders... He could barely breathe through his fat, red lips, which he tried to keep wide open but which kept pursing like a baby's as he wheezed. With both hands, he was holding onto his huge belly, which rested on his thighs like a globe wrapped in a cotton undershirt... There was one other man there who resembled the bill collector from the gasworks, dressed in black and black-haired, with a yellow face. This one was going to stay an ordinary German,

*Take your clothes off and wait here.

a *Volksdeutscher* for sure, because the real Germans were blond…I was something in between, more of a brunet. The other two…the skinny old man and ruddy cheeks who could barely breathe, would probably become *Reichsdeutsche*, because, judging from their skin and their new underwear, which was nice and not patched like Vati's and mine, they were men of a better sort…Vati was moving his lips…he didn't know which language to use…German or Slovene…*"Du mußt dich ausziehen bis zur Unterhose…"** he said. I felt embarrassed in front of these people, but I had to do it. I set my things on the shelves next to Vati's…I hid behind him…The fat man wheezed like a mountain. This was the first time I was together with grown-ups, half-naked men at the doctor's, and it was kind of like being in the army…A half hour later, a nurse appeared from behind the curtain and began reading names off a card in a metal frame…The first one she called was the fat man, who could scarcely breathe. He lifted himself up like the sphere of the earth. Then it was the turn of the skinny old man with the waxen face…The fat man was already stumbling through the curtain…My God, he was in a really bad way now…He clutched at his throat, as though trying to pull off a tight collar, even though he was naked down to the waist…Vati and the dark-haired man jumped up…They helped him lie down across several stools…He was gasping for air so violently that his eyes were bulging out like two billiard balls, their blue irises floating to the top like little gray circles…His whole face was covered with tiny, fine silver droplets…The little nurse

*You have to strip down to your underwear.

appeared with some machine with a face mask, which I recognized as an inhalator. She set it on his mouth and nose and told Vati and me to go on...

At first, I thought I'd fallen amid icy peaks full of lightning, sun, metal and mirrors...It was like in an accident...Everything hurt, not just my eyes...This was the most luxurious examination room I could have ever imagined...There were huge mirrors lining the walls, the ceiling overhead, and even the floor was covered with big reflective tiles...Except, in the middle, there was a kind of bed...no, a leather – or rubber – conveyor belt attached to a motor...probably something for practicing walking or something like that...I could see myself on the walls, up above, down below, with my legs looking like pillars... with wizened Vati next to me...There were nothing but doctors sitting at the table...concealing black boots and officers' uniforms under their lab coats...They were talking and laughing, partly like doctors and partly like commandants, but never, as I was soon to realize, like just one or the other. Everything started to hurt, much worse than during an ordinary doctor's appointment...my head started to throb hollowly...something began slicing at my lungs...my rectum started to sting...the teeth in my gums started to wobble, as though my whole jaw was about to drop out of my mouth...Vati handed over the cards... mine and his...he gave them to a doctor wearing glasses, who held out his hand..."*Die Unterhose ausziehen...*"* the doctor said. Underpants off...in front of them and Vati?...Vati pushed his long johns down

*Let's have those underpants off.

off his legs…this was the first time I ever saw his penis…a long, gray, droopy nose set in a black thicket with some onions gone blue… a real caricature, a gargoyle, the face of a furry monster of roots and tubers…I didn't see it straight on, but everywhere else, from down below, from the sides, from above. I squeezed my eyes shut and next to him saw myself, a dark, skinny body which I recognized only by the shock of hair flopping over the forehead…*"Spaziert ein wenig bis zur Wand…Auch du, Büblein, zusammen mit dem Papa,"** said the doctor in the middle. Vati walked from the table toward the door as though he were walking on eggshells…I went behind him, following his skinny, hairy white ass as though I were following an animal…*"Die Beine höher heben…noch höher!"*** the doctor ordered us in a military sort of way. These guys really did hold the reins in their hands…With extreme effort, lips compressed, Vati raised his weak, skinny legs, which had a habit of tipping over…up to his navel…*"Links herum!"**** We each went our own way. *"Rechts herum!"*****…These doctors were more likely drill instructors disguised as doctors…*"Bauch hinein, Brust hinaus!"******…I still couldn't see or feel much for the glare…I kept mistaking the ones in the mirrors for myself over here…Vati was also

---

*Take a walk over to the wall…You too, boy, go with your daddy.

**Lift those legs up higher…higher!

***Left face!

****Right face!

*****Stomach in, chest out!

heading straight toward the doctors in the mirror instead of toward the table… It was hopeless, no matter how many times over you were multiplied. "*Jetzt auf das Band!*"* Somebody came to help – a military orderly. Vati stepped up onto the belt… He was supposed to march straight ahead toward the exit… while the motorized wheel that the soldier turned on moved the belt back in the opposite direction. This was bound to be Vati's doom! He lost his balance… He would have gone crashing off the track onto his hip if the orderly hadn't first grabbed him by the elbow… It was easier for me, as long as I didn't look down at the moving floor or the end of the belt… Then we had to go back to the table where the gymnasts were sitting… "*Sie sind tuberkulös! Der Junge ist jetzt in Ordnung,*"** said the doctor in glasses as he read from our cards… "*Die Spritze!*"*** The little nurse came out from behind the curtain with hypodermic needles in hand… An ordinary doctor by the milky window got ready to take our blood samples… As the needle approached his ear, Vati darted away and squinted at the doctor… "*Was ist denn mit Euch?*"**** the doctor asked him harshly. "*Nichts,*"***** Vati shook his head. He closed his eyes, moved his ear close… when the needle pricked his earlobe… he jumped on the stool. "*Diese Slawen sind*

*Now get up on the treadmill.

**You're tubercular. The boy is fine now.

***Hypodermic!

****What's wrong with you?

*****Nothing.

dünnhäutige Menschen," the doctor said as he unscrewed the syringe...I twitched just a little...I didn't dare repeat Vati's mistake in front of these overblown egos in lab coats...At the table, the doctors were making notes on the cards..."*Setzt euch!*"** We had to sit on a high stool... One of them pressed his metal stethoscope against me...I breathed, coughed, held my breath, I knew this drill from Urach...while another tapped Vati on the knee with a mallet...Then they switched out...A third doctor examined our eyes and turned my eyelids up...and then another examined Vati's penis...and when that doctor moved over to me and bent down to examine mine...and he probably noticed immediately that I liked playing with my little fuse...he pulled and pulled the foreskin up over the glans so forcefully that I had to cry out at the top of my lungs...and then he squeezed my balls and my belly just above the pee-pee. In the meantime, another doctor was sticking his gloved hand up Vati's behind...I felt so many pain points all over my body, as though I'd been gutted and sutured in multiple places..."*Zum Röntgen,*"*** the bespectacled doctor said. Black door to the right...This bit I knew, it was a relaxing kind of medicine: stand on the marks, press the cold plate to your chest, listen to them call out their calibrations in the dark, watch for the green light, the red light...

Move along!..."*Zum Fotograf!*"****...First Vati went through a

*These Slavs sure are thin-skinned.

**Be seated.

***Take him to x-ray.

****Take him to the photographer.

padded door. I sat on a bench and waited for a long time...When he reappeared, he was completely beside himself...gray-faced, sweaty, stammering..."*Du mußt die Unterhose wieder ausziehen, Bubi!*"* he said in distress...This was a room like one in a photographer's studio... On the floor at one end of the room, there was a gym mat, illuminated from all sides by lighting equipment...mounted on stands, fixed to the walls, placed on the floor, suspended from the ceiling...with a camera and tripod standing in the shadows. "*Lege dich auf die Mitte der Decke,*"** a male voice said from out of the shadows. I lay down and looked up. "*Die Hände weg vom Pimperle! Ausstrecken!*"*** the man said. *Click! click! click!* went the camera..."*Stehe auf!*"****...I got up and hid my pee-pee. "*Die Hände weg. Still stehen!*"*****...*Click!* went the camera..."*Jetzt stütze dich auf alle viere!*"******...I got down on my hands and knees...with the glass eye of the camera and photographer staring me in the face...he had a pale head with a black mustache and a scrim of hair at his temples. He wore a necktie, so he wasn't an officer...He hid his head behind the camera. *Click!*..."*Jetzt drehe dich um! Mit dem Hintern gegen den Apparat!*"******* I turned around. Now the glass eye

*You're going to have to take your underpants off again, Bubi.

**Lie down in the middle of the mat.

***Keep your hands away from your willy. Hold your arms out.

****Get up.

*****Get your hands away from there. Stand still.

******Now get down on all fours.

*******Now turn around so your bottom is facing the camera.

was staring straight into my rear end…and my whole rectum contracted. *Click!*…*"Setze dich!"**…and I sat down…*"Die Hände aus dem Schoße. Auf die Decke stützen."*** Now I had to move my hands away again and expose my genitals. *Click! click!*…*"So! Schluß! Kannst gehen!"****… At last, I climbed back into my underwear and went outside, totally blinded…It was as though I'd been performing at the ballet…Vati looked at me when I came out…but then the door opened…It was the little nurse…*"Zurück in die Kabine! Sich anziehen!"*****…Taking a completely different passageway, we went through the same curtain back into the gray-painted little room, as though coming home after a journey of many days…Others were already there: the ruddy-cheeked fat man who had been unable to breathe before was still sitting on two stools, naked to the waist but with his suit coat draped over his shoulders. He was calm, and although he still had difficulty breathing, his breasts at least weren't heaving up toward his chin…*"Wie fühlen Sie sich?"****** Vati asked awkwardly. *"Schon gut…schon gut"*******…as he waved his hand in front of his face like a fan…Exhausted and frightened of whatever still lay ahead of us, Vati and I both quickly

---

*Sit down.

**Get your hands out of your lap. Set them down on the blanket.

***That's it. All done. You can go.

****Back to the waiting room. Put your clothes on.

*****How are you feeling?

******I'm ok…I'm ok.

got dressed. This time I tied a knot in the rubber band around my shirtsleeve so it couldn't escape out of my sweater...

We walked down the corridor. Every window had its blinds pulled all the way to the bottom, and lamps were turned on. Was it still day out? Just how many cars did this train actually have?...I was curious what was in the next car up ahead...It turned out to be a big office. Instead of desks, it had tables with windows on both sides. At each window there was a longer or shorter line. They were labeled "Balkan," "Rußland," "Italien," "Skandinawien," "Südafrika"...At each of the windows you had to hand over one of your colored slips so they could copy them onto big sheets of paper, then they handed them back... Where were Clairi, mother and Gisi now?...At the next to the last window, all the people waiting in line had to have their fingerprints taken. That went slowly...the people jostled each other, and when each one came bounding out of the crowd, they had the tips of their fingers black. I saw one older gentleman, very refined with a pointed beard, and his wife, who were drowning in tears...What had happened to them?...I was sleepy, hungry, my legs ached, and the fluorescence of all these slips of paper made my eyes glaze over...If grown-ups had to live like this, then I'd prefer never to grow up...By this point, everyone looked broken, drawn and nervous...At the last window, they collected all of your white, blue, green, and red sheets, then put them in a file folder and wrote your name on it very elegantly with a nibbed fountain pen...I noticed they were putting the adults' documents into red notebooks and the childrens' into green ones....

This went on for almost two hours…I went with Vati into the next car, feeling deflated…It was set up as a kind of post office or library. There were packages in brown wrappings and books on the shelves and floor…Even the women were dressed in blue smocks like shop attendants. On a desktop, they used some machine that rang to wrap up the packages and seal the string with red wax. There was a nice smell of glue…

When we drew a velvet curtain aside, what we saw was a regular lounge car…with flowers in decorative planters, armchairs and thick carpets covering every inch of the floor…We were stunned. I sat down in one of the unoccupied armchairs. Vati sat down beside me, because the chair's seat was so wide that the two of us could sit in it comfortably. Someone touched us on the shoulder, and when we turned around, the thin, kohlrabi-colored face of the man in the dormouse hat was smiling at us…"Are you waiting?" he asked congenially…"Yes, I am," Vati said in confusion…"What time is it?" The man pointed to a big wall clock. It was past two…Where was his boy?…A bit further on…Squeezed between two seats, with his hat in his hand, he was standing and nodding off…At the desk, people were talking in whispers. Suddenly, next to the curtain we'd come through, I saw Clairi…I would have recognized her anywhere by the little fringe of hair on her forehead…Gisela, whom she was carrying, looked dully over her shoulder…and next to them was mother, her hair done up with those scorching curling irons. I went straight over to meet them…We greeted each other as though it had been ten years since we'd last seen each other. *"War das eine Plagerei…,"* * mother said. She had to sit down. The veins on her legs had swollen up like sausages. All three of them were hungry and dead tired. *"Da werden wir warten, daß uns das Leben verekelt…"* ** It was already getting on toward three. People were talking quietly, walking back and forth on the soft carpets. Only the crowd around the desk…with the buffoonish Baron Loretto in their midst, of course…was talking more loudly, laughing and shouting. This place was like home to them…I pushed a little velvet curtain behind our chairs aside and discovered a window behind it, with a stack of leaflets bearing the swastika and eagle tucked behind a radiator…A female official called out some names and some people went up to the desk…Then she called out still other names. The man in the dormouse fur hat got up, pulling his wife and son along after him. This was interesting…I went with them up to the desk…The official was sitting there, dressed in a white blouse and black trousers… She abruptly handed them some document that the husband had to sign, and then she handed them three IDs. *"Jetzt können Sie gehen. Alle Anordnungen bekommen Sie brieflich."* *** Nervously, the man tucked the ID into his wallet without knowing what it meant or where he was supposed to go…An SA trooper pulled the curtain concealing the wall aside…there was a big, wide sliding door behind it…he shoved

*Now that was torture.

**They'll keep us waiting here until we're sick of being alive.

***You can go now. You'll receive all further instructions by mail.

it open…a wide wooden stairway with railings had been pushed up against the outside of the car, its icy planks strewn with ashes…It was still daylight, though gray, but most of all cold air flooded the train car…*"Da!"** the SA trooper pointed the way for the three of them to go. As he descended the steps with his boy not yet fully awake, the man looked back toward the desk…Everybody whose names the official called out was free to go home, where they would await further instructions that would be sent by mail…the Jakličes among them…Where was the banker? And the swarthy man from the gas company? Both Jakličes went out through the sliding door with their mother and father…They looked back at me again. What was their point?…Some SA troopers came in from the mail car carrying folders under their arms…one of them pulled the sliding door shut and drew the curtain closed…Something was about to break…some people stopped moving, while others got fidgety. *"Ruhe!"* the official called out. *"Ich bitte die Herrschaften um Ruhe!"*** She began reading a new list of names…People were listening. I caught our names in the list… including all five first names. There was something we had to sign… then the official came out from behind her desk and drew open a heavy red curtain. *"Bitte…eintreten!"****

A tall, stocky blond man with a metal swastika in his buttonhole stood at the entrance. He handed each person two handsome, heavy

*There!
**Quiet! Ladies and gentlemen, please be quiet!
***Please come in.

books...one of them, with gilt-edged pages, was particularly fat... What awaited us after that?...We stepped into a regular reception hall that was elegantly lit...with half-filled wine glasses arrayed on a table...a whole division of glasses in the middle and, on a polished platter on legs, there was a mountain of honey and marmalade cakes, the sight of which made my mouth water uncontrollably...On all sides, the walls were paneled in black oak...a chandelier with candles hung from the ceiling...How was I going to swipe at least one of those honey cakes?...But one by one people came into the car, obstructing the richly set table and pushing us farther and farther away from the door...we had to keep retreating farther back, to the far end of the car..."They're going to eat everything up!" I extracted both books from under Vati's arm...he didn't notice a thing...*Mein Kampf* shone in gilt lettering on the brown cover of one. It was the nicest and fattest. The other, somewhat thinner, was called *Der Mythus des zwanzigsten Jahrhunderts: Auszüge.* So it was some kind of religious book...I tried holding both books between my knees, but because they were too heavy, I had to set them down on the floor next to the curtain... Everybody around us was taller than Gisela and me...I felt as though I were at the bottom of a well where nothing untoward could happen to me, at least that's how it seemed...The upholstered door closed... Who was that standing by the table laden with glasses and cookies? I picked up something red...that was him, that was that louse von Wertbach from earlier that morning..."*Heil Hitler!*" he exclaimed.

* *The Myth of the Twentieth Century: Excerpts* (by Nazi ideologist Alfred Rosenberg)

What a clunky voice. As though he'd been separated from it, or his tongue just wasn't used to moving...All around everyone raised an arm, "*Heil!*"...The jerk proceeded to deliver his speech..."*Ich begrüße euch im Namen unseres großen Führers des großdeutschen Volkes...*"* He got carried away as he spoke, first softly, then rising up to the heights, then down and quiet again. That's how my teacher Mr. Mlekuž had spoken on the king's holiday...except that Mr. Mlekuž's voice carried farther, was smarter, more patient and nicer than von Wertbach's...Hitler and Germany were awaiting us with great anticipation...the people and their leader both hoped that we would earn their implicit trust in all things...Our first duty in our new, real homeland would be to provide assistance to the battle fronts...and our second, no less important, would be education – self-education, of ourselves. Not the technical transfer of know-how, but the transformation of our character, the reinforcement of all those virtues that were dormant in each of us, in our Germanic nature...These were big, adult people, but they were listening to him like schoolchildren listening to their teacher...Ever since the war had begun, everything was backwards...schoolkids behaved like adults, adults like schoolkids...Why wasn't that fine, stocky gentleman speaking, who had handed our books out to us? He had a nicer voice...he appeared to be better educated...He wouldn't have blown such smoke or indulged in such manic outbursts, if he'd been the speaker we wouldn't have had to put up with von Wertbach's unctuous drone...Politicians needed smart, educated people to keep

*In the name of our great leader of the great German people, welcome.

their speeches from degenerating into oral diarrhea...Gisela was standing behind Clairi's back, facing me. I pursed my mouth to show her how incredibly hungry I was, and this made her laugh...Amid all the leather coats, I noticed one tan raincoat...it was on the banker Gmeiner. I pointed him out to Gisela...Gisela looked in his direction, and when she saw him, she burst out laughing again...Von Wertbach kept talking...lots of tempestuous words that gave the impression of one big, extended fit of very violent quacking...Bolshevism is a disease of the blood. Russia is a racially and spiritually sick part of mankind...I'd read all this a thousand times before in the papers and on posters...There was a big portrait of Hitler...the nicest I'd ever seen...hanging high up on the wall...portraits like these were normally reserved for movie stars and put in cinema display cases...Although he didn't look like them, the way they admired themselves in a mirror...he seemed like a big, straightforward guy with a metallic glint in his sharp, wide-open eyes...Then, beneath the picture frame, an artery crossing von Wertbach's forehead appeared...Had he climbed up on a footstool? He began speaking with even greater force..."*Ich habe die Ehre und Freude, euch allen, hier versammelten, mitzuteilen, daß ihr von diesem Moment an die gleichberechtigten Staatsbürger des Dritten Reiches geworden seid...*"* Jubilation! Shouts, waving, tempestuous applause...I couldn't get my head around it at first...Did this mean that we had become real Germans, just like that?...jumped over some hurdle

*It is my great honor and pleasure to inform all of you assembled here that, from this moment on, you are fully fledged citizens of the Third Reich.

without even knowing it?...won some contest? Hands started getting extended, legs intertwined, all the people looming above Gisela and me were grinning and laughing and congratulating each other... shaking hands...Von Wertbach spun around like a soldier to face the portrait and started singing the anthem...Everyone raised their right arm, especially gigantic Mr. Gmeiner, the only one wearing a gabardine...they almost tricked me into raising mine, too. But on command like that, and when everybody was doing it – nah-ah!..."*Deutschland, Deutschland, über alles...Über alles in der Welt...*"* Welt. *Alles,* above everything else...that was something so infinite that it couldn't exist anywhere...Beneath the peaks of the mountains there was air, and above them, there was the sky...the sky had no limit...it reached beyond the moon, that big rock that belonged to nobody...everything was beyond the stars you could see only at night, there was no place where a homeland above everything could be...it didn't exist even in your homeland, except in the places where soldiers or teachers just happened to have been..."*Ich gratuliere wiederholt...Bitte, bedienen Sie sich...*"** Some glasses started clinking toward the front. "*Ich stibitzte ein paar Kekse für uns,*"*** Clairi told me. She had pushed her way through the crowd...I picked up the books...she came back...and delivered a round cookie with jam inside for each of us. When I popped it into my mouth, my body shook with such monstrous pleasure...

*Germany, Germany above everything...above everything else in the world

**Let me congratulate you once again. Please, help yourselves.

***I've swiped a few cookies for us.

Gisela ground away at hers like a machine, Clairi closed her eyes to enjoy it, and Vati's gummed up under his denture... Behind us the train car door opened up, and the fog burst in... Suddenly we were outside... If we hadn't just been naked and poked with needles all over and now back in our fur hats, scarves and gloves... I would have thought I had dreamed it... It was four o'clock and it was twilight... We were hungry, because we'd had to come to the exam on an empty stomach... and we were freezing. At last we had worked our way through that long serpent of train cars... had we come out at its beginning or at its end? Mother looked harsh and angry. Clairi was excited, Vati could barely stand up from weakness, I could have eaten god knows what, and Gisela's leg hurt on account of her brace... she would need to lie down for at least an hour or a half hour without it. "*Ich sage euch eins,*" mother said. "*Ich habe von allem diesem Theater den Hals voll.*"*...And then: "*Ich habe mich entschlossen: ich gehe nicht nach Deutschland... keine vier Pferde bringen mich dorthin...*"** That didn't surprise me, but Clairi, "*Aber Mama, das meinst du doch nicht im Ernst?*" she exclaimed, almost breathlessly. "*Nach allen diesen Schikanen und Plagerei, die wir durchgemacht haben?!*"***..."*Gerade darum,*"**** mother said firmly

---

*Let me just say this: that whole circus made me sick.

**I've made up my mind. I'm not going to Germany. Teams of horses couldn't drag me there.

***But mother, you can't mean that seriously... After all the ruses and torment we've gone through?

****Precisely!

and harshly. Vati said nothing...he just blinked. It wasn't worth wasting words over...We set out through the field toward the streetcar stop...today had been far too eventful for us to go home on foot, even though once we got there we would have to throw some potatoes in the pot and wait for them to boil...I looked through the streetcar window...Was I really going to have to leave Ljubljana?...The Triple Bridge was coming up...suddenly its pillared balustrade seemed as foreign to me as a balustrade god knows where...The delicatessen on Stritar Street was like a store in a foreign city...We had to get off the street car at City Hall because of a barricade...the Italians had set up sawhorses and strung them with barbed wire all the way across City Square to the fountain. They had even set up a machine gun aimed at the square. They were checking everyone's papers. People were jumping over puddles and handing the carabinieri and bersaglieri their passes. Once a man in front of us was allowed to pass, we jumped over a stagnant puddle and showed them ours. As far as Jail Street, there were searches going on in all of the buildings. They were looking for weapons and some bandit...

A NEW DECREE ON REDUCING RATIONS was issued. Now each person was allotted a pound of sugar, a half-pound of noodles, a quarter pound of rice and a pound and a half of lard per month... Vati got four Drava cigarettes per day...two on his own ration card and one each on mother's and Clairi's. You couldn't find any cigarette butts on the streets anymore like there were before the war, except for some disgusting remains of stogies that the *questurini* would toss aside... Vati was nervous. Work wasn't coming along well for him. He was more starved for tobacco than for food... They also started giving out less for dairy and baked good coupons. You had to get in line outside the dairy on Old Square first thing in the morning... It had already happened that, after carefully doling out the milk by seven a.m., there was nothing left for as many as ten to twenty neighborhood residents..., Potatoes were delivered once a month. You had to get up at four if you wanted to get to the outbuildings next to the market by five, when curfew ended, in order to get some... Usually I waited in the courtyard entrance until the clock on St. Jacob's Church struck five, then set out for the market at a sprint. Bunches of running boys and girls, old ladies picking their way, and men carrying buckets and bags were already out and headed to the market. If I ran fast and managed to pass a lot of others, I could be there in four minutes. But out on the square, under the huge advertisement for "Schicht's Stag soap" and "Palm" rubber heels on the side of the Ljubljana power plant, there was a huge crowd of at least five hundred people already waiting outside each of those outbuildings. Where had they come from? Had they slept in the entryways of neighboring buildings? Or did they have night passes?... Not until six did the weighing begin. Each person was allotted one pound. The fat lines of eight people abreast slowly moved forward... My turn didn't come until ten, eleven or twelve o'clock, when I reached the counter of the old shack which emanated a volcanic stench of spirits and rotten dirt. Five pounds of potatoes for five people. You weren't given a chance to double-check the weight or pick through them... even though there were always plenty of black, frozen, smashed, or mealy tubers among them, or ones that had already gone to seed. The newspaper said that the people responsible for continuing the war in our province were at fault for the new limits on sales of rationed foodstuffs. That meant the communist bandits who were hiding in the forests and stealing from our farms... Every park, every last inch of earth would need to be sown and planted. Even Marshal Pétain in Vichy proclaimed that the young people of France would need to take up tilling the soil again. French teachers would once again teach the sons and daughters of the nation agriculture, instead of Latin or math... Even Slovene educators were proposing that every youth aged sixteen and older be required to help out on farmsteads three months out of the year... As always, I kept going down to read the newspapers posted outside the *Morning* printing press building for Vati... we only bought the paper on Sundays. Newspapers were the only thing that wasn't rationed... The submarine war in the Atlantic was progressing... the Germans had just sunk their six hundred and eighty-first ship... It was a cold, dirty, intense fight. In the newsreels, you could see footage of sailors in their wobbly, cramped submarines trying to evade depth charges, or crews onboard the destroyers that navigated the surface in zig-zags, tracking tell-tale sonar signals... The Japanese had occupied the Philippines. Yamamoto, the Japanese admiral, was the hero of the Pacific! The photograph showed a bow-legged man with a samurai sword that was too long and too heavy for him. He had sunk the aircraft carrier Lexington and deployed such a curtain of anti-aircraft fire that, in one hour, fifteen bombers plummeted into the drink... Rommel was at El Alamein with his

Afrika Korps…Over Malta, which had disrupted his army's supply lines between southern Italy and North Africa, sixty English spitfires were downed…But the worst was in Stalingrad: a battle from house to house, and room to room. Territory there wasn't being measured in meters, but in bodies…The rag-tag soldiers of Hungarian, Italian, Slovak and Spanish divisions were shown laughing, as though the sun were shining…And then one thousand English bombers over Cologne…not a single building remained untouched…Berlin, Leipzig, Dresden…*"Nein, da gehe ich mir nicht den Tod holen,"* mother said. *"Schau, alles nur Ruinen."* * And the people, old women and men in tatters clearing away the destruction. Tiles on one stack, bricks on another. *"Aber Moral und Disziplin haben die Deutschen,"* ** mother said proudly…Communist bandits were killing our peasants and setting fire to Slovene homes. One picture after another. Kangaroo courts would publish lists of hostages who'd been shot…they were long lists of names…twenty, thirty, women, men…with their years of birth and their hometowns. The shootings were usually carried out at dawn the day before. "The new order in Europe will be based on the cooperation of all nations. No borders will be needed, because all nations will be unconditionally subject to mutual and universal authority…" is how the *Slovene* described it. "In these trying days, may Mother, Homeland and God be our nation's motto…" the *Slovene* wrote. "Victory does not just mean what the ordinary person imagines it does. Perhaps our

---

*No, I refuse to go tempting death there. Look, everything's in ruins.

**One thing you have to give the Germans: they've got morale and discipline.

victory was born in April 1941…" In the short space of time since the start of the war, it said, the Slovene nation had undergone a glorious rebirth…*A new code of morals*: women and girls were advised to wear one-piece swimsuits reaching down so-and-so many inches above the knee…Despite the war, the newspapers still had a children's section with riddles, crossword puzzles and stories…

One day, my cousin Minka, the daughter of our Uncle Jožef from Cegelnica appeared. She had a job now at the post office. The first thing she told us was that Aunt Mica, the one with the sick leg, had died. Due to the battles that were then flaring up between the partisans and the Italians, they hadn't been able to inform anyone about the funeral…She brought us a pot of lard with cracklings, a bag of white beans and a box of home-grown tobacco…sliced…How were things in Lower Carniola? mother asked her. The peasants were having to protect their fields, granaries and livestock against the forest bands and the Italians…Uncle Karel had signed up with the Village Guards. What, you mean he's a soldier? Yes, but at home, not in a barrack or parsonage, where some members of the Catholic Youth League have begun hanging out so that the Reds can't kidnap or kill them…What about Uncle Jože, Ivan and Ciril? Have they signed up for anything? She shrugged, turning red in the face. That's why she had come. Her father and Ivan were still at home, but Ciril had been put in jail. Could Vati and mother write a petition to the Italian authorities of Novo Mesto, reassuring them that he was a law-abiding boy and a believer and asking for his release?…Of course we will, said mother and Vati, taken by surprise, but will something like that actually help?

Of course it will, Minka said, if mother writes as a German and in German. Minka would see to it that her letter gets nicely retyped by a friend of hers at the post office...Does Karel wear a uniform? I asked Minka. Yes, he does, they wear a black beret with a crucifix and Italian leggings, but he prefers to wear his own hat. That was true...Karel wouldn't even eat without his hat on. And did he carry a weapon? Yes, a long flintlock with a bayonet. He and Jože had stopped talking. She was afraid that one day Karel was going to show up in force with his pro-fascist gang on her father's farm. In the village of Bršljin, some raging women with pitchforks had stabbed to death a member of a forest band trying to sneak home for the night...Things were very bad. One day a town would be under the partisans, and the next, it would get occupied by the Italians and Whites. And each side was paying with lives...Thank god she'd found work in Ljubljana, where things were peaceful...Imagine, in one village a little bit farther on from Cegelnica, the Italians had ordered all the trees lining the Krka to be cut down so they could see the partisans crossing the river by boat, but then the partisans informed the villagers that, if they did that, they would view them as traitors. A priest and an Italian officer had tried to mediate, so they killed both of them. Now the Italians had shot ten hostages in retaliation. I couldn't imagine a war taking place in the field between the woods, the rail line and Karel's house... Nor could I picture bandits and guns and caps marked with hammers and sickles in the forest that was overseen by the woodsman...I could imagine feuds and double-dealing and fights, all right...but battles and shooting? No way...

I went to school every day when I didn't have to spend all morning standing in line... The only teacher who was any good and taught me anything was Mr. Fink, our mathematics instructor. He was energetic and smart... He would come into class like a whirlwind, and, before you knew it, he'd written equations up on the board and class was in full swing, he didn't waste any time... Short, skinny, dark-haired, around thirty years old... Even though I didn't much like equations, his mathematics were clear and accessible to everyone. He didn't distinguish between kids who got it and those who didn't. He would get all worked up if somebody suddenly caught on to a concept, and he showed it... but that didn't mean that student was given an unfair advantage. Similarly, nobody could have misinterpreted his disappointment for disapproval. Aside from fearlessness, he exhibited neither warmth nor anger. Only the slightest trace of derision clung to his dark, mustachioed face, as if left over there from his own boyhood days, and he had to make an effort not to let it show through as a teacher. Also, the way he raised his arm to deliver a Roman salute looked more like he was trying to swat a fly with his gradebook... Unfortunately, physics and biology were easier for me than math. Both were taught by Mr. Anton Vodovnik, a strange individual who always wore a beret, whether in class or in the hallways. His pale face was devoid of all color, he appeared to have prematurely aged, and we never saw him in conversation with any of the other teachers... He gave the impression of always being alone, not out of arrogance and not out of spite, but because he was always depressed. He spoke slowly, he stammered, as though he were listening to somebody telling him what to say. He would walk up and down the classroom aisles, but with his beret on, he always looked like he was about to leave. Whenever he turned his back, the class – all little brats from Two Emperors Road and Žabjak – would start pelting him with tiny paper airplanes. He never noticed them, not even when he turned back around and they were flying at him in little squadrons...One time, he went to the lectern, took off his beret, and bowed his head down to the class. We could see that he had a deep gash in the upper part of his forehead that his beret normally covered. That's how we found out why he wore it. He had gotten the gash a long time ago, before the war, when he took a group of students on a hike in the mountains...There had been an avalanche, and three students were killed. He barely survived. This was a sort of mark of Cain he'd been left with. It was obvious that he couldn't make peace with his role in the students' deaths other than by continuing to teach at the same school. The sentences he produced were so separate from him that you could have sworn they'd been spoken by somebody else. His laughter was like Frankenstein laughing. I would greet him carefully in the halls, although he never replied. Alas, he didn't teach us very much. I had developed a liking for the exact sciences, and particularly physics, on account of models of atoms...those little glass balls that revolved around a nucleus like flames around the sun...Earth...was it really being inflated, as I'd read in the newspapers? The universe...was it really not infinite, as they'd told us till now?...But all he did was draw charts on the blackboard and every now and then show us an experiment, but all of this took place at a time when everyone still knew everything about physics, chemistry, biology and astronomy. But he never told us about the most recent discoveries, the things only experts and specialists knew... Our history teacher was named Stanko Femc. He was also one of the authors of our history textbook... Assyrian wars, Roman empires, clay tablets, Alexander the Great, uprisings, reforms... I would have expected great things from someone purveying riches like those. But no. He would tell us exactly the same things that were printed in his book, no more and no less. Even when he asked the class questions, you weren't allowed to say more. The sobriety he projected paralyzed the entire class... Our teacher of drawing and calligraphy, Srečko Lenard, was not fond of talking. He preferred to show us how to mix colors or sharpen a calligraphy nib, and he liked drawing models of letters on the board. If you copied them well, you got an A... Our Italian teacher was a young Fascist from Milan, Margherita Ardacci. She wore a black uniform and a cap with a fasces patch sort of coquettishly, as though it were the latest, most fetching fashion. She would stand in front of the class and stretch her arm out in a flawless Roman salute, *"Viva Duce!"*..."*Viva!*" we replied, right arm extended. She liked the fair-haired boys best, most notably Požar, the son of a knitting woman from Galjevica. He was blond, almost white as flax, with blue eyes. Sometimes, when she would ask him questions from her seat on the dais, she would put an arm around his waist and press him up against her desk... We all giggled, we would have liked to be in his place, because Margherita really was an attractive, provocative young lady. But she also had a way of smacking your hand with a metal ruler. We learned some of the basics of grammar from her and songs like

"*Firenze dormire,*" "*O dolce Napoli,*" "*Vieni, c'è una strada nel bosco*" and others...The other teachers? Now and then in the halls, I ran into a tall, skinny, older teacher who taught in the upper forms as she paced back and forth outside the teachers' lounge, clutching her gradebook and an armful of Slovene books to her chest. I recognized her as Mrs. Komar, the nice lady that Clairi and I had run into in the red building across from Tivoli that time when we were selling fur pieces, and who, though she didn't buy anything, invited us into her apartment for a break, a cool glass of fruit juice and a chat on that hot summer day. Clairi still remembered her. At the time, Mrs. Komar had said that we might meet again in her class...Now that had actually come true. So I made a particular point of saying hello to her wherever I met her, whether in school or in town. She would say hello back as she might to any student, because she probably couldn't remember the circumstances of how she, my sister and I had met some years before...My Slovene teacher, who at the time was also my homeroom teacher, was Mrs. Püchler. She had the name from being married to a German officer. She was a full-bodied blonde with breasts like two planets. During class, she would sometimes send me to the cleaner's with a ticket to pick up her white shaggy cardigans, dress suits and coats. She always wore white or light blue...Otherwise, she was quite prone to stop anyone leaving the school building during the main recess. "Where are you headed?" she would ask. "Out to get a notebook," the student might answer..."Whenever you go out to buy a notebook, that fact should be written on your face," she would warn. "And then you need to go quickly and decisively..." Everyone who repeated sentences aloud or spoke after her was a good student. She always demanded silence in class. At those times she might stamp on the dais so forcefully that her breasts shook, her belly, her hips, each part on its own, giving the whole class an image they could masturbate to that night. Once she had a heel fall off. She stumbled and limped and stood still with one foot unshod, standing on the dais in her silk stockings, soft and powerless... humiliated, half-undressed. It was as though she wasn't at school anymore, but at home, perhaps in her bedroom, and that aroused our desire even more. I had to take her shoe and heel to the shoe shop on Privoz so they could fasten it back on. What sunny, warm leather that shoe was made of!... Once, when she was sick, I had to deliver some notebooks to her house for her to grade. She lived in one of those buildings with turrets near the courthouse on Tyrševa Street, where Clairi and I had tried to sell Vati's furs. She lived on the very top floor. I rang the bell, but the door was open. She lay, or half sat, on a cluttered sofa. There was nobody in the entryway, nor in the kitchen or parlor... "Mrs. Püchler!" I called out. "Yes. Back here!" she answered from someplace. I followed the voice through a fourth door that was open... She lay, or half sat, in a blue gown on a cluttered sofa with her legs slightly apart, the gown parted up to her hips. You could see all the way up her blond legs in their stockings to the shadow at the top, on which her pudgy hand was resting. I saw her face, her tousled hair, her upper front teeth with the gap between them, her glasses, which had slid down to the tip of her nose. I bowed, "Here are the notebooks"... "Set them down over there," she said in a soft, gentle voice that I wasn't used to hearing from her... She was pointing to some brown shelf with banknotes on it. I set them down. But I felt like throwing myself on her and starting to knead all the curves that were causing her gown to bulge like batches of overcooked macaroni. I came back out onto Tyrševa Street somewhat lightheaded...

Otherwise... aside from a few conversations with Kemperle, a flunkee from the previous year whom I sat beside in the back row... school was mostly an unbearable, unnatural, artificial environment where you couldn't make any real friends. There wasn't anybody for me in Old Square, either, just a black-haired guy with a big mole, the son of an antique dealer named Kocmur who lived in one of the central buildings on the square. Once, we spent several minutes talking about model ships outside our front door, since he liked to assemble them, too. That was a nice conversation, sort of a short-lived mutual fawning... The son of the dairy owner was older than me, and he painted. His oil paintings were set out with prices on them in his mother's display window. But I wasn't interested in painting.

O NE SUNDAY, I WENT WITH GISELA, limping in her brace, out to the movies. Fani and her mother went with us. Old Hirol was utterly beside himself with rage. He wouldn't let them waste time on trivial things. In order to escape from the house, they had to pretend they were going out to visit somebody... *The Magic Bird* was showing, the first color film in a long time. People were saying the most incredible things about it. Even connoisseurs who'd been around the world described the movie as something inconceivable. They would never have been able to imagine anything like it!... That morning I got in a

line for tickets that wrapped around the movie theater two times…
with a wait that took more than four hours. There were people in line
who had seen the movie three times, eight times already… They were as
happy as children who had been to some unknown land to visit a fairy
and were suddenly allowed to return. On top of a cliff that looked like
a mountain cloaked in a wedding dress, there nested a magical bird…
one morning a little girl and her brother set off through the talking
forest alone… Enough magical things happen to them along the way,
let alone at the top… A gigantic *cremeschnitte* cut into fantastic slices,
surrounded by balconies full of Gypsies wrapped in flags, music and
a million little lights… A glass gallery as big as a cathedral hangs in
the sky, full of miraculous machines and kettles, each as big as three
houses combined, which whistle as they emit a rainbow of steam in
all directions… The South Pole, where some explorer resembling
Captain Scott in a big fur coat quietly explains that he's found a gigantic hole in which the earth's axis revolves on ball bearings made of
ice… Seen from a great distance, long rows of delectable orangeades
with cream in enormous tumblers approach on conveyor belts toward
the viewer… A cannibal and a python in a cage cook a huge ostrich
egg together. He spits at the python, and the python vanishes… In
the darkness of the movie theater, it was beautiful… all beauty always
takes place at night… one body pressing against another. The whole
theater was looking up spellbound, unwilling to miss a single scene,
in love with the people up on the screen, in love with love itself…
Thank god there were no random searches or air raid alarms during
the movie, perhaps because it was a children's film and it was Sunday…

Outside, a cold September rain drizzled as we pushed our way through the side exit toward the Ljubljanica...It was a beautiful movie, with the story constantly taking place at high altitudes, even when life in a poor hovel was being depicted...People shouldn't be allowed to exit movie theaters, to exit that rapture, they should be made to stay there forever, contained within four walls, and not until night falls and darkness merges with the earth should they be allowed to come out...but never while it's still daylight...What pathetic creatures everyone was! Not a single person dared to look another in the eye...I would have gladly lived forever in that sort of enchanted stasis. That was probably my soul's desire, which wasn't keen on the idea of having to keep on hanging around street corners and school with my body...

That's why I began recounting a thousand and one details from the movie. Even Gisela, Fani and her mother started talking. Details that were accurate and details that weren't. I told some genuine fairy tales. They're also a part of your education, Mr. Fink had once explained to us in class...Each time, I described new, extraordinary things with the same ease as taking a breath. I myself was surprised by that... "See, mama, Bubi is giving us a completely different view of what we saw," Fani said...But my magic was finished as soon as we reached Old Square...There, in front of the pharmacy, Hirol was standing, already as drunk as a skunk. All at once, there were no words for the situation. He was so drunk that his head drooped over the cane he was holding, and his whole body shook when he finally came to...Fani's mother's face transformed into a scarecrow's..."Just wait, just wait, I'll show you..." she hissed with malicious glee...and went running across the tracks with such swift, if very short, steps that Fani could scarcely keep up with her. I thought the old ghoul was going to turn and attack them. But he didn't. Fani tried to hug her mother by the shoulders. "Leave him alone, mother, it's not worth it…" she said…"I have to knock some sense into him, the old boozer. This stone should do nicely." She was holding a stone, a handy one – like the stone one of the neighborhood delinquents might have just thrown at somebody, but missed, so it wound up on the pavement. "Just let him touch me one more time and he'll see," her mother yelled. "Of course, mother, of course," Fani said. "You'll show him. Please don't get angry. Let's go home and fix supper…" Hirol was out of commission. Perhaps he had seen them. He spat in their direction like the cannibal in the cage spat at the python, and in two or three bounds, he was in the shelter of the Crap Café…"He vent to ze tavern!" Gisela gasped. "Quiet," Fani called out. Slowly, she led her mother back to the door. "I coult take him on, ma'am." I said. "Be quiet, Bubi," Fani said. "I vas chust zayink…"…"But you mustn't say things like that. A child shouldn't even think things like that." "I'm not a chilt! I'll pea fohrteen in Nofembah." "You *ah* zdill a chilt!" Gisela shot out. Fani had to suppress her laughter. "Let's go, come to our place for pudding!"…That was a soufflé made with some powder or other, a synthetic substitute… Fani took it off the sideboard, sliced it, and distributed the slices on plates. We were eating it when we heard Hirol's cane in the hallway outside…"It's him!" her mother shrieked. "Mama!" Fani instantly took hold of her. I looked at the door which had a beater hanging on it and a calendar with a chimney sweep…The door started to shake.

"If he wants anything, I'll throw this iron at his head," Fani's mother said. In her delicate hands, she was holding one of those toothed coal-fired irons like the one we had... The door flew open with a terrible bang, at the center of which stood stocky Hirol, yellow-faced, in his black solicitor's suit, with one withered arm hanging at his side and the other firmly, demonstratively on top of his cane, which resembled a real cudgel. "You sluts! You whores! You cunts!" He stumbled into the kitchen, the wind-up monkey, and just as he was about to reach the stove, I grabbed Gisela and ran... At the instant I pressed on the door handle, all hell broke loose in the kitchen... I could hear Gisela limping up the stairs, then a shriek, the clatter of chairs being overturned, and crying... and then *whoompf!* when the table already set with dishes for supper was overturned... That was the spirit of life!... "You peek!" I shouted... I was shaking... I could have killed him... I could have plunged god knows how big a *khanjar* up to its hilt into his bristly neck... How on earth had that baboon ever managed to trick Fani's mother into falling for one of his lime sticks?... It couldn't have been about money... So it was just a mistake! A delusion! In any case, women were always in too big of a hurry. It was the same with Clairi. Always taking the first guy who crossed their paths. The first dung heap down the road was fine by them. The same as for flowers. The prettiest ones needed the stinkingest shit!... But the fair weather never lasted for long. And then how they cheated! I had plenty of examples of that! Vati and mother, for instance. But women never gave up! That was their spirit! The spirit of life!...

The door opened... for a moment I saw the Turk standing in the middle of the kitchen...and then somebody slammed the door shut again...Fani came out into the hallway. At first I could hear the sound of her breathing, then I saw her, and she also noticed me by the window...She didn't pause but came flying straight toward me until I felt her collide with my ribs. In her clutching embrace, I was practically hidden and crushed...under her lips, which kept kissing my cheeks, my face turned to rubber...I couldn't breathe anymore. She was stuck to me, complete with tears, hands and furry sweater. I wanted to free myself, but not in a way that confused her. I tried to contract so I could crawl out from under her...but she hugged me again, kissing me on the cheeks and sobbing and pressing her forehead to my shoulder... With my mouth and everything I had, I pressed against her face for support...This was like some sort of sickness...I stroked her head, her temples, her forehead, those eyebrows...I didn't know what tricks to use to try to envelop her and short-circuit her pain. Her face shone in the dark like a penitent's face through the grille of a confessional..."Fani...Fani," I said..."What?" She was sniffling. I backed up and, in the light of the nighttime sky, I saw her pale, almost childish face. She rested her forehead on my shoulder again...I moved my face downward, and though I had her part right at my lips, I didn't dare start sniffing and licking her hair. I had to say something, even though my happiness and turmoil were almost overwhelming. "Fani, I loff you!" There, I'd said something I'd never said before. The letters constituting those four words remained in the air, they didn't drift out through the window into the dark..."I love you, too"...Oh this insane, crazy woman!...to blurt out something like that!..."You mustn't cry!"

I hurriedly replied, to avoid blurting out the same thing again...“I’m not anymore.” She looked up...it was true, she wasn’t shedding tears anymore...Oh, how much I wanted to kiss the corner of her mouth, on the right side, where that miracle of her smile resided...“Did he scare you, poor boy?” she asked. Suddenly, I was filled with rage... how could she think something like that! “No!” I answered angrily. That was too harsh...“You’fe kot to ket out off ziss house,” I said. Who had just blurted that out? Me? Yes, me!...“Somevehr zo fahr avay, zat your fahzer can neffer peach you akain. I haff sree onglez in Lower Carniola...no, chust von. Ze ozer two aren’t fehry nice...Ongle Ruti liffs in Bolitsa. You can hite viss him. Voult you koe viss me?”...My God, what next? “Yes,” she nodded. “Koot,” I said. “It’s nice zehr, viss a hill ant a fohrest. Vee hat a nice rappit fahm zehr!”...I didn’t want to say anything more, for fear she might reconsider...She grabbed me by the shock of hair flopping over my forehead and began smoothing it back over my temples. “You’re much handsomer like this,” she said. I had goose bumps running through all of my hair follicles, my head was trembling so much. “Really?”...“Of course, have a look!” She took a mirror out of her pocket and drew me right up to the windowpane, where it was lighter. In her hand, she was holding the mirror, in which I could make out a white forehead...“I ton’t know.” I didn’t know... Having my hair combed back seemed much neater to me. But she was for sure the authority. “It’s true...I once studied to become a hair stylist. I’ll do your hair. You’ll be so handsome, you won’t believe it...” She was holding my shock of hair in her right hand...despite all the hugging and kissing before, this was worth so much that it felt like she was touching me for the first time...Oh, if only she'd tell me again that she loved me, that she was in love...with me, perhaps. "Fani," I said. "What?"...No, I didn't dare. "I'll alvays help you," I said...Suddenly there was silence at the door...a silence as though it were midnight... From the kitchen came the sound of ordinary talking...quiet murmuring..."Psst!" Fani said. She ran to the door, listened and looked through the keyhole...She was back in two bounds..."We'll talk again tomorrow"...She put her hand on my shoulder...then she turned around and calmly went inside...I listened, ready to burst through the door at Fani's first shout if the Turk started to slug her...Noises, rustling, water pouring, footsteps...Nothing else. Had they finally managed to put the old man to bed under his crocheted comforter?... Still, I stayed there. You could never know...I may have remained standing there for a whole hour. I couldn't move, and I didn't feel well. I waited for the light to go out under the door...I hadn't been struck by lightning, but by love's grace...I pinched myself, but nothing helped, I was still dreaming and alert with my eyes open...When the darkness became deepest, I went to sit on the steps near the water pipe leading upstairs, to us. I felt as though I were sheathed inside an egg, a shell... inside which there was life, buzzing and swarming...only inside it... if I stretched out my hand and set it on the step, for instance, things would start fizzing and glittering there a bit, too...But just a few inches above my head or away from my body and everything was quiet and motionless...That swarming beehive moved with me. If I were to get up now, go to the wall, and set my hand on it, it would probably sink through it like fog...I tried, because I knew I'd be disappointed, and

it would hurt. I went to the wall. No, I wasn't able to soften it up…
Mornings to the dairy, then school, classes, like beautiful pictures out
of an atlas. I couldn't go to sleep, either… Everything went by so fast,
as though I were watching it from an express train. Not one thing
was interesting enough for me to notice. Mr. Fink called me up to the
board, and with an ease I'd not known before, my hand produced a
perfect equation… In geography class, I was asked to mark the loca-
tions of all the mines of the former Drava Province. As my hand passed
over the map, I scratched out the precise location of each of them. The
teacher graded me *very good*, which for him meant *outstanding*, but it left
me completely unfazed… This was true love at last, because Fani was
already going on eighteen or nineteen. She was a real woman, a real
girl. She comported herself like my ideal – overcoat, fine hats, purses.
She wore makeup and powder and the subtlest touch of lipstick. She
had a job, her own salary and her own passion, which was singing…
She knew how to cook and bake delicate pastries, and those little
aprons that she would tie to her waist suited her perfectly. She wasn't
some teenage schoolgirl. She wasn't one of those louse-ridden girls
from Žabjak who spent all day racing around on their father's bikes and
hollered like market hawkers. She wasn't like girls who didn't know
anything, had no idea what to do with their time, and were forced to
beg from their parents for every last lira to go out to the movies. She
wasn't like the girls who got perfect grades at school and whose first
and last wish was to collect as many *A*'s as possible on their flawless
assignments… No, Fani was a mature woman, a real lady… I lacked
only a few degrees of longitude before I could attain the core of her

world...a few years, some form of independence...my own capital, clothes, the necessary social connections...If only at some moments she could just shrink and grow younger, take on a school dress and pink cheeks and start attending the class across from mine, then after school I could walk her home and kiss her on the corner for all the world to see...Then when she was back home, within four walls, she could turn back into a real, adult woman...It would only take a few miracles, a few years forward or back, to even everything out...

Once, during class, on a map pasted inside a book cover labeled "*Provinzia Lubiana*" which had all the larger towns and outlying villages marked on it, I blocked out Grosuplje along with the train line and the road through the fields and woods to Polica. Then I enlarged it and copied it out onto a sheet of DIN A-format paper. I could hardly wait for class to be over. I left Kemperle, with whom I usually walked home as far as his house, alone outside without offering a word of explanation...I ran straight home. I grabbed a pot and the bucket and went to get water. But first I had to wait. I didn't dare take the key to the water, for fear of starting too soon. Better to count up to who knows how high before reaching my hand into the niche. I took my age times ten and counted all the way to the end. I may have been counting for a full hour. It was possible she wasn't home due to choir practice. Then, finally, I poured the water. I first filled the pot, which I carried upstairs, then the bucket...There was still no sign of her... Then I waited by the window and looked from the garret toward the curtain on Hirol's kitchen window...It didn't budge, nobody drew it aside...so there still wasn't anyone home. Then, before dark, I went back down for more water. I waited. Then I took out the key. Again I waited. Shut the water off. Waited. Hung the key in the niche and waited. Picked up the bucket and listened... It was dark, evening, when a light went on behind the waxed paper blocking their window. I went down the hallway with the map I had drawn and sat on a crate between two wardrobe cabinets... toward the back. I kept rubbing my hands against my short-sleeved shirt to warm them... rubbing my knees, since I was only in shorts... I was as hard as though poured in a mold... Then, as though the entire building were coming to life, the door finally opened and out she came... Wearing one particular apron that I liked because it made her most attractive of all... I emerged from behind the wardrobe and through the open door could see the Turk, with his trouser legs rolled up and his feet in a basin... Fani unlocked the water pipe and saw me next to the wardrobe. She turned the faucet on full force, and a powerful, deafening stream began filling the aluminum kettle. I sat on my crate, got up when the stream of water cut off, sat back down as she twisted the faucet and got up when she put back the key... "Fani, vill you come pack out into ze hall?"... I could tell from the sight of her cheek in the twilight that she was angry... and scowling. As she went to the door, she said, with the back of head facing me, "I've got no time," then closed the door behind her... My God, what had happened?... "*Oof,* my feet are so stiff!" I could hear a contented Hirol exclaim from the kitchen... "I'll wash them with vinegar for you," Fani said... Then I heard her "*Ow!*," followed by a table being overturned. I dashed to the door... "*Ow!* Don't you go dutch rubbing me with those whiskers like that!" "Oh, no? We'll see about that!"

"No, you won't! Mommy, you get this bull under control!"...Oh, I was familiar enough with that. The old man was fond of rubbing his whiskers against Fani's cheek...I'd been present before to see him chase her around the table, or her running away from him into the living room and then back again, or jumping up on a chair and hiding her face while she squealed...He behaved like that when he was in a good mood..."*Ow!* That hurts! Go away! What are the other girls going to say when I come to work tomorrow all red-faced and raw?"..."*Oof,* that's got me nice and warm!...We've had a good time tonight, haven't we, girly?"...Next was her mother's voice..."I've put camphor oil in it this time. Mrs. Amon said I should give it a try," she said..."Is the footbath water warm enough yet?" She sang all this like a song...I stayed out by the water pipes for a while longer. Then I went to have a seat on the staircase, because I assumed Fani would ultimately come out when she remembered I was waiting for her here.

SHE DIDN'T COME...Not that first evening, or the next, or the one after that. The hallway remained quiet. I sat on the stairs and looked up to see the darkness above me...to figure out once and for all what a real night was like...The door by the water pipe opened and closed. Like some sort of crazy clock that keeps time with a hotchpodge of sounds...the snap of a door handle, the glow of a lightbulb, a stream of water. If it was her, she could see or hear me...I would shift my feet in the dark or take a breath like the prompter in a theater...it was easy to notice me. Nothing. The hallway went dark again when she shut the door...In our room, I stretched out on the table behind the cast-iron bed that the other three slept in. My eyes wouldn't shut. I turned my head toward the wall...toward the bucket...once I stayed lying on my stomach facing the window...what a gray framework of woe!... another time on my back, looking up at the pipes from the gas lamp at the ceiling. Somebody who was inside me, between and under my bones, the fabricator, the liar, the spirit that filled everything to the tips of my fingers and toes...argued with my body that something terrible had to have happened...Sparks, fireflies of hope flickered through the dark hollow...I had to catch them, keep them, at least one of them. Maybe tomorrow would be different...I didn't want to go downstairs anymore. I asked Gisela to go to the faucet. But she could only bring water back in a small pail because her brace forced her to use one hand to hold onto the railing. For larger quantities, it was just me. I took the biggest containers we had...three at a time. I turned on the faucet as far as it would go, until it was thundering like a waterfall. I looked only into the container, waiting for it to fill...Still, Fani's mother came out into the hallway. "You've gotten the floor wet, Bubi," she said. Her bare, gray eyes shone like the glow of morning in winter...Was I just fooling myself that only I saw them that way?...I raced back upstairs for a rag to wipe the floor dry...But now old Hirol was there, too, glowering out of his overgrown face, as though his last thin shell of decency were just about to crack, and any second he'd be aiming that stick of his not at the floor but at me..."Hello, Fani," I said the first time we passed each other on the stairs. "Hi, Bubi!" she answered cheerily. She was wearing nice gloves with bright stitching...a kerchief around her neck...a salt-and-pepper sport coat...nice shoes...and clutching the collapsed canopy of an elegant woman's umbrella in her hands. She went down the steps…a grown woman, so mature and decisive that I couldn't begrudge her anything…If I'd shouted, she wouldn't have heard me, and if I'd run after her, I might have broken my legs, but there's no way I could have caught up with her…

GISELA HAD A GIRLFRIEND named Olga, who lived on Upper Square. One day she dragged her straight off the street, where they'd been playing, into our house. Outside, in the sand around the fountain and the statue of Mary, the neighborhood girls liked to meet and play with their dolls and baby carriages…Olga resembled Tatjana somewhat. The same bright yellow hair, the unwholesome face, the watery eyes, she even had a slight limp. But she was younger than Tatjana and roughly a year older than Gisela. After that first visit she started to come regularly, all by herself, even when Gisela wasn't at home. She came in without knocking. She went up to Vati and watched while he sewed. Then she picked up the tailor's shears, and Clairi had to pry them out of her hands so she couldn't hurt herself with them. She would put on collars that had the minimum possible number of stitches in them so they could be tried on for size, then stretch them so tight that the stitches burst and the collars fell to pieces. Then she sat down at the chest of drawers and starting playing with Gisela's toys… one day she even began rummaging through the shelves…Vati seemed silly because of his curls and wart, mother seemed crazy because she curled her hair with hot tongs and Clairi seemed stupid because she only knew German and always had such a startled expression…One evening when she came upstairs, I felt profoundly humiliated when she saw how Vati had bedded down with furs on the work table and discovered my very similar sleeping situation on the kitchen table… Who knows, maybe she and her parents and sisters lived in similar circumstances, or worse, on Upper Square. They lived, as I learned later, on the corner between St. Florian's church, the bakery and the American Tavern… in a building full of little drunks and day laborers that was also inhabited by a crazy old lady, an old hooker named Mici… all I knew was that they had plenty of milk at home, because the residents raised goats in the courtyard… She came one Sunday when Gisela and I were already in the midst of putting on a play for our family behind the built-in shelves… I was playing a customer, and Gisela, wearing Clairi's smock, was the store owner… It was a farce about a close-out sale that we had made up ourselves. As the customer, I had been standing outside the store since first thing in the morning, impatiently waiting for it to be eight o'clock and wringing my hands, while the store owner was taking her time applying her make-up. "*Haben Sie Erbarmen, die Dame.*"* When it finally turned nine, she opened the door… I burst into the store like a whole herd of customers, burying her and her goods beneath me. Then the store owner turned into a customer named Gisela. She put everything – from shoes and furs to pots and pans – on her head until she couldn't see anything and then burst out of the store with a victorious whoop. Then both of us turned into ladies out on a shopping trip. We fought over the only item

*Take pity on me, m'lady.

remaining, a blanket… Each of us took turns yanking it toward himself until we finally ripped it in two and fell to the floor… Then I turned into a thief. I stole the cash register, father's till, off of the counter. Gisela turned into a policeman. Wriggling out of the blanket, she blew on her whistle, arrested me and took me off to the hoosegow… At this point, the store was empty and the crushed store owner lay powerless under the counter. Then one last, latecoming customer appeared. "*Ich muß um jeden Preis etwas kaufen, ganz gleich was*. I must buy something at all costs, no matter what…" I kept repeating this phrase, alternating back and forth from Basel Swiss to Lower Carniolan dialects for so long that the whole room started repeating it with me. But wherever I looked, there were only empty shelves. Then, on the floor, I noticed the owner of the store, passed out. I grabbed hold of her, hoisted her up over my shoulder, and carried her off, sighing, "*Für etwas wird es schon taugen.* It's bound to be good for something," while the store owner replied in a drawn voice, "*Wenn für nichts anderes, dann zum essen.* If nothing else, then maybe for eating…" Everyone was laughing. Suddenly I noticed Olga, who was sitting on the cast-iron bed with my family. She was laughing along with the others; actually, she was laughing derisively, as though she had just discovered some shameful secret. Disgusting! Her mouth twisted to one side, and her face, as always, took on the mean, crafty look that I knew from grown-ups… Offended, I climbed out of the old clothes that I'd deliberately put on to look goofy… I didn't want to make it that much easier for her. Even before this, I'd been hoping Gisela would stop spending time with her… "What's your real last name?" she asked Gisela… "I don't know… Iselin…" "It's the same as ours, only backwards," I snorted. The little girl screwed up her face like some grown-up delinquent. "Backwards, huh?" she said and with her fingernail scratched our name on the wall beneath Vati's paper patterns…"So, Čičavok…you're the Čičavoks!" she laughed. I was so mad at myself I didn't know how to respond…"That's right, we're the Čičavoks!" I spat…Olga announced the new name all over Old Square, Žabjak and Karlovška Street all the way to the Tribuna factory, where they made baby buggies. When I came back from school and the little girls from Upper Square were out playing under the statue of Mary, they squealed, "Čičavok! Bubi Čičavok!" Soon, when I went past the Gruber Palace, across from the green where boys would scrimmage at soccer, even the Žabjak kids would call out, "Či-ča-vok! Či-ča-vok!" Or they'd say, "That's the house where the Čičavoks live," instead of that's the house with the Salaznik Café…That vile nickname stuck to me like a plaster…It was something comparable to, "*Jeder Ruß ein Schuß! Jeder Britt ein Tritt!…*"*

THAT SPRING, GISELA HAD TO GO for another operation, one of a series of procedures…She lay in a ward of mostly adults next to a window through which you could see the yellow building of the St. Peter's Barracks, which had now been converted into a prison for partisans. Once her condition was stable, she was transferred by recommendation of the medical commission to the Children's Home on Streliška Street, which also looked after children convalescing from

---

*One bullet for every Russian. One kick for every Brit.

illnesses. She had her meals and slept there and, along with the other children, had a doctor's examination every day. She wore a flannel gown, and though she was one of their most seriously ill patients, she was also one of the most boisterous. She would have been out hopping and skipping around with the others if they hadn't put her leg in a cast again. I visited her every day, because I knew from experience how rough it is when you don't get any visitors and how perversely your fellow patients can treat you if you're always alone. I also sensed that I needed to protect her, because the other kids took her for a German on account of mother and Clairi, and sooner or later…the opportunities were endless…they would find a way to make her pay for it. I felt so relieved each day when I first saw her, holding onto a chair in order to walk and smiling amid her peers who, like her, were dressed in the same sort of gray breeches and flannel overalls with big pockets sewn onto them…. The Children's Home was run by a convent, and the playroom on the first floor was presided over by a young, exceptionally fun-loving nun. She was scarcely an inch taller than me. I'd never met a nun like this before! She was so buoyant, it made you forget she was wearing a hundred and one heavy nun skirts, with one of those starched airplanes on her head. She was constantly joking… with the children, their parents, me, the other sisters…and all the while her face was so expressive, and her eyes shone so unabashedly that you couldn't believe this was a nun. I had to be careful, because she was incredibly sly, and somehow I became aware that her jokes had multiple meanings…"Gisela tells me you know how to draw," she stopped me one day not long after Gisela had been admitted there.

"How would you like to draw us something for the playroom? As you can see, the walls are bare." Indeed, the playroom was bare, all they had were a few toys in one corner and a blackboard on one wall for the children to draw on. "Could you draw us Snow White and the seven dwarves? We would provide you with paper and paint." I didn't have to be asked twice, because my help would mean they would treat Gisela that much better than they had until then... Giggling, the fun-loving nun immediately took me upstairs to meet the director. The director was installed in an office that had black leather easy chairs and smelled powerfully of tobacco. He was a sturdy man in a gray suit, with a gray mane of hair and thick eyeglasses on a tanned face that made him look as though he were just back from Africa. I could read two things on that face: precision and goodhearted kidding. "Sounds good, sounds good!" he said amid deep laughter, his chin pushing against his thick tie and revealing small, bad teeth. Together with the happy-go-lucky nun, whose name was Kajetana, I measured the playroom... My concept for it was to depict the whole story of Snow White and the seven dwarves in a series of images up at the ceiling: the first scene would begin over the door, and the last one, ending the story, would be over the blackboard... I even got a whole stack of big, high-quality drafting sheets, three feet by three feet, seventy of them, two boxes of paints, a clutch of brushes... I barely managed to drag all that wealth on my back and head home to Old Square... I got started immediately. I worked for seventeen days, including three Sundays in a row. Every afternoon, alongside a row of glasses filled with water and then, when Vati went to sleep, on the workroom floor next to his brass lamp...

The grim castle of the old queen on top of the mountain…the magic mirror flashing in her boudoir…the lousy hunter…Snow White… with deer, owls, rabbits, weasels, hamsters and white snakes with crowns tagging along behind her…I copied and reworked all of them using photographs from father's old fur-trade magazines, the *Kürschner-Zeitung* from Leipzig…the dwarves in the gold mine… seven little beds in their shack…By day while I worked everyone had to take care not to step on my sheets or kick over the glasses of water… each evening, I worked late into the night, undisturbed…if I made a mistake, I could paint the scene from scratch on the reverse side of the sheet, but I was careful not to, because the sheets were calculated to cover exactly the space in the playroom…When everything was ready, I had to take the drawings to the Children's Home on a rented handcart…When the hour came for the children to go out for recess and then come in for their afternoon nap, sister Kajetana, another nun and I used a ladder to tape the drawings to the walls…Nine feet up from the floor, just under the ceiling, the broad strip of my illus-trated story began…from doorframe to ceiling…concluding in a wedding ceremony over the wash basin next to the blackboard…Thus, when you opened the door to the playroom, the first thing you saw over the window was Snow White and all seven pudgy dwarves. Not until you were inside the room did you see all the other scenes on the opposite wall, and to the left and the right…the animals, the wicked queen, the huntsman who in his human frailty couldn't kill Snow White, the glass coffin, the young prince on his white horse…Every-one came to the opening…all the nuns and the director…Gisela was excited that I had decorated the room and proudly told the other kids that her uncle was the one who had made all the paintings...I was pleased, too, and for weeks afterward kept stopping by to see how they were holding up...The director had me called into his office and handed me a hundred and fifty lire. That was an actual workingman's wage, which I could use to buy something on the black market...But that wasn't all. The friendly eccentric added that I was welcome to come have lunch with them every day, because their kitchen made more than enough food, plus I was welcome to take leftovers home...That was too much, so I promised to paint a new series of pictures...Little Red Riding Hood or Hansel and Gretel or Cinderella. "Now that's something new!" mother squealed in delight. Finally I'd brought something home!...I was in seventh heaven. Now every day after school, I headed straight to the Children's Home...with a thermos and two containers in a basket. Sister Rafaela, the head cook, was such a good soul...Her sallow, rather careworn face had a big black mark, a regular little cushion, like the noblewomen in old paintings...maybe that was the mark that identified good people?...First I stopped by the kitchen to say hello to her...The kitchen was full of white-clad sisters of mercy. Even sister Kajetana, still laughing of course, was among them...and the mother superior, a tall, skinny woman with whiskers who also wasn't gruff all the time, even if she was thin and remarkably tight-lipped. I could already hear their laughter from the ground floor entrance...and when I showed up at the door to the kitchen so she could see I was there...the kitchen was already full of nuns, young, old, in between. They were guffawing and teasing each other and running around so much that the whole place rattled with rosary beads and crosses and aerodynamic wimples... The mother superior was just barely able to keep chaos at bay. I had never come across so many entertaining nuns in my life. Even when I showed my face, they didn't miss a beat... they just burst into louder laughter, with a chorus of hellos, waving of hands... The fun-loving Kajetana, that crafty circus performer, once even pinched my cheek really hard and grinned so wickedly as she did it that I had to seriously doubt she'd really been a nun before I met her. Then sister Rafaela would bring me my lunch out in the foyer... whole bowls of vegetable soup, glistening spaghetti and salad, each course in its own deep dish, then at the end she'd take my basket back to the kitchen so I could take leftovers home. Every day, there were different dishes. On Fridays, for instance, there was a sweet tomato sauce with sculpted potatoes and fish steaks floating in it. Whenever the door to the office opened and the director came out, I always got up and gave a respectful bow... not trying to butter him up, it came from the heart. A few times his wife was there visiting, too. She was a thin, somewhat older, heavily made-up lady with a long nose, always dressed in black velvet and red sweaters... Sometimes she would pleasantly return my bow, but at others she ignored me and gave no sign of acknowledgment, depending on her mood that day. "*Das ist eine...*," Clairi once started in about her, because she'd also met her in the office the day they brought Gisela there from the hospital. I quickly put my hands over my ears... I didn't want to hear it, least of all some women's needling... Occasionally I would have as company at the foyer table some student or beggar, who might smell so bad that it took my appetite away. One day, a fiddler came climbing up the steps – the one who looked like Frankenstein whom I knew from the yard of the conference of St. Vincent de Paul, from begging on Fridays, from the Harborside Tavern... He stopped beside the railing, took his battered violin out of its worn canvas bag and began playing in horrible squeaks... *furioso... pizzicato... crescendo*... and again *furioso*... His face was as white as a shoebox, with tiny black eyes, hardly any mouth worth mentioning and hair falling onto a bulging forehead as yellow as a canary... *Brrr! Brrr! Yi-yi-yi*... Still, out of decency and compassion, the nuns would come to the door and applaud him with their little hands... sometimes the director came, too. They served him a bowl of tomato sauce, potatoes and salad at the other end of my table. I would say hello to him, but he wouldn't answer, or even nod... clearly he didn't recognize me and didn't know where to put me... Always, when I finished eating, Sister Rafaela would bring the basket back to me full... sometimes, in addition to the thermos of soup, a container would be stuffed with rolled dumplings, which I made sure went to Clairi... Then, once back downstairs, I'd check in on Gisela again and stop by the playroom to take one more look at my paintings... Life, it seemed to me... in proximity to kindness, without any traps... was somehow evening out... Around the Public Kitchen there was always a crowd, lots of people, and sometimes there were random searches... On the sidewalk next to the building, there were leaflets bearing a blood-red star and a triangle with *LF* printed over it... Who dropped them there? When? Last night, or early this morning? It could have been anyone... the ones jostling each other here in the Public Kitchen, or up the street in one of the better cafés. You could find them across the Ljubljanica and on Jail Street, too. It was more dangerous to pick them up and read them than it was to distribute them. "Long live Tito!" one of them said. "Long live Stalin!" "Long live Roosevelt!" "Long live Churchill!" "Long live the Anglo-American army!"...Sometimes flyers with longer text or even entire little newspapers lay on the ground...Once, I found a ripped flyer with the headline "*Christmas Communique*," which I stuffed in my trousers and read at home..."...the fact that we Slovene Christians have allied ourselves with the communists does not mean the end of political diversity for the Liberation Front...We believe that if the essence of communism is being realized today, then our essence will be realized tomorrow..." I didn't understand it, except that it meant something different from what the flyers and papers with the red star, hammer and sickle were saying. There were also flyers on the ground with messages that could just as well have been published in the papers..."Fellow Slovenes! Anyone who trusts the communists will pay dearly for that trust. When Red Ivan comes galloping in from the steppes of Asia, you'll endure calamity surpassing what the God-fearing Russian nation has endured for the past twenty-five years... Slovenes! Be smart! Don't trust the communists, who believe every-thing they can prove and prove everything they believe." This was a war of flyers that battled it out with their punctuation and words or stood off to the side, the way some individuals do...The slogans, signs and pictures on buildings and walls were similar...Like hoodlums, the bandits also cut phone lines, chopped down telegraph poles, riddled the tires of ambulances with holes and dumped offal on monuments... But that was nothing. I wanted to meet the guy who hung a flag with the five-pointed star on the church tower. That was a hero! Or the guy who disarmed two Italian officers singlehandedly... Though I suppose that didn't take all that much courage. I would have liked to disarm one, myself, off in some side street... I knew how quick they were to go wobbly and hand over their kits with their grenades, pistols and daggers... But planting the flag on top of the church. Now there was an acrobat! A mountaineer of the highest, most death-defying order... Thank god, at least Ljubljana hadn't been bombarded... Over Germany, the flying fortresses were laying carpet bombs day after day until their cities were theater cutouts and their streets heaps of rubble and people had no idea anymore which way was home... Pretty soon, bomb craters would be all that was left!... Even here over Ljubljana, the air was sometimes filled with the wail of sirens "*wwwwaaaahhhhh*" and the "*dotta-dotta-dotta-dotta-dotta*" of small salvos... Those were the anti-aircraft artillery firing up in the air. Searchlights would illuminate the sky and buildings as though it were daytime, luring people out on the street, so that sometimes ten or twenty might be standing on a hill in the glow of a cone of light, looking up through the clouds at the streaks nervously painting the sky... With a single pocket flashlight at night, you could set off a whole anti-artillery battery, because the Italians took every little glow in the dark for an American paratrooper... *Boom! Ba-room!* hummed the flying fortresses way up above, five miles over the city, each carrying seven tons of munitions and a highly accurate bombsight. They had a much homier sound than the

Heinkels or Messerschmidts...*Bzzz!* went some Mosquito, the fortresses' pathfinder, as it dove down in loops, as if on a lark...once... then once again...And each time it dove, just for fun, it set off twenty or thirty phosphorus flares that rocked and sailed...from one cloud to another...they were determined to see everything!...the flares crackled, shot up...they could see everything, more clearly than in broad daylight...trees, rooms, the steps up to the castle, carts, housewives standing outside their houses, Salaznik watching them from the grass in the courtyard...What a theatrical spectacle they presented to us! And the anti-aircraft defense force, banding the sky to the north... the south...and the west with hundreds of cones of light, looking for bombers, was just as stupid as some local traffic cop: they needed to light up the gaps and holes between clouds...And then, once the planes left, the cones of light subsided...from the clouds down to the people...at a slant...first one...then the rest...That's what you called clear vision. You could see through bushes...everything looked granular, buildings and bricks and women in nightgowns looked like snowmen in the dazzling brightness...only their mouths remained black. And then the siren announced the all clear...

WHEN I GOT TO THE END of the fence surrounding the Children's Home, I always went to the other side of the street. There, on the other side, was where a gigantic maple grew, and behind it, there was a tall, brand new apartment building with big balconies...What a treat for the eyes when I saw on those balconies nice-looking, richly dressed kids, like from before the war...hobby horses, including a gray like

I'd once had myself...elegant ladies all made up, wearing gowns of all colors...carefree young housewives...all as if there were no war at all...as if here, at this building, it ended, leaving only peace to prevail...What kind of people lived in that new building was something I was never able to figure out...

One day, however, I had barely reached the end of the fence in front of the Children's Home...when suddenly, there was a sound of *brrrr! ping! brrrr! ping!*...My God, that sounded like an automatic rifle at least, if not a machine gun. The street around the Public Kitchen, which had just then been full of people, emptied out in an instant...suddenly it was abandoned, like a playing field after a game...I crouched and froze, ready to jump, but then, in spite of the fact that everything else had come to a stop, I walked on...The people in front of me, in the crowd pressed up to the wall, squashed and stiff, gave off a sour smell of stale clothing and bad food from the Public Kitchen...There, at the point where the path began its slope up the rampart toward Castle Hill...toward the little convent...I could see, from a distance, lying on the pavement...hunched over like a kid...a gentleman with magnificent white hair dressed in a black suit...his hat had blown out into the street, revealing his snow-white head and ruddy skin...He was lying in the mud and gasping...and some nun from the convent came running down the rampart toward him, shouting in all directions. The people pressed back up against the wall of the Public Kitchen, they were totally rigid and pale. As if in a dream they were all wriggling backwards into the warm entryway of the big, stinking dining hall. None of them had eyes for anything that was going on in front of them, each could barely feel his own physical presence...and not until the entryway, where they were out of hearing range and in the dark, did some amount of murmuring begin...though not very loud...Where had the shots come from? From the old peasant house across the way or from an upper floor of the Public Kitchen?...Virtually that same instant, the Italians drove up in a truck and a limousine. They unloaded and set out tank traps, and suddenly there were more soldiers around than grains of sand...They closed off the street with sawhorses, scurrying back and forth in their gunny sack uniforms...the cooks from the Public Kitchen came outside wearing their white aprons and hats... holding their knives and ladles, their mallets or the handles of cake servers...Someone had shot a priest, word came from the crowded entryway...a bigshot, the famous Dr. Erlich...They knew him. Every day, they saw the doctor out on the steps. He had his office upstairs from the Public Kitchen...Murderers, spies, bandits! The Bolshies had rubbed him out!...The cooks started wailing and moaning. *Uhuu!* If they could have gotten their hands on a bandit now, they would have bashed him to death with the handles of their slicers and ladles. They were the only ones who dared to cry...A black van drove up, I knew it, it was the morgue's, then an ambulance, and a doctor jumped out...The leftovers were starting to get cold in my bag, I could feel it, because they weren't burning my hip...Several Italians went toward the Public Kitchen, and, using their rifles, started shoving people back inside the building; but they left two guards and a tank trap outside the door...Several other kids and I were allowed to stay outside...The men in the entryway were shaking for fear that they were about to be sent off to prison camps. They were shouting, "Damned Antichrists! Communist murderers!" only in order to save their own skins…The steam billowing out of the Public Kitchen brought all these inanities out into the open…Within an hour, the barricade was removed, and the street was open again and full…Just one soldier carrying a rifle was left by the side of the road, at the place where the priest had fallen…I went to have a look, but the soldier was too nervous – "*Via! Via!* " – to let me get close. At the place where he'd fallen, there was some sort of dark but already smudgy spot…but the low stone wall was still covered with lots of fresh drops of blood, sprayed on it like confetti out of a paper bag…"The communists have committed a new crime," the newspaper reported the next day. "The communists are relentless in their criminal schemes. Yesterday, around midday, Dr. Erlich, the spiritual leader of the Guards in the Storm, was the latest target of one of their bullets…" The leaflets that appeared on the railing of the St. Jakob's bridge showed a five-pointed star dripping blood and said, "There is no way to negotiate a united, democratic struggle for Slovenia's liberty with the communists. The murder of Dr. Erlich is further proof that they are undermining all efforts, proof that the communists are determined to stay in charge at all costs and pervert the dignified restraint of the Slovene people into violent revolution and civil war…"

Once again, a continuous onslaught of blockades and random searches dominated the life of the city…at the Matica Cinema, right in the middle of a movie, a colorful Cuban musical, the lights went on. Arditi were standing beneath the screen on the stage, with three machine guns pointed straight at the audience. They ordered us all to put our hands up and keep them over our heads. The older men had to squeeze their way out of the rows and go in single file up the aisles and out the theater's main entrance, where ramps led up into the flatbeds of transport trucks. No distinctions were made...whether teamster or medical doctor in a pince-nez...all of them were suddenly expendable...All the women accompanying them to the show... girls, wives, stood outside crying from the theater to the university... a regular wailing wall of lament...solid, to last a thousand years. An old woman wearing a hat dropped to her knees and pulled at an Ardito officer by his coattails, "*Prego, signor, prego.*" She pointed to her son, a boy in a ski cap who was already standing under the truck's canvas roof. The Ardito suddenly slammed his fist in her throat, and she let go. All of the women were screaming...the Ardito pointed his automatic pistol at them, ran to the truck's cab and climbed in next to the driver. One after the other, the column of trucks took the men to St. Peter's Barracks...The word was that some damn traitor was sitting there, hidden from view, who told the Italians which of the men were secretly with the LF as they filed past...

Then early one morning, there was a blockade on Old Square, during which the Italians stopped people on the street and searched the neighborhood house by house. Nobody could go out or come in...I hid my bayonet under a heap of coal that we kept on the staircase between the top floor and the attic...The building was quiet, a lot more so than most Sundays...Clairi was muttering something...

counting the echoes...she had a whole slew of rituals and tics... she was acting like a machine...as if "*im Traum...Jetzt sagen die Leute alles über jeden. Jetzt wird uns das halbe Haus anzeigen...Alle Pelzchen werden sie nehmen.*"* "*Ich habe einen Mann auf dem Dachboden gesehen... er hat im Schrank gewühlt...es ist klar...aber wer war es? Ein Partisan, Kommunist?*"**...Then she muttered the whole time, "*Wie ruhig ich bin! Wie ruhig ich bin!*"***...She asked me, "*Bist du auch ruhig, Bubi?*"****... I tried calming her down..."*Ja...ja!*"...I stared and stared through the round, paned windows of the attic...nobody! And there was nobody hiding in or around the old wardrobes...maybe he was in the spot where there wasn't any window and it was all dark...That would be just great if they found the fugitive and my bayonet nearby! Then the whole lot of us could face a firing squad, or be sent to a rock quarry, or taken out to the Marsh...Clairi couldn't bring herself to stop peering around on the stairway..."*Kannst dich nicht ausschielen?*"*****..."*Nein, ich kann nicht.*"******..."*Bist du immer noch ruhig?*"*******..."*Oh ja, du*

---

*...in a dream...Now people will say anything about anyone. Now half the building is going to denounce us...They're going to confiscate all of our furs.

**I saw a man in the attic...he was hiding in one of the wardrobes...that much is clear... but who was he? A partisan, a communist?

***How calm I am, how calm I am.

****Are you calm, too, Bubi?

*****Can't quite sneak enough peaks?

******No, I can't.

*******Are you still calm?

auch?" *…"Ja!…Mach keine Komödie!"* ** I didn't want to provoke
her anymore, to keep from waking her…she said she was dreaming…
fine! I'll leave her to it…Then suddenly we heard a commotion from
the courtyard. Salaznik, who was ordered to climb a ladder to show the
soldiers what was in the attic of his courtyard building, his warehouse,
noticed from the top rung that his pretty wife and an Italian officer
were hugging and kissing on the far side of the building…The officer
was holding and fondling her under her clothes…Old Salaznik began
shrieking at his wife…he crawled up the tiles to the peak of the roof…
then slid down the other side on his butt and into the yard…He went
flying at his wife, letting loose at her with his right while trying to
grab onto the Italian's arm with his left…But all that grabbing of arms
caught him up, and he overturned a whole shelf full of flowerpots…
and marmalade jars. Then suddenly, he was at rest…holding his wife by
the hand like a child…wheezing…and with the other hand scratching
his belly…the Italians were shaking their heads…they left the courtyard…and came back into the house…Then we heard *squok! squeak!
squok! squeak!* on the steps…An Italian officer, a different one, not the
one from the garden, came through the door to the attic…as handsome as a movie star, wearing deer hide gloves, covered with medals
and ribbons, with a neat little pistol in his holster and binoculars on
his chest…His bayonet was well hidden…but then, what is a bayonet?
If he'd had a hand grenade, one of those red ones, it would have been

*Oh yes. You too?

**Yes. Don't make a scene.

worse...Except that hand grenades weren't suited to urban spaces, they were the equivalent of a circus dancer in a church...Pistols, sure, you could use them to shoot at people around corners...At best bayonets might come in handy in taverns, for use in scuffles with drunks...The handsome officer flirtatiously smiled at Clairi as he looked through the furs in their boxes and searched for a weapon. Vati stood with his hands clasped behind his back and watched wordlessly...he didn't care for the spaghetti eaters...Clairi was worried about the furs above all...you never knew how many things your neighbors might denounce you for to the authorities, people were born snitches...At the same time, she was keeping one ear cocked for whatever was happening outside, on the top floor...Because Salaznik wasn't right there with his keys, the Italians had broken down the wide door, came stomping in under the rafters, stirred up whole clouds of dust...sneezed...jabbed with the knives on their rifles at rags, sofas, old armchairs, inside the wardrobes...The officer and a helmeted soldier went with Clairi into the main room...the soldier examined the baker's shelves...that was the only place where something could have been hidden...he probed with his bayonet among the pans and cups...banged on the wall. The officer had a look around the room...now this was exemplary poverty...The cast iron bed and stove, the table...That gave him courage to stroke Clairi's hair. "*Un bacco!*" he said, pressing her head to his shoulder and placing his lips on hers so that her face got squished into mush on his epaulettes...Then there was a gunshot...In a split second, the soldier aimed his rifle at me, the officer ran with his pistol out of our room...and we all came hurtling out the front door...False alarm...

Some Italian had fired into a big spider web in the rafters of the top floor, thinking it was a bandit hiding up there... They managed to fling a regular funeral mound of junk from the wardrobes, chests, sofas, crates, rags and draperies onto the attic floor. Were they planning to douse it with kerosene and set it on fire? Some soldier had already struck a match behind a folding screen...which lit up all the roofing tiles. No, they just wanted to create a mess for us to have to deal with... now each party was going to have to find their own junk in that chaos. But thank god they'd done it just with their stuff and not with their bodies, they'd shot only at cobwebs and not at some poor wretch hiding up here in the attic...What made the whole business even more fun was the way all the soldiers laughed on the steps...Then from downstairs, there was the sound of a whistle, then a trumpet...A throng of soldiers came flying out of the houses, as if on rockets...with pillows, sheets and blankets under their arms...that was always the first thing they stole! The officers handed out orders to them...Old Square was opened again, the sawhorses vanished...the streetcar made its first appearance after all that like a circus wagon on an opera stage...but at the Salazniks, the old man and his wife were at each other like cats... In all of the staircases, you could hear her shouting "Help! *Aiuto!*"...in the course of their tussle they burst out onto the staircase, where they continued to grab and bite at each other...*zzzzip!* went her houserobe from bottom to top, leaving her naked...But outside, there was also quite a lot of commotion and drumming...outside Ljubljana a battle with the bandits was taking place...Machine guns rattled...mobile artillery thundered *Badoom! Badang!* their tongues buried up to the stocks in ruts that the cannons made in the mud beneath them...tank grenades announced themselves with a thin, birdlike twitter *Pheeoooeee-Wahh!* A day or two later outside the dairy, there was a covered truck that had driven up from Lower Carniola. Legs, the legs of civilians poked out of it...some had lost their knees...the trousers ripped and the rest planted god knows where in the dirt...heads caked in dried mud, also smashed...and, on top of this mound, there was flesh... gigantic chunks of it! in two forms, rags and slush squeezed together in one...Slaughtered bandits!

At this point, I would have preferred to do nothing but draw day and night and earn money. Lots of money, which I could use on the black market to buy all kinds of things to eat, plus a few yards of material, so Vati could sew me the coat that I still didn't have...We were hungry and freezing like marmots in winter...

Asipi Abdulhari was an Albanian who had been a shoe shiner and restorer before the war. Now he didn't work out on the streets anymore. He had bought a property next to a barbershop, which had once been owned by a corset maker. But he also bought a smaller one on St. Peter Street which, under Yugoslavia, had been the state lottery. He put it in his wife Hajrula's name, so that the taxes wouldn't be too high...What a place that became, once he renovated it! It was like walking into Arabia!...Furniture varnished a dark red...rows of little drawers reaching up to the ceiling with black silken tassels...glass trays placed atop embroidered runners on the counter...ranged low on the walls to the right and left, mirrors around which tiny bulbs shone day

in and day out…a cashier stand with an ultra-modern cash register…
thick carpets on the floor…a two-piece red plush curtain in the display
window, which he would draw shut on Sundays…Where had he gotten
the money? Had he inherited it from some rich man? It felt like a sin
to walk into such exquisite surroundings in wartime! It made your
head spin, as though you were dreaming awake. But when you looked
closer, it was all kitsch. Like a sweetshop…In wartime, it's the traders
and gypsies who have the biggest stashes of money and throw the most
extravagant banquets, mother said…Even Asipi himself had changed.
Thin, swarthy, mustachioed, before he had always had colorful spots
from shoe polish and various leather dyes. Now he wore a black suit
like the salesmen at Škoberne's Carpets down the street, because in
the better stores they looked down on blue work smocks…At any
rate, Asipi had heard that I had a talent for drawing, and he wanted to
have some posters made for his display windows that would list all the
services he offered his valued customers. Not just cleaning, shining and
dying shoes, but also special applications for water- and cold-proofing
your footwear, wholesaling used shoes, galoshes, soles, special inserts,
minor repairs, replacing heels…even appraising shoes. The posters
needed to be effective in bringing people in off the street, and besides
the text, they had to have clever graphics…He didn't just need two
posters for the store here but also some for his wife's store on St. Peter
Street, plus two more for his buddy who shined shoes on the Triple
Bridge, and two more for some other relation of his who plied a brush
outside the train station. Those posters for the sidewalk operations
were more than anything supposed to trumpet his two stores here in

town...So all together, it was going to be eight posters, for each of which the society of shoe shiners was going to pay me from twenty-five to thirty lire, in addition to the cost of materials, of course...I got to work right away...I copied all different kinds of footwear for various seasons out of Vati's pre-war catalog...children's and orthopedic... for snow, for rain, for pavement or grass or slush...going up over the ankle or not...I stuck funny dwarves and little girls into enormous shoes...I made a whole procession of feet of both genders, young and old and of various callings, which you could see only up to the instep... The reflections on the shoes shone like straight razors...Finally, after a week's work I delivered four pairs of all unique, flawlessly executed posters to Mr. Abdulhari, who liked them most of all for the way they boldly exaggerated his craft...He gave me 250 lire, which was more than half of a warm winter coat...

Around the time I was delivering my designs to Asipi, I ran into Andrej again, who was living in the same building where the shoe shiner had his shop...I went with him upstairs to say hi to his family. His mother and Neva were happy to see me. Neva had a boyfriend whom she was planning to marry, and Marjana down the hallway was doing much the same as before, only now with soldiers...but in these times that was nothing out of the ordinary, when nearly every second woman who had a husband at home or in prison went rutting around with handsome Italians...All of them were doing pretty much the same as before, except for their mother, who was having health problems. She had grown sick of Italian movies and missed the American and French ones, which were always full of ballads and ditties...But something exceptional had happened to Andrej in that time. He had fallen in love with Adriana, who was no more and no less than the daughter of the Italian police commissioner...He had met her one day in the Star Park, at the water fountain when he was taking a drink...She rode up on her scooter, which she wanted to wash...dressed all in white...a white cloche dress, white shoes, white stockings, and a white straw hat. She honked the horn on her scooter and when he turned around, he saw the prettiest girl he had ever seen. Andrej's voice outright shook in his little mouth as he told me about it...Then it came about that she invited him to her birthday party in a villa next to the girls' lyceum. Lots of Italian boys and girls were invited, almost all of them the children of generals...My God, how magnificent she was!...she was wearing a blue dress with white lace and little blue shoes with heels like a grown woman's...They wound up the gramophone, danced, ate birthday cake...The two of them went out in the yard, and in the gazebo, she put her head, all done up in big, grapelike locks, on his shoulder...He was wearing his white trench coat the whole time, even when they were inside, because he didn't have anything else that was decent to wear...And then they kissed...He still had the scent of her hair, her scent, on his trench coat. His mother had already tried several times to take it to the cleaner's, but he wouldn't let her...And because she wouldn't give up, he had to hide it in the attic...He wanted to show it to me so I went with him. It was hanging on a pole that was hidden behind a vanity chest and wrapped in newspaper...He told me to sniff it around the left shoulder...It really did smell strongly of perfume or eau de cologne.

A tiny flower was still tucked in its buttonhole. She had given it to him as a parting gift after plucking it from their garden...He really was in love...He described the party, the lanterns, the drinks and food, the candles and little flags...She had received a whole roomful of gifts, which made him feel ashamed that all he'd brought her was just one flower. She also got a new red scooter. He told me how nice her father was to him, even though he was such a bigshot...Now she and her parents had gone back to Italy, far away...He pointed through an attic vent at the mountains on the horizon...it was funny, the way infinity could get stuck like that on the tip of your fingernail...a gesture... between heaven and earth...That conversation was so interesting that we sat down on the steps to continue it, and he told me the whole story again from the beginning. From the moment when he was getting a drink at the water fountain and she squeezed the horn on her scooter...until the point where he rang the bell at the front door of their villa...Everything, scene by scene, as if in a movie...He even sang the songs that he heard from her guests and her gramophone records..."Has she written to you?"..."Well, she promised to send me a card..." I envied him...If I'd been that handsome, had eyes and hair like him, I could have experienced a fairy-tale love like that, too.

Right at the time I was doing the posters for Asipi's store, I met an older high school student whose last name was Šcšck. He also drew. He invited me over to show me his drawings. They consisted entirely of battles, tanks, infantry, air raids...explosions that verged on bouquets...Far more than the drawings, I was intrigued by the house. It was old, stood next to the Kolman building, and was full of walkways and passages. Most interesting of all was a veranda looking out over the Cobblers Bridge and the embankment...For the first time, I got to see the Ljubljanica from a unique, almost bird's eye perspective...The water flowing under the bridge, which you couldn't hear down below, next to the wall where I used to meet with Karel and Ivan...up here almost roared, thundered so much it was deafening...This view from the veranda, which swayed and shook slightly, as if you were on the deck of a river steamer, suddenly made Ljubljana much more intimate and interesting to me...it opened it up...It reminded me vaguely of some particular spot in Basel...that's it! that's it!...from which I liked to look out at the Rhine, which would roar, eddy and foam around the piers...Where exactly was that?...I definitely wanted to figure it out...I asked Šešek if I could come back sometime. I sat on the deck of the veranda with my legs dangling out between the bars of the railing and stared...All that time, Šešek's old father, a widower and a retired banker...fat, flushed, with age spots and whiskers like the Emperor Franz Joseph...sat behind me near the open door of his room, which was full of old gramophones and contraptions, cutting out ration stamps and pasting them onto a sheet of paper for the grocery store...I stared at the foaming water, listening to its roar and the voices of people that were angrily making their way up, and I felt a dizziness and shakiness that encouraged me to fly...I was completely entranced...but I kept drawing a blank on that damned place in Basel where all of this had transpired and been heard before...

I've already said: I was drawing and painting like crazy...
Mother, Clairi, Vati, Gisela, the castle, to the extent I could still
see it at all from our window, the notched tower and clock with its
Roman numerals...which had dazzled me so upon our first arrival
in Ljubljana... The garden with its shed and the trees by the wall
that had bricks falling off of it...Pigeons in the gutters and cats on
the roofs...all of them mouthy, black, half-breed angoras, one of
which once swiped our whole monthly ration of meat, which mother
had set on the window sill between two plates...With the look of a
highly trained athlete, black-furred Jaka just padded away over the peak
of the neighboring house with the piece of beef in his mouth...Vati
wanted to catch the whole clutter of them, skin them, and sew their
furs into a three-quarter jacket that he could probably sell to some
produce vendor at the market. Only once did a different type of cat
appear outside the window. It was a kitten...white, with a tiny head
on its skinny neck...*psss! psss!*...Who was it that painted women who
looked like it? Botticelli?

Then I took up stories in images..."*Bubi, du zeichnest also auch
Comiks?*"* mother asked...Yes, comic strips that began to circulate
among my classmates...in exchange for their lunch! "The Journey
of the Flying Whale around the World"..."In the Wild Jungles of
Africa"..."A Bridge on the Prairie"...On every page of an unlined
school notebook I would draw up to twenty pictures with text printed

*Bubi, so you're drawing comics now, too?

in little clouds...tiny figures painstakingly drawn, with all their equipment, belts, pistols, and pith helmets...apparatus and technical details...I borrowed some atlases from my classmates, checked some reference and history books out of the library...I learned from those books that, in the old days, the wars, both world and civil, and revolutions weren't called what they are today...they called them migrations of peoples and tribes...One people would arrive from somewhere, and another would have to yield to them by heading south, north or east... one people retreated into the mountains from the invasion of another and wound up driving the moutain dwellers someplace else. The latter settled in a valley and displaced those people...And thus, all the way up until who knows what year, peoples kept exchanging whatever territory they happened to occupy for as long as some was still left...In the zeppelin, the flying whale that I knew from Basel, the people in my story were traveling to the North Pole, and among them there was this really big villain who snuck out of the passenger gondola into a space that contained the cyanide for the mixed fuel and the helium for the filled balloons, in order to destroy one of those fifteen gigantic inflated pears that were, so to speak, the water wings of this whale, and along with them, of course, everything else, so that then above a certain point of the Arctic Circle he could jump out with a parachute, a tent and a supply of canned goods and plant the flag of his country Luciferium at the Pole...I drew and described the complete welter of aluminum and steel, the flutter and pop of the shell of the aircraft during its flight, the revolting gas smell of almonds, and the steps and ladders over which the villain had to be chased...In the jungles of Africa, a white man named James battled carnivorous plants, snakes, cannibals and sorcerers until he broke through to Victoria Falls and sailed away to New York, where he became a doctor...The ledger for the bridge on the prairie included its hero Buffalo Bill and his two hundred redskins riding bareback on horses, who were battling the cowboys and cavalry of the USA...far and away most important was Bill, who for instance could shoot an egg in two at a gallop...My classmates read these comic strips like starving people...even their parents at home read them... They offered me apples, potatoes, flour not cut with gypsum to continue them...Their parents were part-time farmers or expert black marketeers who had from eight to twelve ration cards each...Flour and potatoes were serious business, and if I wanted to get a loan in the form of foodstuffs or a meal, I had to work really hard and be extra conscientious about my plots...I wanted to put together a story about space, about interplanetary travel...about how our world kept getting inflated, as the articles in the science pages of the newspaper said... like an "explosive grenade"...and about how the spiral galaxies were getting farther and farther away, and the fact that the farther away they got, the faster they went...so that we were living in both a politically and physically explosive world. In my class, Mikec – a little, bony kid with bulging eyes, one blue, one gray – was also an excellent draftsman...a lot better than me, in fact. He also tried his hand at comics... his drawings were a lot more detailed and refined than mine, a lot more legible, but my stories outdid his for plot development and suspense. Even one of the other classes in my form had a good draftsman named Bajželj, a stocky athlete...he dealt with flying and sailing themes in his stories...The three of us now got together and talked quite a bit about putting together a really big comic strip, maybe even publishing a whole book of stories in pictures and trying to cash in on it...We admired the paintings of old masters that depicted wars of old...there was no good way of drawing a modern war, they were too dreary for pictures...What were cannons and tanks when you could have catapults that hurled huge boulders or burning canister shots...what were the uniforms of today's soldiers when compared with knights' armor?...And what about religious, church painting?...Sure, as long as there's lots of action...Samson from the Old Testament, who, when they bound him to a pillar, brought down the temple, or let's say Judas when he's with the disciples, hiding behind his back the bag of silver that he got from the head rabbis for his act of betrayal...But I liked it all. Especially mural paintings fascinated me...With brown and black watercolors, you could produce fine and very effective paintings on walls...The walls in our room were horribly dirty...they'd last been whitewashed long before we moved in. Mother gave me permission to paint them...At the window behind the bed, I produced a Creation of the World. That was the first full-page image from the catechism that continually fascinated me anew. The spirit of God standing above the waters amid the sun, moon, and stars at the precise moment when God created heaven and earth, separated darkness from light... The painting was powerful, but what came off particularly well was the transparency of the water...On the wall opposite, I painted paradise lost ... the Garden of Eden, surrounded by four rivers...the plants gentle on the eye and good to eat, the animals, and Adam and Eve beneath the tree of knowledge…On the narrow stretch of wall next to the baker's shelf, I did Christ on the cross: the head…with respect to the beard, mustache, and curls it resembled Vati's, though not in the length of its locks, and thorns from the crown were constantly piercing the forehead…a nail was hammered into the center of the palm! At the point where all of the lines for life and fate converge… drops of blood flowed down his dirty face…he was crying, *Eli, Eli, lama sabahsthani?* Lord, my Lord, why hast thou forsaken me?…Behind the shelves above the hotplate, I painted the Last Judgment: the first signs on the sun and the moon…the fearsome sound of the sea…the people paralyzed in fear and anticipation…that was just the framing! Inside, in the middle of the painting, was the Son of Man on his throne, with eternal life to the right and people bathed in the glow of white spirits… to the left, I showed the underworld with fire, blackened people, and their angels with bare wings…The pictures had the effect of frescoes in a small church or some sort of chapel, just the wall over the bed and table remained empty, only now revealing how greasy and grimy it had become…

One day, our teacher Srečko Lenard asked Mikec and me to come to the teachers' lounge. Our stocky friend Bajželj was already sitting there. Mr. Lenard told us that GIL, the Fascist youth organization, was working with the National Gallery to organize a drawing contest involving all the high schools in Ljubljana. Each school was supposed to submit work by its best draftsmen. As our drawing and calligraphy teacher, he, Mr. Lenard, had already arranged for us to represent our school at that event…There were going to be monetary prizes for the best three. Perhaps one of us might even win one of them? Most of all, however, Mr. Lenard said, we had to take care that we didn't bring shame on him or our school... All three of us were excited... The only thing about it that stank was that GIL was organizing the contest. GIL was a revolting organization... the only member of GIL in our school was Požar, whom our Italian language teacher Margherita Ardacci liked so much. Sometimes Požar would come to school in his black uniform, particularly if he had to go to a meeting after classes... or drill sessions at Kolezija... Their uniforms were made using good material, and supposedly Mussolini himself had sketched its design!... we had to admit that we envied Požar his Sam Browne belt, dagger, and even the medal that he got for excellence in military maneuvers... He was the only kid that most of the school disliked, though on the other hand you had to give him credit for a certain amount of courage, since he rarely came to class without his black GIL *csako* with its silver fasces pin... There weren't many members of GIL... most of them went downtown, to the Youth Center on Kolezija, where orphans lived with no parents, boys and girls who were physically or mentally retarded, slow growers or even semi-invalids... There were firing ranges in the Youth Center's courtyard... in the morning, they'd raise the flag to "*Giovinezza*"... they even had their own little brass band with drums... then, under the supervision of adult blackshirts, they'd practice jumping hurdles, crawling under barbed wire, digging trenches, throwing wooden hand grenades... stabbing bags of straw with bayonets... from morning to night, the whole time wearing their black GIL uniforms, which they would have to launder every day to get rid of the dirt and grime... That place stank of poverty, disadvantage and death all the way to the street. But the most horrible thing was that everyone in the neighborhood had those poor devils in sight, day and night…that none of the kids running around the Center's courtyard in their black-clad parades could evade the vigilant eyes of the local idlers…that no one was going to be able to get past anyone unscathed…

So much for GIL, but *hm!*, the contest was also being organized by the National Gallery, our athlete Bajželj said, and that changed everything, because that's a Slovene institution, as his father had told him… After school, we went walking around, down Two Emperors Road, toward Wetland Meadow…but not too far, because the beautiful wetlands were mined and full of barbed wire…Mikec explained, "I know how it's going to turn out…I'll win first prize, Bajželj will get second, and you'll come in third." That burned me…*hmpf!* third!…last prize, in other words, but all right…On the day of the contest, the three of us were excused from classes…The event took place on the street in front of the National Gallery. There was a sign over the museum's side door, surrounded with garlands of spruce: GIL AND THE NATIONAL GALLERY…Around that side door the most talented draftsmen from all of the city's high schools had gathered, girls and boys…Such elegance, particularly for high school students…everything from before the war…Žiri-made hiking boots, Tivar suits, flannel Ts, white dress shirts with high, stiff collars…the handsome sons and daughters of better families, nurtured and cared for in a way you could only envy!… In fact, there weren't many, if these were the good draftsmen from schools all over the city, there were twenty or twenty-five…but if you considered that there was a war on and that everything everyone did was watched by thousands – no – tens of thousands of invisible eyes! somewhat congenial, but more often than not downright hyena-like... then actually, quite a few of us had turned out for the drawing contest, if not too many... But even these chosen ones were worried... they stood off by themselves... by the fence, on the other side of the street... far away from the door with the sign, so that people wouldn't identify them with that, in order to avoid being conspicuous... They looked up at the sky, at the ground... nobody was talking to anybody. Gee, if they'd been wearing GIL uniforms or the brown riding breeches of the village guards... they'd almost have stood out less, been perfect for telling who's who... but to get noticed like this, for drawing, a minor specialization... that was wrong, it could prove fateful for many, more so than throwing bombs... I paced the gravel paths in front of the gallery... since Mikec and Bajželj still hadn't come... but also because I had no connection to any of these upper class youths... Ljubljana was a regular jail!... at last you got to see the faces of all those adolescent kids from the banquets and better homes!... their true nature! and not just the faces of the ones in the slammer!... no, the whole crowd on the street!... their true eyes... their complexes! their parrot-like, jackal-like faces...

Bajželj, Mikec and I were the last to go in, because we were from a lower-class school and poorly dressed... Everybody in front of us seemed to have headed down to the basement... Some scabby kid my age wearing a suit that looked like it had been cut out of an old Yugoslav army blanket was hanging out next to the stairway railing... a real no-neck who looked like he was from here, maybe even the janitor's son...As we headed downstairs, the brat stuck his tongue out at us..."Fascist bastards!" he shouted...He probably hadn't bothered to say *boo* to the ones in the Tivar suits, but he felt free to shoot his mouth off at us..."Wait right there, jerk, I've got something to give you!" I yelled back, but he turned away...He was gone in an instant... fleeing upstairs or down some winding corridor...I ran up the steps two at a time and got to the staircase with the stained glass window through which you could see the street down below...I knew he was hiding somewhere close by and shaking like a reed. "Show your face, if you dare!" I shouted so loud my voice thundered down the folds of the staircase with its stucco and plaster...I went back, he wasn't anywhere, as though he'd plowed straight into a wall...boy, would I have liked to show that shithead, and I'll admit, I was no better or worse than he was. But it got me worked up. Why, though?...I ran back downstairs, to the basement...Mikec and Bajželj were already pushing their way through some narrow, dimly lit corridor...past gilt statues with jutting arms, stacks of frames with no paintings and canvases without frames...At the next significant doorway, there was an Italian GIL member dressed in his black uniform...A GIL senior cadet...Pale, raven-haired, fawning on all of us, as slimy as some cookie that's dropped into a teacup...He had a bunch of slips with numbers on them which stood for particular subjects; he was the one who decided who was going to draw what and in which medium... watercolors, tempera, charcoal, pen and ink, pencil...The first two or three rooms were set up for still lifes with flowers, still lifes with fruit, still lifes with a mandolin and sheet music…cherubs from an altarpiece…a live model on a plush, movable throne…some old man dressed in a top hat and cutaways…I either drew or was assigned as a subject a human skull on top of a book and a white candle in a gold candlestick against a black backdrop…Above and around the subject, there were rows and rows of paintings, chairs and tables with ornate legs, brocade, tablecloths…the room was crammed so full of priceless rummage that there was scarcely any air left to breathe… I picked out a pencil…there were lots of them, erasers, too…the sheet of drawing paper was clamped tightly onto a board…The GIL representative gave a speech…he introduced the jury sitting at a table…two Fascists and three poor schmucks, drawing teachers dressed in their black smocks…then, at the sound of a hand-clap, we began…All right then…the skull, the book, the candleholder…I drew, agonized and erased…that was allowed by the rules. Mikec was doing the same at a small round table covered with a moth-eaten plush throw that reached all the way to the floor…His composition went beyond an exact, proportional rendering…with its exquisite shading of the candlestick's ornamentation, the dark cavities of the eye sockets, the rictus of the fanged jaws. A regular Doctor Faustus. And he had accomplished all of this not with a drafting pencil but with an ordinary piece of sharpened charcoal…while here I, despite all my little hatch marks as fine as a needle, hadn't succeeded in extracting all those tendrils and buds wrapping their way up the candlestick… It was beyond comprehending, because Mikec's hand was so cloddish and unrefined that you'd sooner expect to see it holding a club than a pen...The jury went walking around...the slimy tea biscuit, the other two Fascists, all three drawing teachers in their black smocks... stopping at each group of contestants...in the auditorium to the left, the room to the right, and here...first at one, then another, and a third...Looking at Mikec's work, they nodded their heads... "*Primissimo*"...As they looked over my shoulder, first the three teachers and then the two Fascists, I could sense their discomfort...all they did was breathe down my neck without saying a word...I was in an agony of nerves, because I couldn't stand having people behind me... Suddenly, while we were still working, we heard military commands being shouted..."The high commissioner of the Ljubljana Region Mr. Emilio Grazioli has honored us with a visit," somebody called out in a piercing voice...Everybody got up from their subjects...and stood almost at attention...And indeed, there in the doorway stood High Commissioner Grazioli with his entourage, looking just like his pictures in the newspapers...wearing a high-peaked cap with the Fascist insignia, black uniform tunic and gold belt...with a red parade dress stripe running down the sides of his riding breeches...and a saber...in the elegance of his white breeches and white kid gloves... I looked the high commissioner straight in the face...and I could feel my heart skip a beat...you only get one chance in your life to look a king, a duke or a prince-bishop in the face, since they spend all the rest of their time behind the walls of their castles and palaces...and then nothing as unforgettable as that happens again!...Even his entourage knew that!...they weren't giving him time to ask anything! they were answering his questions before he had a chance to ask them!...

there was a regular forum around him...each one outshouting the other! each one had the right to be heard by the commissioner!...He was the most important one!...all the others gave the impression of just bunglers!...The photographers ran ahead of the group...*click! click!*...went their cameras...Grazioli walked past...everybody applauded...the drawing teachers raised their arms in the Roman salute...down here in the basement they were safe, hidden from the unforgiving eyes of the bandits!...He would casually raise a hand and give a pleasant wave with one of his gloves, which he'd taken off... He had a whole column of people following behind him, half of the National Council, half of the Regional Government, from the most eminent down to the most common, who in Grazioli's presence came across like pale damsels flocking to Napoleon...He was also accompanied by his white dog, Agar. All of Ljubljana, the whole den, knew his dog...*Pst! pst!* Agar! people would tease him in Tivoli Park. Grazioli had a face that looked scrupulously groomed...his boots didn't squeak...they were made of the finest leather...If I were to tell my family about this, that I'd seen the high commissioner face to face, they'd fall on their butts laughing in disbelief...To see such a royal personage like that out of thin air, and then to be amazed that nothing happened as a result, that you survived...unchanged!...

Then came the awards ceremony and lunch...right in the middle of the gallery, amid paintings of old masters, darkened oils and pinkish, freckly portraits of people who'd been dead for centuries...who were alive way back in the day before dried beans in a bindle, when you carried rice cooked in wine in a little bag that hung from your belt...And in fact, there really was a big table set with all kinds of treats, like the one for my first communion...as though they intended to spoil us!... a whole mountain of slices of white bread slathered with butter, four platters of margarine, cheese and salami, sardines out of tins...The older GIL representative announced the awards...first prize, second prize, not until third prize did Mikec get named...all the rest of us, including Bajželj, got boxes of the very best Italian colored pencils as a consolation prize...During the banquet, I went to look at the pictures by the other contestants. Such oil paintings! watercolors! pen-and-ink drawings! charcoal sketches! All of them, every single one was better than mine by I-don't-know-how-much...there was just one case where I couldn't decide which drawing was worse, his or mine...How could I have been so presumptuous as to let myself be persuaded to enter this contest! how could that idiot Lenard have been so undiscriminating as to choose me as one of the school's best draftsmen!...All it took was one quick glance at the flowers...like flames ablaze on the canvases and boards...one glance at the black-clad old gentleman in the top hat seated in the scarlet-draped sedan chair...or at Mikec's skull done in charcoal...at the apples, red, yellow and green in their baskets...such gifted people! And how pathetic by comparison was my draftsman's skill!...

I FOLLOWED CLAIRI TO THE LIBRARY...should I keep drawing and painting, or not? That was the question that tormented me ever since the ordeal at the National Gallery...Mikec could dash off a comic book in three days...while it would take me two weeks to daub out as much…What if I wrote stories and stuck in an illustration here and there?…But what kind of stories? Romance, detective, adventure or humorous?…I vaguely sensed that I'd reached some sort of crossroads and that I had to decide which way to go…But the times weren't particularly supportive of choosing careers, since finding any work at all was no mean trick…I went around with Vati, who was otherwise loath to leave our attic apartment, inquiring about possible jobs… we stopped by all the furriers and sign makers and house painters in the area to see if they had openings for an apprentice now, before I graduated from school…No, at the moment there wasn't much going on in those trades, not even during the high season…and what things might be like in two years was anyone's guess…

Clairi kept checking out nothing but books by A.J. Cronin…*The Stars Look Down* and others like that. All of them with long titles, blockbusters that she could read for two, three months…half a year at a time. She would read a bit here and a bit there…sometimes finishing half a chapter or even a whole one…massage the book as though it were some sort of cat…put the thing back on the shelf and then ponder…That way she always had some other life at her fingertips, available for her to open and see how its fate was progressing…Then she'd ponder some more, weighing the arguments for and against espoused by various characters in the book, as though these were actual people…and once she had processed it all, in her sleep or while sewing, she would take on her next helping of potboiler…Each time she checked out another Cronin, even though Cronin only had five or six books…

The library was on Congress Square...downstairs there was a barbershop and a hair-styling salon, two elegant, old-fashioned businesses with little mirrors affixed to the glass of their display windows. Their owner was named Perm, and if you put an S on the front of the gilt lettering of his name that ran across the mirrored sign over the entrance...The library was located on a mezzanine. Even the hallway outside stank of dust, old books, glue, disintegrating spines and greasy marbled bindings...thousands and thousands of writers were dug in there, up to the ceiling, in long alleys of precarious shelving. I checked out fairy tales for Gisela, stories of forest sprites, the fates, dwarves, Netek the famished wanderer, and midsummer night... together with her I began learning about folk legends, unchristened dusk spirits, ghost riders, the Golden Hag and the Golden Horn... There was a counter with books by Slovene authors on one side and a table of foreign authors – English, German and French – on the other...For myself, I would check out Arsène Lupin, Sherlock Holmes, Jack London, *Poor Folk*, *Notes from the House of the Dead*...All of these books had something in common: they described the misery of life at the bottom, or at least offered some glimpses of it...and even the books themselves as objects were vile...dirty, torn, full of greasy thumb prints and stains of egg yolk or spilt coffee, even whole shopping lists penciled in, as though the people who read the books before you had used pork chops or big pieces of bacon as bookmarks...I expected a lot of that ex-convict and wretch Dostoevsky...but he was so obscure and twisted in places that it was a strain...But the *White Nights* alongside the Neva...that was good, like misery transfigured by the brilliance of a sub-Arctic summer... It was beautiful... All those Lenochkas and Ninochkas, pale young girls in their shabby rabbit fur coats... One scene in particular stood out in my memory, where a young girl who feels persecuted by the adherents of some revolutionary cell takes refuge in the home of some friends, and how there, in the safety they offer her, the fear she has just had to endure petrifies her, turns her into a statue, a mask... in other words, it shows her going mad right in front of her friends... The Karamazovs... the only one of them I understood was the son of some dying captain who had to fight it out with the other boys, one by one. Cankar... I had to read him for school. If those were supposed to be stories, then give me poems. Admittedly, his style was more florid than Dostoevsky's... whom you could devour like a newspaper... but in spite of that, the Russian was the better writer... Hamsun's *Hunger*... even the cover design in brown was revolting... but hunger was something I knew. It was true, when you don't have a scrap to eat, you become as light as an angel and things start to become so clear you can see through them...

There were always lots of people crowding around the counters... of all ages, genders, every possible calling... Some railway worker would always come with his leather traveling bag, like the ones doctors have, only much bigger... he would scoop thirty or forty books off the counter straight into it with his elbow... there were little old ladies who had gone completely white and smelled bad from constant, motionless reading in their armchairs... There was a long line of people stretching all the way back to where you paid your borrower's fee, and a whole multitude, fifteen feet deep, outshouting each other with titles and writers' names.... The librarians in their black work smocks made a point of taking their time as they walked with slips of paper from one overstuffed shelf to the next...or stood at the counters piled high with whole warehouses of books...romance novels, murder mysteries, how-to manuals, tales of adventure...all jumbled and stuck together in an impenetrable gray mass...They had fish eyes from doing nothing but reading, and they looked down their nose at the hoi polloi of unsophisticated readers...There was a man working the cash register who was said to be a poet. He had curly hair, hairy hands, and always wore too short a shirt...He would fill out and stamp the checkout slips and borrowers' cards...*ka-slam! ka-slam!*...without once looking up.

There was a tiny, gray-haired woman with glasses perched on the tip of her nose and always wearing lipstick who worked in the foreign book section...Mrs. Jeranko...She spoke excellent German, French and Italian...and would chat with the foreign customers as though it were nothing...She was well educated, and what a memory!...Christine von Pisan, Luise Labe, Marceline...French women poets...She could name all of them! even recite them! did I ever have respect for her!...One day at her counter, I ran into the lady in the white hat and black earrings that they called the Christmas Tree.... so she hadn't left for Germany, either?...She was checking out a stack of fat books and chatting with Mrs. Jeranko at length. Once, when Clairi came with me, the two of them spoke about all kinds of things...

They were in the midst of a lively discussion, when suddenly the lady recited some verse, "*Die Flucht war vergeblich; überall fand ich das Gesetz: Man muß sich ergeben: öffne dich, Pforte, dem Gast!*"* ...Very beautiful! And apt!...

In both sections, for Slovene and foreign literature, there were stacks of illustrated weeklies and monthlies at the ends of the counters... *The Family Friend, Bazar der Zeiten, The Slovene Illustrated, Illustris-Brotin, Gentleman, Ullstein Stern* ...the illustrations were from god knows how many ages ago...in their pictures and texts they preserved fashions, recipes, documents, events and stories from the years before the war...They were bound into annual, semi-annual or biennial volumes, or separate and unbound...I would borrow two full shopping nets of them at a time...carry them home, open them up on the floor, leaf through them, read some...then take them back to get more...The first automobile...big world fairs...new discoveries in science...technology...Only now did I discover the differences between this time and the one I had lived in as a little snot between 1928 and 1938, about which I knew next to nothing...not to mention the time before I was born...Occasionally, the paper had already deteriorated into mush...after all those years the printer's ink had dried up, taking with it that peculiar smell of color, and leaving only the meaning...There were thousands of advertisements, jokes and riddles...who invented the toothpick? How long is the Great Wall

*Fleeing was pointless; everywhere I encountered the same law: you must submit; open, gate, for the guest.

· 180

of China?... crossword puzzles, party games, various tests of your knowledge, memory, concentration... There were questionnaires: What would you rather be? A revolutionary or a rebel? As revolutionaries, they listed Robespierre, Marx, Lenin, and as rebels Danton, Bakunin, Trotsky. I opted for rebel. On the last page they explained what that said about your personality... for a) Revolutionary: You have definite goals. You are a bureaucrat of utopia. And for b): Your goals are hazy. You are quixotic and prone to jousting with windmills... Here I found the stories of Rockefeller, Vanderbilt, Rothschild... the richest men in the world. About the King of England, the Duke of Windsor and the divorcée Mrs. Simpson... there were photos of the Illyria Women's Club playing throwball, a variation of handball for women, and pictures from some cooking contest held at the foot of castle hill in Ptuj... a big portrait of Lord Morny wearing his sky-blue monocle, an international swindler who had tricked a whole slew of governments, stock exchanges, race tracks and companies all over the world... There were gruesome stories from Red Russia, from the time of the revolution... about the members of the Tsar's family who had been massacred, about his daughters, the grand duchesses, who'd had their breasts cut off... about the millions of peasants who had been driven out of their native villages and lived for months, from one day to the next, at train stations with just their samovars. A reporter wrote about how the conductors on special trains for foreigners distributed big pieces of cardboard to the passengers, who were supposed to use these to cover their windows, so they wouldn't see the heart-rending scenes of misery on the platforms as the train passed through a station... Or:

at carnival time in Berlin, a man named Ehrendorf went to a dance, where he met an attractive, svelte blonde. She was wearing a broach with a swastika and was just nineteen or twenty years old, innocent, fun-loving, even-tempered…the perfect young woman for Hitler's emerging new order…After the dance, Mr. Ehrendorf convinced the girl to go with him back to his apartment, where she was more than willing to submit to his wishes. Then, at the crucial moment, she straightened her elbow, reached out her right arm and fervently gasped "Heil Hitler!" as passion engulfed her. Poor Mr. Ehrendorf practically had a stroke!…Once he collected his senses, the adoring young blonde explained to him that she and her best friends had solemnly sworn to each other that "every time, at the holiest moments of their lives as women, they would remember the Führer"…Then there was a long serialized story about the Russian spy and assassin Vlasin Progorov, who stayed in the most luxurious hotels of Europe as he tracked down the émigrés that he would dispatch to the great beyond…In the photos, he was shown wearing a striped bathing suit, in a life preserver out on the sea off the Lido with some countess who would later become his victim…What is that song of songs about love that Russian poets write?…"The eyes of my beloved are like tall stoves in the steppe, her lips are etched boldly like a canal to the Arctic Ocean, her shoulders yield like dams on the Dnieper, and her back is as long and straight as the Trans-Siberian railroad…" "Why did the Reichstag really go up in flames?…Fat Field Marshal Goering set the fire himself…" The trial of Dimitrov…Pictured here: Communists and Nazis in 1930 joined in the struggle against the Prussian parliament...The confession of a communist: I approached communism as a source of fresh water, and I left it as a poisoned river that sweeps away the ruins of flooded cities and the corpses of the drowned...The Night of the Long Knives... Hitler responsible for killing thousands of his adherents in the SA...Hitler depicted in a mud-spattered leather coat helping his chauffeur push their famous limousine out of some ruts...slight and not at all leader-like...It was as though you were looking at a crystal ball of the world...various humiliations and absurdities...more real than the history in books...Oh, of course there were other kinds of episodes, too...life in Paris, street singers playing the accordion and fiddle in courtyards and picking up francs off the ground...the making of the movie "The Boxer Rebellion in Peking" with thousands of extras, lions, horses, marines...the horse-drawn omnibuses were crushed by the enthusiastic crowds of onlookers in the Bois de Boulogne... That was in peacetime, and the people had faces like wax...

Old photos from 1928 and '29...What had happened in the year I was born and shortly thereafter? This was a sort of horoscope, a horoscope of the world...King Feisal of Iraq was the most famous man...he sat in the octagonal throne room of his palace, supported by eight marble pillars...he sat on a divan wearing a black, two-cornered Mesopotamian cap, had a pointed beard and sharp facial features... The most famous man in the world...Some peace-loving Arab from Jerusalem, who on a Friday afternoon during Ramadan had been peaceably chatting with his Jewish renter, went to the mosque, where he heard a cleric speak, then ran home and butchered his renter and the man's wife and children with a kitchen knife... Here was a news item about how, during a summer heat wave in France, a truck freighted with eggs ran into a truck full of butter and flour... There were no casualties, but in the heat the flour, eggs and butter fried up into a gigantic omelet weighing several tons... A car race sponsored by the Daimler factory... that consisted of all black automobiles honking amid the buggies and horse hitches... a shirt made of lace with the caption: the best smell for your white things is the smell of lavender... monogrammed handkerchiefs were back in fashion... On November 14, 1928, at 6:30pm at the Crystal Palace in Geneva, the Colonial Indian Exposition is scheduled to open, featuring native hunters performing their war games... And so on. The whole volume, to the extent all the issues were there, with its pictures and texts resembled an orchestra that was just now warming up, while the conductor refused to appear... But a fall issue had a story from China. "The Executioner Wang Lun"... During some distant dynasty this executioner had been a great master of his art... His fame reached to every province of the empire. At that time, there were a great many murders in China, and sometimes it was necessary to behead up to fifteen or twenty people per day. It was Wang Lun's practice to stand off to the side of the block, whistling some sweet little tune... while concealing his curved sword behind his back, so that even as his victim was still coming up the steps to the scaffold, he could behead him with a lightning-quick stroke... For years and years, this Wang Lun had a certain unquenchable ambition, which it took him no less than fifty strenuous years to realize at last. His ambitious wish was to be able to execute his death blow so quickly...in accordance with the laws of duration...that the severed head would remain atop the body, the way dishes remain on a table if you snatch the tablecloth out from under them quickly enough...Wang Lun's great day came when he was seventy-eight years old...That day, he was to dispatch sixteen clients from this world to the world of their ancestors...As usual, he stood at the foot of the steps, with eleven shaven heads having already dropped into the sand at masterful blows from his sword...It was the twelfth that delivered him his triumph...Just as the man was setting his foot on the lowest step, Wang Lun's sword sliced through his neck with such speed that the head stayed right where it had been, and the man kept climbing the steps without realizing he had already been dealt the lethal blow. When he paused at the top, he turned to Wang Lun and said, "O, fearsome Wang Lun, why do you prolong the agony of my anticipation, when you dispatched the others with kinder, more merciful skill?"...When Wang Lun heard these words, he knew that his life's ambition had been fulfilled. A spritely smile played across his face as he said to the man, with exaggerated respect, "Why don't you give a bow?"...Beneath the headline, it said, "At a time when fear and uncertainty dominate our lives...when nobody knows if he'll be the next to lose his job and income...when the victim is the last one to learn of his fate, read this story, one of the few jokes out of China"...A terrible story...but the Chinese drawing of Wang Lun that accompanied it was as harmonious as the design on an Easter egg... In general, there were two kinds of drawings in these magazines... either they were gentle and light, as though women had drawn them... or they were coarse, final and violent, as if the work of butchers... All of this was my earthly horoscope, the force field in which I'd been born, and the influences that were to shape my character and fate... I didn't completely believe it... there were still the old, medieval stargazers, the prophets and sorcerers in their pointed hats and cloaks studded with silver... they had deeper insights into the laws of fate than anything that was written or depicted here... But it was impossible to deny everything that was going on... the automobiles, the politics, the murders... it was impossible to deny that you'd come into the world at a moment when great wars were in the making...

AT HOME, IN THE BEDROOM, I wrote "Two Suitors and One Bride"... a very funny story... One after the other, I put the sheets of drafting paper on the bed to dry... It was a huge pleasure for me to be able to use my school pen to scratch out something other than stupid homework assignments... When I reached page 42 of my manuscript, I made a pair of hard covers for it and bound it as a book... Vati, Clairi and mother spent all day in the workroom, where it was warmest... the stove maintaining a temperature of about forty-five degrees. Vati and Clairi both worked at the table in their overcoats and fur hats, with a kerchief tied around their heads... and every now and then they'd go over to the stove tiles to warm their hands, on which they wore gloves with the tips of the fingers cut off, so they could sew... Vati laughed a lot as he read my story and simultaneously translated it for mother and Clairi…That suitor…what name did I give him?…Tripitz!… now there was a good one…the way he set up hammocks all through his apartment, strewing them with flowers…azaleas, hydrangeas, chrysanthemums…a regular flower shop, a true hanging garden!…so he could steal a rich widow, hunchbacked Mrs. Kratschmann, out from under the nose of another suitor named August…Vati laughed, which meant there was something to my story…but there was something else occupying his attention…Stalingrad!…Here's what had happened: after the Reds had penetrated the defense lines of the Romanian division and the LVF, the Légion des Volontaires Français, the Sixth Army under General von Paulus was cut off…surrounded by the Russian army…in a so-called "pocket!"…They were beyond fighting over ruins, at this point they were fighting over heaps of bricks. From his headquarters, Hitler gave the order for them to fight to the last…On the 30th of January, he had von Paulus promoted to Field Marshal… and on January 31, 1943, after a failed attempt to break out or retreat… out of ammunition, with 91,000 starving soldiers, all that was left of an army that had once numbered three-hundred-thousand men, the general surrendered…The next day, the Führer pronounced von Paulus a traitor to the Great German Reich…The soldiers, he said, should use their last bullets to take their own lives…Even General Rommel had been driven to the far edge of North Africa…in Stalingrad, not a single building remained intact…All of this was printed black-on-white for us to read. Vati kept turning the pages this way and that to learn more…but there was no more…*"Jetzt weiß man alles,"** he said…*"Nicht alles, aber genug,"*** said mother…Stalingrad was burning…worse than Cologne, Dresden, Berlin…worse than Manchuria, the Philippines…Malta, Tunisia…Worse than the stoves all over Ljubljana and the farmsteads in Lower Carniola…There was a thick layer of snow on the roof that made the workroom bright…and still it kept snowing. Vati went over to the stove…he was angry…he was squinting and blinking…*"Stalin ist hundertmal gefährlicher als Hitler. Jetzt wird die Welt staunen, was es heißt, wie ein Menschentier zu leben…"**** "Laß das alles, glaube nichts, wir sind alle den Wahnsinnigen ausgeliefert,"***** mother said. "Ich bitte dich nur eins: nicht vor den Kundschaften das Maul aufmachen! Die Wände hören ab, jedes Schlüsselloch hat ein Auge, überall nichts als Spitzel…"****** "Die Frau Berger, Zalokar, die Frau Bon?"*******… father asked angrily…"Natürlich! Diese wissen nicht mehr, was sie sagen sollen…wen sie verraten sollen…sie wissen es wirklich nicht…"********

---

*Now we know everything.

**Not everything, but enough.

***Stalin is a hundred times more dangerous than Hitler. Now the world will find out what it means to live like a human beast.

****Drop all that, don't believe anything, we're all of us at the mercy of madmen.

*****I ask just one thing: keep your mouth shut around our customers. The walls have ears, every keyhole has an eye peering through, there's nothing but snitches everywhere.

******Mrs. Berger, Zalokar, Mrs. Bon?

*******Of course! They don't know what they're supposed to say anymore…whom to betray…they really don't know…

Our customers were not numerous...despite the ads we put out that we repaired, refurbished, remade every conceivable item...out of old overcoats, little fur pieces, throw rugs and aprons, out of calfskin bags, sheepskin covers for arm rests, the skins of house pets...a lot of dirty work for not much money, as though we were cleaning the public toilets under the Triple Bridge...all the mold, stench, and mothball dust that shook out of those linings! On every floor, I posted a sign with an arrow so any new customers could find their way through the dark building up to the furrier's shop...from morning until curfew, a light bulb shone from the top of the staircase, and for the front door, I used wrapping paper to draw a picture of a tiger growling...

We got all kinds of customers...Mrs. Zalokar, for instance, a tall blonde-haired lady, truly refined, the wife of the postmaster who lived in the red building across from Tivoli...An exceptional beauty: blonde with dark eyes!..."The war will be over soon, Mr. Kovačič," she said as she walked from the stove in her refurbished opossum fur, which Vati had converted from a loosely hanging jacket into a nicely fitting three-quarter length coat...several days and nights of stretching it with the help of my muscles and Vati's painstaking needlework were behind this handsome product of ours. All of us looked at her, sizing it up...If mother spent the finest days of summer sewing marvelous dresses...but so painstakingly! airy confections with such masterful stitching, solidly made!...then Vati was the master of furs of every conceivable kind...As ever, he would kneel in front of the customer, then from behind...putting in pins and favoring lighter fur inserts here and slightly darker ones there. What legs Mrs. Zalokar had!

Straight, long and slender like an Englishwoman's. "Oh, you'll see, soon it will all be over, soon we'll all be able to breathe again..." She would chat with Clairi and mother...and always brought some surprise for Gisela...once it was a fan that she had painted herself... when she was young, all the girls learned how to paint...ah, but soon you wouldn't be able to get paints at any price anymore!...She was more of a friend of the family than a customer...When I delivered the finished items to her at home, I saw all the company she had visiting in her living room...a big assembly of relatives...the old pharmacist from the Hotel Slon...two colonels of the Home Guard...fathers, mothers, children with puppies...postmaster Zalokar, a pleasant, swarthy man with remnants of dark hair...somebody from the Opera sang in a deep bass...she accompanied him on the piano, exceptionally well, without any score...operas, songs...And the way she struck the piano keys!...combined the notes into chords!...first at one end of the keyboard, then at the other...Mrs. Zalokar was too proud and too unafraid to be spying on us...

Another of Vati's customers was a fat lady named Mrs. Nikolič... who was so hysterical that you couldn't imagine her thinking anything over calmly for even a minute...when she picked up something with one hand she would drop whatever she'd been holding in the other... Or Ruža, the wife of Sergeant Mitić of the Home Guard. She was still as vivacious as ever, and she still wore big hoops in her ears, even though she and her husband didn't live in a villa anymore but a small room in an ugly old farm house on Streliška Street, where in the summer they would store mountains of watermelons for the traders, and in the winter bags full of beans. They barely had enough room for themselves... Mrs. Bon was a different story, the wife of a short, rotund dentist who wore a pince-nez and goatee, to whom Vati sometimes sent Clairi to have dental work done in his private office in exchange for some work he'd done on his furs. Mrs. Bon was a tiny, harsh woman with bristly hair and eyes... she had two grown-up sons, regular giants... and such a vast kitchen it could have been in a hotel... It was at her house once... where, all combed and neatened up, I was delivering a newly knitted cardigan, that I saw in the foyer, on a table, a photograph of a skinny, bearded man in a beret and cloak, carrying a rifle, whom I recognized from the newspapers as the organizer of some Home Guard bases around Novo Mesto... I couldn't quite believe it or trust my eyes... an organizer like that was neither fish nor fowl... carrying a rifle, but not dressed in a uniform! To some extent, I felt contempt for him as a traitor and someone who was collaborating with whomever or whatever, maybe with all sides!... Once Mrs. Bon told me to step into the hallway and call for her husband to come out of his office... By mistake, I opened the wrong door... and saw a room full of men... both younger and older, sitting or standing in all parts of the room and looking through a tobacco haze at a map on the wall, and there were both adult sons and some bandaged general or other... before the door slammed shut right in my face... *"Die machen eine große Politik... etwa eine blaue Garde, habe ich gehört,"** Clairi said. *"Wenn du dorthin gehst, mußt du nicht nur aufpassen, wie du dich benimmst, aber*

---

*They're engaged in high politics there... sort of a blue guard, is what I've heard.

auch, wohin du schaust…"* That was an unpleasant house…as though prisoners, volunteers, deserters, rebels and traitors were living in it side by side, all jumbled up…I always felt a high degree of discomfort and tension when I pulled on that doorbell…ready at any instant to discover some hole dug in the floor, a tunnel with a whole band of masked conspirators carrying guns and with various insignia on their caps that I'd never before seen…Once the elder of the Bons' two sons called me into his room when I got there…He closed the door…and reached under his jacket, as though he were adjusting his trousers. He kept a pistol there…Was he going to kill me? ("*Sobald man aus dem Haus schreitet, wird man ein Spielballm*,"** is what Clairi had said.) "No, no, I'm not going to shoot you…at least not yet!" the young giant laughed. A regular clown!…"Draw this for me, so I can see how good you are…I'll give you thirty lire for it," he said…It was a skull from the doctor's office…like at the GIL contest! He gave me some paper…It was easy, even though I made some mistakes…"Great!" he said…"Look at how many pictures I've got, but none of them real." It was true, he did have a lot of pictures, but they were all reproductions…I made a bee line out of there with my thirty lire, as fast as my feet would go…There were also two younger women, Milena and Emilija, who would come to see us, two sisters, friends of Clairi's from Beethoven Street…one of them

*When you go there, you don't just need to mind how you behave, you need to be careful where you look.

**As soon as you set foot out of that house, you become a ball that's in play.

was slender and blonde, the other one stocky, with glasses... The first had a job at the courthouse, while the other, dark-haired one taught kids musical instruments... I have to say, they were both cheerful and pleasant... But more than them coming to our place, Clairi and I would go visit them... In the hallway, they had nearly a hundred Chinese pictures in identical frames, a priceless heirloom from their father. The whole time we were there, Clairi would keep admonishing me not to lose control of myself and touch any of them. If just one of them broke, all the rest would become worthless... There was also the wife of a merchant who had a delicatessen in a round building near the railroad overpass, and she would come visit us. But she was always so downtrodden and defeated that not much came of her visits... you practically had to drag the words out of her... Mrs. Berger, who came to town twice a year from her villa at Bled, in early fall and then in the winter... She was one-half lady of the manor, one-half delivery woman. Strong, tall, ruddy and healthy! She would bring whole suitcases! and bags! not just bundles! of all kinds of furs, sweaters and collars for Vati to mend or rework for her and her friends... She would pull out some fur that was six feet long... an entire bear, a boa, a whole troop of foxes... a veritable flood of all kinds of pelts... worn and shiny, or black as blueberries... the whole workroom stank of mothballs... we ran out of air and light. She would bring father razor blades from the Reich, from Sollingen... and big, round lollipops for Gisela... Who was she? *What* was she?... That was no castle she lived in, but a regular manor house... We didn't quite know what her story was... She was a *Nazifrau*, true, she wore an NSDAP pin on her blouse, identifying her as a party member... but, now and then, she would say things to the effect that chaos and disorder ruled everywhere. Moosburg, that was the name of her manor... *"Ein ganzer Hof voller Leute... Frauen, Männer... Gefangene... Freiwillige... sogenannte Deserteure... alles. Bolschewiken... Bibelforscher, unsere Wehrdienstverweigerer, wissen Sie... zwei Berliner Prostituierte, Liebchen von unserer Dienststelle... außerdem französische Arbeiter... die sind erbitterte Nazigegner... recht bösartig... werden sie nicht mögen, wenn sie einmal zu uns kommen..."** Now that was a colorful life, much more colorful than in our house, where you also had no idea who was living under the same roof as you... Then there were other customers... not as complicated... Ana the waitress, a fat woman who struck me as exceptionally pretty... a caretaker named Praček, Salaznik's brother, who had one fur hat after another made for him, leading Vati to suspect he resold them or supplied them to the partisans out in the forest... and then cousin Minka, who never wanted to say where Ciril and Ivan were and what had become of Karel, and her friends from the post office, who none of them, by any means,

---

*A whole manor full of people... women, men... prisoners... volunteers... so-called deserters... you name it. Bolsheviks... Jehovah's Witnesses, some of our conscientious objectors, you see... two prostitutes from Berlin, the sweethearts of our army post... And some French manual laborers to boot... Bitter foes of the Nazis... really nasty people... they're going to be none too happy if the Germans decide to move into this place...

ruddy-cheeked and wearing their thick work coats, gave the impression of being born yesterday...

The end of the war, or at least a truce!...some of our better customers knew this first-hand...on the best authority! straight from the general staff! from the government!...The Mongols might well come galloping in, but more likely the Anglo-American forces would... and perhaps we would have a chance to live in our Europe in peace, after all!..."If anyone calls you into their office," mother instructed me..."go, but don't say a word...people always tend to say too much!...If somebody tells you, 'It looks like the end is coming, don't you think?'...tell them that you haven't seen or heard a thing...That's the best answer!" "Do you know what happened in Poland in 1939?" the perennially quiet Zalokar asked once when he and his wife came for a fitting..."No, what?" father cautiously said, because mother was there..."They occupied half of Poland, and all of Finnish Karelia, they seized Lithuania, Latvia and Estonia on the pretext they were theirs...Stalin is going to pry all of Europe out of the Allies' hands and turn it into his Red colony..." *"So wie es der Hitler auch möchte?"* mother asked..."Far worse...That Tatar, or whatever he is, has a more ravenous appetite than Hitler..." Once again the streets were littered with flyers, cheerful and red..."Stalingrad! The fatal blow to the Axis from which Hitler will never recover!"...The Germans had taken on too much, once again! Hitler had aimed too high...set his sights too

*The way Hitler would like to do?

far out. The Reich was going to have to impose a new draft…as they had done in the past, in the time of Napoleon! A horrible people!… One evening, a deep voice suddenly hollered, "Long live Stalin! Down with Hitler!…" And then it was silenced…It was Hirol…"*Blödsinn! Mach die Türe zu!*"* mother said. Clairi was worried and upset. "*Und wenn sie ihn einsperren?*"** Had she honestly not figured out that Hirol had staged that for the benefit of our attic…that it was intended for us up here, mother, Clairi, Vati, even Gisela and me, and not the rats in the attic!?…Hirol now started giving me provocative looks whenever we passed each other in the darkness of the staircase…he would brush right up against me, letting his stinking, sweaty suit stick to me, so that I could hear the snot popping in his hairy nostrils… he made no effort to conceal that he was on the verge of raising his cudgel against me any instant…*whack!* and *smack!* and *clunk!*, sending half of my head flying…His wife came out…gray, with her hair done up in a bun, looking mournful…she came the instant I turned the faucet on and checked under the sink. "Good evening," I said, but she didn't respond or even look at me…I waited outside the toilet while somebody was inside…I went away and looked through the screen at Salaznik's garden…The door opened. It would have been futile to try to address her…the toilet smelled freshly of perfume, and the vent was left open…Fani hadn't been seen for several months. "*Vielleicht*

*Rubbish! Shut the door!
**What if they lock him up?

ist sie zu den Partisanen in den Wald geflohen," Clairi suggested...*"Oder, wie die Richterin vom zweiten Stock erzählte, hat sie einen Italiener geheiratet, und ist mit ihm durchgerannt..."** Maybe she'd married that mountain artillerist, the *Ardito* whom she'd met two years before and who came to the building looking for her... She wasn't going to wait for the partisans to take the clippers to her head and shave it, as they did with all women who went out with Italians, so that they had to wear kerchiefs all summer and winter long until their hair grew out again. There's no question but that they would have shaved her head, unless they spared married women... For the time being, we knew nothing about what had happened to her... Suddenly, no one had seen her for several months, and then she was nowhere to be found... Perhaps she'd gone to Calabria or Sicily... lots of women went there... word was that over there the war would come to an end sooner.

I STILL HAD PERMISSION to eat at the Children's Home, even after Gisela was released... At last, we'd laid hands on a wheelchair for her... at Kocmur's second-hand shop on Old Square. The Kocmurs were the parents of that kid who assembled model ships out of plywood... Husband and wife both looked at us slightly askance... all three of them had the same, identical birth mark... which was weird!...

---

*Maybe she fled to the partisans in the forest.

**Or, like the judge's wife on the third floor suggested, she married an Italian and fled back to Italy with him.

Oh, they knew everything about us already...there had to be lots of talk about the Čičavoks going on in these houses and rooms! even though we tried to be as inconspicuous as possible...talk about those immigrants, the Germans, those deportees, that Swiss family had to be echoing off all of these walls...But when they saw us, Vati with his goatee yellowed from smoking, me, and especially Gisela with her club foot and hip brace made out of reinforced leather and steel rods, they felt sorry for us...Their little dog Betty had just died...and that was a severe blow for their son...here, under the chestnut tree by the water, is where they buried her...She suffered a lot as she was dying...she'd had cancer or something...she always sought out the coldest rooms in the house to lie down...their son held her head in his lap the whole time...Those eyes! What a beautiful dog she'd been!...flawless...her coat, her shape, her balance!...she was beyond compare and could have held her own with any thoroughbred!...Ever since the city had been divided into sectors and surrounded with barbed wire, Betty had missed Upper Carniola...St. Mary's Hall...Grmada Hill...ah, Jezersko Valley...a dog needs forests and meadows full of rabbits and deer and ducks...here all she could do was prance underfoot when we took her for walks in Tivoli, and it took a visible toll...She was unhappy, this was a terrible life for her...They had spoiled her for sure...she ate off the same plates as they did, but later, when she was dying, she suffered terribly...The veterinarian ran out of morphine... she spent fifteen days lying in their bed...she didn't complain, she just didn't have any strength left...One morning, she wanted to go out... she was determined to find the coldest spot outside that she could...

which turned out to be a cement hydrant...she bedded down...and began wheezing...as incredible as it may seem, she lay down facing in the direction of her favorite memories...Upper Carniola, Grmada, Jezersko...She stayed that way, like a regular hunting dog...pointing toward her green spaces. Say what you will, people have lost the gift of that kind of beautiful, modest, loyal death...they always put up too much of a fuss...though this would be the most honorable, the simplest way for them to go...Gisela and I felt moved...we went with their boy to look at the grave under the chestnut tree...but Vati was gone by then. When it came to animals, all he cared about was whether their pelt was healthy, whether their fur was thick and their hide was intact...

We got the wheelchair unassembled...it was a special chair for young cripples from the days before wheelchairs for children became widespread, so this was a true antiquarian item! Two cushioned boards with springs for the seat and back, and a third for the head...It consisted of a high frame upholstered in blue-green leather and stuffed with seaweed...it was kind of disgusting and probably jam-packed with fleas, vermin and crab lice...We had to scrub the thing down five times, wash it with rags and disinfect it so Gisela wouldn't catch anything...Its four metal wheels came separately...There weren't any pins, and the threads for them were practically stripped...so we took some tubes of furrier's dye that had hardened and boiled them...and used nails instead of pins...and now it worked. I took her outside...up and down and this way and that...out to the Point on the Ljubljanica, to Tivoli, toward Golovec Hill and to visit some friends...

We went to visit Trnovec, a classmate of mine, whom I would help with drawing in exchange for his help with math...He lived in a house that was halfway up the path to the castle, looking out over St. Florian's Church...He had lots of sisters of all ages, which really appealed to Gisela...They served us up some preserves made of cherries from their own garden...Now that was something!...to have your own fruit trees...or even just one! Miroslav's sisters were every single one of them blonde and adventuresome...They would leap from their second-floor walkway down to street level and go dashing on little carts or sleds down the side of the hill to the church...across the streetcar tracks...and beyond, all the way to the pillar of the Virgin Mary... Gisela and I played with them a lot, and I got along particularly well with Darka. Once, on their walkway, she accidentally left her hand in mine...for quite a while! until it was no longer accidental...and for her name day, I gave her a picture that I'd painted on a wooden board... Once we went to St. Florian's Church to hide out...it was across from the American Café...and was open day and night...In the middle of the nave, there was a heap of beams mixed with mud and snow... and amidst the pews, there was a bell whose rope had broken. Aside from the main altar, a few dark blue tablets with psalms and a pulpit entangled in wild grapevines and ivy, there was nothing interesting or churchlike about it...I left Gisela outside and went with Miroslav up past the altar...I was always filled with curiosity and dread as to what was behind the altar and tabernacle, the holy of holies, the angels and chandeliers...There was nothing except a wall...no, there was nothing but big, coiled patties of shit ... old ones that had acquired the shape of belltowers and fresh ones, still bloody from diarrhea… The drunks from the American and the kids from Upper Square had been coming here to relieve themselves for quite a few years… I went back out through the entrance, which was inscribed "Porticus" over its arch… I had the devilishly distinct sense that I was a far bigger coward and more fearful of blasphemy than the delinquents on Upper Square… On the sidewalk outside, at the foot of the steps, Olga held sway with a pack of her girlfriends… The instant she saw me, she let loose with "Bu-bi! Či-ča-vok!" and the whole swarm of them began chanting after her, "Bubi Čičavok!"… I took a step toward them with the wheelchair… and the lot of them retreated into an entryway, where they continued their hyenic outbursts and stuck out their tongues, which were incredibly long!… Gisela paid them no mind, while I… *Zhoooo! boom!… splat!…* as they mocked the sound of cows mooing and pooping… No, that wasn't them! no!… that came from above!… out of the air!… and especially from the castle tower!… those were the flying fortresses up in the sky again… And once again civil defense had managed to miss sounding the alarm! And *brrrr! brrrr!* some Mosquito fighter unloaded a whole charger at the bridge… into the Ljubljanica… so you could hear the geysers all the way up here… My friend and I shoved the wheelchair from the Trnovec house uphill with our backs… somewhere in the clouds high up above, there were flying fortresses, regular industrial factories that floated in air… greetings from the free world!… from England and Canada! America and New Zealand!… they had pilots in leather jackets with thousands of zippers!… and were full of chocolates and caramels like in *The Magic Bird*… All of my friend's sisters were out on the walkway, waving to the sky with their scarves..."Don't be stupid," their blonde mother shouted at them. "What if they see those scarves of yours and decide to drop a big bomb on our heads!" Trnovec and I hid behind a tree trunk...*boom! whoosh!*... the fortresses kept flying, but where? To Greece? Crete? North Africa? The Nile River Delta?...

The street was deserted...there were no people, no wheelbarrows, just crazy Mica wandering around Upper Square, so worn out and delirious that it looked like she was never going to be able to stop... She was smiling...her eyebrows were white...and she was wearing rubber galoshes...which she always had on, summer or winter...a kerchief tied under her chin and a hat on top of it...the partisans had shaved her head in some entryway...She always laughed with just one side of her face...Whenever you asked her something, she would stop and mutter, "Oh my, help me, sweet Mary"...or more often just laugh...she seemed big and stout in her overcoat or her homespun smock...Praček the custodian once used two slices of buttered bread to lure her into his mess of a room...When the door closed, her squeals could be heard from outside...Once Miki, the painter's son, and I locked her inside the courtyard outhouse of Salaznik's café...But first Miki lifted her skirt with a stick...all these women are ridden with sickness and crap, he said...actually, his father had told him, all women were carriers of disease...you could discover a whole latrine pit under their panties...Then he locked her inside the loo..."What do you do with the Italians?" Miki asked her through the opening at the top...She laughed and whimpered..."Is it true that the Italians pee in your bottom and leave lire in a bowl for you for letting them do it?"...Suddenly she started whimpering so much that I had to let her out against Mikec's will...she emerged and headed out to the street, as though she'd just been nowhere in particular...

I would take Gisela over to the Cloisters, because they had some swings, teeter-totters and sandboxes there...One day, I ran into Tatjana outside the grocery store...She was walking from the butcher's shop toward Roman Street...she was exactly the same as she'd been two years before...no taller, no prettier, she even still limped...I waved to her, nodded my head...she didn't acknowledge me...Some incredibly short Italian in riding breeches like balloons was hobbling beside her...they were chatting as they walked alongside the ivy-covered Roman wall that she and I had once walked past...I felt a wave of heat surge to my head.

I took Gisela to play under the chestnuts outside the school... where I met two of my friends...The first was Julijan Mohar, who was two grades ahead of me and already an apprentice...He lived near Prule. His parents were custodians and gardeners...City gardening is what they had printed on a sign over the gate...and then you passed through their garden, and then came their house behind it, and behind that was their winter garden, with seedlings and greenhouses...but it was in their garden out front, facing the street, where everything was lush and burgeoning...even kohlrabi and turnips...His mother was a petite, nervous woman and his father a stern, toothless little man... but both of them always spoke so fast that I never understood a word they said. Julijan's brother had served in an SS tank division...he had been killed...and his uniform was sent home along with two Iron Crosses...Sometimes his mother would walk through the courtyard and garden carrying that uniform in her arms...resting her head on it...you could see on the uniform exactly where he'd been hit...he'd just raised the flap on one pocket and *bang!*...In Russia...She would take the uniform with her upstairs, or out to the shed...Sometimes she'd have a seizure...collapse on the kitchen floor...kick the floorboards with her feet...trying to break through them!...her clothing would rip, giving her even more momentum..."You! You! Russians!" she would shriek..."Murderers!...Animals! Mongols!" She wanted to break and destroy everything. Julijan showed me the uniform, which was kept hanging in the attic next to an autographed portrait of Hitler...the uniform was made of black leather, and the helmet was leather, too, like a pilot's...There was a photo of his brother taken next to his tank. Against the background of his armored vehicle, his hair seemed flaxen and almost white...pilots, submariners and members of tank crews were an elite made of the same stuff. Next to him was another crew member...a friend of his brother, the fiancé of Julijan's sister. The Germans always managed to denigrate their comrades-in-arms of other nationalities...the French, Romanians, Italians, Hungarians, Spaniards and Croats...they saw them as traitors and had greater respect for the Russians and English, and most of all for the Japanese...but his brother had been an exception and one of the very best tank commanders...Julijan had apple trees in his garden, as well as pears, plums and apricots...their garden was so full that Gisela and I felt like we were back in Jarše or somewhere on the banks of the Krka…just in better, more hospitable circumstances…Julijan's sister, a slender, blonde girl, brought Breda, a rambunctious tiger-striped cat, out to the garden for Gisela to play with, along with a bowl of fruit…She had already been to visit her boyfriend…had ridden with him in his tank on the eastern front…and gotten such dirty finger- nails from riding in it that she still had trouble getting them clean, even with kerosene…Julijan had a writer's streak in him…He was a broad-shouldered guy, an athlete with a big, blond head. Amid the overgrowth by their fence, there were plenty of nooks to hide in and talk. We agreed that we were both going to enlist in the Home Guard the first chance we got…Once a week, we would write our novels… real adventures and whodunits…Out in the garden, on either side of a table with a pile of fruit in the middle, we would sit and write… some really neat stories…he was working on a blockbuster mystery novel about gangsters in Chicago…I was writing "The Hunt for the Muktar Diamond"…a tale of adventure from East India…The first page had a drawing of a ship as it approaches Ceylon, with a pair of lovers embracing, their backs turned to the reader…Above them, there was something perched in the crow's nest…that was the object of the plot…Julijan brought a stack of maps and atlases down from the attic which we used to trace our protagonists' adventures…They showed parts of the world where there was no war…North America…espe- cially South America, or Australia…You could see how a continent would practically die of boredom with no war going on…but as soon as the trumpets sounded, the real glory was about to begin!…universal glory! bathed in blood, at that!…and never-ending travels!…armies constantly on the move this way and that!…then clashing and rolling and rolling!…until they explode!…transports, locomotives and trains, tanks! armored equipment carriers…and on and on!…Every hour, Julijan and I would read to each other what we'd just written. Julijan had more imagination than I did, that much I had to admit… during a police chase, his gangsters would vanish straight through the pavement into subterranean garages…while with me, it took several pages just for my protagonists to disembark with their luggage…

Martin Gorjanc – Tinček – was my other friend from school. He was a poor but well-kempt peasant kid who always came to school in a white shirt and green hat. He had red, almost dark brown hair and a broad, freckled face…He wasn't an A student, but at school, he could figure out anything, the way peasants somehow always can… He had fled from Lower Carniola to the city with his parents and little sisters, to get away from the partisans…They weren't real collaborators or real members of the White Guard…but his oldest brother had been a secretary…a judge's bailiff and secretary at the county courthouse…The partisans shot him dead during some local court proceeding…and then they came out to the family's farmstead… burned their house down…the stable…the barn, everything!…They hid out all night in a field of clover…His father, mother, sisters and him…the forest brethren sprayed the field with machine gun fire… searched for them in the village…these were field partisans!…that's what they called the ones who holed up near their home villages… they came within a hair's breadth of not getting away! They crawled on their bellies for a whole day and half of the following night...they were rescued by a Fascist armored vehicle...then they hid out in the home of first one, then another relative...none of whom could put them up for very long...they had to explain to each of them that they were innocent, all while trying to hide from the partisans, yet they kept getting exposed or snitched on...They lost everything...At the seat of the provincial administration, they had an audience with General Leon Rupnik...the chairman of the association of Slovene mayors... lots of peasants showed up at the government building that day...his father was given work in some warehouse, and the family was assigned a room on Salender Street...His father worked a shift in a cold-storage facility...he had stopped trying to explain anything about himself and his farmstead to anyone...his mother was just a peasant woman... All they knew was life in the country...the building's owner let them raise chickens and rabbits in its courtyard...All six of the surviving kids were with them...Their room was full of beds, one right next to the other...two or three of them together would be covered with big tarps that had been sewn together...they took up two-thirds of the floor space...in the other third, they had just enough room for a table and chairs, a cookstove, and a small, additional table next to the window that looked out onto steep Salender Street and where Tinček and I would occasionally do our homework...His sisters would open the door...for their father, their mother, Tinček or me...all five of them together...this was no joke! They didn't laugh for a minute while doing it...it was a huge door! and heavy! as if out of some castle...they always had to take care...and first peer through the keyhole to see if maybe their visitor was someone from their village, or even a partisan from there...There was always the chance they could track them down in the city and shoot them!...Everything in their big room was clean and fresh, like in a sacristy. The pillows, the tablecloths, the sheets – all of them white...the floor was always scrubbed down to the knots in the boards...not a single bit of straw, not the tiniest fragment of coal was under their cots or around their stove...a candle was always lit by the devotionals, and the walls were covered with embroidered hangings...the girls were always sitting on their beds, mending or knitting or braiding lace...they didn't giggle and they didn't gossip or pinch or tease each other...they didn't touch anything if they weren't first given permission...they wouldn't even pet a cat on the street... and when they were outside they didn't look at anyone...they were always just fixedly set on their tasks. They weren't fun-loving and daring like the Trnovec girls, so they didn't appeal to Gisela as much... They wore long, flannel dresses that reached almost to the ground and were covered with ugly, old patterns, like Aunt Mica from Cegelnica... high shoes that laced up to the ankle, big kerchiefs that they knotted under their chins; even in summer they wore long-sleeve blouses... they actually looked like a bunch of little old peasant wives. But they were healthy, sturdy and ruddy-faced, not one of them pale, weakly or melancholy. We sang a lot together. Especially the church hymns they liked best...for instance, "Sing, Ye Mountains"...You could talk and sing with them like you would with any devout person...there was no need to go falling in love here...Tinček knew how to make willow whistles, a skill I'd already lost...to entertain ourselves, we'd play monkey wrench on the floor between the beds using different colored beans... I trusted Tinček. He was honest... oh, a heck of a lot more than I was. He would never have played me like Firant had... he would never have betrayed me... We helped each other... I helped him with his writing and he helped me with my math... In class and in chapel, we sat in the same row. For decency's sake, his sisters always went with their father and mother to mass at the Franciscan church... they never once went to the cathedral, which struck them as too grand... For Easter, Tinček gave me an Easter egg that he had painted himself... I repaid him by drawing him a humorous calendar for every week of the year...

"ON THE ANNIVERSARY of Hitler's dastardly attack on the USSR"... the leaflets announced... no resident of Ljubljana was supposed to venture outside between 6 and 7 p.m. on the 22nd of June, 1943... During the previous year, the leaflets had announced some misinformation, driving everyone out of all the buildings in Ljubljana toward Aleksandar Street. Even Clairi and Vati in their lair upstairs learned most of what they knew from the leaflets... "*Besser die Nase nicht aus dem Haus stecken. Man weiß nie, was denen einfällt...*"* Going outside at the forbidden hour, in broad daylight, was as good as walking through a pitch-dark night with traps set all around... You could feel a hundred eyes trained on you... Where were they? Up on

---

*Better not stick our noses out of the house at all. You never know what that lot's got up its sleeves.

the roofs?...At the vents in the attics?...Suddenly we were forbidden to go out...that meant scurrying from one corner to the next as if at curfew, to get home as quickly as possible...Could you see it on the faces of the people still out walking the streets?...The stores had to stay open...so get going, first off to City Square...At the delicatessen, where all they sold anymore was macaroni and rice for ration coupons...people would zap! just vanish...two or three overweight housewives carrying baskets...porters...Whoever was still out on the streets was a heretic...a traitor...perhaps an informant for the Reds, or for the Whites? There were patrols out walking toward the open-air market...carabinieri...*Arditi* wearing fezes...Home Guards...they doubled back toward the bridge taking the same route...If you so much as looked at them, they lost all control...Blockheads...I got as far as the bridge...at any instant *zing!* something could hit you... On the far side of the bridge, people were out walking around...across St. Mary's Square, around the Prešeren monument...Loyal citizens... members of the White forces...adherents of Rupnik? There weren't enough of those to fill up the square...Fear drove people inside their houses to avoid being marked out and killed next time, blown up by a bomb...everyone was looking out for his own bones, his own head, his own stomach...for ration coupons...both of the opposing forces were exerting pressure on people. I would have liked to see one of those organizers at work...Staying at home for one hour was better than losing your head...then the hunt for turnips and carrots could continue, mother would say. By seven, the wolf was full and the goat still alive...And a new list of sinners got drawn up...and twenty, thirty, forty years later people who hadn't even been born at the time would read your name from it with menace in their voices…

One day around lunchtime…I had stopped by the Children's Home as usual with basket in hand…Sister Rafaela came out of the kitchen looking downcast. The director had given her orders, she said, that as of the following day they were not to give me any more food, neither for my own lunch nor to take home…In the kitchen the nuns were kidding each other and laughing as usual…the loudest of all was Kajetana, of course…Sister Rafaela looked at me, her face as pale as could be…I liked her a lot, not just because of the food, which was important, but because I could sense that she was thinking of me…From then on, I had to conceal my visits, she told me in a whisper…and under no circumstances come upstairs anymore…I was to wait for her at the door downstairs…at one o'clock every day, and she would bring me some food from the kitchen…and the next day she would give me a fresh pot of food, while I was to hand her the empty dish from the previous day…and so on, back and forth… and along the way somehow we'd figure out a better system…Precisely at one, I was to ring the bell once and hide in the corner…She would come running out and bring me the leftovers in her basket… she would dole out the contents or better yet just exchange pots with me…I'd better not forget: one o'clock sharp! one ring of the bell! From now on, the food would be worse, much worse…she had to make a hundred meals of turnips and carrots each day, and she was going to have to take care that the children didn't get diarrhea, and we should take care, too…she would have everything prepared ahead of time and set it aside...It was obvious to me...we had a friend!...Sister Rafaela...more than we could have ever hoped for, given the circumstances...You never know, not in wartime or peacetime or in times of misfortune, where to turn with all the stomachs and lungs and livers! there are boxcars full of them ...but the hearts? they're so incredibly rare! over the course of five hundred million years there's no counting all the stomachs and gullets, but the hearts?...those you can count on the fingers of one hand!...At home, Clairi was incensed. *"Das hat diese aufgedonnerte Frau Upravnik angestellt!"*..."*Und ob.*"*...Now I waited outside their door every day...in the corner between the facade and the entrance...from the pavement all the way to the top, there wasn't a single window, just bricked-in casings...I lightly pressed the doorbell button...and set my ear right up against the wall to hear when the key turned in the lock, but even then I was supposed to remain perfectly still until I heard *"Pssst! Pssst!"* or saw the hem of her white habit... Sometimes Sister Rafaela was relaxed, at other times not, but each time she seemed a bit more nervous...The fact that she was violating the director's orders was a sin...She negotiated those three flights of stairs...quietly, wearing a cape, beneath which she carried one or two pots of food...She would glance back over her shoulder to see if she was being followed...sometimes we would exchange pots, while at others she would have to pour the contents of hers into mine...she was so nervous that she would spill some on her habit, on my clothes, on my shoes...she shook like some eleven-year-old girl worried that

*This is that dolled up Mrs. Director's doing. Still, ...

· 212

someone was going to roar at her any minute...she would hide the pot under her cape, lock the door and go running – *clip, clip, clip* – back up the stairs...both of us had to run, she and I, each in our separate directions...if they ever caught her at this, she'd pay for the two of us...

I always took the same route to the Children's Home...across Town Square, past the bishop's residence, down Streliška Street...I had timed my route down to the second...with ten minutes to spare, in case I was forced to wait somewhere or look at something...At that time of day, there were lots of people out on the streets. There wasn't much worth looking at in the display windows...The appliance store had stoves, Šmalc had fabric for ration points and cabinets full of straw hats...here and there at the delicatessen there was a jar of mustard or artificial honey, but mostly just some ferns in planters, the same as at Škoberne's Carpets...Except for the optician's window next to the shoe store, on the ground floor of the building where Marko lived upstairs...The optician regularly changed his display using color ads from before the war...One day, I stopped on the sidewalk outside...his display had ads for different kinds and models of glasses, all perched on dummies' heads...for bad eyesight, to protect your eyes from the sun, for pinces-nez and monocles...the ads showed palm trees on beaches in the south seas and brilliantly lit streets in big cities...a theater balcony with a lady holding a lorgnette and a man looking through opera glasses...all of it reminiscent of the pictures of places and people in old issues of the magazine *Bazar der Zeiten*..."Right, right, it must be some joke!"...a tall, healthy, ruddy-faced gentleman dressed in an expensive suit and standing outside the door to the shoe store said in parting to the people inside...Closing the door, he gave a slight bow as I kept looking, when suddenly...*ratatatatatatat! ratatatatat!*...flung me in the air and the glass of the window shattered in front of my face...I turned to find the gentleman who had just been talking into the store lying across the street, on the sidewalk at the entrance to Locksmiths' Street...at the corner of Šmalc Manufacturing...and I could also hear a car racing at full speed down the embankment... On the square, where at first everybody had frozen, all of a sudden they all started to run...some toward the market, others toward Old Square. I got squeezed at the display window and carried off by some people who decided to turn around and run back...they were all familiar with the order of the Eleventh Army Command, according to which anyone found within five hundred meters of the scene of an assassination was to be shot on sight...Everybody was running. I saw Lukman, the tailor, the tiniest little man, being carried off by a crowd, and the old barber Matijevič trying to sprint, though out of practice for decades...I ran with the ones that were headed toward Old Square, but halfway there I realized I was running in the wrong direction...People were running right down the tracks, with their hands held up over their heads..."Those damned idiots," a tall man in glasses shouted, "why do they do that!...they know how many of us get shot for each person they kill!"...The frontrunners stopped on Jail Street and were looking back...some were trying to force their way into Asipi's shop, but the shoeshiner had blocked his door with a table...he didn't want any assassins hiding in his store...the barber secured his double doors with a chain and stood shaking his head at the people outside, refusing to let them in…others were dashing up the stairways of various buildings to hide in their hallways…On Cobblers' Bridge, a crowd had gathered around something next to the railing…A military truck drove up, and its driver approached… the square was even emptier than on that anniversary of the invasion…agents were leading some woman at the double out of some shop…tiny, fair-haired, wearing a white smock…from a distance her muscular legs and potato-like nose made me think that I knew her. A hair stylist? A saleswoman from the delicatessen?…It was the wife of the man who'd been shot…She pried herself loose from the agents and literally fell over a gray dress that lay on the ground…she fought off the soldiers who tried to lift her up…Everyone was looking on from a distance…I couldn't afford to wait, because Sister Rafaela was just then getting ready to head out of the kitchen…I went back toward the square…past the shops, past Škoberne's and Hamman's, the watchmaker's, the optician's…my pace neither fast nor slow, so that no one would be tempted to shoot me…When I got to the shoe store, I saw people on the other side bent over the gentleman, a man in civilian clothes, either a detective or a doctor…but no one was anywhere in sight, not even peering out the windows…I reached Roth's, then the appliance store, and not until the arcade of City Hall did I set off at a dash…It was two minutes to one…I ran the whole way…reaching the wall around the Children's Home at a minute past the hour…I told Rafaela, who brought out two pots in her nun's traveling bag, that just a short distance from there some elegantly dressed man had been shot dead by the partisans…like a speck, left lifeless with the other specks...I'd been trapped, unable to move forward or back...Sister Rafaela froze, trembling with fear...she lifted her face up, whispering as she crossed herself, that day she was the calmest person of all...I ran back, and when I reached Šmalc's, on the sidewalk where the man had been lying, I noticed a black spot...and nothing else. That car they had shot him from, which then went racing down the embankment...careened into a young mother out walking her baby, which went flying out of its buggy, smashed into a wall and was killed on the spot...that's why there had been so many people gathered on the bridge before...then down the Gallus embankment, overturning the second-hand dealers' mattresses and rocking chairs as it went...then down the Trnovo embankment or up to Roman Street...There had been four of them, killers dressed in their Sunday finest...Nobody knew anything about the man who'd been killed...a few days later, the little hair stylist with the wide fringe of blond bangs and the potato-like nose was back working in the salon next to the delicatessen...now she was a marked person, too. Had that man been a traitor? A real one, or not? A White, a Red, or a Blue?...Such a good-natured man...

Two days later, weapons were discovered in a small house near the dam on the Little Graben canal...Bombs were tossed through the windows, the residents were shot and the house was burned down... Was that where the assassins from the car had hidden out?...Tinček and I went out to see it...the house didn't have a roof anymore, just a few walls with more holes in them than bricks...the furniture, stove, clothes, dishes and tables – everything was mixed up together...some legs were poking out of their trousers...there was a bloody corpse lying next to the wall outside...its head looked like it had been attacked by hornets...nothing but red abrasions, with the forehead bashed in and a lump of dough hanging out of its mouth, its brains, which had been blown out its nostrils. A guard had been posted who didn't yell at passers-by...he was a lanky Italian who stood at the corner, looking away, toward the dam...there was nothing but ash, as though from burned cardboard, floating in the water...Tinček looked at the dead body without any feeling...It was terrible, yes, I could have vomited in disgust...I felt a stinging hole in my head, as though I were about to disgorge marrow out my nose any instant...but there had been a time when I felt even greater disgust...at the tips of my fingers, when I had to shake hands with that revolting Firant...What was horrible was that I was guilty of this, too...not just because of the revenge that would overtake me, but because I myself hadn't been killed...but then again, that wasn't why, either...

A week after the start of the new school year, to my great surprise, we got a new homeroom teacher, that thin, strict Mrs. Komar, the Slovene instructor...and Italy surrendered...it put its hands up under the onslaught of the Anglo-Americans...

AT THIS POINT, it was as though everything started to fly and nothing was fastened to the ground anymore...The Italians fled by cover of night from the St. Jacob's barracks into the forests...crossing Golovec toward Mt. Krim, Black Peak, Mokerc...others hid out in various buildings in town, disguising themselves as civilian tramps...

some of them were captured or had to surrender…Through the barracks' open main gate, all over the entryway and out into the middle of the street, there were bags lying around, boxes with mortar sights, blinkers for donkeys, wooden carbine stocks, duffle bags, knapsacks and flash pans…It was like April of 1941, when the Yugoslav army fled and the Italians hadn't yet reached the city…"Those damned spaghetti eaters," Vati said. "Whoever has them for an ally is a goner from the get-go"…A bunch of disarmed Italians huddled in the hallway of the Zois house…without their gun belts and with their army caps turned backward, or wearing civilian hats…smiling coquettishly and nodding or bowing to the people on the sidewalk. At an open window on the other side of the river, two of them were putting on costumes…this was a sort of props and wardrobe room for the St. Jacob Theater… they were putting straw hats on each other, and fringed necker-chiefs…a couple of regular gauchos…authentic clowns of the Second World War…In a passageway, where the stench of galvanization was strongest, three of them asked Havliček the electrician for some old work overalls…they begged, they apologized…I knew it well…of all the humiliations of exile, the most mortifying is that eternal begging and apologizing…for this! for that!…one day all you're left begging for is everyone's pardon…you're in everyone's way, a burden to everybody…even once your misfortune has passed, you can't change yourself…A bunch of Italians were lounging all over the second-hand dealers' armchairs and beds set out under the chestnut trees…some of them already changed, the others waiting for the shopkeepers to bring them some rags from their supplies…a few girls from Žabjak, daughters of the second-hand dealers, hung out close by...they were singing, accompanied by a guitar...now nobody would be able to force them to have their heads shaved in a dark entryway. Now they would be free to stroll with their boyfriends in public, as custom demanded, until they got married during Lent...now they wouldn't have to go looking for dark places to make out, or lift their skirts without unnecessary words, unspoken or wasted, and without the face they could see in the daytime...Patrols of Germans, Home Guards and Blackshirts would chase the deserters through the streets and lock some of them up in the barracks...And what scenes those were on the streetcars!...barely would the ticket takers dressed in Home Guard uniforms get in front, than the half-disguised Italians would start jumping out the doors at the back...it was like a game of cops and robbers...one of them jumped out of a streetcar at the Triple Bridge into the Ljubljanica and managed to survive...The St. Jacob's Barracks were open and turned upside down...three soldiers who were sick and barely conscious stayed in the building, its windows stacked high with sandbags, and slept, unable to move...meanwhile, the neighborhood delinquents were going systematically in and out, as if under orders, and emptying the place...they carried out crates, blankets, bags and footlockers until the Home Guard arrived and set up sentries...Just yesterday, Julijan said, when Italy capitulated, they were fighting the partisans from the bunkers to bamboozle the Germans...not just to kill some Slovenes, plenty of them were killed, too, but just so that the deception would be that much more convincing...For their generals and leaders, as for people without any fighting spirit in general, the guerilla was their enemy. They needed his courage about as much as his love...A statement by Marshal Badoglio was published in the newspaper, to the effect that Italy had asked for a truce and that its "proposal had been accepted..." General Gastone Gambara declared a state of emergency in the city...Peace and order must be maintained! the regional adminstration reported...These Italians...their mighty, imperial army had fallen from the clouds like a ripped paper kite...And the Anglo-Americans had penetrated their boot all the way up from Sicily, and the new government had seized Mussolini and whisked him off to a hiding place on top of some craggy mountain...

Toward ten o'clock that day, we watched out our classroom window as a column of wagons driven by peasants began crossing the Prule Bridge and entered the city to escape from the partisans...Horses, oxen, cows, calves...wobbling in their midst was a shapeless wagon painted all colors...yellow, purple, pink, with *Dopolavore* written in huge letters...a Gypsy wagon, a regular monument in three or four parts...with lots of windows...countless wheels with rubber tires and two engines driven by a powerful wood-burning generator...then peasants, horses and oxen again...The head of the column came to a halt under the chestnut trees on the Trnovo embankment, with the whole parade following suit behind it...stretching from the Gradaščica canal and the old landing around to the Point...over Prule Bridge and up north on the roadway...along Karlovška Street and aross the bridge over the Gruber canal...along Lower Carniolan Road to Rakovnik, Škofljica and on from there in two branches...reportedly all the way to Kočevje and Grosuplje...A gigantic parade consisting of countless rigs, buggies, covered wagons and livestock...with pigs in crates, geese, ducks and hens...Never before had so many peasants been in the city at one time...all of Lower Carniola stretching all the way to the partisans...Frightened by the city, the streetcars and people, the geese huddled under the wagons and honked, or dozed, their heads tucked under their wings...So who was right now? The Whites, who asserted that the peasants were on their side, or the Reds, whose leaflets proclaimed that the whole rural population was behind them?...It was strange...here was this gigantic crowd...an endless column bearing everything possible in their wagons, from foodstuffs to big wooden cabinets...that lived just a stone's throw away from the bandits, the Blue Guard, the Black Hand of the White Guard...and here it was, fleeing the Turks...Seeking shelter in a city that was ready to release swarms of bees and pour boiling oil on them from atop the church ramparts?...They knocked on all the house doors along the embankment asking for water for their horses and livestock...some people gave it to them, while others who were staunchly behind the partisans shut the door in their faces...Tinček and I went exploring the column from the chestnut trees down to the bridge...He was looking for relatives, hoping to run into an uncle or at least some friendly face from his village...There were no less than eight cows hitched to one wagon...not exactly fat ones but not emaciated either... horses and colts were tethered together in herds, by village, and were grazing around the bomb shelter...Townsfolk were already out bartering...offering trousers, coats and shoes, all of it cheap stuff, in exchange for flour and lard...The wagons were loaded down with everything possible…foodstuffs, down comforters, bales of hay, bags of flour, pots of lard, barrels of wine, smoked meat…Little old grandmas and small children were sitting on top of heaps of beetroot, stacks of hay, mounds of alfalfa…Some of the kids were frightened … while others were out doing somersaults on the Point or playing "Who whacked me?"…Tinček and I were practically slapping our thighs while we watched them. Once you're no longer a kid, you get jaded, despite the fact that the movie theater of the world doesn't change one bit…What do you have left to get so happy about? You have to get pretty damned hammered for anything to seem like fun anymore… These kids were having the time of their lives…throwing chestnuts at each other, girls against boys…in a year's time, they'd all be worried about damaging their shoes. Gorjanc and I were laughing our heads off…what a great age, when you don't yet have to watch out! and *zing!* here comes a projectile, and another…The older boys, aged sixteen and above, had probably stayed home…in their barracks or rectories…The younger farm wives were making regular trips to clean the churches and rectories, where the oldest peasants and children were spending the nights…"They said we had to go or else they were going to set our houses on fire and kill us," a peasant explained to one of the townspeople bartering with him. The Ljubljana resident made a face like curdled milk. "And you believed their propaganda?" he said, incensed…"Hey you there, mister, if you don't beat it this instant…" said a woman in the next wagon over, lifting a pitchfork…The ducks were quacking…they tied their feet together and set them in the Ljubljanica…letting them graze while they held onto them from the riverbank by a string...At the Point, peasants were carefully harvesting the grass that grew in-between the concrete steps, so as not to damage them...Several wagons corresponded to several houses in a village... there were kitchen crocks full of meat, potatoes, real lard...they were cooking these over small fires...our dinners of boiled macaroni had long since lost any aroma or taste, but out here it smelled like Sunday afternoon at one of those country inns on the outskirts of town that in better times Ljubljana dwellers flocked to...The Gypsy wagon was parked on Two Emperors' Road...It had *Dopolavore* inscribed on both sides...they had probably provided entertainment for workers and soldiers by dancing, singing, mind reading and fortune telling...Were these our Gypsies or foreign ones?...Leaning out the wagon's window was an old Gypsy man who had four rings on his fingers...with the gemstone settings turned inward, facing his palm...a ruby! an emerald...and a sapphire on the third finger...on his little finger there was a "blue diamond"...some Gypsy women were perched on the far side...speaking all different dialects, from all different tribes, caning chairs while they cooked...Julijan's mother invited some peasants into the courtyard of her "Urban Gardener," so they could sit down to their meal in the shade..."If the Germans don't get them," one person said, "the black hand will"...Tinček and I walked out as far as the Church of Don Bosco in Rakovnik, then back along the other side of the street...There was dried meat tucked into the empty pegholes of brussels-sprout stalks, bags of boiled beans...it was like a big country fair...We hadn't yet come across a single person from his village. Was it because they supported the partisans and had stayed? All of this still seemed strange and unreal to me...all this canvas, pigs in crates, flocks of children...Home Guards were out patroling the columns on foot...peacekeepers, *ha!* making sure that no fires, scuffles or fights broke out...Most of the peasants would have to sleep in or under their wagons, thank god the nights hadn't turned cold yet...all of these people who owned parcels of land, forests, fields, meadows and barns back home had to make do with a few square yards of ground and a tree branch above them...They had brought scythes, sickles and axes along...even muskets, in case anyone tried to attack or rob them during the night...some even had their dog on a chain under the wagon...Winter Relief workers distributed blankets, tarps and medicine...When Tinček and I got back, the geese on the Trnovo embankment had become emboldened...They went padding across the road into the nettles, heedless of the people and cars...the little ones were already starting to get bored...To everything there is a time...take the Capitol, for instance: if the barbarians had come a twentieth time, the geese wouldn't even have bothered to look at them...There was an announcement in the newspaper: From the Führer to the German people..."Therefore I have judged it my duty to take every possible measure to protect Germany and its allies from the fate that Marshal Badoglio has inflicted on the Duce and the Italian people"...Slovenes! The treachery of the Italian royal house has forced the Great German Reich to take your homeland under its care...There was an announcement that the Krim Brigade of the Home Guard would join with German units in escorting the fleeing peasants back to their villages...

When I stopped to look at some horses on the way back, some sturdy blonde girl approached me. I'd seen her before. She lived somewhere on Old Square or close by. She said, "Hey there!" She wasn't out trying to barter food for old rags... "I'd like to ask you something," she said and motioned to me to head toward the bridge with her... This calling me aside didn't sit right with me at all... "Yeah?" I said. "I'll bet you know how to get out of the city..." "Through a checkpoint, of course," I said, turning away... "I know that much... But I'll bet there's some other way..." I shrugged. "Where is it you want to go?" "Out of Ljubljana..." I headed home, and she followed me over the bridge and beyond. She had a ruddy face and big breasts, and beneath her checked dress her shoulders were as powerful as a wrestler's... How old was she? My age?... At the grocery store across from the school, where we got our noodles, lard and soap with ration coupons, there was a fight... People were standing around the store entrance. Some male voice was roaring so loudly that it was raising the dust in the entryway... "Get away from my house, you whore!" the voice bellowed. A body came tumbling down the steps into the entryway... the grocer's daughter-in-law, a pretty woman... despite having two children, she'd been seeing some Italian captain... At the top of the steps stood a man, the young grocer, her husband... haggard and pale with a long, jutting chin and the slightest of mustaches... three whiskers!... like some gangster... He must have just then returned home from jail, because there'd been neither sight nor sound of him for several months... He was only half dressed... he kept on kicking her, out of the entryway onto the sidewalk... Now people were pressing up against the wall... now that the

Italians were no longer our enemies, evidently this had stopped being a political matter and was strictly a private affair... The grocer was wearing some sort of shaggy long johns, suspenders and a hat... "Go be with your tenente, you whore!"... The only people laughing at this were a patrol of police volunteers... especially the slight, blond leader of the patrol, who was probably a student, a skinny rascal with white glasses... he was showing all of his teeth, jumping around and slapping his thighs, as though his laughter had incapacitated him, while his two peasant colleagues stood by, grinning like wolves... *Bam!* the door slammed shut and the key turned in the lock... The pretty, pale, dark-haired woman was left half-lying, half-crouching on the sidewalk, all smudged with bruises and dirt... I felt sorry for her, because she had always been so friendly as she served her customers amid the store's half-empty shelves... and I especially liked her thick, dark hair against the white nape of her neck and her regular facial features... Then a little, slouching lady with a gray perm stopped next to her... about whom it was also common knowledge that she'd had a relationship with some young Italian from the St. Jacob's Barracks... She started to comfort her, took her by the shoulder, lifted her up. "Come with me, Katarina..."

That blond girl had not budged from my side. From there she crossed the street with me, too... "You have to know some way out of Ljubljana..." she kept pumping me relentlessly... At the streetcar crossing, a patrol of Home Guards appeared... using the crosswalks. Julijan and I were going to enlist in the Home Guards... and at the first chance we got, we had decided, especially now that they were in such a fix. I knew where their recruitment office was...next to the Bata shoe store, right behind the Pelikan stationery shop...The young blonde kept walking with me. She was laughing and tossing me glances that left me confused, probably she was a big moviegoer. "Come on!" She was pushing me to go upstairs with her, to meet her family...She lived across the street from the Albanian sweet shop. Their name was Topel, as I saw from the plaque on their door. She had a mother, also ruddy-faced and blonde, and a younger sister, who was pale and just skin and bones. She led me into a real living room...with white chairs, tables, a fine rug, a dark lacquered Chinese cabinet like the one mother had back in Basel...For the first time I realized that the disgusting rooms we had on Old Square could also be beautifully furnished... not just with cots, dust, broken chairs and wardrobes full of smelly clothes...I stopped at the door, which stayed open...under no circumstances was I going inside..."He's going to tell us how to get out of the city," my new acquaintance said. Me? How? Was she crazy? The only way out was through the checkpoints in Rudnik or St. Vitus...and that way led to Germany!..."Through Wetland Meadow, then across the Little Graben canal, but the whole place is mined, and there's barbed wire," I said. I turned around on my bare feet and went downstairs... God, what did they want from me? Maybe they'd confused me with some kid who worked for the partisans and knew secret ways out of the city...

On Jail Street, I ran into Bug, a schoolmate, a lanky guy who lived on Breg on the other side of the river in an attic room with his mother, who was a cleaning woman...He was carrying a cardboard box with a lead seal...he pretended like it was some big secret, but in fact he was going to the post office at the railway station to pick up a package...We went together...The station was packed...the entryway, waiting room, platforms and open spaces outside all the way to the co-op...and probably even farther on, to Zalog...There wasn't a single train that could avoid passing through the station...military transports of German soldiers, transports of prisoners, transports of refugees...Lots of pregnant or overweight women, dressed half in folk costume...Bosnian? Istrian?...stood around or squatted with their big travel bags, carpet bags, bundles and wicker baskets all the way out to the streetcar stop and the Miklič Hotel...We barely made our way through one of the five entrances...Trains arrived bringing army units, while others departed...trains bearing soldiers passed through, while trains bearing civilians didn't...They got switched here and there onto side tracks...A regular waltz of switch tracks and buffers, with people in motion...this ballet didn't take place just in the sky but on rails as well, train by train...endlessly long transports... Germans, Hungarian draftees, Home Guards...all of their armaments...Mongols, Vlasovites...small, slouching, sallow soldiers with wide, lascivious mouths...captured, shoeless Italians...sitting in cattle cars, their legs dangling out, hungry, singing, swaying or toppling over as the trains lurched...And armored trains with artillery that could shoot down giants...regular munitions dinosaurs with three locomotives out front and more and more cars connected behind...Advance guard formations, artillery! and transport after transport...a multitude under arms, wearing crew cuts or pompadours…with coquards and death's heads on their caps, a whole drafted goulash of the Balkans…They were wailing for someone to send them women, the fat female partisan prisoners on the platform… The war had claimed its young in every tiniest corner of Ljubljana… all of the trains were full, all the embankments, all of the jails, all of the barracks, all of Germany, of Europe…people of every age…White Guards…Bulgarian, Serbian, Croatian, Lithuanian and Latvian soldiers…fighters, traitors, rebels, Jews, left-behinds, Mongols… rations consumed under a hundred flags! A terrible traffic! If you took quick count of all the countries fighting against the Russians and the Anglo-Americans, how many armies…you came up with twenty-eight easily! If just one flying fortress came overhead now, it would have been child's play to drop a bomb from a thousand feet up…and blow the whole train station to smithereens. Turning the lot into mush, mincemeat…You could tell things had to keep going like this, that there was no alternative…The worst of it was that all of the trains had to get shunted onto side tracks right there at the station and nowhere else…for hours at a time, whole nights at a time back and forth at the station, with the main line shut down and the switches destroyed… women, whether pregnant or grandmas, cooked something else here than on the other side of the Ljubljanica…bacon with bran, goat cheese in water…There was a crowd outside the shack of the post freight office. People were exchanging fleas, lice, crabs…Bug had to wait in a long line that got jostled by the crowd milling around…for a package of food that his oldest aunt had sent them from Upper Carniola…We had to mind the Mongols, who would swipe anything that wasn't screwed down or that they could tell you weren't holding onto tight...That's what railway stations are like when nations collapse...perhaps life on earth began at a train station, at the moment when transports besieged it...Long lines of women were sitting on benches on the platform...from big cities, blonde, made up, in nice worn coats with purses, manicured nails, all of them looking alike... they kept scratching their handsomely tanned legs, which were covered with scabs...these were probably sick people or whores...there were Vlasovites standing around them...sweaty, stinking, in thick, crumpled Russian uniforms..."*Lieb! lieb! lieb!*" they kept repeating...The SA, the train-station gendarmes, kept order with canes and night sticks...they'd go running across the roadbeds, disentangling the chaos amid the transports. There were too many people on the tracks, which kept the trains from departing...So now it was the turn of the gendarmes to restore order...with their truncheons and big Mauser pistols...Some girls who looked like they might be Gypsies were leaping across the tracks like deer, fleeing the SA in the direction of a black railroad overpass...No one was permitted to get off a train that had arrived from Lower Carniola...They had come from parts south by zigs and zags, encountering bombs on the rails and bridges blown up, ragged, their eyes febrile and bulging from everything they'd seen and experienced...in bullet-ridden, singed train cars...they had no idea in which switchback, what tunnel or what part of of the country they'd been under fire...They reluctantly reboarded their train, but they had no choice...all of them, without exception, were singing "Lili Marlene"...a real song that weathered all cyclones and accomplished the most that a song can do...it was sung in every trench on this and other fronts...There were probably thousands of tunes that had more meaning to them...the Slovenes, Bulgarians and Czechs, for instance, with all their tunes sung in five-part harmony...but only this song had reached every corner of the world...*Chug! chug! chug!* a new locomotive pulling a transport heading back south started to pull out, but then stopped...there were southerners sitting on the tracks, civilians and women, grandmothers minding children...none of them wanted to travel back there...they wanted to move on...toward northern Italy, to Switzerland, Germany, Scandinavia...they sat down under the train cars, let the train run them over, but they were staying...In the main hall of the station, crowds gathered around the timetables, and in the lobby with the ticket windows, there was a big map of Europe...but the ticket windows were closed, no more tickets were available...It was only with a great deal of trouble that Bug managed to get his package from the freight depot...both of us carried it, pushing our way through the waiting area on the platform...from one bench to the next, past mess tins, invalids and gendarmes...There was so much commotion in the buffet that you couldn't see anything...Singing. "Lili Marlene"..."The Gang's All Here"..."The Watch on the Rhine"... Both civilians and soldiers...The singing never stopped and the trains outside didn't either...If a plane flew overhead now and the sky came crashing down on the station...it could make short work of the whole city in just fifteen minutes...the Triple Bridge, the castle on the hill, the skyscraper, the cathedral, all of them would be turned intro the-atrical flats, husks of their former selves...All you could see in the buffet was beer in mugs and laps...fat girls...Gypsy girls...those blonde ladies with the scabs...Soldiers in square caps...Hungarians...were joking with each other...meeting in the doorway... stealing the sausages from each other's mess tins...clowning around... senior officers with spurs and shocks of African black hair, as if straight out of some operetta, walked past with women holding onto their arms...they danced a quadrille under the station clock. Suddenly *bang!* one, two gunshots...one of the Krauts had been downed, a German... in the middle of the ticket lobby...the poorly aimed shots had come from the SA...they had meant to shoot at a Gypsy who had swiped an officer's raincoat...blood was gushing from the man's gunshot wound...the stream of it jerked in time with his pulse, up his back toward his head...blood was gurgling from his mouth, he was a Vlasovite from a tank division, disguised in his chameleon uniform... all of his protective coloring was soaked..."Long live Stalin!" somebody shouted. The SA stood stock still, at attention, in front of the body...An officer came up and led away the gendarme who had done the shooting...

There was also a small unit around the Robba Fountain...two or three jeeps with a one-inch gun and a motorcycle with sidecar...the crew dirty and grim, with helmets down to their noses and machine guns hanging across their chests. They brought order to the area around City Hall in an instant...all they had to do was aim the gun's barrel...and, in a second, green tongues of flame would be flaring up under the feet of the people by the bridge or on Jail Street...One of them came trudging past us down the street...there was a dent in his helmet, from a grenade?…Bug suddenly burst out laughing…in a flash the German was up on the sidewalk and had him by the shoulder. *"Du lachst mich aus?"* he bellowed…*"Soll ich dich über den Haufen schießen?"** he shrieked…God, what a face he was making…flushed red, eyes bulging, Bug went white as a sheet…on top of that, the soldier had a Colt Browning pistol at his hip with the safety off. *"Bitte schön, Herr Soldat, der Bub ist mein Freund…er wollte nichts anstellen…nur heute ist er lustig, weil er ein Paket mit Lebensmitteln von seiner Tante bekommen hat…"*** The soldier let go of him…his face changed, and his eyes opened wide in surprise…*"Was…du redest aber gut deutsch…Bist du ein Deutscher?"*** …*"Ja, mutterseits, sie ist aus Neunkirchen bei Saarbrücken, Faist…"***** I rattled off as fast as I could…In the meantime, Bug had beat it to the other side of the street…leaving me to calm the soldier down…*"Das geht mir nicht in den Kopf…eine deutsche Seele…"****** My God, he was happy, even though his face was still red…*"Ich zeige Ihnen, wo ich wohne."******* …We walked a few paces together, still talking…I showed him our house, if he wanted to come visit, in case he was going

---

*Are you laughing at me?…Shall I just shoot you here on the spot?

**Please, Mister Soldier, this is my friend…he didn't mean anything by it…it's just that he's happy today, because he just got a package of food from his aunt…

***What?…your German is good…Are you German?

****Yes, on my mother's side, she comes from Neunkirchen near Saarbrücken, name of Faist…

*****I can't get my head around this…A German soul…

******I'll show you where I live.

to be staying in Ljubljana for any length of time...I knew from my own experience how he must have felt...as though he were suddenly back home, with Germany around him...I walked him back downtown...as people cast nasty looks our way...not at him, but at me... and furtively, at that, which was even worse...when we reached the Zois Pyramid, we shook hands...Man is his language, I would keep telling myself twenty, thirty years after that...

A few days later, the white fortress at Turjak fell...the Home Guards inside had to surrender under sustained artillery and mortar fire to a force of partisans and Italians that was two or three times their size...When the attackers had the advantage of numbers it was easy to win...Alcatraz had fallen under the might of the Reds... and the prisoners were transported to the northwest interior...in the city, a new government was proclaimed: General Leon Rupnik, with a white goatee similar to Vati's, became president of the regional administration...

Everything was tending to get worse rather than better. The movie theaters started showing German films starring Hans Moser, and finally French ones again, from Pétain's Vichy France...you could see Versailles and Paris again, the Champs Élysées with the sound of *chansons* sung in the shadows of gas street lamps...the shooting out in the streets had come to a stop...a German patrol began walking our street right down the tracks...all boots, ribbons and Iron Crosses... ramrod straight and gruff, like some statue made out of metal... Food rations were reduced to the absolute minimum...if we wanted to survive to the next harvest, the papers reported, we must limit ourselves to the utmost extent...There was almost no meat...A thin slice of black bread and a mound of mashed turnips qualified as an excellent meal...Other people may have eaten better or worse within their own four walls...some of the other people in our building, the market vendor's family and the Salazniks, didn't look starved like us at all...behind closed doors they must have been depriving themselves of their share of boiled macaroni, what with their supplies of cabbage and sausage...it smelled too good on the stairways and under their open windows...they must have been trying out all kinds of different dishes, it smelled so delicious everywhere...you could just see the thick beef soups...the hams with dumplings swimming in butter, the chicken in aspic, the bowls of fruit salads and platters piled high with cheese strudel...Sometimes you stood transfixed, your nose sniffing and your ears picking up the clinking of knives and forks...and you ate, stuffed yourself, drank along with them...Were these the friends of officers from the barracks' depots?...black marketeers?...did they go out raiding warehouses by night?...I could imagine every possible thing...a flame burning in three ovens at once, with bowls and dishes arranged all around...

At school, our chemistry teacher, a Russian émigré named Lesnov, talked mostly about the chemical make-up of various food-stuffs and dishes...causing our mouths to water...that was the extent of the chemistry we learned from the dwarfish Russian with the narrow face and eyebrows thick as paint brushes...Nor did we learn any more about physics from the other science teacher, Mr. Vodovnik...the only thing that was useful or interesting was that he brought an old radio receiver to class...without its housing...so we could at least see how it was put together and some day wouldn't make use of the devices with the same level of understanding as cannibals, lazy people or women, for whom knowing that kind of thing was beneath their dignity... But when we asked him about splitting the atom, which was most likely the basis of the new secret weapon that Hitler kept promising at the top of his voice...he told us that we would learn about atoms in the upper forms...he didn't even mention in passing what turmoil atoms were in – far worse, in all likelihood, than the turmoil of the universe...I knew about lots of experiments from reading popular magazines...and about the three physicists...Brasch, Lange and Urban...who tried to split the atom at a time when there weren't any accelerators...using a current of several million volts. To achieve that, the three young physicists built an experimental power station several thousand meters up on Monte Generoso in the Italian Alps...a promethean challenge to God like that couldn't go unpunished...one of the young physicists, Arno Urban, plunged from a cliff to his death... But those were the forerunners...how many names of physicists were to follow...Rutherford, Soddy, James Jeans, Planck, Einstein...we heard nothing about them...About what could happen when forces with an energy and ferocity previously unknown to man were released inside tiny tubes dipped in oil? Could those mysterious powers that reached earth from the universe and were known as death rays also strike from those flashing boxes?...Who was going to discover those hidden forces of matter dancing their infinitesimally tiny dance of electrons...how much time would it be before they exploded?...

It was a beautiful fall...Ever since the airfield at Jarše, I had developed the habit of looking at the sky while lying on my back...One day, when I lay down on the bench by the window that we used for stretching out hides, I was able to look up without the roof or the castle getting in the way...the uninterrupted, boundless, transparent blue filled my eyes...and I was flooded with a fabulous feeling, a state of natural enlightenment that I had felt on many occasions when I looked at the sky...especially in Nove Jarše, when I would wait with a sack at the edge of the fields for the peasants to harvest their potatoes so that the Balohs and I could clean up after them...

In the midst of this vast feeling, the paradox of infinity grazed me so abruptly and painfully that it was like getting stung by a wasp...I imagined an arrow released with such force into that blue that it pulled free of the earth's gravity, flying past the moon and defying the pull of the sun...and then? It traversed the curve of interstellar space, other suns, solar systems, milky and honey ways...and then? First it passed spiral nebulas and new solar systems, and there was nothing that could stop it...there was no border, no end to space and time...and the worst of it all was that this was reality and not fantasy. It would be entirely possible to create an arrow like that...comets with their parallel, open tracks were naturally formed versions of just such an arrow, rising and falling in unbounded space...both of which were the same thing and only served to heighten the intellectual strain...The sky had no right to look so contented and bright if its smile was concealing such a terrible secret that it was unprepared to reveal...like those smiling adults who decided to keep their secrets, ruthlessly violating a sacred right, the right to know...

Next to Mr. Fink, my homeroom teacher Mrs. Komar wasn't just the best teacher in the entire school, she was also a good person. Now and then as our homeroom teacher she had to say something harsh about our behavior, but in those cases she really kept it to a few words instead of delivering whole lectures...She was strict as a teacher...particularly with respect to grammar...But she knew how to explain things like few others did, as though she were explaining how some machine worked...as though she first took an empty housing, into which she put more and more parts, insights and reflections...and sometimes it was even as though she were opening some package in front of us and taking out some previously unknown contents...I couldn't get grammar...especially conjugations and declensions...diagramming sentences...I expected integrity from words, just as I did from sentences...not some nit-picking dissection into the elements of formations and sub-formations; a word had to have the solidity and indivisibility of a precious stone that endures – that's it; and at the same time it had to have a tone...a music that floats in space...actually we shouldn't study language at all if we intend to speak it joyfully all our lives...Mrs. Komar gave me bad grades for grammar without the least trace of condescension or derision and excellent grades for my compositions, but without any particular praise...I wrote my assignments fast, in a few minutes, as though

I were rolling unhewn stones and simultaneously banging on some noisemaker...But in some unconscious way, Mrs. Komar was also pretty. With other teachers...during our classes we had plenty of time and opportunity to get to know something about grown-ups...the thing that hovered above their collars, a head with a face, the mirror of the soul...overlaid with a smile, tears, a knitted brow, a contorted mouth...was a sort of quizzical gesture on just one more extremity, separated from the body, which behaved in its own way. Not so Mrs. Komar. Thin if not skinny, dark-skinned, with freckles on her face, arms and legs like an Indian, dressed in a dreadful schoolteacher's smock with the narrowest collar, wearing shoes with no heels, her legs and arms gangly, she was fetching in her every pose, movement and gesture...writing on the blackboard with such concentration and in such a hand...the way she knew how to leaf through a book attentively and set it back on her desk like a reliquary, the way she leaned back in her chair, paced back and forth on her dais and came to a halt when she wanted to emphasize something important...in her figure, from her emaciated, weakened legs, her concave midriff, her shoulders that hugged the teacher's desk, her slender neck up to her head, her brow, the alert and earnest look of her eyes from under her reddish-brown hair...everything was part of a single, coherent picture, a soul. There was nothing marginal or secondary, all of it was her, everything was of equal importance...Mrs. Komar was what they called an intellectual laborer, and anyone would have been tempted to marry her in a heart-beat, because there was nothing and yet so much that was feminine about her...she was never cross, willful, hard-hearted or greedy...she was always the same with respect to her focus and exactitude...And what diction! Coming from her lips, the language was beautiful... every last dull concept of grammatical jargon...each example of syntax, word formation, morphology, each single word...*pail, peak, water, linden*...had its music, as many facets as a diamond and a variety of aggregate states...She didn't turn Cankar's sketch "A Cup of Coffee" into Lord knows what...like Mrs. Püchler or Mrs. Sajevec from the school in Graben...she didn't sing it, although she did read the story like a composition, she just didn't let herself succumb to Cankar's monotonous, repetitive melody...she used her voice and diction to make her own music...as if she were playing some composition for violin on the trumpet, for instance...or vice versa, as though she knew how to use a block of wood striking a fence to perform a piano sonata...good God, if I wrote about myself the way Cankar did... about my experiences...about how I'd once lived in Basel...about that house in the Gerbergäsli with the shop on the ground floor... the stuffed tiger next to my bed...the apartment in the city center, the noise in the evenings, the colorful ads, the cars, the casino... about the peacefulness of Rue de Bourg, where we had a Christmas tree that reached all the way to the light fixture that hung from the ceiling...about the old building next to the police park...the mission school that had such bad memories for me...but also my tramps along the bank of the Rhine, on steamboats, through orchards or the zoo...about Mardis Gras parades and celebrations outside the Helvetia...why, it was all like some paradise I'd been driven out of... another world where I scarcely recognized myself anymore...I was like a record, one side of which has been buried underground for so long that its underside is completely effaced, grown-over, forgotten!...I'd had a double life, several of them, hundreds of them...but that life from Basel was really vivid!...For instance, that bit that I seemed to recollect since forever...was that my birth or was it a dream?...those stripes that were at the beginning, from behind which faces eventually appeared that until then I'd only heard?...Those repeated phantoms next to the balcony curtain...where? on Elisabethplatz...when I was still in my bassinet and courting the plaster muses as they cavorted across the ceiling?...If I could write something about that...and show it to Mrs. Komar, who wasn't just an expert, but on top of that a... I could only imagine what...

We'd been assigned to write a composition...about some book that we'd read. I wrote about Dostoevsky's *Poor Folk*...I'd wanted to write about *The Idiot*, which I'd checked out of the library in German translation and tried to read in that atrocious, dense Gothic script, but couldn't, as much as I desperately wanted to...Some days after that, when Mrs. Komar brought back our graded notebooks, she told me to wait for her in our classroom once school was out that day...We were alone amid the empty rows of desks...She sat up on her dais...a ruddy, freckled, thin, pretty Indian squaw. I walked up to her desk..."Isn't fourteen a little young to be reading Dostoevsky?"..."I'll be fifteen soon," I answered. "Is it that you can't answer your teacher's question, or do you just choose not to?" she asked with a smile. I shrugged awkwardly, because I didn't really know...She: "Are you absolutely sure that you understood what you read?"...The answer burst out of me…"No! That's just it…" Mrs. Komar smiled. "If you know there are things that you don't understand, then at least you know that…" "I do understand what they're saying and doing, it's just that…" "Just what?" she asked…"What I don't understand is the hidden meaning…" Her: "The hidden meaning?"…Me: "You know what I mean… the hidden meaning. The secret behind it all." Mrs. Komar: "And what sort of secret do you imagine that is?"…Me: "Oh, you know, there's just the one secret. The secret of everything…" Mrs. Komar started to blink. It was apparent that the secret I was hinting at could only be love…Then her face flushed red under her freckles. My God, what an awkward misunderstanding!…"It's the secret of man…" I rushed to explain. "Why we're on earth…what's in our heads, our dreams…" "Ah, I see," she said more boldly this time. Now I could relax. "That's what I want to write about…seen from childhood." "Really?" she said with the same eagerness…"Once it's done, I'd like to show it to you," I stammered…"I would like that," she said cheerily. "Come see me whenever you want. I'll be happy to help you anytime." She collected her things…the notebooks and grammars, the jar of ink for her pen, the gradebooks…there was just as much of her in those things as there was in herself…just as much charm and attention, even though it was all somber and strict…but it was precisely the gloom and severity that attracted me…

So I began my first big attempt…I tried to write…It wouldn't come. It was hard. More impenetrable than rock…which at least preserved its wild docility in contrast to what had been written. I thought I had to write about some third person…not about myself…Not about the unbearable temperature I felt inside, and all the thoughts that were crawling like ants all over and inside me...And especially not about the music that now and then ran riot inside me. I tried to immerse myself in the grammar, so as to keep from annoying her with my ignorance... It would never have occurred to me to tell her about the time we'd met at her house, in her kitchen, when Clairi and I were out selling furs door to door in 1939...

EVENTUALLY THINGS REACHED THE POINT where my parents bought some material on the black market for a coat that Vati stitched together for me in two days...It was for casual dress, with big pockets sewn on the outside, wide lapels, a belt...As a product of the war economy, the heather fabric wasn't of particularly good quality, with bits of wood and even whole splinters caught in the fibers...God forbid I get caught in the rain wearing it, because there was too little protein in the weave...but the coat was new and, at least for the time being, flawless...I went out dressed in it to show off a bit...which was silly, I realized, but to be able to walk through town without disapproval, even pleasing in the eyes of civilization...for an hour or two, being able to mix with the crowd at the opera, on the promenade, and in the skyscraper as an equal part of the decor and without raising eyebrows...ha, now this was a pleasure!...I went from there to the movie theater, the Union, which was a cut above and resembled a concert hall. They were showing a French movie. Jean Gabin and Michel Simon...that big lunk with the bovine eyes and outsized potato face who was somewhat reminiscent of me...I got a good seat…I had groomed myself for the occasion, scrubbing my face, combing my hair and putting on a fresh collar…mother, who gave a woman's touch to everything I wore to school or to mass, had made several collars for me that I could attach with fasteners to my sweater…and trick everyone…except my gym teacher and the doctor at the dispensary…into thinking that I even had a shirt on under my sweater…I buffed my shoes to a high sheen, using Asipi's technique… until they shone dazzling against the sidewalk…The best-heeled kids in town held court at the Union Cinema, which with all its pillars resembled a palace…the sons of well-placed civil servants, at least, if not entrepreneurs, lawyers, bankers and owners of the biggest, most prosperous stores…all of them living in houses alongside the promenade, the theaters, cafés and parks in the heart of the city…all of them pale, with pampered skin, dressed in Tivar suits, elegant gabardines and the narrow ties that had just then come into fashion…but most of all with that pronounced arrogance that I felt all youth must have if it intends to be taken seriously as youth, and that I never could carry off…I draped my coat across my knees…it seemed to me as though I had approached my ideal with dispatch…to the right and left of me there were dozens of young girls from the same social sphere as the fellows…Dressed in pastel sweaters, wearing earrings and necklaces, and with furs draped over their knees and nice-looking purses resting on them…however much I longed to be part of the society in which they circulated, I was even more repulsed by the conformist instincts of the girls my age…they behaved too disdainfully, giggled unbearably and judged good looks on some animal husbandry scale from zero to twenty...the nose, the eyes, the hair...they expected boys to wear their hair long and constantly demonstrate their athletic prowess, strike poses on the promenade, dance...maybe they even secretly expected them to work for the partisans like some masked hero from days of old...They wanted to see everything in color, and each fellow to be a handsome prince...that wasn't me, the idiots!...quite the contrary... Michel Simon played a cripple, a castle servant, ruled over with an iron hand by Jean Gabin, who wants to force his own austerity on the whole village. As a result, he doesn't just starve himself but all of his hired hands and especially his wild dog Iago, who grows more and more bloodthirsty from one day to the next, because he's not fed... Iago won't let anyone near the steps to the castle...Michel Simon has to think up all kinds of ruses to trick him and reach his quarters in one of the castle's towers...One evening, as he's returning to his room carrying his modest supper in a small dish, the dog refuses to let him pass...At that point, Michel calls out, "Iago!" and sets the dish down on the floor...Iago's steamshovel of a tongue laps at it twice...and it's gone!...then he sets down a second dish, this time of potatoes...three smacks of Iago's tongue, and he's emptied it..."Hi, Iago!" Michel calls out from then on, and they're the best of buddies! if he hadn't played the Lord God himself, righteously handing out treats, the cripple would have succumbed to bitterness, because fury at his master was already eating away at him...The next evening, I headed out to the opera in my new coat...the standing room in the balcony...*Carmen*, *Cavalleria Rusticana*...The fact was that theater was far more alive than the movies...you could watch actors of flesh and blood...even off in the wings as they got ready, and the musicians at the foot of the stage, which was like an engine room below deck...sometimes you could even pick up the smell of their makeup as it wafted off the stage... Sure, here as well there were lots of the same girls and guys from the promenade, students at the classical high school...a closed society indulging in pleasure and cavorting about with its own kind, as if in a warm bath...a breed, a tribe to which I absolutely did not belong and never could...and that filled, as I've said, all of the movie theaters, swimming pools, tennis courts, sweet shops...ski slopes...I didn't belong with them, and I didn't go anywhere, either...If someone were to ask me if that most beautiful chandelier with the little polished pyramids in the Café Evropa used to be lit during the war...I would have no idea what to say.

The week after I got my new coat, I headed out with the handcart to the fuel store on Roman Street to pick up our monthly ration of kindling and firewood...wearing my gabardine, of course!...I set a chair down by the front door and carried the wood out to the shed in the courtyard...when I came back the third or fourth time...my coat... which I had carefully folded up and set down on the chair with some other things...was missing...I couldn't believe my eyes...I went to check in the woodshed...up all the steps, in case I had hung it over the railing...then behind the front door and out in the courtyard again... a thing like that was enough to drive a person crazy!...only after I'd checked and felt through every last obscure corner of the house did I dare come out with it in the workshop... A whole hurricane exploded! I had to go to the police, my parents demanded, on the other side of the Karlovški Bridge. Now…with the war on, and bombardments and massacres taking place, to go and report the theft of a coat!… why, all the cows and snitches would laugh at you from their attics. Who were you to go dumping some little private problem on people who were buried in work! Mother insisted. War or no war…laws had to be enforced regardless of circumstances…if there was a mistake in your accounting, you had to hold the accountant responsible, and if somebody defaced a public monument, you had to let loose at the vandals, punish the child who had broken a glass pane…So I went… In the turreted building on the far side of the bridge and the train overpass there was a police station, inside of which a bunch of old cops with big bellies and tiny little pistols in holsters were trying to keep warm around a cast-iron stove…That station of theirs stank so bad you couldn't breathe…One of them with a bushy mustache took my information, all of it…When I answered where my mother was born, "Neunkirchen…Saarbrücken"…he looked at me as if I were the last person he wanted to see there, or as though he was in bed with the partisans…"Come back in a week," he said grimly, but I could tell then I was never going to see my coat again…maybe some partisan somewhere was already wearing it…I'd gone out just three or four times in my coat…and shown it to Sister Rafaela, who was beside herself with delight…and then the couple of times at the Union and the opera…and then it was gone…Now I was back to wearing Clairi's long knitted cardigan sweater and Vati's thirty-year-old suit coat, and once again I stuck out like a sore thumb…If I didn't want to seem completely out of place, I had to behave humbly, dressed in those clothes...and when I converted the cost of my coat into calories...I realized that all five of us could have lived for a good three months on that money and still had enough for the electric bill. Only fools dress up during wartime.

Because our path certainly wasn't strewn with rose petals now... we'd turned all our longtime customers' clothes inside out at least twice over and repaired and refurbished their every last item of fur...despite all our ads, we weren't getting any new customers, period...and we had to make do with the bare minimum of food that ration coupons got you...Despite the dry kindling that I collected wherever I could... around the castle, on Golovec, near Rožnik...all of the wooden benches there had been stolen by then, as had all the fences that faced onto the Ljubljanica...we had to ration our fuel. Only two logs and three small scoops full of coal per day...by evening, the attic was so unrelentingly cold that we had to walk around in jackets, scarves and caps...Vati still refused to touch opossum furs, which were good for making jackets at best...He was saving those for the day when our circumstances became so dire that we had no alternative. Should we go back out selling furs door to door?...I took some with me to sell at the market...hiding them in my school bag, to avoid having to pay market rent...my family gave me a detailed price list...this much money for a cap, or X amount of potatoes, Y amount of flour, Z amount of tobacco...The vendor next to me was selling every imaginable thing...rusty nails, soured milk, ripped blankets, poured leaden snails, wooden Easter eggs, heels and soles ripped off of shoes...I went to see the shoeshiners...at last Asipi ordered a new set of posters from me...for which he paid half in money, half in shoe polish, which also worked out...I chopped wood for Ana the waitress...and suddenly I was stopping at every house that had stacks of wood or heaps of coal waiting to be chopped or put away. I would ring the doorbell and offer my services...respectfully... along with my tools...an obedient little helper...unprepossessing and cheap...and as quick as a weasel. There was a big pile lying in the snow in front of the paint-and-dye store on Old Square. They had a grown son in the house...a giant with a big belly and three double chins...but he didn't feel like doing the work, or else he was sick...The wallpaper hanger on Komensky Street had a mountain of logs in his courtyard, and while I was there, his neighbor, a retired voice instructor, had a bunch of firewood and coal delivered...I had work for four days in a row until sunset, till curfew. On New Square, I helped the servant of one of the better families who lived in the mansions there shovel two wagon loads of lignite into their cellar, which was as gloomy and vast as a torture chamber, and then split up a whole cartload of wood-chips...I earned money everywhere...and at one place I got an old sweater...but nowhere was I given bread or anything else edible... One time, Karel and Ivan joined me...In the Kolman warehouse, they helped me unload some wagons and put stuff away. Karel and Ivan hadn't changed much...outwardly they had even more pronounced pouts and the lips in-between were pasted into a fleshy wrinkle... After all the time that had passed, I felt sure that all three of us may well have been made to be acquaintances, but not friends under any circumstances...We extracted porcelain, plates and glassware out of straw...it was cold and we had to be careful...and put them in

their places on the shelves...Karel was, hm, how to put it...sort of
turned inward or something, even though he was chattier than usual.
I couldn't understand how I could ever have felt so bound to him...
The wagons arrived one after the other...all week long, from Monday
through Saturday. You had to work carefully: lying down on your stomach on a kind of sawhorse, a plank that was laid across both sides of the
cart, and then carefully feel your way through the clumps of straw...
then pull out a plate, then another, a third...all the way to the bottom
of the crate, setting them on a part of the plank, one end of which
rested on the wagon hitch and the other on the warehouse door...
and then carry them upstairs, where you had to set everything back
down in compartments filled with straw...It was a bit reminiscent of
pitching hay into a manger...It was tricky work...you had to mind
the balance of your torso one moment, and the balance of your ankles
the next...Around then, I also got to see Iva and Cvetka again, and the
old dressmaker...who was still as inconspicuous as ever...One afternoon, when Karel and Ivan hadn't yet arrived in the warehouse...we
worked a production line...with one of us digging through the straw,
the second carrying things, the third setting them down where they
went...I couldn't do anything all by myself, so I went straight up to
the store...The owners were upstairs...those two brothers with their
plump, ruddy faces...they were playing "Lili Marlene" on the piano...
but singing different lyrics, in Slovene...something like this: "Fritz
isn't going to beat Ivan, he'll just get his arse shot on the run...hurrah,
Lili Marlene..." One of them looked at me through the window and

gave me a big, contented grin...was he trying to provoke me because he thought I was German? He was smarter than that...he was over thirty, or maybe he just had too much time on his hands...When I saw Ivka coming out of their storefront, aside from recalling the rabbit furs, I felt no pangs at all...she was dressed in a coat and one of those woolen caps that women had begun wearing then...which covered the head, ears and neck and was tied under the chin, resembling a bonnet with a little point at the crown, causing the face to seem sculpted as it looked out from under the cap...her little curls were hidden from view, and though she was still thin and had the same light, piercing eyes, she seemed somehow gray and clumsy...she neither overshadowed nor illuminated the houses on the embankment the way she used to, and I felt just as much for her as I did for any of the other random passers-by. How strange, even though the earlier experience remained firmly in my memory! After six afternoons of work for the Kolmans, we got paid: each of us received a set of glistening glassware – a pitcher complete with polished stopper and six small glasses...no money, much less anything edible...we were only allowed to choose what color of glass...Blue, green or yellow?...A set of glassware... but none of us had families where alcoholic drinks were served...and the glasses were too small to use for milk or water. We were insulted and protested...we wanted money...nobody had said anything about money, the warehouse manager lectured us, just payment...So if there wasn't going to be any money, then instead of this glassware we wanted something serious, like pots or platters or plates...We wanted to speak to the owner, who was rich…they wouldn't let us into the store to see him, they said he was gone, although he was there, except that we didn't know if the man in the store upstairs amid all the porcelain and chandeliers was the owner or just the manager…Each of us took home his useless glassware, which wasn't worth all that much either…if we'd been given tin reliquaries, at least we'd have something of decorative value…but the blue glassware sitting on the shelves next to our tin dishes and bent boxes looked like a castle looming over a village of serfs…

Another job, which I got thanks to Bug's mother, was better: six straight weeks working in a basement from seven in the morning until eight in the evening, including a lunch of tea and sausage. This involved cleaning the rooms and straightening the files, old binders, ledgers and documents in the vast basement of the palace that housed offices of the regional government. The archives of all possible banks… cooperative, maritime, coal-mining…credit unions…clubs…organizations. First I had to get all the sheaves and bundles of papers off the top shelves…set them down in the hallway…remove all the cobwebs and use a scraper to get any mold off the walls…scrub down the shelves and cement floor…then wipe all the dust off the bindings and envelopes, arrange them by size, number and color…shred any other, extraneous papers into tiny bits and then burn those in the metal bins and grills out in the courtyard…we would gather up chestnuts, and while the other two were downstairs, the one in the courtyard would roast them…It was cold, dusty and slushy, and as soon as we took our hands out of the hot water they started to freeze in the icy air...the filth on the floor entangled our feet like entrails...we were overseen by some sort of archivist in a black work smock whose breath stank as much as the words written in the registers and bundles of papers, which were disgusting...Work like that in cellars like those, where there wasn't a living soul around, just piles of bank and company files that had to be transferred from one cellar to the next, might have been bearable enough, if only real people at one time or another hadn't been forced to do business with them...But here you sensed something: that one day the extent of the rot would become overwhelming, because the same filth that had been recorded in these bundles of papers day after day also poured forth out of human beings...Gross! But the pay was good...for cleaning the cellar of those filthy banks and companies all three of us, each one separately, got as much as a well-paid worker earned in a month...I got more than Vati and Clairi combined would have been able to scrape together in two months...

It was something, but not enough with five mouths to feed...I would have had to rob a bank or loot a food depot...One day, the old cleaning woman from the first floor...I had no idea how much she, like the other residents of the house, hated us...asked me to deliver a bag of potatoes to her daughter...a stunningly beautiful blonde lady who sometimes appeared in the stairway window...all the way out to Bežigrad, where there was no streetcar line...The beautiful lady walked with me...The sack contained potatoes, this I could tell from its lumpy contours, but it was so unnaturally heavy that it felt like it must be full of chunks of iron...I had to set it down several times and rest...which upset me on account of the young lady, because that must have made her think I lacked endurance and muscle tone...She walked ahead of me...by ten or fifteen paces at least...so I had no choice but to study her from head to toe the whole time...I'd never seen such a delicate, angelic figure before...more beautiful than any I'd seen until then...more beautiful than Fani, Ivka, Enrico's mother...Was it even possible for such a gentle, light, practically weightless creature to exist in this life? Even if I'd seen her in a movie, she would have seemed too beautiful!...maybe she could exist in heaven, but only there...This slender figure in her black bell dress, swaying on her elegant legs... and that tousled abundance of blond hair, cascading like tow from her head!...The same panel of her coat kept lifting up each time she moved...then dropped back down the same way each time...always within the same limits...like the rustling of leaves in the crown of a tree...And her face: gentle, pale, not powdered...with dark eyes and a delicate nose...her lips only slightly more pink than her skin...was there anyone anywhere who could live with a hyacinth like that?... When I had to set the bag down again beneath a clock that hung over the street...she turned around from the sidewalk on the far side of the street and smiled at me...she wasn't angry or disappointed with me at all...Because she was wearing a black coat, her face seemed even whiter and her hair took on the color of white gold..."Why don't you take a break," she called out to me...It did me such good to hear that... Then I hoisted the bag up again and followed her step by step...across the street...down the sidewalk...a long way past the stadium...then down some path through a field to the left...We came to a house...a new, white house…its rooms recently plastered, the walls as fresh as that morning's bread. I could see trees out the window, like in Nove Jarše or on the farm…it was a magnificently simple place for looking, pondering, making plans…nothing but lightweight white furniture, lightweight armchairs, benches…a little starter house for newlyweds…The beautful young lady paid me handsomely…a very large sum of money, for three such trips by foot…and to top it all off, she poured some fruit juice into a crystal tumbler for me…If my future turns out to be anything like this house…but making any plans was out of the question…the beautiful lady already had a husband…a handsome, dark-haired fellow, deeply tanned, who resembled the maharajah in *The Tiger of Eschnapur*…No sooner had we reached the fence, which had also been recently painted, than she gave me a smile good-bye…When I put the money on the table at home and told Clairi how I'd earned it, she knitted her brow…"*Man redet, daß ihr Mann, der in einer Druckerei arbeitet, unter einer Decke mit den Roten steckt…*"* Oh… my God, that sack really had been heavy…Several years later, when the new regime revealed some of the tricks it had used as part of its underground work in Ljubljana, I recalled it again. The sack had been as heavy as lead, and because the beauty's husband was a printer, well then…perhaps I had lugged across town part of a printing press or the contents of a type case, buried amid the potatoes…Those sly foxes had used me, perhaps thinking that if I got caught, I'd be released because I passed as a German, and even if they arrested me, they wouldn't

*They say that her husband, who works at a printing press, is in bed with the Reds.

catch them. But what if I'd ratted?...Or maybe I just imagined it all...
I wasn't offended a bit...I would have headed two or three miles
uptown again in an instant, hauling another bag of potatoes like a
donkey...if I could have had that forest sprite skipping around ahead
of me like that...

O̶UR STUDY GROUP AT CHURCH was led by Mr. Becele...We
met every other Saturday for three hours in a parish assembly room.
We didn't talk about the war, or the partisans, or the communists, or
the league of Home Guards...all that hocus-pocus of events, facts
and substitutions beyond the walls of our brotherhood was constantly
merging and consuming itself so fast...everything was on top, on the
bottom, higgledy and piggledy all at the same time...there was no way
any of it could inspire confidence, trust, or any degree of faith...If we
talked about wars and revolutions, it was always those distant, ancient
ones that had long since petrified into history...They were like prayers
that made no mention of the pain or death that had just befallen us,
but rather a sort of distant, diluted mourning, sorted into centuries
and mummified...The room in the refectory where we met had pews
and a little altar to the Sacred Heart, which was always kept behind
drawn curtains and closed shutters because of the cold and the air
raids...The first order of business was a prayer, then we learned some
new hymns, which Becele drew in black and red calligraphy on scrolls
that resembled ancient Egyptian papyrus manuscripts...Next came a
reading from Antonio Fogazzaro's book *The Saint*, a discussion of some
chapters from the Old Testament...an interpetation of some images

of the prophets, as well as some events from the historical and didactic books…the Gospels, the Acts and various letters of the Apostles… Revelations…and then questions like "If Jesus commanded us to love our neighbor as ourselves, how could he then drive the money changers out of the temple?"…It was an interesting discussion…Everyone was also supposed to say something about himself and his problems…but that was no good, because Becele practically had to use tongs to drag the words out of everybody…another reason it was impossible to be frank was because then we would have had to talk about everything that was going on…the war, the massacres, the terror, the informing, the hunger, the rationing…The best part of our study meetings were the lectures with overhead projections…Becele didn't just teach religion, but chemistry and painting as well…He announced a whole series of lectures that were supposed to present a general survey of painting… his respect for art was so great that he often fell silent while showing a picture…As soon as a painting appeared on the screen, he would say just two or three modest sentences describing the image and then not speak, so as not to get in the way of our connecting with it on a deeper level. Which was a shame, because he explained art far better than religion and whatever he said determined what we found inspiring and developed an affinity for…

At our very first session, he showed us some slides featuring mythological motifs from ancient Greece. It was like some sort of drug. All kinds of images started to appear on the screen, rather like when you flip quickly through the pages of a fat book…Venus, Ariadne, Galateia – to whom none of us ascribed any fleshly significance – began rising up off their pillows, gathering fruit in the grass, concealing their sorrow, letting flowers drop from their hands, telling each other their dreams... Venus to Mars, or Venus to Cupid, lying on his side with a rabbit, two doves – one light, the other darker – at the foot of some landscape that dissipated in the distance... Procris leaping out of the bushes, collapsing flat on the ground, and already bending over her was Cephalus, her hunter husband, with one ear elongated and frayed, allowing him to detect hidden prey; who because of one tragically thrown spear became her murderer... Next to their battered sandals sat a handsome black dog, whimpering... Then still other worlds appeared... Andromeda, Atalante, either asleep or expectant, bare except for the animal skins they had on, draped with pearls and blossoms, seated before their mirrors... And though couples may have been depicted embracing, each individual seemed very much alone and self-contained, not one of them appeared to transcend himself and his ample, pale flesh... The Galateias arrived on dolphins, leaving huge seashells behind, some of them emerged onto dry land alone, while others were accompanied by mermaids and centaurs. And there were always doves everywhere, snakes, seashells and peacocks. What we were experiencing retreated into the background... only the pictures were vibrant... some sort of shadowy dreams in the dark... They drew you away. His physical eyes reached as far as castles, columns and synagogues, but his sorrow reached much farther, deep into the land, the forests, to the peaks of the mountains, into the evening... the imaginary... she wouldn't be coming back home, she'd stay there looking for something that was already destroyed... And then, in another picture, she would be saying goodbye beneath the lights of a shattered night sky that were drawing her away again, far away, but this time toward home…

It wasn't, however, just the figures of the nymphs and horses with human heads that affected me, it was also what Mr. Becele had to say about the painters themselves…stories from real life, vivid aspects of their personalities. Their relationship to kings and princes, the hatred, their young years…I found even their faces appealing, as though that aspect of them alone had predestined them to work with brushes and paints…Yet somehow you couldn't compare them to people…when our catechism instructor showed us some folios containing big reproductions of their frescos…I realized that these masters hadn't been people at all but something between centaurs and prophets…

There weren't many of us in the study group…between ten and twenty…Tinček and I were the only ones from our grade in school… The brotherhood's secretary, Mr. Becele's right hand, was Lado Pšeničnik, who was a senior at our school…A tall, slender, dark-haired fellow who wore black trousers with gray stripes, like seminary students…pale, with his hair combed to one side and wearing a big, floppy hat…always with a bow tie or necktie…and never without his black briefcase, made of the finest leather, at his side. He would take roll, keep minutes, prepare lectures, and note down the topics of the sessions to come. He had a high-pitched, artificial, cooing voice… he was capable and responsive to the priest's needs to a fault, but imperious toward us…Sometimes during a session he might sternly admonish even Mr. Becele himself, if he happened to have omitted anything…Clearly he had a gift for administration…he would come

259 ·

up with assignments for each of us, but keep the easiest jobs for himself…in a word, he was efficient and slimy. If Becele hadn't used him as his assistant, there probably would have been more of us in the study group…Word was that he'd met the greatest living poets and that he wrote poetry himself and got it published… I'd even read one of his poems in the monthly *Light*…a sonnet about the heroic end of the famous commander of a crack brigade of the Home Guards, Captain Meniščanin…That was why I found Pšeničnik intriguing, but I didn't dare try to get to know him better…

The meetings lasted three hours…after that we would go to confession in the Trnovo church, just as we did on every last day of the week…I still didn't feel like telling the father confessor anything serious…the smell on the other side of the grille was too antiseptic for me to mix my sins with it, and then I would have had to believe, as everyone did, that you were absolved of your sin, which stayed with your confessor. But the worst of it was that you couldn't even talk with him openly about your infractions, impressions and plans…that even in the confessional, trust didn't prevail, not even for an instant… Everyone and everything was suspicious, everywhere there were blabbermouths and snitches, both outside and inside the confessional…On Sundays, the church would be full. I would approach the altar bearing the eucharist in a group of adults, but most often with my classmates. Except for Tinček, I didn't believe that any of them were pure. Not one of them had ever said anything that made any damn sense about the war, the Reds, the Whites, the Blues…every single one of them avoided expressing any opinions at all...every last one of them was a gossip...barely would one of them absent himself, than the others began slinging mud at him...by nature, man is an informer, a snitch, that's how he was made, he can't do any different!...if he steps out for a bit, leaves you alone, don't bother giving much thought to where he's gone...he's gone to call the teacher, the cops, the priest, to tell them he's seen you...doing this and that...I didn't have the gift of trusting people, I had to protect myself and maintain as little contact with them as possible. It beggared belief that people actually went to mass on account of their faith...and not just so that the priests and their ass-kissers in the refectory would see them, thus neutralizing their secret, forbidden activity...and this left you wondering whether each person wasn't just fighting for his own purity of soul because he had to, because otherwise his body would implode...The person in line ahead of or behind me didn't concern me one bit...even less at the altar than outside. That put me off about myself, as much as it did about others...In church, we ought to have all been equal right here, right now, the way we were going to be in heaven...the last (i.e. the first) ought to acknowledge the first (i.e. the last) in church at the very least...And the prayer that rose up afterward. It was the most efficient, most insincere conversation with God imaginable...Everybody in church put on this inward face that frightened me as much as any knowledge that remained out of reach. The old women...whom I loathed because they didn't have to make decisions anymore...excelled at everything. They sang the psalms...twisting, uplifting, widening their mouths like trumpets…prayed louder than anyone else…and served as the roadbed that supported all of this ballast. All the noise in the world wouldn't have been enough to drown out the praying intensity of just one of them…they were determined to make it up there, into heaven, the light, by any means necessary…And every so often… the looks they would cast our way if we weren't behaving like them… they wanted to uglify and age us by sixty, seventy, eighty years, just so we'd be like them!…One defense I had against the dangers of choral prayer was to focus on contorting my lips the way their mouths were moving…There was no soul to the prayer, it was just a function of the mass, like part of a game…if people prayed to more than one god, then at least the prayers would vary and they would have to practice long and hard before each one…What's more, each person was using his prayers to beg for something that he wouldn't have been willing to pass on to anyone else. The prayers…were a desecration of God, the most loathsome of sins…For each prayer you prayed, you ought to have done a lot of penance…

At home, I tried praying all of the prayers that I'd passed on in church…I prayed them until my mouth went numb, but even then they weren't able to offset anything…they didn't course through me or the sky outside our workshop window…Finally, I tried praying in my own way, using my own words…jerkily, singing, with long pauses, in a kind of trance…but I doubted that this personal hermit's prayer accomplished anything…if it was able to rise up at all…Once, during a storm, when the whole attic was shaking like a shack on the edge of a volcano, I decided to test whether God liked me even a little bit…

When lightning flashed, I stretched out my arm and...no thunder came. At the next flash, I reached out my arm again: and again there was no thunder. At the third lightning flash, I didn't dare try to do it again – and that time all hell exploded...which left me not knowing what to think, and I doubted the noisy lightning strike as much as the silence that prevailed before.

DURING AN AIR RAID spent in the school's bomb shelter, I got to know Pšeničnik better...Ever since Italy's capitulation, the Anglo-Americans were constantly flying over the city...all you had to do was look at the clouds that their wings grazed!...but they were decent...they didn't do loops down toward the street! then swoop! and back up!...they flew high up, perhaps cowed by the flak, they didn't dare bomb us...maybe they left us alone because the big cheeses at one of their many international conferences had made that decision...But every day...two, three, four hours spent under alarm...finally you got to the point where that constant, threatening, tumbling game of musical chairs...the thundering of the "fortresses" over the rooftops...that stupid rumbling made you sad...and you felt hopeless and beaten... edgy, because you weren't getting enough active recreation!...because when you were under the RAF's merry-go-round, you didn't get one extra minute to think...First the sirens!...The whistling!...And then the explosions!...And so we would sit for two, three, four hours a day, wedged in between sand bags and the roof of the cellar, which was propped up with beams...sick of each other, all we could do was be bored...

Although Lado Pšeničnik's personality repulsed me...with all his servility, bowing and fickleness...the fact that he wrote poems and got them published...and most of all that he knew the greatest poets of our time...attracted and fascinated me...Even some of his habits intrigued me, the way women might beguile me with comparable tics...the way he put on and took off his gloves, one finger at a time!... or carefully fastened and unfastened the brass clasp on his expensive briefcase, which had everything conceivable inside, from beautifully bound volumes of poetry and dictionaries to the stamp of our church study group, which was as big as a fist...the elegant case that contained the clippers and files with which he tended his nails...the magnificent square watch on his wrist...his well-tailored suit, which was always neat and pressed, etc., etc.... I didn't know if this was a way of growing up, a sign of intelligence, or if he was just another Bug who was playing some game...the fact was that everything about him attracted and interested me, the way the shopkeeper's display window next to the bishop's palace did, crammed full of everything, from Bibles to comic strips..."I hear that you write," he said in a falsetto in his sing-songy lowland dialect. "That's right," I answered. He was thinking, he said, of establishing a literary circle for everybody who wrote. It would meet at his house, so he was inviting me to go visit him on Thursday...he would show me his poems, his library, his collection of rare autographs...

He lived with some distant relatives or other...on the floor over a former restaurant called The White Wolf...out front, the building still had a sign affixed to it depicting a wolf in sheep's clothing...

The owner was an ailing, elderly gentleman…a baron, as Lado told me, who had been elevated into the nobility. A little, ninety-eight-year-old man who was served by a cook and her niece, a robust, ruddy-cheeked girl named Katarina, who got room and board in the old man's apartment, the same as Pšeničnik. The stairway was dark, polished, immaculate…there was an engraved plate on the door that read Anton von Ukmar…When you go someplace like that to visit… an old, famous building, it's as though you've arrived at a castle… The distrust that prevails among people outside, among the stinking houses clustering around castle hill, vanishes in a domain like that… where you probably wouldn't have to regret confiding in anyone… confidentiality suited those picturesque, chatty, sleepy times of good digestion that the old gentleman came from…not even a single spark of all the commotion, spying and slaughter could make its way through a sky full of airplanes in here, much less find gunpowder to land in… His niece Katarina let me in the front door. Even though she was quite ruddy-cheeked, she was dressed severely, without a trace of extravagance. She led me down a long hallway that on one side had a statue of Mary standing in a recess, with the kitchen, pantry and bathroom on the other…She opened a low door…this now was an anteroom…a window with woolen drapes and a wide table under a chandelier… and little porcelain figurines everywhere, small statues, vases…old fashioned and pretty…She knocked on a vaulted door to the right and out came Lado in a dressing gown, with a black bowtie around his neck and a beautiful lock of hair as hard as ebony curling around his left ear…It had been ages since I'd seen people living like people…

and, in particular, I'd never before come across a peer of mine quite this dressed up…a sixteen-year-old kid, actually…I was stunned, as if confronted with a child dressed in adult clothes…But then…if I thought about it…we actually had quite a peculiar collection of boys in my class at school…Kemperle, who with his incipient, Errol Flynn mustache could almost have passed for a young married man…and on the other hand Mikec, diminutive, physically stunted, who would have fit in with elementary school kids, or Marn, for instance, who was tall, overweight and slow like a director in his fifties…and then there was me, still wearing shorts that made me look like a regular imp… the whole lot of us felt stupid of head and awkward of body…but we all went to the same class at school like a wolf, cow, fox, hen and owl all going to the same barn to sleep…

Pšeničnik showed me his room. It had once been the veranda of an inn, that years before had been closed in with brick and a bit of cement, leaving panes on three sides through which you could see some of Wolf Street, with a shop sign on one side, part of the roof of the neighboring house on the other, and out the middle window what had once been the restaurant's outdoor seating area in a lush, green court-yard, where people played bocce and musicians performed. Pšeničnik had an amusing collection of church handbells and a shelf on which his volumes of poetry were attractively arranged…all of them typed out on high-quality white paper and bound in notebooks…Poems that resembled what real poems should be…about sunrise, visions of war, the summer sun, conversations with God, misty mornings in the city…I leafed through them while he ducked out into the hallway to call for something... and then Urška the cook, wearing a bonnet, arrived with two cups of fruit juice on a salver... I discovered something else in a separate black notebook that he showed me... a play titled *Ladislav and Katarina*... he said she was his unrequited love... quite tragic... she was, alas, both a relative and a baroness, while he was just the son of an ordinary peasant... Now he was working with some old instructor of classics from the teachers' college to translate the whole play into Latin... it was a drama in verse and took place during the first Roman Republic, in the time of Brutus... It was five acts on 120 pages and a total of 2,098 lines of blank verse. He spent two hours working on it every evening... surreptitiously, because it had to remain a secret... next year, for Katarina's seventeenth birthday, he was going to make her a present of his tragedy twice... first in Slovene, then in Latin, written out in his best calligraphic hand, at that... and he was going to include a letter with his gift... I felt moved by this... and for a long time after that I saw a very different person in him... He had other interesting things hanging on his walls... pictures, diplomas, photographs from the old baron's younger days... Here, for instance, was a shot of von Ukmar in Paris outside the Sorbonne, when he fought in the war of 1870-71... which meant he really must be just under a hundred years old now... he had served in the cavalry... the picture showed him dressed as an uhlan with gold spurs, a saber and sashes across his chest... another photo showed him at a ball at the opera... then skating at the famous Winter Palace... But the thing that impressed me most, apart from his tragedy, was a rare prize that he had standing on a small, round table... a framed portrait of the poet Oton

Župančič…inscribed by the poet himself: "To my dear young friend Lado Pšeničnik…" and next to it yet another, almost cinematic photograph with the same kind of inscription, signed by the soprano Valerija Heybal in the role of Turandot…and then yet another photo…this one of the poet and judge Alojz Gradnik, wearing that high, gray, almost blunt hat with the wide hatband…an image that everyone knew… also inscribed…Was this even possible?…"Do you know them?" I stupidly asked…"Of course," he replied in his high-pitched voice. "I get invited to their homes to visit. You can come with me sometime, if you want…" Now his stand-offish behavior didn't surprise me anymore… He knew all the most distinguished names of the day! geniuses of the highest caliber…Župančič, Gradnik…two real titans of poetry…and not only did he know them…no, no…he was even on friendly terms with them…Still others had inscribed his album of autographs…the novelist Fran Saleški Finžgar, the architect Jože Plečnik…and lesser lights, too…Silvin Sardenko, Pater Chrysostomos…and not small fry by any means, but really decent poets, critics, editors, leading scholars in various fields…the compilers of various encyclopedias… university professors…Dr. Tine Debeljak, Joža Glonar, Dr. Rajko Nahtigal, Anton Gojmir Kos, Ivan Pregelj, Marija Nablocka…All of these things around me…the notebooks, the diplomas, the photos… the sacristy cord with the bell by the door, given to him as a gift by the priest and writer Janez Jalen, which he used to summon Urška from the kitchen or Katarina from her room…I felt weak, speechless…now I believed everything…I believed in all his abilities and talents…I understood why he had to dress, behave and speak as he did, why he always seemed to be walking on eggshells…it was obvious, he lived among these deities, these giants of intellect…it was obvious that this changed your life; obvious that it cast you out of the wretched day-to-day struggle…good God! that at last you got to stroll up to that high point where everything was just a single, unobstructed view and you didn't have to deal with any of this crap anymore…What wouldn't I have given to be able to occupy his place…

Pšeničnik coughed…he pressed a black-bordered handkerchief to his mouth…"It's my lungs," he said…"consumption quite possibly," and then he dabbed his face with the cloth…But it couldn't have been bad…as long as the cough was that short and compact, close to the mouth…maybe he was just imagining it…I could have talked to him for several hours about lungs…a year in hospital in Basel and a year at the Langenbrück sanatorium in the canton of Urach…Comfort leads minor illnesses astray into worse ones, precisely the way it seduces you into scheming and talking drivel…He should have seen Vati…the way he would double over when he had an attack, lose his breath and his ability to see, and how we then had to shove him literally halfway out the attic window so he could gasp for a few stray gusts of fresh air… But there was something else on display on his shelves…all of the first editions of the turn-of-the-century poets Dragotin Kette, Josip Murn, Simon Gregorčič and Anton Aškerc…by the publisher Kleynmayer & Bamberg…all those brownish, unbound editions with the big type face and uncut pages that you would see in the display windows of used book stores…for instance, at bearded Mr. Sever's store on Old Square…"I'm toying with the idea of, you know, establishing a literary circle. We'd meet in that antechamber." He showed it to me...it was the same room I'd come through earlier...with figurines, a big table with a woolen tablecloth, the chandelier...and a window that offered an unusual view of Wolf Street...you saw the corners of buildings as if at broken right angles...Anyone who lived in this kind of luxury and with those kinds of connections could establish whatever he wanted...if I had been him, I would have founded something, too... anything. "I know some fellows who write...a girl who lives on the Poljane embankment...We could meet here and read our poems... stories, too, of course...discuss things. Urška would serve us fruit juice..." Oh, it'll go fine even without the grape juice, I said and waved it aside...Suddenly we heard a groan from the room next door...it was Mr. Ukmar..."Hold on, I'll introduce you," he said...He knocked on the door and led me in...this was a genuine hunting-lodge room, light and dark at the same time...there he sat at a bureau, wrapped in a blanket...nearly a hundred years old, poorly shaven, ill disposed, with a cap on his bare head and sullen..."Baron," Pšeničnik called out loudly, "let me introduce my friend, a young writer, so you won't wonder who's walking around in the next room." There was a greeting...followed by the crackle of saliva in his mouth...*"B'jour, b'jour."* That was in French. I examined his face from up close...all wrinkles and stubble...but still, a fine face, not revolting at all...almost feminine, like an old lady's...gray, utterly gray eyes...he was staring at me, but not as an old person would...No, he wasn't falling for Lado's claim that I was some sort of writer...There were rifles and antlers hung on the walls...but what drew my attention most was the window...

What a view that was, of all three white bridges at once and of the black figures of people walking across them...all of them like black paper cut-outs, with even their facial features so clear in their walnut brown color that it seemed I was looking through a magnifying glass instead of a window pane...It was indeed something extraordinary, especially this height...ten feet off the ground...like in my dreams when I looked out from the basket of a low-flying hot-air balloon...

I would visit Lado every week, if I hadn't already walked him home after school...Each time their cook Urška, in her old-fashioned kitchen, would boil me up some juice made from dried fruit and peelings. Each week, I got a mug full of hot juice that both warmed me and rinsed my stomach...Urška would heat up her metal hair curlers in the big brick oven...The baron's niece Katarina, an exceptionally taciturn girl who lacked a title of nobility and lived on the next floor up, which one reached through a locked cage gate...would cut Lado's hair and curl it with hot tongs...which was how I found out that he didn't have naturally curly locks. I sat on a bench in the entryway while he perched on a stool in the kitchen and had Katarina curl that shock of hair that flopped down over the left side of his forehead, obscuring somewhat his eyes and an ear like a curtain of ebony...Add a fez and you'd have an Egyptian fellah. But it was undeniable...even at first glance, he looked like a poet...lithe, pale, handsome, with jet black hair, always impeccably dressed and shod...Out on the street, Pšeničnik was constantly having to tip his hat and respond to greetings right and left, linger with one acquaintance and then chat with another...On one occasion, the acquaintance in question was Pater Chrysostomos stepping out of a phone booth on the Triple Bridge…Pšeničnik chatted with him as though they were equals, if not a shade condescendingly…on another occasion, he was stopped by a tall, older woman with a voice like a man's and dressed in a woolen suit with a skirt that reached to the ground…"Who was that?" I asked him. "Manica Komanova," he said, turning his nose up. "'The Children's Friend.' 'The Aunt with a Basket.'" Well, what about that! I'd already read her stories to Gisela. And she'd liked them…Once, while out walking, he lingered for a while with a gentleman wearing a small hat on his head and a pince-nez on his nose…"Professor Janez Tomažič, the German literature scholar," he explained to me afterward…The next time it was a refined gentleman in the middle of Congress Square…a man of the world from head to toe…with a cane, wearing light gray gloves and puttees…I stood off to one side, near a musical instrument store, while Lado chatted with him. When they at last parted, Lado didn't tell me who the man was, although he had struck me as familiar…So I asked Pšeničnik…"Lajovic, the composer. And academician," he replied, somewhat put off…That's how we'd go zig-zagging down the street…in the town center or as soon as we approached some public building…the opera, a church, the Academy, the university, a gallery… here would come somebody whom Lado knew personally. I played the role of the barbarian at his side…the delinquent…and I was even dressed for the part…jacket, scarf, fur hat, shorts with an elastic band sewed inside the legs…so-called "shtrousers," to which I'd attach leggings that were already heavily patched around the knees and heels…

At last, the day came when Pšeničnik took me along to visit the great poet Oton Župančič…it was going to have to be a short visit, he kept drubbing into me, because the famous man's health was in a delicate state…I was beside myself…I washed up, combed my hair, shined my shoes, put on Vati's trousers…but everything in my wardrobe was so pathetic and careworn that I didn't look even close to presentable…Lado had a freshly curled shock of hair and wore a nice striped shirt with a bow tie…a vest and a pocket watch on a chain with an ivory Egyptian head on the cover…the baron's watch, which Katarina had lent him…Fine, he could be dolled up however he wanted to be…as slim, handsome and tall as he was, he'd look good in anything…even a tarp or an old gunny sack…while I, squat, undernourished, with a face like a potato, wouldn't have been helped by a bespoke suit, much less one that came straight off the rack…oh, I'd been able to size myself up as I went past empty display windows… my body had long since become my secret sore point…At least now, as I accompanied Lado on his visit, it was as though there weren't any war…it was a splendid day, the kind that fills you with confidence and contentment…I was hurrying to keep pace with Lado's black briefcase with its gold lock, and the bag, suspended by a bow from his index finger, that contained a gift of pork cracklings that he was taking along for the poet. I was just afraid that some unforeseen event – an air-raid alarm, a random search or some coincidence – might get in our way and keep us from arriving at our destination on time…We went to the Schleimer Building…which housed a deluxe sanatorium…a smooth, modern building…without those superfluous gewgaws that cause you to break your knuckles…with a long, wrought-iron fence consisting of lance-like rods...and forsythias in bloom on both sides of the courtyard...with two cement pots in front of the entrance that were so big I could have crawled into them...Pšeničnik rang the bell first, then knocked...then he went inside, closing the door behind him, to find out how the poet was doing before announcing me... I was a bit worried that maybe he'd tricked me and on his previous visit hadn't mentioned to the poet at all that he'd like to bring someone along next time...Suddenly I had an urge to get out of there...Then he opened the door a crack. "You can come in," he said...The room I entered was bright, if furnished with monk-like austerity. Behind a smooth table beneath a big, modern window, wearing a blue brocade dressing gown sat the poet himself...spindly Oton Župančič with spectacles perched on his beak-like nose and rumpled hair over his high, darkened forehead...The poet that all the textbooks were full of...whose portraits hung in every school hallway...and sometimes even appeared on the first page of the newspapers...whose poems weren't just published in the *Morning*, the *Slovene*, or featured in book-store display windows, but also got printed on the leaflets and mimeographed newspapers that the partisans scattered around town...A great man...the people's favorite...as victorious on one side as he was on the other...in town as well as in the forest...with the Whites and the Reds, and the anti-Whites and the anti-Reds... which was virtually impossible, because they'd been slaughtering each other forever...I'd seen it with my own eyes...those rumbles out on St. Martin's Road...when they'd attack if one side so much as looked different at the other...A raw, bloody history..."Come closer, come closer," the great poet called out to me in his deep voice…"Introduce yourself," Pšeničnik told me…I almost passed out…I could scarcely say my name…I reached my hand out and felt his light, slender, veined hand in mine…He shook it, smiling at me through his spectacles like Vati with his blue eyes, which were as round as chocolates…I took a seat behind him…on a chair that Lado pointed me to…that spun around like a piano stool, and because I was shaking, it turned even more…first left, then right…it had a mind of its own…The two of them were engaged in conversation…about what, I had no idea, because my ears were buzzing so much…all I could hear was Lado promising to bring him some flour next time from his brother in Lower Carniola, at the same time as he handed him the bag of cracklings for Mrs. Župančič…Then he took some of his new poems out of his briefcase for the great poet to read and critique by his next visit… All I could do was listen, because I was incapable of following their conversation – his deep, thundering voice as it echoed in that small, white-painted room…or sneak glances at him…his wrinkled, gaunt, birdlike face…which was just like his pictures…except here he was alive and moving…his wide mouth and arched nose, which didn't have a bunch of gray bristles growing out of it like Vati's…speaking of which, Vati's trousers were here, on me, also visiting…Although Vati was older than him, or perhaps Vati was younger, but I couldn't work the numbers out for sheer nervousness…I looked at him, but couldn't memorize his face as a whole…only that big crease by the nose, and the furrows and spots dotting his forehead…I did manage to figure something out…that he didn't have a brocade scarf, as he seemed to have in his pictures, but that it was just the high, wide collar of his light blue silk dressing gown turned up...and that the bow around his neck was in fact a black bow tie, like the one Pšeničnik wore...His head turned from profile to facing me and he asked, "So you write stories, do you sir?"...Sir! And stories! My God...It was as though some famous old monument had turned to address me...I couldn't comprehend the question at first...it got flung in my face like a stone gets flung into rapids and carried away...I blurted out, "Yeah"...and then corrected myself to "Yes, sir..." Who in the world had ever just sat like this chatting with the great god of poetry?...he was more than a high commissioner and a prince-bishop combined...I blushed and got anxious, because I'd reacted so stupidly...Yet he turned toward me again. "My friend Lado tells me that your family came from Switzerland before the war?"...He looked at me somewhat mockingly through his horn-rimmed glasses...sure, Switzerland was tiny and it didn't have any wars, so people were always making fun of it...yet also curiously, as though I were some sort of rare bird. I felt my head swell up like the reservoir of a spirit lamp...oh, if only Mrs. Komar were here, she would have known what to say..."That's right, in 1938," I said...Then at last...Lado got up and adjusted his hair...thank god!... and then there was a knock at the door, and a young, blond fellow came in whose cap barely stayed put on top of his thick, curly hair. He greeted the poet cheerily, almost as if they were old friends...and nodded to Pšeničnik, who nodded back, as if the two of them were friends and, at the same time, servants to the great man...The only unusual thing about the blond guy, who was widely taken to be a traitor...was that he was dressed in a brand new uniform of the Home Guard Legionnaires, with a patch on his sleeve showing the blue eagle against a white coat of arms...He had brought some sort of paper scroll for the poet with a carnation wrapped up inside...the look in his eyes seemed clear, bright and open...and the poet was obviously happy to see him. "Oh, it's you! I've been expecting you." That sort of welcome from the great man, who in all likelihood had been a Falcon in his younger years, both confused and intrigued me...But the visit was already coming to an end and I hardly had any breath left in my lungs...At last, when we were outside and had turned the corner, I asked Pšeničnik who the young guy in the uniform was. "He's a poet," Lado answered. "He's written a wreath of sonnet wreaths, if you can imagine that!"...I couldn't quite put it all together...assembling sonnets was a science verging on mathematics and demanded the utmost intellectual resources of a person...

On April 20th, the city was full of flags...At the stadium where the papal nuncio had once held an open-air mass...the new army of the Slovene Home Guard swore its oath of allegiance...General Leon Rupnik, the Slovene Pétain, was there...two steps behind him was Gauleiter Rösser...and far out in front of both of them was Bishop Rožman with two canons of the cathedral...The bleachers were empty...there hadn't been any soccer games for a long time and the gymnastic tournaments organized as part of Dopolavore had ended... Ten-thousand men swore an oath to the leader of the Great German Reich, Adolf Hitler, on his birthday...and kissed the new Slovene flag with its blue eagle against the white coat of arms...The new flags began appearing on the fronts of buildings alongside the German ones with their hooked crosses...a sort of forced hybridization, a devil's brood...if the former seemed flag-like and authentic enough, the latter were simply harbingers of death...a sort of banner borne by crusading bowmen and lancers...There wasn't a soul in the streets... Around eight o'clock, a parade started to form...high school students marched down Bleiweis Street...carrying at the head of the parade a long, narrow sheet of canvas with an inscription in blue: "Long Live the Home Guard Army"...General Leon Rupnik stood on the balcony of the government building...waving his glove...the young people chanted in chorus "Long live the Home Guard army!...Long live General Rupnik!...Long live President Rupnik!"...At least a few of them actually supported him...maybe around two hundred!...they showed some guts, because participating in this parade really was in nobody's interests...it couldn't have frightened the Reds or the anti-Whites particularly...At noon, the ceremonial review of the infantry and cavalry took place...everyone in my school had to line up along Tyrševa Street...I was acutely aware of how few people there were... some student patrolmen, anticommunism instructors, assigned us our places, but our ranks were thin...we were the crowd lining the street, but just one person deep...on both sides of the street, all the way from the stadium to the main post office...On Ajdovščina Street they had them standing so far apart...that you could have stuck at least five more people in between them...and I could see way down Our Lady Street...the tracks, the signs, the church, the retaining wall by the railway overpass...the Bellevue Hotel atop Šiška Hill, where the Gestapo academy was, all bathed in sunlight...Some of my schoolmates tried to slip away...while others tried to make themselves invisible behind the backs of their neighbors, behind buildings, in entryways, between their hats and upturned collars...nobody knew if the person next to him or across the boulevard might be spying for the Reds or the Whites...any single one of them might be an informant, a time bomb...some of them pretended to be curious bystanders... shifting their weight in the cold from one foot to the other and anxiously craning their necks to see to the end of the street...First came the standard bearers...two riders on horseback...this was something real...two battle flags, a German and a Slovene one, both of them torn and stained...the first one god knows where, at the Eastern front, most likely...and the second at some White Guard outposts, in rectories, churches, or castles...possibly Grahovo, where France Balantič, the young poet, had perished in a house on fire...Next came the honor guard marching in parade step...a unit of German officers wearing helmets, adorned with ribbons and Iron Crosses...the SS Führerkorps marching with bared sabers that they held close to their chests...So upright and precise! Like one man!..."That they are," two fellows said, doubled over from the cold and the pangs of their empty stomachs...All together now in parade formation: legs up, legs down...despite the uneven paving stones and the streetcar switch at the crossroads. *Click! clack! Click! clack!*...Not fast, like Carmen at the opera...and not slow, either...but medium speed...just one perpetual right angle, performed by heart...All together now! I could watch them for a whole hour and not get bored... Like a comet flying past... "Our country boys are up next," a man who had been scratching himself – for fleas? for lice? – said disparagingly... Not quite!... The first to appear was an officer on horseback... the chief of the general staff. It's not that they were marching badly, it was just that they didn't have the same impact, since they weren't wearing boots, and they didn't have helmets, just caps, and made out of inferior fabric at that, the same as their uniforms. They marched, squad after squad. Two or three people would applaud, perhaps under duress... everyone preferred looking down the road and across the street to see who was there... At that instant, a bunch of flowers dropped onto the tracks... lots of them, not just a few... everybody looked up, then down... who was throwing the flowers?... had the better-dressed types been hiding them behind their backs, under their coats, or had they dropped from the windows?... The units marched past... Assault troops, sappers, engineers, the unadorned infantry... one march step after the other... all picture perfect. The young, the older, the old... All of them terribly thin, poorly shaven, peasants, workers too, students, farm boys... I examined their faces... somnolent, bored... Next up was the cavalry... A black horse in the lead... followed by a bay. Rifles slung over their shoulders... their heads covered by helmets... As I made my way to Lado's place, a squad of cavalry came clopping down Wolf Street... a young girl standing all alone amid the wide pavement of the Triple Bridge... aside from me and a bootblack there wasn't a soul... shouted "Hurrah!"... and ran out toward the officer riding a white horse... she reached up on tip-toe as he bent down and tucked her bouquet under his Sam

Browne belt... The cavalry went clopping across St. Mary's Square out onto Miklošič Street, which was deserted... No rally followed... Toward evening, Sergeant Mitić showed up at our door... he came to greet all of us, but especially Vati, wearing his officer's uniform of the new Slovene army with its silver second lieutenant's epaulettes... Soldiers, bureaucrats, clerics... have no problem making the transition from one flag to another...

The new flag was hanging over the entrance to the headquarters of the Home Guard Army, located in the former Rotary Club palace, and there was a soldier in its guardhouse, which had been painted in the Slovene tricolor... officers, messengers, and enlisted men were rushing in and out... At last, it was time for Julijan and me to volunteer for the new army... We went to the enlistment office, which was in a tiny storefront next to the big Bata shoe store... where a flag with the blue eagle reached down to the sidewalk... and on the wall outside, there were posters showing a Home Guard pointing his finger at passers-by, "You... have you enlisted in the Slovene Home Guard Army?" The building had two entrances... we first went in the wrong one. An older sergeant was sitting in the darkened shop, which had posters and wrapping paper stuck to its display windows... it was hard to make out his face in the gloom... We said that we were ready to enlist in the Home Guard Army... "How old are you?" he immediately shot back... We told him... in seven months I was going to be sixteen, and in less time, just three months, Julijan would turn eighteen... "Bring me signed, written permission from both of your parents, or at least one... You won't need written permission once you turn eighteen, but you won't be eligible, even with your parents' permission, until you're sixteen."…We went back outside…deflated. What were we going to do?…Julijan wouldn't have any problem joining the army, his parents would give their permission without his having to beg… and, in the worst case, he'd be in uniform in just three months…But what about me?…I didn't know what to do. Naturally I was going to have to finagle my way in as soon as I could…I decided to give mother a blank piece of paper to sign, then I would add the missing text… "I, the undersigned, Elisabeth Kovačič née Faist, give my permission for my son…born on…in…currently residing at…to enlist in the Slovene Home Guard Army…" Mother didn't know Slovene…and she didn't even know what kinds of requirements the school placed on its students…so this was going to be a cinch…I gave her a blank sheet of stationery that Margrit in Basel had written something on… after blocking out how much space I'd need for the text…*Was ist das, was ich unterschreiben soll?* * she asked…*Etwas für die Schule…daß du mir erlaubst, in die Ferien zu gehen…* ** I said. She called Vati over…what did he think about this…Vati had no idea and showed no interest, either…*Ich unterschreibe kein leeres Blatt,* *** mother said…*Wie du willst…dann kann ich halt nicht in die Ferien gehen,* **** I said angrily, tearing up the sheet of paper…Incredible! What could I do to get

*What is this you want me to sign?

**Something for school, saying you give me permission to go on a school trip.

***I refuse to sign a blank sheet of paper.

****It's up to you. That just means I can't go on our school trip.

away from home?...When Julijan went back to the enlistment office, they told him they didn't need his signed statement of permission yet, because he first had to submit a written request and include his birth certificate...In wartime, there only needs to be a year's difference in age...less, a few months...between you and your friend, and that's enough to determine completely different fates for each of you... There was the real question...if I was also going to have to submit a request...of just how I was supposed to come up with my birth certificate...Mother guarded our documents like the apple of her eye... they were our proof of existence...a sheaf of the most important ones which she kept in her purse was always kept hidden in her immediate vicinity...but where?...I didn't dare hand Vati a blank sheet of paper to sign...he was so unresourceful, absent-minded and helpless that I didn't have the heart to deceive him, just like I couldn't have brought myself to trick Gisela...But then there was mother's handwriting... that dense, slanted, ornate Gothic script that she'd inherited straight out of the thirteenth century from Bishop Ulfilas...there was no way I could forge that...any attempt to reproduce it would have screamed forgery...One early afternoon when I got home from school, in hopes of taking her by surprise, out of the blue I set my math notebook in front of her, opened to a blank page for her to sign opposite a page of my homework..."*Warum?* "* she asked..."*Weil ich auf der anderen Seite die mathematische Aufgabe ungenügend geschrieben habe...*"** "*Dann*

*What's this for?
**Because I got a bad grade on that assignment.

unterschreibe ich mich halt unter der Note."* And she signed in the margin of the assignment itself...

Good grief...what was I going to have to do to be able to get away from there? To keep from leaving Julijan in the lurch! One evening, our cousin Minka came to visit again, bringing us a jar of fat from the farm...They've killed Uncle Karel, were the first words out of her mouth. What?...We all jumped to our feet, each of us remembered Karel for something...mother, Clairi, Gisela and I, all of us for the same thing...but Vati...started to blink and tremble, Karel was his brother, the baby of the family...They axed him to death...he'd been found on the steps down to the cellar...outside the door facing the well...Somebody chopped his head off...and dastardly as they were, they had hacked away at him before that!...as he lay on the ground! bursting his stomach ulcer and causing him to bleed to death...Who is responsible? Vati asked, the color gone from his face...Not her father, Uncle Jožef, or her brothers Ciril or Ivan...no, that would have been going too far! even though they hadn't gotten along, because they were Reds...Ivan and Ciril reportedly even officers, heroes!... Some people were even saying his step-son had done it. His step-son? That's right, Joži...Karel was seeing some woman from St. Jernej, who had an illegitimate, adult son...she and Karel had been planning to get married...it was probably her son, who had always been good for nothing...he wanted to get his hands on the property fast...that's what they were saying...Now nobody knew where he was, in order to

*Then why not sign next to the grade?

· 284

question him...maybe he'd joined the partisans in the forest, or was hiding who knows where...Whether we liked him or not, none of us wanted him dead...we'd bring him back to life if we could...But Vati! He began sewing like someone obsessed, then he would just sit with his hands in his lap and look out at the castle...so downtrodden and maidenly slight that we just let him be. "*Das haben die Roten angestellt,*" mother said. "*So wie mit dem russischen Kaiser...Sie sind immer kaltblütig und im gleichen Moment gefühlsvoll wie die Messalina...*" *

I went over to Julijan's house...he had gotten permission, his parents had signed it for him, and he had already passed the preliminary conscription. He would be joining the army next month...he showed me his blue army ID. When the heavy fighting began, he reassured me, I wouldn't need any papers...any army post would take me in with open arms...It was just two months to the end of the school year... I composed a request and a letter of permission and forged Vati's signature without the least twinge of conscience...and if I was really good, they'd grant my plea to let me serve in the same unit as Julijan... Julijan went with me...he and his army ID would lend me support if things got complicated...This time there were other, younger soldiers on duty at the desks in the front office...sitting under a portrait of Rupnik and the blue eagle coat of arms...moments before we walked in they had been pelting each other with spitballs, eating from their mess tins, pushing the drawers in and out...all of them right at that

*This is the communists' doing. Just like they did with the tsar. They're always so cold-blooded, and at the same time as sentimental as Messalina.

age when they relished making fun of kids who were sixteen, like me…
Some of them had already been through a lot…fought in battles…had
medals dangling from their chest…with their first trials by fire behind
them…at age 19, 20, 23…They studied my request…and the signed
permission…they didn't ask if I had my birth certificate. They were
very decent, I have to hand it to them, and they recognized Julijan by
sight…"Did your father sign this?" one of them asked. I was standing
at attention. "Yes, sir!" I said…"Fine…we'll send final notification
to your home address…" We went back outside. Had I succeeded? I
waited one week, two weeks, three…and nothing…then at the end
of May, I suddenly got sick.

SUDDENLY I BEGAN LOSING my balance, came down with a fever
and started to vomit…All at once, the whole world turned chaotic, and
every object became much too vivid…the sides of a street car came to
life like membranes…a truck with its huge gray tires came bounding
toward me like an elephant…everything was transformed, and I along
with it…I was amazed at how readily this took place, without any
involvement from me…Wow, I might even enjoy living like that, if
only it didn't hurt so much…At the clinic the doctor said, this is probably your stomach…but still, I want you in the hospital. I went there
with mother. I could barely walk…We waited for a long time at the
hospital's registration desk, which was bedecked with so many metal
plates that it looked like we were in some traffic-licensing bureau,
until finally the doctor on duty led us into her office…Mother immediately…in the doorway, all agitated, and in German, of course…

told her what was wrong with me...and the haggard doctor, whose hair was combed flat against her head, turned gruff...She tapped my belly..."Does this hurt?" or "How about here?" She handled me so jerkily that I started to hurt everywhere...She bent her face, hard and sallow, down over me...her hatred for Germans, for mother, for me was so palpable that there was no need to explain it...I felt the same hatred for dark-skinned, hirsute people...I just didn't understand why she was treating me like some officer weighed down with iron crosses and medals...which made her seem kind of slow and juvenile to me...She prescribed some tablets and chamomile tea and sent me home...That night as I lay on the table, I vomited the tea back up...the only thing I'd been able to get down...everything I had eaten for the past several months, the entire year, god knows how long, came flying out of me by the quart...I couldn't lie down or stand up or lean against the wall...I just clutched at my stomach and barely made it through until morning, the end of curfew, when the streetcar bells started to jingle again...Mother and I got back on the streetcar outside Krisper's...with me cradling my belly like some huge head of cabbage...A very dignified, old, gray-haired lady gave me her seat...my head and everything around me was spinning, but this kindness touched me, and once seated, I started to look all around the packed car for the little old lady, to thank her, if only with a nod of the head...In the emergency room this time, there was a male doctor, thank god...who immediately, without a moment's hesitation, sent me to the new part of the hospital...a three-story building that wasn't painted yellow like the rest but grayish white...I leaned on mother as we spent an eternity making our way over the winding paths of the park to the building…"*Über diese junge Doktorin von gestern werde ich mich bei dem Krankenhausvorstand beklagen…*," mother began to swear. "*Und wenn ich von Pontius zu Pilatus laufen muß…*"* "*Nein, mach das bitte lieber nicht,*"** I begged her. I was afraid that if she complained about the doctor, the whole Red rabble would come crashing down on us…and blow us away…her, me, Vati, Clairi and Gisela, like dandelion fluff… The glassed-in waiting room was packed full of people…someone put a thermometer in my mouth…and the mercury rose…102, 105…106 degrees…with a temperature that high I could well be dead…they took me into a room…ripped my clothes off…and put a linen shirt on me that was split down the front…mother stood in the doorway in her flower-patterned dress and her white hat from Basel, flushed red and crying…I felt sorry for her to the depths of my soul, and I could see that now, with death threatening, as we said good-bye to each other, she really loved me…They quickly put me on an operating table, and one of the assistants placed anesthetic over my mouth and nose…"Count out loud for as long as you can…" I counted one, two, three…up to seven. The doctors were washing their hands, I could hear a stream of water, interrupted by hands being placed under it…the stream became a waterfall whose roar got louder and

---

*I'm going to complain to the hospital administration about that young doctor yesterday, no matter if it means I have to run to the ends of the earth.

**No, please don't do that.

louder…curiously, the sound of the waterfall retreated at the same time as it got closer and engulfed me…

Suddenly, out of nowhere, I woke up…had I been dreaming?… I was thirsty…somebody's hand was holding out a small glass of fresh water…it was dewy from the tiny, cold droplets all over it…I reached for it, but the glass pulled away…and laughed. It was a young man dressed in white, with a narrow, dark, suntanned face…I must have been dreaming…"Give it to me," I told him. "You want this glass? Some water?…Nah-ah!"…"Just one drink," I pleaded…"Water! The bottle! The glass!"…"Forget it!…You lying scum…Black hand!"…I didn't want to be beholden to him. "Clown! Syphilitic! Stinker!"…One blow after the other! "Traitor!" he shouted. "White guard! German pig!"…"Lickspittle!" I answered him. "Bandit! Fartface!"…"Little shit!" he roared…"Big shit!" I threw back in his face. "Cockroach! Rat!"…It must have been audible miles away, I was howling so fiercely…A nurse…fat and red-faced…was adjusting something near my head. "What are you muttering?" she asked. "I'm answering that troll over there," I said. "But there's nobody else here," she said, along with a few other mundane, sensible things. "Worm!" the demon shouted…"Prick! Bastard! Asshole!" I caught sight of my foul-mouthed abuser and woke up…He had his hair cut hedgehog-style and his face was reddish…he was wearing a striped hospital gown and holding a glass of water at the foot of the bed…as he grinned, he exposed every tooth in his head…and he held out the glass…"Here you go, have a drink"…and pulled it away again…It was hot…the window on the far side of the beds was open...I was parched with thirst...and felt terrible pain somewhere in my abdomen...There was a whole cluster of flies perched on my bedspread at the level of my stomach...so thick you would have thought it was a muff made of mink fur, or pine marten... I couldn't move my arm to brush them away, so I tried blowing... two or three rose up, but then settled back down...*brrrrr*...like miniature whirligigs...and merged with the others...brown head, black thorax...white flesh, if you cut them open...little modular bellies, transparent wings...I had never really considered them vermin...they were simply bugs to me, the same as the ones living in trees, wherever I was...in some room my parents had locked me in...they kept me company...they were house pets, room pets I could play with...and I hardly ever found them disgusting...I remember how, at breakfast in the green house on Gerbergäsli when they flew in circles over the table, I would daub some marmalade with a knife on the edge of my plate so they could have breakfast with me...Today I know: a childhood without animals is no childhood at all...

I stank like the plague...When the nurses came on their rounds and the fat nurse and young one changed my dressing, I could see all the pus I was producing...my appendix had burst...and its thick, yellow discharge stank even to me...a rubber tube jutted up out of my belly, with a safety cap on top, to prevent it from slipping into my stomach, inside the wound...there was a regular tunnel down there...and the stuff would come surging in waves out of the little hose, then congeal on my abodomen...I was parched...I crept to the foot of the bed...the young, sunburnt patient holding the glass of water was still taunting me, as if in a dream, only now he was vivid and palpable...he was the only one in the ward who could get up and walk around...the other, bedridden patients laughed at his jokes, which also involved me...They were probably laughing at me because of my family...mother, Clairi and Gisela, who would come to visit and talk to me in German...not that I could say anything back to them..."Water, water," I ranted, idiot! until that big, fat nun who weighed roughly a ton came lumbering into the room..."Quiet!" she barked, as though I'd plied her with some obscenity...and, let's say, pulled her skirt up over her head!..."I've told you a thousand times, you mustn't drink any water..." She dragged me back toward the head of the bed with such force that my whole body exploded. No, this was no Sister Rafaela, or Kajetana, or mother superior from the Children's Home, and not even that old custodian from the conference of St. Vincent de Paul, let alone a nurse from Urach...This was some crude, overblown toad disguised as a nun...some produce huckstress from the public market...At last, I managed to raise my arm and drive the flies away... they weren't used to me putting up a fight...on my first try I managed to catch a whole fistful of them, scraggly as weeds and buzzing malevolently...they escaped through all my fingers at once up to the trapeze bar, where they reassembled immediately...on the fourth or fifth day, the orderly placed a half-filled cup of fruit juice on the nightstand... that jokester at the foot of my bed had stopped taunting me with water...now, every two hours I was allowed to swallow a teaspoon of it...if I took a sip of the juice, the old godmother would instantly come barging in and take the cup away...somebody in the ward must have been diligently providing her with reports... Whether children or adults, when people are sick, they're all juvenile... Back when I'd visited Vati in the hospital before the war... the patients had seemed so tame, not dangerous or aggressive at all, the way healthy people are, and that made me feel comfortable around them... it also made me want to become a doctor, because that way I'd have a peaceful life guaranteed... but when I looked around me now! at the ones in this room!... Whenever I needed to use the bedpan or urinal and rang for the nurse... and a red light over the door lit up, like in the hospital in Basel back in 1933, it was very similar, the fat nun lifted me up like a log and I'd groan, causing the whole room to laugh or get mad at me... If it was the young nurse coming to help, I'd recognize her more modest, white-clad profile through the glass and relax... She was more accessible... even though she never spoke to me, she was more careful about lifting me up, and it didn't hurt.

Finally, ten days passed, and I exchanged my first words with the other patients... there were six of them in the ward with me... Vati came to visit, and we chatted... and this was the first time they realized I was Slovene, because until then my only visitors had been Clairi, mother and Gisela... Vati was dressed in his best blue suit, which he had ironed only an hour before... he stank up half the room with the remains of old food in the suit coat that he'd steamed up... He brought me a piece of a cake that mother had baked... but how had she managed to get the eggs and baking powder for it?... The other patients became friendlier toward me... the young demon that had been continually taunting me with the glass of water...had I dreamed it or was it real?...even came over and sat on the edge of my bed to exchange a few words with me...I explained to him, and by extension to all the others, that we weren't Germans, but Swiss, in order to soften his scorn, insolence, hatred...By day fifteen I'd managed to get my stick legs out of bed for the first time...and the whole parquet floor began to dance under my feet...The young guy rushed over, took hold of me and taught me to walk...He asked me where Vati was from... Cegelnica near Novo Mesto, I told him. "Then he's a lowlander!" he exclaimed, beside himself. "I'm from Trebnje!" His face brightened... taking on those familiar, local village features that made people look slightly bovine and crazy...I'd liked him a lot more before that, when he was playing the devil...

Then, once three weeks had passed, I was allowed to bathe for the first time. The big nurse led me to the bathroom...full of all kinds of doors, wooden ones, glass ones, all labeled...but cold, which was very nice, because outside it was hot. She turned on the faucet and ordered me to undress...completely, and in front of her, at that...I refused to budge. "Let's go!" she said..."I'm not getting undressed!" I said..."What is this?" she shouted, standing arms akimbo...She came straight toward me...to her I was worth less than the broom in the corner, a scrap of paper on the floor...I clutched onto my hospital gown and shirt. "Get out..." "You little toad, you snot...you're telling me what to do?"..."Get out!" I shouted...Damned two-ton harpy! "You've done it now...I'm going to get the doctor...and the director…and they'll show you a thing or two!" It was then that I exploded…"Get out, you old witch!" I'd lost all control…I grapped a sponge, a rag, some soap off the bath stand…and started throwing all of it at her…*Boom! crash! smack!* at the door! at her wimple! at her gigantic boobs!…She slammed the door shut behind her…and went bellowing down the hall in her bass…I took my clothes off and climbed into the water…outside it was quiet…a few minutes passed in the cramped bathroom, then the door opened…and the thin, gray, smooth-shaven doctor stood there with his lips in a pout…"Listen to me, you little snot: what kind of behavior is this? How dare you attack the reverend sister?…You ought to be grateful to us for saving your life!"…I looked back down and kept scrubbing away…I knew who he was…that smooth, sporting face of a Falcon…today he'd be called a liberal, a coalition member, present everywhere and nowhere at the same time…You can't get anywhere with people like that… it's as though you were talking to a damp wall…"Once you've finished bathing, we're going to dimiss you at once. Report to the ward manager at the end of the hall. There's no place in this hospital for thankless brats like you…" "You're a doctor…you know!" His lips started to tremble…*brrr! brrr!*…the nerve of this little toad! I could tell he wanted to smack me…but then I would have splashed him… Once the staff at the far end of the hall changed my dressing…a completely different nurse and a different doctor, I was given a piece of paper that said I couldn't attend gym classes for three weeks…That was good news…a fascist named Buffarini was the gym teacher at school, a martinet in a black uniform who was always ordering us to do push-ups and more push-ups…with the exception of Požar, who was still regularly attending GIL…it was a huge pleasure to be able to shove my doctor's excuse in his face…For ten days, while the others were doing their push-ups, I just stood in the gym like a telegraph pole… On the last day of classes, a short, pale university student lectured to us about the dangers of communism…in the next school year, that was going to be a class all its own!…in the gymnasium, our catechism teacher Mr. Becele presented a slide show to the entire school about the desecration of churches…especially during the French revolution, when crowds carrying red flags marched through the streets. Then the Jacobins placed a naked woman of easy virtue on the altar to replace God…everybody strained their eyes to see her…but in front of the tabernacle, among the statues and candlesticks, all we could see was a white smudge…which was supposed to be that naked prostitute…

"Achtung! achtung! *Wehrmachtsender Laibach!*" *…the announcement came from Town Square at an unusual time of day… now there were loudspeakers, big trumpets affixed to the fronts of all public buildings, transmitting news from the radio, and now and then music…"Achtung!"…Instead of Beethoven's Pastorale Symphony coming from the speakers, the sirens began to wail… No, this wasn't an air-raid alarm. For that the sirens used a whole different signal. And then came the fanfares…"*Achtung! Achtung!* Attention, attention!"…Were they about to announce a victory?…

*Attention! Attention! This is the radio station of the German Army in Ljubljana.

but that was impossible...For the past two years, all they'd done was retreat...Kursk, Italy, Normandy, North Africa...the whole chain of fortresses encircling Europe...from the English Channel to the Apennine Mountains and Aegean Sea in the south and the Vistula River in the east, had fallen like dominos...Or was a separate peace with the Russians being announced? That would be possible...it was certainly talked about...Heads appeared atop the castle tower...the German crew occupying it. The loudspeaker on City Hall...on its balcony, amid the palm trees and flag poles, was too far away to hear...you had to be in Town Square...No, it wasn't a victory. *"Achtung! Achtung!"* There had been an assassination attempt against Hitler...at precisely 12:37 p.m....a time bomb. Everybody looked up. All the heads atop the tower had disappeared...hiding deep down in the castle...and suddenly there wasn't a single German soldier to be seen or heard anywhere...I ran home to share the news..."*Sie sagen aber nicht, ob er tot ist,*"* I said. Vati got up, wiping his hands on his smock...he began pacing the room...he was nervous..."*Wenn er nicht tot ist, wird es was schönes geben...,*"** mother said. It was toward the end of July and very hot...people were out swimming at the Point, the public pools, the Little Graben canal...not a soul in this paradise knew anything yet...shaken and in tears, schoolboys and girls from St. Vitus and Kranj carried bouquets of flowers to the monument to Hitler...But he wasn't dead...That evening over the loudspeaker...came his voice,

*But they're not saying if he's been killed.

**If he isn't dead, there is going to be hell to pay...

not some substitute's...Some officers had plotted a coup!...all of them had been caught...they would be marched in front of a court of the people...He announced a new offensive against Russia...a secret weapon: in the coming days, long-range rocket bombs would utterly destroy England...His voice soared with such menacing power, shook with the rage of a swarm of provoked hornets, bellowed with the hollow roar of a hurt lion, conveying a ferocity that made your hair stand on end..."*Jetzt wird es nicht mehr die geringste Ordnung in irgend etwas geben...*" mother said. "*Hätten sie ihn umgebracht, so hätte Ordnung geherrscht! Jetzt wo er mit heiler Haut davongekommen ist, sind wir für immer in die Unordnung geraten...*" * It was a beautiful summer in spite of the war...out in the wetlands near Rudnik, I cut peat...in an area where there were no land mines or barbed wire...I carried it home in bags to dry in the sun outside the woodshed...it would make excellent heating fuel in the winter...The newspaper had photos of the subterranean conference room that had been blown up at Hitler's headquarters in East Prussia...more than eighty feet underground... with libraries, a map room, fans for ventilation...two or three floors full of typists and Telefunken operators...all of it in ruins...Hitler... slightly singed, deafened by the blast, holding onto his injured arm... showed Mussolini...haggard and pale, in a black coat and black hat... the destruction...the walls, the tables, the ceilings...So this is what

---

*That's the end of any order in anything anymore...If they'd managed to kill him, we'd have order again. But now that he's come out of this unscathed, our lives are going to be unending chaos....

had become of the both of them...their own people had turned against them...and yet the war went on, regardless...The V-1 and V-2 rockets were falling on London...six thousand killed, 75,000 buildings destroyed...The Anglo-Americans were breaking through the Atlantic wall...in France, the French were settling accounts with each other... collaborationists were being shot on a massive scale, they were being killed one by one on every street corner, lynched at every streetcar stop, their eyes gouged out, their heads cut off...the newspaper had big photos of that...columns of Anglo-Americans were on their way toward Tuscany...ten thousand airborne troops parachuted into Holland...the Germans shot them in mid-air...there was an uprising in Warsaw...the Germans launched a counter-offensive in the Ardennes Forest...Budapest resisted the Russians...everyone – children, women and old people – participated in the defense of the city as the Mongols surrounded it...a noose was tightening around Japan as young Kamikazes began barreling into the decks of convoys around the Philippine Islands...We saw them in the *Wochenschau*,* preparing to take off...bowing to a portrait of the emperor, tying white strips of cloth around their foreheads...clambering into their little planes, human torpedoes...all of them young, barely twenty years old... There were also photos of Stag Hollow...a mass burial site...where the bodies of Home Guards bound together with barbed wire and then executed by the partisans had been unearthed. After the mass grave at Katyn, where the Germans had discovered the bodies of 5,000

*German wartime newsreels

Polish officers shot by the Russians at the start of the war, this was the biggest massacre yet...*"Aber die Deutschen sind nicht besser,"* mother said...*"Ich habe gehört, daß sie in den KZ-Lagern die Juden mit Giftgas ersticken lassen und aus ihrer Haut Lampenschirmen machen..."* * But that was just hearsay...this about Katyn and Stag Hollow filled a whole newspaper and covered whole posters with photographs...a huge ditch full of skeletons and still-decomposing corpses in uniform...the soldiers standing at the edge of the ditch looked as tiny as gnomes...a huge mound of excavated dirt...whole flocks of sparrows and ants... you had to be a bird to pick out the tiny worms...the whole sky was flapping...a regular feast day!...with robins, titmice and crows too... The end of the war was approaching...you could reach out and touch it...the front door to the house was left open, everyone was silent, nobody nodded to anyone on the steps anymore, and even Hirol had stopped making his threats...a settling of accounts was approaching that would send thousands of bodies hurtling into pits.

Helmuth jens was a sergeant in the medical corps. He was part of the crew assigned to the castle...He and Clairi had met in a drugstore...Either he had heard her speaking German to the saleswoman or he had been asking for some ointment and nobody who worked in the store could understand him...in short, that's how they met...She was away from home for several afternoons...

*But the Germans are no better. I've heard that they use poison gas in the concentration camps to kill Jews and then make lampshades out of their skin.

Then one evening, she stayed out late…way past curfew…Vati began muttering from his corner that she was probably out whoring again… Gisela was afraid and mother was worried…she sent me downstairs to keep watch by the front door…It was already half past ten and the street was deserted and quiet…I opened the door just a crack to have a look outside…it was already September…When I heard footsteps, I drew back behind the door…through the gap I could see Clairi and the shadow of a tall soldier in the wide collar of an army overcoat, its front unbuttoned, revealing its lining as far as the epaulette…I was on pins and needles…They were speaking German…whispering…I could hear Clairi's voice…pitched just a little too high, sounding plaintive, and a shade too sweet…then right above me in the dark, they kissed, and I could hear the smack…Clairi had her arms draped around his neck…I didn't like this, because I cared what happened to her…once again, this was something she would pay a price for, she was going to get cheated again, was her life never going to be normal?…Reluctantly she and the soldier parted…then she went upstairs…and I let her, hiding in the shadows so as not to startle her. Vati scolded her like some underage child…in order to bring peace, she promised to bring her friend Helmuth up to meet the family next time…

He came toward evening. He was a tall, stocky fellow with woolly blond hair. At first, I didn't like him…he seemed harsh and taciturn. He was fair-skinned, with a dash of color in each cheek and a big, crooked nose. He wore the badges and epaulettes of a medical sergeant. His hands were gnarly, curls the color of wheat covered his head, and his voice was deep. He wore no gun belt and carried no weapon…I liked that, because it proved that he wasn't afraid. He sat down in a wicker chair opposite Vati. Without a word, he set a package of English tobacco down on the table for him. Mother fixed tea. This was the first time a real soldier had ever sat in our house...as opposed to some mongrel like Mitić. He and Vati talked about the military situation... Vati asked him why the German army was retreating from Russia so fast. Jens laughed...*"Sehen Sie, mein lieber Herr Kovačič, den Rückzug aus Rußland verkehrt herum...Rückkehr! Rückkehr! Oaahaha!..."** And he laughed. Mother laughed, too, and then Jens turned back to face Vati. *"Nein, entschuldigen Sie, im Ernst...die Taktik ist so: die Ukrainer sollen nur säen über Herbst und Frühling...zu der Erntezeit kommen wir wieder mit den Güterwagen..."*[**] When the grain was ripe and the Russians were ready to harvest, they would go back to cart all the grain back to Europe. Why should the Germans and their allies toil in the fields? Let them do it! When harvest time comes, they'll be back for the grain...That was really a good plan...if you could carry it off...*"Ich war selber in Rußland,"* he said...Huts with thatched roofs...*"famose Öfen aus Backstein, mit dem Kamin duch das Strohdach..."*[***] One village after

---

[*]My dear Mr. Kovačič, you should look at the retreat out of Russia the other way around. It's a return! A return! *Wa-ha-ha!*

[**]No, I apologize, seriously now...the plan is this: the Ukrainians should be free to plant in the autumn and spring...by the time the harvest comes around, we'll be back with our freight cars.

[***]I was in Russia, myself.... Incredible red brick ovens with their chimneys sticking out through the thatched roofs.

the other...aflame, endless fields...churches with onion domes every color of the rainbow...sleigh bells...the Russian cavalry decimated... freezing cold, hunger..."*Wir haben die gestorbene Stute geschlachtet...mit Hackenschlagen in den Bauch und die Schädel...dann haben wir sie zerlegt... ein Glied nach dem anderen...und dann auf das Feuer gelegt...das waren große Braten...die besten Beefsteaks von je!* "*...And just what is the Russian army like? Vati asked. Is it powerful?...And what about their weapons, I asked..."*Auf einen deutschen Soldat kommen zehn russische Soldaten...,*" Jens answered. "*Was die Waffen betrifft...ihre Feuerwerfer sind sehr gut und auch die Amphibien U-Boote...*"** But the most dastardly thing about Russia was the war being waged by the partisans...just like here in the Balkans. He had served some time in a ski division fighting the partisans...all of them uniformed in white. The Russian partisans had a particular way of engaging in battle: their marksmen would sit in the treetops and fire on the columns below...Their women also perched up in the trees and had the best nose of all...Even though they were all dressed in identical white jumpers...with no insignia of rank at all... the women's proverbial intuition allowed them to sniff out the leader of the pack in a heartbeat...and they would take him out first..."*Man sieht*

*We slaughtered an old mare...by hacking into her belly and skull. Then we dismembered it...one limb or quarter at a time...and set them on the fire to cook... those were enormous roasts... the best steaks ever!

**They've got ten soldiers for every one of ours. As for weapons, their flame-throwers are very good, as are their amphibious vehicles.

nichts…es blendet vom Schnee…alles ist im Weiß, Bäume, das Gestrüpp… und auf einmal: Paf! und schon liegt der erste…der Leutnant am Boden… Ja, das ist dieser berühmte weibliche Instinkt!"* …Clairi flushed red and took him by the elbow…in many respects she had begun acting like a young girl…but as gone as she was over him, she would immediately catch herself and retreat back into herself and her chair…

Jens didn't carry a weapon, but he did have a big cigarette lighter made out of a machine-gun cartridge. *"Und wie sieht es jetzt in Deutschland aus?"*** mother asked…*"Wie ein Vulkan, der sich selber hundertmal herumgedreht und bombardiert hat…"* he said…*"Keine einzige Stadt mehr ganz, Hospitäler voll, Vertriebene…in Berlin die furchtbarsten Leichenhaufen, die ich sogar an der Front nicht gesehen habe…Aber die Leute… die sind diszipliniert…ich kann mir einen Franzosen oder Balkaneser unter diesen Bedingungen nicht, gar nicht vorstellen…"**** *"Wie gut, daß wir nicht nach Deutschland ausgewandert sind,"***** Clairi said…But I can

---

*You can't see a thing…. you're snow blind…. With everything covered in white, the trees, the underbrush…then suddenly, *bang!* And the first one down…is the lieutenant…That's feminine intuition for you!

**So what does Germany look like today?

***Like a volcano that has spun around and bombarded itself a hundred times…There's not a single city left intact, the hospitals are full, refugees everywhere…piles of corpses in Berlin far worse than any I saw at the front…But the people…they're disciplined…I simply can't imagine a Frenchman or Balkan type withstanding conditions like those…

****Thank goodness we didn't emigrate to Germany.

imagine, mother said, that the people don't dare voice any doubt in Germany's victory or say anything critical?..."*Ja...sie müßten seit einiger Zeit nur sagen, 'Rommel ist nicht ganz sicher, ob er den Kanal halten kann,'...oder 'Wann kommt endlich diese geheime Waffe zum Vorschein'... dann war ihr Maß voll...Sie werden nie wiedergesehen...wie viele sind so verschwunden, weil sie sich ein bißchen skeptisch gezeigt haben...Aber ich sage euch: warten sie ab, daß der Rote aus der Mongolei kommt...dann werdet ihr etwas erleben, da werdet ihr staunen...Sie können der größte Held sein und sich nur den geringsten Zweifel anmerken lassen...schon sind Sie am Schafot...Was für Lager ich gesehen habe!...Da waren zwei, drei Baracken bei Kijevo...mit Selbstverstümmlern. Alle hohe Offiziere, einmal Helden, Parteimitglieder von 1905, 1917...Einige dieser Häftlinge haben sich die Stirn tätoviert mit der Inschrift 'Ein Sklave Stalins'...Die Ärzte haben ihnen einfach eine Lape Haut herausgeschnitten und nähten die Stirnhaut mit einer groben Naht zusammen...Da hatten sie sich wieder tätoviert und schrieben auf die Stirn 'Ein Sklave der UdSSR'...Erneut wurden sie operiert und zum dritten Mal schrieben sie über die ganze Stirn 'Ein Sklave der KPdSU'...Auch diese Inschrift wurde im Krankenhaus herausgeschnitten. Nach drei Operationen war die Haut ihrer Stirn so gespannt, daß sie nicht einmal die Augen schließen konnten..."* *

---

*That's right...lately all it takes is for you to say something like 'Rommel isn't sure if he'll be able to hold the Channel'...or 'Are we ever actually going to get to see this secret weapon?'...and you're done for. You'll never be seen again...noody knows how many people have vanished like that, just because they expressed a little skepticism...But I'll

Self-mutilation like that was horrible. But what had been perpetrated in the concentration camps... in Dachau and Buchenwald? And what about the fate of the officers who had conspired against Hitler?... But nobody dared to ask about that. *"Ich sage nur eins: dieser Krieg dauert zu lange..."** mother said. Jens laughed. *"Ich schaue den Krieg immer vom medizinischen bzw. von dem epidemischen Standpunkt aus,"* he said. *"Sehen Sie, im ersten Weltkrieg... vor 1918... drei Kanister Wasser über den Durst! und man fand die wildesten Kohorten alle vergiftet wieder... jetzt nitschewo!... Ich bekomme jeden Monat einmal Berichte aus der Reichskanzlei... überhaupt keine Epidemie! zwei Typhusfälle bei Tzara-Plava... einige in Titos Reich... eine einzige 'Galle' auf Salamis... sozusagen*

tell you this: just wait until the Reds arrive out of Mongolia... that will be something like you've never experienced before, it will leave you speechless... no matter if you're the greatest hero in the world, if you let anyone hear the slightest doubt in your voice... it's the scaffold for you... You can't imagine the camps I've seen... Several barracks near Kiyevo... with prisoners who had mutilated themselves. All of them high-ranking officers, Communist Party members going back to 1905, 1917... Some of these prisoners had tattooed the phrase 'Stalin's Slave' on their foreheads... The doctors simply cut out the skin bearing the inscription and sewed up what was left with a coarse thread... But then they tattooed themselves again, this time with the inscription 'Slave of USSR'... Again they were operated on, and again they tattooed onto their foreheads 'Slave of CPSU'... This tattoo was cut out in the hospital too. After three operations, the skin on their foreheads was so taut that they couldn't even close their eyes anymore...

*I have just one thing to say: this war has gone on for too long.

gar nichts...verglichen mit den Epidemien von 1917!" *...Up in the castle, he said, he had a reproduction of the Dürer woodcut in his medical atlas...the horsemen of the apocalypse...these days we can cross out two of the horsemen, at least...plague, which has vanished, and hunger, which is no longer as devastating as it was...In Dürer's time, this war would have ended in two years...now all of these horsemen have been immunized twice over, ten times over against everything... the germs have all gone on strike..."*Der Krieg mit Hilfe von Blutbädern ist eins, aber er bringt keine Lösung...wenn die Mikroben das Interesse verlieren...dann Gnaden allen Soldaten...sogar ein Atomkrieg wird ohne Mikrobe niemals zu Ende gehen...In den fäuligen Oasen kein Fieber...zwei Flecktyphusfälle in Zagreb...ein Fall von Windpocken in Chicago – sogar im Vardartal nicht eine einzige Ratte...Nicht die Marschäle noch die Diplomaten diktieren den Frieden, sondern die Flöhe und die Ratten...wir haben zuviel geimpft, dieser Krieg wird nie enden."* ** ...That was how he saw things and, unfortunately, so far everybody agreed with him...

---

*I always look at the war from a medical or, let's say, an epidemiological perspective. Look, in the First World War...before 1918...all you needed was three barrels of water to quench the soldiers' thirst and you wound up with endless cohorts poisoned...but now, *nichevo*! [Russian: nothing]...Every month, I get reports from the government's medical office...no epidemics at all! Two cases fo typhus near Tzara-Plava...a few in Tito's domains...and just one case of cholera on the island of Salamis...basically nothing...compared with the epidemics of 1917.

** War carried out by blood bath is one thing, but it doesn't lead to any conclusion...if

Jens was an interesting guy. As a civilian, he'd been a math teacher, but in the Wehrmacht he'd gone through a year of medical training. If at first I'd disliked him on Clairi's account, now I actually liked him and stopped being jealous...Once when he invited her up to the castle to join them at mess, I got invited along...To go walking through town with a German sergeant like that, and up the hill, no less, to the castle garrison, to their super-citadel, was to expose yourself to all the countless seen and unseen eyes...doing something they would remember for years to come...People always suspect more, they always judge based on their imagination, the capacity of their dreams. In all likelihood not just our whole house, but the whole neighborhood knew about the dishonor of Clairi's relationship with a German non-commissioned officer...All those countless unknown persons at three and four removes deciding your fate...Up at the castle, that crumbling fortress, there was no trace anymore of Sandy, Škerjanc or the old castle gang...just soldiers, weapons and more soldiers, and long-range artillery installed at the battlements...I was curious to find out what the buildings were like on the inside...The big courtyard and rooms filled with bunk beds...Jens showed me his unit's quarters, their big

the germs lose interest...then it's the soldiers' gain...and even an atomic war without any germs will never come to an end...No fever in even the most polluted oases...two cases of typhus in Zagreb...a case of chickenpox in Chicago – not even a single rat in the Vardar Valley...It's not the field marshals or diplomats who dictate the peace, but the fleas and the rats...we've all been immunized too much for this war ever to end.

radio receiver and transmitter and the air-raid alarm...the gas masks and leather kits hanging on the wall...I'd still had no word from the Home Guard recruiting office...if I could explain to Jens what the problem was, perhaps he could help me, but then it would come out that I'd forged Vati's signature...Jens showed me the quarters of the gunnery crews that had arrived from Russia...like all the rooms in the castle, theirs was propped up with beams...their automatic rifles and chargers hung from the foot of their bunks...Each of them had no more than his own bunk and his own locker, an austerity that appealed to me...My request about signing up for the Home Guards hovered on the tip of my tongue, but on the other side of a space divider, in Jens's first aid office, Clairi was setting a table for supper...goulash in three mess tins, with a salad of cabbage in their lids...She and Helmuth had probably made love in that whitewashed room, which had stretchers and a cot made up with a sheet...On a shelf, there were some medical books, issues of a military magazine called *The Alarm* and some other books...two of the authors there, Schopenhauer and Kant, were already familiar to me from some newspaper stories I'd read...After supper, Jens invited us to go with him to the top of the tower and enjoy the view of Ljubljana...it was still light. I'd only been up the tower once before...when our teacher Rosa took our class there... that time there was a glass-covered table at the top that had labeled drawings of all the mountains you could see...but now it was gone... It really was a gorgeous view just before twilight...and now everyone in the woods down below and the houses on the hillside could see

Clairi and me...Up here in the open air you had a clearer sense of the war...the partisans in the mountains...Budapest resisting the Soviets...even that unbroken front line running from Switzerland to the Atlantic, which the Anglo-Americans were holding at the Rhine, felt like it was just over the first range of mountains. Jens pointed out the northern constellation to me ... he didn't call it the Big and Little Dipper, but used its Latin names, *Ursa major* and *Ursa minor*...they were like little, flickering faces...lime white and light blue. "*Wenn die Kanonen schießen,*" he said, "*dann ist es so, wie ein Lichtschleier, der am Horizont murrt.*" * ...Clairi joined us. "*Helmuth, du bist ein Sternenfreund...*" ** "*Wie gut, daß es noch eine Unendlichkeit gibt.*" *** Jens shook his head. "*Da irrst du dich, Clairi. Nicht einmal eine Unendlichkeit gibt es...*" **** "*Gott ist unendlich,*" ***** Clairi said ..."*Auch darüber irrst du dich, Clairi; es gab einen Dämon von wesentlich grausam teuflischem Charakter, aber auch er existiert jetzt nicht mehr...*" ****** "*Du lasterst...*" ******* A scale of stars drew a thin silver brow through the sky..."*Wie denken Sie sich das, Herr Jens...*

*The artillery fire makes it seem like there's a veil of light grumbling on the horizon.

**Helmut, you're a star lover.

***It's so good that at least infinity still exists.

****You're wrong about that, Clairi. There's not even an infinity anymore.

*****God is infinite.

******You're wrong about that too, Clairi. There used to be a demon of a profoundly, gruesomely devilish nature, but even he no longer exists.

*******You're blaspheming.

nichtunendlichen Raum?"* I asked…"*Unbegrenzt*," he replied, "*aber nicht unendlich. Eine Kugeloberfläche ist auch unbegrenzt, aber nicht unendlich…*"** "*Man kann doch eine Zahl nennen? Für das Durchmesser?…*"*** "*Er schwenkt…dieser Raum pulsiert…*"**** He spoke about a third dimension, about imaginary triangles, about parallels and tangential planes…I couldn't understand all of it…It was cold, so we turned up our collars…he took a helmet that rested atop the wall and set it on my head as a joke…He started to talk about the ancient Germanic god Wotan and other pagan heroes. Sadly it didn't mean much to me personally, just as werewolves, forest sprites, the fates and the legendary King Matjaž, asleep in the mountains for centuries, didn't mean much to me…and I was always amazed whenever people would start talking so passionately about these phantoms of legend, and I would feel deprived for not being on such intimate terms with them…

JENS WAS A GREAT HELP to the family. He would come to visit two or three times a month…always surreptitiously, so as not to provoke indignation in the house. He had a map made of thick leather, badger

---

*How do you mean that, Herr Jens, non-infinite space?

**Unbounded, but not infinite. The surface of a sphere is unbounded, too, but it's not infinite.

***But there must be some number they've come up with? For the diameter?

****It vacillates, this space, it pulsates.

hide, military issue...he had a whole set of them...and you could spend weeks on end examining any river you wanted, how it flowed through the centuries and all the corners it turned during that time... He and Vati would discuss all four fronts over that map...Once Jens arrived with a pistol holster attached to his belt, but it was filled with tobacco..."*Den habe ich in unserem Magazin geklaut...*"* he said in all candor as he shook it out onto some newspaper...

Vati's condition was getting steadily worse. He had stopped eating, he was turning green, and suddenly he had to go the hospital...his ration card went with him...The small room on the ground floor of the pulmonary ward where they put him was crammed full of patients, and on top of everything, there was a Home Guard stationed outside the door...a regular giant dressed in huge trousers and an enormous tunic, holding a finger over the trigger of his submachine gun...because in the corner next to Vati's bed there was a captured partisan, battered, with a critical lung condition, strapped into bed. He was a young, underfed boy with a shaved head and both arms in casts, stealing frightened glances at the other patients and the visitors...Where had they captured him? In what forest...Vati talked to him as much as allowed...took care of things...and felt sorry for him..."Bring him some more," he said..."More what? We don't have anything!"..."Some fruit"...I brought two pears. For the duration of visiting hours, the guard...they were all giants here, wild boars in

*I nicked this from our supply room...

uniform...stood in the room the whole time...you could feel him at your back as though a tank were parked there...word was he only stepped out during doctors' rounds. When I came back to visit soon after that, Vati whispered to me in German..."Go to Second Street in Rožna dolina and find the Klepec household...tell them that Ivo is here in the hospital..." So I went. It was a chilly day...the start of November...and a drizzle of sleet bit into my nostrils...Here and in Mirje was where the most affluent residents of Ljubljana lived...all of them likely supporters of the partisans, which made me feel like I was in some sort of dangerous embrace. On both sides the houses stood back from the street, with gardens out front...villas bearing names like "My Peace," "My View"...slightly darkened from the precipitation, like cardboard boxes...Clairi and I had also come here to sell fur muffs and hats...a German shepherd that started barking in the fenced yard of a house where I stopped for directions provoked all of the dogs nearby so that soon half of the neighborhood in every direction was barking...Klepec lived in an unstuccoed addition to a brown wooden building resembling a gingerbread house...A middle-aged woman wearing a brown smock opened the door...I told her that Ivo was in the hospital in the bed next to my father's, kept under guard, in room number five...I said that Ivo had asked Vati to have me deliver this message to them, so they'd know where he was...The woman probably worked for the Liberation Front...her eyes, the swollen bags under them as dark as though they'd been inked with a brush, looked at me so grimly that I was sorry I'd told her anything...She said, "We don't know anyone by that name!" and slammed the door in my face...On visitors day, I told Vati what had happened...*"Ganz richtig...das Weib mußte sich so verdächtig benehmen, weil sie nicht wußte, wer du bist..."*

Vati didn't stay in the hospital for long, barely ten days...They were no longer able to help him as much as before...so they sent him home, because they needed the beds for other patients...In the office, a nurse handed me his ration card, but a few days later, mother determined that the hospital had cheated us...two extra rations of bread, two tabs, each good for a hundred grams of bread, had been torn off...She sent me back...The nurse had a whole drawer full of little tabs like the confetti you throw at Mardi Gras paraders...but she explained that she couldn't give them back to me, because the patients got additional pastries and snacks...On the way back, I opened the door to room number five..."What do you want?" the gigantic legionnaire barked on the other side of the handle..."Sorry"...I said...Ivo...nothing but skin and bones...was still sitting strapped into bed...nothing had happened yet...the partisans still hadn't liberated him from the hands of his jailers, as they had so many others...*"Ist halt ein armer, junger Teufel,"* mother said. *"So einer interessiert niemanden..."*

Once he was back home, Vati was unable to do any work...The needles kept slipping through his strangely bloated fingers...even larger objects dropped out of his hands...He had to keep going back to the window to gasp for air...Jens suggested that we set up his bed

---

*Rightly so. The woman had to be suspicious like that, since she had no idea who you were.

**Poor young devil. He's of no interest to anyone, injured like that.

there…So at first we assembled some bedding for him on two wicker chairs next to the window, where, dressed in his suit, fur hat, scarf, and gloves, whenever he needed to, even unassisted, he could pull on a wire that I had tied onto the window handle to draw it open and capture a fresh stream of air…He wasn't under any circumstances supposed to smoke, but still he managed to puff away his daily allowance in the course of the morning…sometimes Jens brought or sent him some via Clairi…a cigar, a pinch of tobacco…I had to scour I don't know how many streets just to collect a miserable heap of butts which I used to roll two, maybe three cigarettes for him…He would have given half his life, all of his bread for one pack of Dravas, particularly since he had no appetite anymore…there were just two things, neither of which we had, that would have posed a dilemma for him…choosing between a pack of cigarettes and a full bowl of hearty beef soup… Three days later, he was no longer able to sit up in the two chairs we'd arranged for him…he was feeling pressure on his chest, the small of his back ached and his two stick legs swelled up with fluid so much that we couldn't get his socks on him…We had to move his bed back onto the table…some furs, a mattress, a stack of pillows and behind them my drawing board to block the draft from the open window… Now he lay on his side with one hand under his cheek and watched as Clairi, wearing her overcoat and with a blanket wrapped around her legs on account of the open window, sewed items that he had left only half- or one quarter-finished before his trip to the hospital…Every now and then, he bellowed…"Whoa!" if she missed anything…Clairi, who was freezing and shook even more at these shouts…had to hold the fur right under his nose...so he could use his finger to point at the problems...and it was true, Clairi's stitches weren't by a long shot as exact and microscopically precise in the leather as his...they warped it...the fur on the other side didn't blend naturally as it should have, to make the finished product look like it was made from a single piece instead of a bunch of disparate smaller ones...These days, what he did would be referred to more as a kind of plastic microsurgery than fur trade...she had to rip out all of the stitches...carefully! carefully!... to avoid damaging the hide, not to mention the fur, rub the leather down with grease and talc...before starting all over again...

There wasn't much Jens could do to help. But it was enough for him to come visit and sit with us...tall, stocky, confident in his green uniform, handsome and blond...and exchange a few words with Vati now and then, listen to mother's complaints, and to my sister's...It was enough for Clairi just to be able to feel his uniform touching her sweater...He would have liked to be able to bring Vati some medications...but aside from the antiseptics, aspirin and bandages, he didn't have anything...the main dispensary where they kept morphine was controlled by an SS officer...Jens advised mother to write Margrit in Switzerland...he would use the military post to get the letter dispatched as quickly as possible...But unfortunately the border was closely monitored...and it was impossible to get anything from there...We looked at his map printed on thick leather...he drew a precise line showing where it could get through...across the notorious border stream...between the sixth and seventh tree...where smugglers got through..."*Da fressen und saufen sonntags alle zusammen...*" he said, "*die Polizisten, SA, Helvetier und Maquis...Wenn ich nur einen der Grenzübergänger kannte!*"[*]

Dr. Kahn, a fat physician assigned to us by the office of public health, was Jewish. Vati didn't like him because he had "no tolerance for clerics or kikes," as he put it...Dr. Kahn only paid us house calls begrudgingly...unbeknownst to Vati, on the sly, Mother and Clairi had enticed him with a lamb's wool hat that suited his fat head perfectly and protected his little ears from the cold...yet even so, each time I had to show up at his office and beg from three to five times before he'd actually consent to trudge up the steps to our apartment on the fourth floor..."*Die Medizin kann in diesem Fall nicht mehr helfen,*" he said to Mother with an expression of disgust on his face at having to use the language he detested..."*Und auch die betreffenden Medikamente, wenn Sie sie auch aus der Schweiz bekommen, könnten ihm höchstens um ein paar Wochen das Leben verlängern...*"[**] This he said in the doorway before leaving...red-faced, broad, and neckless between fur cap and collar, just like a square.

One day, however, it looked as though Vati had suddenly been saved...He was sitting up on the table without any support...his eyes were clear, and through his stubble, the features of his face were

---

[*]That's where they eat and drink together every Sunday... the police, the SA, the Helvetians, and the Maquis... If only I knew one of the smugglers!

[**]The medical profession has nothing to offer in this case...Even if you do get the medications from Switzerland, at most they'll give him a few extra weeks.

smooth...he was happy to see every single one of us, even Gisela...
he said in a clear voice, "This flour soup is really delicious"...he ate it
all by himself, unaided...and he even tossed the end of his scarf over
his shoulder, to get it out of the way as he spooned up his soup...
But toward evening, his energy gave out...and we had to carry him
from the workroom to the cot in the bedroom...He was choking...
we had to help him off with the vest that he'd had on all these days...
pull off his undershirt, his scarf, open the window...only frigid air did
him any good...his legs, from the ankles up, were like two lumps...
In the midst of an attack, he lost consciousness and, though I could
see the blanket rise and fall with his breathing, he lay completely
motionless...

Mother said to me..."*Geh schnell den Pfarrer holen...*"[*]

That was against Vati's principles...But the way she looked at me
said that that there was no time left for prejudices, that the truth was
as unshakable as a rock...I put on my scarf and fur hat...I took my
time getting downstairs...all of the doors were closed...the market
vendor's, the judge's, the café owner's...it wasn't the silence on the
stairs that was significant now, it was the closed doors that reminded
me of something...In the entryway, which was dark over its big cobblestones, everything around me began to change and music started
to sound in my head. I got frightened. At any instant, I might fall on
the pavement and start frothing at the mouth and thrashing around.

*Quick, go get a priest.

I had to get out fast!...Hugging the walls of the buildings, I headed uphill. All of this was against Vati...but needed for God, up there, in the dark...it was needed for this journey to nowhere, to Jerusalem... damnably treacherous to the one person who couldn't defend himself...fiendishly servile to God, who didn't expect any of it...And I was supposed to knock myself out in order to make this shit happen... It would be best if I didn't obey...but barely had I told myself that than I could feel the fire in front of me...as searing as those tongues of flame out of a machine gun...There was nobody at the refectory, a gray building on Upper Square...the priest was in church performing the evening pieties...I couldn't deal with the light, the walls... I told myself that I'd wait downstairs at the door...in the side street across from the building on the corner where crazy Mica and Gisela's obnoxious friend Olga lived...As I stood there between the refectory and a wall covered with posters that faced out at a right angle past the refectory door, I suddenly remembered having once been in some other corner just like this...In Paris, when I was two and a half years old...mother and both of my sisters had taken me with them on a short business trip...I always swore I had no memory of it, and in fact I didn't...but now it came back for sure. I was sitting like this in the evening, at dusk, in overcast weather, all alone in some side street... possibly outside the hotel we were staying in...on one side there was a black door, probably to the hotel, and behind me there was a wall with advertisements posted on big boards...my sisters and mother had just then left me alone in my stroller, in order to duck in someplace just for a second...and everything there had been exactly the same as it was here, at this moment on Upper Square...the same time of day, the same staging, all of it had come back...I sensed this distinctly as a kind of acute, benign jolt, an invigorating shot intervening to deaden my horror...

I went back downhill to wait for the priest outside the church, but I couldn't shake that pleasant sense of displacement that pervaded me from within...I saw the red facade of our house, illuminated up to the second floor by the blue light of the streetcar stop...the silhouettes of people walking straight toward each other without colliding...I saw the street leading uphill, the broad sidewalk, the store, the streetcar in twilight...but the whole time that light, pleasant, rare surprise that had sliced me in two kept rolling around in my head...When some old ladies came out of the church and started to chat, I was suddenly seized again by that previous sense of horror...it lay on the ground... wafting from everywhere...I caught sight of the priest just as he was coming out of the assembly hall of the St. Mary's preschool...I stiffly approached him and said, "Could you please come take confession..." He had a face that resembled a bust portrait of Julius Caesar...massive lips, long eyelashes. The children looked on curiously. The priest said he'd be right back and that I should wait for him under the trees...and when at last I saw him again, he had that box in his hands, and when he approached me and asked where we were going, I nodded my head toward our house...

Briskly across the street, through the door, into the entryway, that malevolent dark...from one floor to the next, I kept going on autopilot...the priest right behind me...this was the first time I had brought such an unusual customer home…Candles in ceramic holders had been lit in the workroom…regular grave lanterns on the counter, the work table, the side table…this was mother and Clairi's work, inspired by that "unerring" feminine instinct for what's appropriate on this or that occasion…When the priest came to a stop among the flickering flames, he must have felt as though he'd entered a chapel or come home…I saw Vati's shaggy head amid the bedposts…mother and Clairi quickly cleared everything away from around him…he was gasping for air and his face was as sweaty as a soaked mask on the verge of disintegrating…When I bent over him, he looked at me intently, with no sign of confusion…

His bedside lamp was switched on and casting light on my frescoes…the Creation, Paradise, Crucifixion, Judgment Day…now I felt ashamed of them, because here an expert was about to see them… there were also some candles burning on the corner of the kitchen table…Today, no matter how many times I try to recall that scene to mind, I make comparisons and I can sense: those stripes, the light and the dark ones that I seem to recall seeing at birth, were identical to the ones surrounding Vati as he bade farewell to life…as he went off into the dark…The priest put on his stole and came in to take his confession…mother shut the door – only she was allowed to stay, because she wouldn't understand anyway…It took a long time…every now and then, Vati would moan…Finally the door opened, and he was praying penance…"Oh my God, I am heartily sorry…" he prayed, repeating the words after his confessor…without his dentures, which left his tongue flailing around in his structureless mouth…So he had let them beat him... The priest didn't want any tea, not even a taste... perhaps to avoid dishonoring himself to some unseen eye... I led him downstairs to the door, through the dark... I couldn't get rid of the feeling that he was taking with him whatever Vati had confided to him in private... perhaps even in that little black box of his... something that belonged only to Vati, his own secret...

Vati lay at the very bottom of the bed, having soaked it entirely... he always peed long and copiously, like a big horse, which was something I'd always admired about him ever since I was little... We dressed him in fresh clothes and then, without disturbing how he was lying, we pushed a blanket under him, lifting him up a bit... Clairi at his head, mother at his feet, me in the middle... He lay at the bottom of the blanket, shriveled and as light as if we were carrying Gisela. Only on the other side did the blanket evidently yield to his weight... We brought him into the workroom and set him down on the table with a stack of pillows at his head, so he could breathe and look around the room..."*Ist dir kalt?*" Clairi asked..."Do you want something to drink?" I asked..."I'm not thirsty," he managed to say in a resonant voice through all his wheezing..."If you suddenly feel bad overnight, bang on the wall. With my yardstick." I held it up in the light for him to see. He watched me as I bent over him to lean it against the wall... I wasn't afraid of him because, at heart, we'd always understood each other. And then there was the fact that I'd been working like crazy for the past three years... though that impressed nobody so much as me...

*Are you cold?

That night, Clairi woke me up…*"Schnell! Schnell!"*…Vati was having a serious attack!…We tore the newspapers off the window and shaded the lamp, so that we didn't attract an airplane or lure some idiotic bandit into shooting his gun into our room…We took hold of him, got him into a sitting position, then each put one of his arms around our shoulders…his lungs and his throat were rattling…his arms were as cold as stone…*"Luft! Luft!"***…He tried to open his mouth but suddenly got choked up inside or outside…he made some signs with his fingers…and slumped with his head on my shoulder…*"Er ist tot… tot,"****** Clairi wailed…with an almost joyous expression on her face. I looked at him…his eyes were closed, in fact. I pushed his scarf aside and listened under his limp shoulder…*"Er ist nicht tot."***** I helped her set him back down and straighten his legs…*"Hol' die Mama."****** But mother was already there…right behind me. *"Vati ist gestorben,"****** Clairi said…Agh, agh, agh! was all that mother got out…she started to sway, and I jumped up to keep her from falling…Gisela was talking in the next room, she'd woken up…*"Er wollte noch etwas sagen, bevor er starb,"****** Clairi said…I brushed that aside…but then didn't…

*Come quickly!

**Air! Air!

***He's dead…dead.

****He's not dead.

*****Go get mother.

******Vati is dead.

*******He wanted to say something before he died.

all of that was just a dream...he hadn't wanted to say anything, that was delusional, a fantasy...and you had to guard against fantasy... which ought to be ashamed of itself, considering what people had to go through..."*Beten wir...da beim Fenster*," she said. "*Knie nieder!*"[*] I knelt down...I wanted to make her happy...When I'd managed to pray several prayers from the sad part of the rosary...Clairi tried responding to me...she said, "*Er starb wie in einem Buch...*"[**] Ridiculous...books, with their damned formulas always written following the same style...Cronin's!...couldn't provide a model for anybody to die...if he even was dead. She went to the window and looked up toward the castle..."*Wie könnte ich das jetzt dem Helmut mitteilen, Bubi?*"[***] she asked...Then she looked at me. "*Gehe ins Nest*,"[****] she said. It was best to obey her. I went into the other room, but I couldn't keep my eyes shut. I got back up. She should go try to get some rest, I said to her; I can't sleep, I said, I'd wake her up later...

When she was gone and I was left alone, I tried to study his face... it was like stone set in a block of cement...I tried to listen...I wanted to pick up any voices coming from wherever he was now...I sat there, and by studying the pupils peeking out from under his eyelids, I could see along with him whatever it was he was seeing, guess at who was approaching...Karel...Mica...his mother and father?...Some

---

[*]Let's pray...over there by the window...Kneel down.

[**]The way he died was like out of some book.

[***]How can I let Helmut know about this now?

[****]Go to our nest.

figures...some sort of angels in disguise...their white faces...the gigantic robes they were clothed in...Who are you? And then suddenly Vati recognized him. Oh, it's him; and he hugged him...they hugged each other..."So that's you, you..." Then another hug, heartfelt... Karel! What a surprise! He's happy to see him here. Everyone here is like that...Where are you coming from?...And you? It had been ages since they'd seen each other. Don't speak too loudly...You're here. And mom and dad, too...Some people approached...figures circulating this way and that...for as far as you could see...I could only see what was in my thoughts, and my thoughts were about light coming from there, but I had no idea where, and about the people I knew... I knew this was my projection, that this wasn't that, because it didn't work, trying to see things together with him...that he was far from there...probably still waiting in some booth or compartment for his turn to come. His hands were so firmly clasped over his stomach that I couldn't pry the blanket out from under them. And if I lifted them...? I tried...but it was like turning the crank on that contraption of Karel's by the Krka...hard...if he was really dead...but then I managed... Clairi came out of the next room...she told me to go get some rest... she also wanted to spend some time alone with Vati...Again, I couldn't keep my eyes shut. I saw a scene that had either really taken place or I had just dreamed...in Cegelnica!...in the hollow...it was big...Karel was sitting in the hollow with his hat cocked jauntily to one side, as he had at the fair in Bršljin, and there were others sitting behind him, and whenever I walked past, Karel would grab me by the ankle and pull me down, into the hollow...I went again, after cutting myself on a scythe that lay in the grass, and again he grabbed me by the foot and dragged me down toward him... I walked past a third time, and again he grabbed me by my instep and dragged me down... this scene kept repeating endlessly... it felt like I was going crazy, and my head kept tossing back and forth on my pillow because I was getting sick... I got up and went back into the workroom. Clairi was sitting at the head of the table... she wasn't crying, but her cheeks were red and swollen from tears, and she probably didn't have any more to shed... When I got to the counter, the way she looked at me made me want to turn back around, rather than have her get angry at me again...

THAT MORNING, Vati lay on the table as he had during the night... his mouth open, his hair lying in separate strands on the pillow... He was grayer and more rigid than before... it seemed as though he must have woken up around daybreak and moved a bit away from the wall... Clairi and I tidied him up a bit and then caught the streetcar to Holy Cross... to arrange for the grave and burial... By our reckoning, the family's entire iron reserve of cash would be needed for both... The priest at Holy Cross looked more like a grave-digger or peasant, he was wearing boots up to his knees and blue work overalls. He looked at us blank-eyed and sullen, probably because Clairi was speaking German and I did a bad job of translating... my Slovene was neither soulful nor vivid enough. He only half understood us, but then he wasn't really inclined to listen, either... wordlessly, he put a big piece of cardboard down on the table... A map of the cemetery, full of tiny rectangles bunched up on one side and a big blank space, an empty field, on the other...Clairi wanted a grave in the more populated part of the old cemetery, so that Vati wouldn't be left lying alone..."There aren't any more plots," the priest said, sounding irritated in the extreme...Now, with the war on and so many corpses everywhere, it basically didn't matter where our dead Vati was going to lie...At the coffin maker's, a salesman showed us caskets on display in their attic...white ones, brown ones, even blue ones. Through their window I could see straight into the foyer of my old school, Ledina, which was across the street... We had to pick the cheapest one and buy it on credit...it had just one decoration, a kind of silver spiral on the lid, and all the way home, Clairi had to keep telling herself how nice it was despite the low price...

In the meantime, mother and Ana, who helped her, had washed Vati...all they were waiting for was for us to come home – actually me, so I could try on his two suits...the blue one and the black one. One of them would go in the coffin, while the other, nicer one, would become mine...I tried on both of them...then mixed them up: trying the trousers of the black one with the coat of the blue one, and vice versa...the one I tried on first, the black one, was chosen to go to Holy Cross...I had the impression that Vati, lying next to us on the table, was frowning because he didn't agree with our judgment...Clairi and I then went to see Milena, who worked for the courts, and her sister Emilija...to get veils, black stockings, dresses and coats...for her and for mother, and then stayed for tea and cookies, which they offered us in their heated kitchen.

That afternoon, people from the building came by to sprinkle holy water on Vati...Mr. Praček, the market lady, Ana, the judge's family, Salaznik and the cleaning woman...the mother of that pretty young blonde lady who was married to the handsome printing-press operator...only the Hirols didn't stop by...I brought the holy water straight from the christening font in St. Jacob's Church...Later that day, Tinček, Ivan, Karel, Marko and Franci came by...Julijan didn't, because he'd been posted somewhere in Lower Carniola...Just before they arrived with the coffin for Vati...Firant, with that pincer-like jaw of his, appeared...The two men from Holy Cross who came to get Vati arrived with a different coffin...not the one Clairi and I had picked out at the casket maker's that had the silver serpentine on its lid, but a plain, ordinary, black one with no spiral, which looked terribly dreary...Clairi began arguing with them...But it wasn't the men's fault at all, one of them was from the city sanitation department and the other from the coroner's office...they told Clairi that the casket they'd brought was just for transporting the body and that the one we'd bought on credit that morning was waiting at Holy Cross...The minute you have anything to do with salesmen, Clairi said, you get swindled, it's like some sort of rule...That evening, Jens came by, after holding off in the afternoon on account of the neighbors...he brought a candle, some sort of eternal flame in a thick, green jar. Vati was gone from the table...we rolled up his mattress and his red, patched blanket, tied them up with string, and then set them on the heap of coal and peat in the stairway leading down from our workroom.

First thing the following morning, Clairi and I went to the grove of the dead at Holy Cross...Vati was lying in the St. Andrew's Chapel... The casket hadn't been replaced...judging from the lid, which had been placed upright next to it and lacked the serpentine, we could tell it was the same one the two men from the coroner's office and sanitation department had brought the night before to take him away. Clairi went storming off like a fury to the coffin maker's...I stayed there...This was a genuine place of death...I went strolling from chapel to chapel to look at the dead people...I had gone to see them once before in that garage by the St. Joseph's institution...They were rich, poor, middle class, different kinds...and all of them men. Thank god, because women have always struck me as unnatural in death, they love life so much...The dark circles under their closed eyes were like traces of death, if not death itself...I was alone in this little city... I started making up roles...one role of the dark circles was as shameless shoeprints...another was as invidious traps, still others were cannibal bite marks...I exhorted some of them to be decent, others more open, and still others to be more considerate of the people they'd left their mark on...There was one little chapel I couldn't get into at all, because there were so many wreaths and flowers...I expressed my indignation out loud, when suddenly I heard the footsteps of people entering the grove...I fled behind the chapel so they wouldn't discover my childish secret...

There weren't many people at the funeral...the procession moved as if in a haze...Mother had sewn a black veil onto her black hat, but you couldn't see through it very well, which made her look like an Arab woman and caused her to trip...The procession consisted of Ana, pretty Mrs. Zalokar, Tinček's and Marko's mother, our cousin Minka wearing a big yellow coat, Franci…and a few little old ladies whom I'd never seen before…

I knew the cemetery from when we had lived in Nove Jarše…but now Vati was traveling on the shoulders of the black-clad men…flying like a zeppelin over a miniature New York…All the individuals lying here…dead in 1796…1883…1905…old, young…even the poor newborns in their plots who had barely lived a few months and probably got to be winged creatures as a result…how were they going to welcome Vati? The way we'd been welcomed in Cegelnica…Nove Jarše…Old Square?…The grave was hardly any bigger than our basement room in Mr. Perme's house…which was just over there, half a kilometer on the far side of the fence…There were two or three tombstones close by, and I could make out their years…The life of one of them had stopped twenty-two years before Vati, another had seen time stop just nine years before…Vati was older than them by exactly the number of years each of them had been dead…he had seen, known and experienced exactly that much more than they had…Maybe that's why they were also shyer than the ones crowding around us…perhaps that would be a reason for them to be more forthcoming and kinder about welcoming Vati, because in the old days people visited and confided in each other a lot more than they did today…I wanted to stay by the grave. He had also stayed over with me in the sanatorium when he brought me to Urach…but when it got dark, I was seized with a panic over that huge parcel of tombstones. Vati was lying down there in the open grave, amid roots, sand and worms that were so tiny the birds scarcely noticed them... Twenty-four years later, I wrote a fat book over four hundred pages long about all of this. I set it in a different time, because I wanted to describe death itself... because I was pursuing a different approach, different tracks, a different framework... Maybe I'll describe it again someday in some different form, but for now, I'm surrounded by other signs and other tracks...

When I arrived home, mother was sitting up in an unusual posture... with one shoulder hanging down, as though she'd just had a stroke... We couldn't get her to shift the way she was sitting. We turned the light out over the door and drank some tea... it didn't much matter, given the lack of customers... Fewer and fewer people wanted us to have anything to do with them or their furs anymore, despite our meticulously crafted advertisements... The stretching table was empty... We felt ashamed... We felt guilty... We didn't talk, in an effort to protect our sorrow... For the first time, mother was at a loss... she no longer looked like the lady of the house... Clairi sat crying at the table. Gisela, who didn't like Vati, was crying for her sake. We didn't feel hungry. We didn't feel like doing anything in particular. As it was, we'd never taken up much space, but now we shrank even more. We would have gladly asked anyone for forgiveness... we had forgiven each other everything. We reassured each other in tones resembling an oath that we loved each other. We were terrified of the prospect of losing another one of us... Ana, Mrs. Zalokar, Salaznik the café owner... at the graveside, all of them had urged us to be brave... as did some passers-by in the cemetery... We set out for Holy Cross. We stopped at a florist's shop to buy flowers. Only the most beautiful ones... with the last of our money. You couldn't get flowers on ration cards, or lettuce... The candle burned every day... We couldn't get used to its not being there... Even Gisela, who was already going to school, felt moved by it... I dragged myself from one chair to another, from bedroom to workshop, from workshop to bedroom. As it was, I scarcely weighed seventy-five pounds in those years, and now I lost another six. I shrank. The fish oil that mother gave me made me throw up... I even managed to stupidly squander my access to meals at the Children's Home... when I rang the bell and then saw something white approach, I came out of my hiding place too soon... and found myself face to face with the director dressed in a work smock... His eyebrows shot way up behind his glasses when he saw the thermos and tin in my hands, and I noticed Sister Rafaela standing on the steps behind him, clutching onto the railing and looking afraid... "What does this mean, Sister Rafaela?" the director asked... "He's come for the scraps that we'd otherwise give away for pig slop," she lied. "Didn't I tell you..." and so on... I felt badly for Rafaela... All I could do anymore was wave and say hi to her... she was probably upset with me for behaving so stupidly... Jens arrived and comforted Clairi... "*Du mußt dich freuen, Clairi. Diese Trauer, so wie dieser Krieg, wird nicht ewig dauern. Ihre Macht ist riesig, aber begrenzt. Daher auch ihre Lebensdauer. Man muß entkommen, man muß verneinen...*"* Today I know that Jens got that last part about retreating and denying from Buddha and Schopenhauer...

*You should be glad, Clairi. Like this war, this sorrow won't last forever. Its power is enormous, but limited, as is its duration. You have to escape from it, you have to deny it...

The workroom gradually went to seed...Clairi completely gave in to her pain...She was unable to finish anything on time, not even the few orders that she managed to beg for herself...she kept hearing Vati's voice telling her what to fix and how to sew...and when she looked up, of course he wasn't there...There were even downright ridiculously simple things that she couldn't manage anymore...there wasn't a nickel left in the house. Not one customer coming with a sizable order. You could actually talk things over with Vati, but not so with Clairi. I made the rounds of some people we'd once been in contact with to beg them for cash advances on jobs...Dr. Bon, Mrs. Nikolič, Milena and Emilija...Anywhere I saw a pile of wood lying around, I went to ask if they needed someone to chop it. And I still had to run to that damned school every day, even though I got nothing out of it...We liquidated our supply of skins by selling them to various furriers. Every one of them studied each lira ten times before letting it go, weighed each piece of bread a hundred times before using it as barter...We barely scraped up enough money to buy food with ration coupons...We took Vati's half-used ration book to the grocer...the young one who had kicked his wife Katarina out of the house the year before over her affair with an Italian officer...and we bartered it for coupons for bread, the cheapest of all foodstuffs. For Christmas, the Germans made walnuts, butter and other holiday strudel ingredients available for coupons...we couldn't afford them. Mother would sit for hours on end in a state of paralysis. When she got back up, her legs would hurt...and she'd have to regain her balance...there was an unresponsive look in her eyes... I began to be afraid something could happen to her... I went with her to the market so she could bargain... but first she curled her hair, to buttress up her performance, so she could be more assertive... she was quite pretty, and I latched onto her arm... with fatigue and gratitude she closed her eyes. Thirty years had to pass since that time for me to finally appreciate the startling and sad realization, which I've come to repeat to myself ever since: that you and your loved one are two separate beings, no matter how much you may love each other... A half-finished Persian lamb's fur coat that Vati had made by snipping off some little piece, some stray little tab from every Persian lamb's hide that a customer brought in for him to work on, or by sewing on another half-inch from the scraps... was something we refused to sell... it was sacred, something untouchable... We didn't have any jewelry that we could barter or take to the pawnbroker's... There was less and less merchandise in the shop, and what there was was worse, lower quality, ratty... there was nothing that we could show to a customer... Father had understood quite a few things... he had made lots of pieces by hand that, by comparison, even the most modern automated fur-making equipment could only produce at the level of a first-year apprentice... Clairi made a point of showing how totally frayed her nerves were... to spite Jens, whom she told she had just two options: to become old and fat or to hit the road like a gypsy... She was afraid to sew at the worktable at which Vati had worked and on which he had died... I tried to sell anything at all at the market in exchange for beans or flour... I succeeded a grand total of once…when I managed to barter us some lard, but that success was never repeated…Then one day, Minka came to visit…bringing with her a little money, some flour, some lard…that was supposed to be compensation for Vati's part of Karel's estate…All we could do was stare…all those fields, meadows and woods, the house and the livestock…and what she'd brought us was supposed to amount to a quarter of that? There was no hope of taking this to court…one day Novo Mesto would be occupied by the Whites, then by the Reds, after them by the Blues…That money and food saved our lives… Clairi got somewhat better. But I knew that all of this had to come to an end sooner or later…there were three women, all of them sick or disabled in one way or another…I was going to have to drop out of school and start working full time…after all, I was the only man in the house…And then, on top of everything, this happened: one evening, Clairi didn't come back from the castle after she'd gone up later than usual…Typically she was back by midnight at the latest… Now it was one o'clock, then two, then three…Mother sent me back downstairs…I waited behind the door to the courtyard, since going outside was out of the question, the patrols would shoot you on the spot, especially the Vlasovites, who took no excuses…Finally, Clairi and Jens came strolling back. They were talking. *"Noch eine Stunde!"* * …He kissed her…*"Gib mir noch einen Kuß!"* ** Clairi said, sobbing… He kissed her reluctantly. Was it over between them? I wondered,

*One more hour.

**Let me have one more kiss.

terrified…She went upstairs crying…Jens remained standing on the sidewalk. Like some sort of blue stone…holding a box of matches in his right hand…then he turned around…and only after I heard the door to the workshop close upstairs did I lock the courtyard door and run home…That was the last time Jens and Clairi saw each other…At 4:25, he had to catch a troop transport to the front on the border with France, between Nancy and Bremen. The operation he was dispatched to was called *"Die Wacht am Rhein"** …

THE SEELISBERG LOOKS OUT over Lake Urner…This is where they once brought me to stroll through the Rütliwiese…a meadow full of intensely aromatic cyclamen, bluebells, hyacinths and other flowers…this is where Wilhelm Tell lived, they told me, this is where the Swiss people swore allegiance to each other in their resistance, this is where Switzerland with all of its cantons had come into being… Wilhelm Tell was a brave man for me…one of the greatest archers in history…who, in order to demonstrate his prowess, didn't even flinch at the prospect of sacrificing his son by setting the apple on his head that his arrow halved at a distance of sixty feet…I didn't associate Tell at all with the formation of the cantons of Switzerland, just with that meadow full of cyclamen, and the fact that he was the greatest archer of all time…in my mind, comparable to Peter Klepec, who lived in a

*"The Watch on the Rhine" – a German patriotic song dating to the 19th century, and later the German military code word for the Ardennes offensive of December 1944, resulting in what is known in English as the Battle of the Bulge.

pasture and hurled enormous rocks...Martin Krpan, who dragged horses out of their stalls by their tails...or King Matjaž with his beard wrapping around a stone table and slumbering with his army inside Mount Peca...

Now, after Vati's death, I started to write...I tried to describe Vati's death...Tatjana, my first love...and then my childhood years in Basel...I came to an agreement with my Slovene teacher Mrs. Komar that every Tuesday I would bring some of my writing over to her house for us to read and correct together...I wanted to start at the beginning...with how I first encountered the world, lying on something high and white...with mother, Vati and my sisters on the Elizabethenplatz...with the shadows that they would eventually emerge from...I knew...this would be hard, too hard, almost like describing a dream where there was nothing firm you could seize onto, but also nothing so fragile and elusive that you could firmly place your hand on...Even at the moment when I had a blank sheet of paper with that assignment in front of me, everything was as though I'd just woken up, realizing, noticing that I was surrounded with things and people, and if I looked very carefully at the sky or at the wall or at the floor or at my hand as it wrote, or didn't write, it would happen that I got the feeling I was seeing all this for the first time. Then I would wonder or I would ask, as if for the first time, "What is this?" I would look around and ask, "What are all these things? Where am I? Who am I? What is this question?"...At those moments a sudden, powerful, blinding light would flood everything...allowing the shadows of my concerns, all shadows of any kind to vanish, in other words all the walls that had the effect of causing me to imagine or invent differences, distinctions or meanings... I was no longer able to formulate any questions, no matter what kind... because I couldn't get past that first, basic question, past the brilliant, dazzling light that arose from that question, a light so powerful that it encompassed everything, consuming it and causing it all to disintegrate... Only some crazed action, some mad heroic deed or mad love would be able to respond to the question of that blinding light, and that mad love or heroism would change everything, growing in an enthusiasm that would fling the whole universe into the fire...

I had to give up... I had be more modest, more childlike... I had to start somewhere that was more tangible and ordinary... my first wanderings through the streets and gardens, the stores, the display windows... the French-speaking sunglasses vendor, the market vendor who sold candies shaped like the boats on the Rhine who was a Swiss German... The visits to the zoo and the way the zebras, ponies and lamas seemed like people who'd put on animal masks down to their shoulders, because those were human eyes moving behind the mask slits... The carnivals with their big floats and masqueraders, the confetti and streamers that rained onto the carnival parades... The wells in Basel... of which there were at least a hundred, each of which I drank from using the ladles, until I finally came down with such a bad case of pneumonia I had to be taken to the hospital... Life in the hospital right next to the Rhine, which I escaped from one day and ran home... and then the year spent at the sanatorium in Urach... the blue building with doctors and nuns and never a visit from home...

I sensed how happy they were to have gotten rid of me because I was so active and because I'd always doubted that Vati and mother were my real parents...For two years, I was a patient and nothing else...at first the kind that was strictly confined to bed, and then a convalescent who could get up and walk around dressed in a robe...The young doctor from Germany whom the patients called Hitler and who I felt sorry for...so I would go seek him out in the cafeteria, where he ate alone after everyone else had eaten, so I could cheer him up, entertain him by making faces and telling jokes...The steamships on the Rhine, the tugboats, the big freighters, the river gulls that hovered over my head as I snuck onto one of the tugs with their iron bars, the "*Fleur des carrières*"...Helvetia Day and the August parades that we would dress up for in the guise of various old-fashioned trades and estates...the floats that were made up like zeppelins or castles with draw-bridges... Christmas and the time I saw the baby Jesus out our window...in fact, in diapers on the balcony of the room next to our window, where the balcony turned a corner and continued on the other side of the building, facing another street...the red school of the Christian Brothers, reminiscent of Ljubljana's Church of the Sacred Heart, our black-clad teacher, the nuns, my fellow pupils and the way little bells in the tower announced breaks, not bells in the hands of the school's servants or some electric clock...And then there was Basel itself...with its many streets and intersections, its traffic heading in all directions...there was so much to describe...now I could see that...but, now that I had submitted to and accepted my childishness, I wanted to write an idyll full of spring and meadows and cyclamen...but so much had accumulated in the meantime that I didn't want to take anything from there in isolation from its connection to something else, which in turn was connected to yet something else...in a regular chain of various big, little, light and heavy rings...I'd devoured such a wide variety of things in the first part of my life which, in spite of countless events, had actually been a single uninterrupted present...

Mrs. Komar and I worked in a small room that she referred to as her office. Both of us sat at a desk, she next to some cabinets, me next to the wall...I could see Bleiweis Street out the window...An old house in a garden, surrounded by a wrought-iron fence and the corner of the tall, gray government building...but especially the bare limbs of a row of trees jutting toward the windows, and the way the raindrops slid down their black branches...First I would read my essay, which Mrs. Komar and I would correct for grammar as I read, then I would read through it again in its corrected version..."I wasn't able to write it the way it happened," I said. "The part of it that's behind the event, the part that's unusual, strange, unreal..." Mrs. Komar listened to me attentively...not as in class, where we were asked questions... and she would still give me F's for not knowing the grammar or for mangling the language of a written assignment...what was taking place between us on Tuesday afternoons was something different from school, and class was completely separate from these Tuesdays...At school she always looked straight ahead when we answered...here in her office, with her hands supporting her head and her long, fine fingers supporting her thin, freckled and bronzed face, she looked me in the eyes...This was an unexpected change, and I was thankful to her for agreeing to these extra sessions, which became events for me…I was happy to have her to myself, which was probably the last thing I could have expected from any of my teachers…"You'll find a way," she said. "You just need to grow up. You'll be able to see the material delineated much more clearly, and you'll be better able to distinguish different feelings…" Me: "But by then I'll have forgotten it all. I have to write it now, while I still remember it clearly…while I know what it was like…hot and cold…But I'm limited, and it's so far off that it hardly seems like me who experienced all that…" She: "It doesn't hurt anything for you to organize the events from various perspectives…even if awkwardly. It's practice. Work always progresses by stages. When you're older, you'll have this part behind you. And when you reread these essays, you'll know immediately what you did wrong and what you wanted to say…" Me: "I don't know…perhaps you're right…But the other thing is that, in Slovene, I'm not able to describe everything the way it actually happened…It's as though that was one reality, and what I'm writing in Slovene is something else…I suppose I don't know enough expressions yet, but when I read books, I get the impression that our language lacks a lot of expressions…" I said this haltingly, with reservations…because I knew that Slovene was the language of her love, while it had been implanted in me at a late age and with real pain as a second mother tongue…This has determined the difficult nature of my language…to the present day, and all I've wanted is for this language to become not just a source of torment for me, but one of happiness, if not of pleasure. That's why it was good that I was taught not by a man, but by a woman…"Slovene is rich…

you'll see…" she said without the slightest trace of offense. "For every feeling, we have dozens of terms, and there are more shades within each feeling than we know…and we have terms for those shadings, too…" Me: "Maybe so…I don't know all of them, especially not all those local colloquial terms that mean the same thing…" What I was trying to say was that in our readers and in Slovene class we mostly talked about the language as though it were some fully developed classical orchestra, where all the familiar instruments of the philharmonic were included…from the piano and violins to woodwinds, drums and trumpets…and even some instruments that had a less balanced auditory range…the celeste, triangles, bells…But by contrast, there really were noisemakers of a different sort…simple, unusual, local ones…made of wood, fruit, horsehair…that weren't a part of the classical repertory we studied and learned how to recognize…Me: "Slovene doesn't have the expression, the meaning or the space that the years of my childhood had…" She, with a wry smile: "Are you still looking for the meaning behind everything…?" Me: "Yes…You say that here I need to write 'I was filled with a sense of melancholy,' and that I shouldn't spend so much time describing that feeling… but what I felt was something very clear and specific, while here all we've written is that I felt sad…in order not to disrupt the story or violate a sense of proportion…? What's more, I didn't 'judge' in this spot, as we've corrected it; this was something that leaped out of me, angrily…" In some sense, I was fighting to save the innocence of my writing…She: "I understand, what's at stake here is your truth…What would it be like in German? Could you say what you want there?" Me:

"I don't know...I know German even less than Slovene, because I've been determined to learn Slovene at all costs...I only know the most common words, and they're not good enough for these truths... Plus, I'm also a little mixed up...these two languages don't like each other...and here I am, thinking half in one, half in the other, mixing them up..." She: "That will pass...that's why we're practicing...Try to read some more of our books so you can polish your language..." Me: "I'm not just trying to learn how to write correct – grammatically correct – Slovene, I want to be able to say what's pressing on me... how I look at myself..." She: "That's true, you and I have only been studying how to write correctly. But you know, if you want to break the rules, you first have to learn what they are..." Me: "I have to get clarity about what's happened, Mrs. Komar..." She: "Good Lord, why are you in such a hurry? You have so much time..."

I undertook a systematic reading of Slovene literature...Josip Jurčič, Fran Levstik, Janez Kersnik, Fran Saleški Finžgar...the thing I admired about these writers was their clarity and finely wrought detail, as though they were writing about some accomplished tribe that lived in harmony with the seasons and God, who dealt with them according to his laws, like a strict father with misbehaved children... Their detail encapsulated peasant life from sunrise to dusk as it had been for a hundred, for two hundred years, together with things that had happened long before that...This literature made me feel like a clown dressed in rags, not just a beginner who had barely got past the alphabet...But it was impossible to squeeze my life into the consciousness of language like that...all the internal points of view that kept getting turned upside down, or lost, or never got expressed due to panic and disorder...It wouldn't have worked, and even if it did, it would no longer have been true...Ivan Cankar!...was a nattering writer. The music of his writing reminded me of dance-hall tunes from the turn of the century that people in my mother's time used to dance to... Aside from the exaltation of some vagaries and a stack of indictments, I got nothing out of his books...There were yet other writers who had described where they had come from and where they ended...but most of them had come from Upper Carniola or Prekmurje or someplace, and for ages practically each and every one ended up in Ljubljana... No, I couldn't graft my experience onto them either...Cankar had also been rather unwell...disagreeable, angry, vituperative, and then suddenly gentle and full of praise...those were the only two states I could discern in him, but that was far too little for the countless distortions that life was capable of...So I sought out other writers...I'd already read Dostoevsky...his characters were a little sick too...they thought a lot in their heads about religion and about how God saw them in his head...but despair also drove them to carry out assassination attempts against life and the world...Jack London: in fact people weren't just brave and courageous, like Amundsen or Captain Scott...Tolstoy: in some cases, when he was describing his trust in God and conversations with him, it was similar to the feelings that I had...Hamsun was close to the time and experiences I was enmeshed in...Gide's *Strait Is the Gate*...was a strange see-saw that teetered back and forth from heaven to hell and back...it was rarely on earth...except when somebody lit a lamp or climbed a fence or did anything else that was connected to the world . . . Still, these books remained living creatures for me, with living people, whether I liked them or not . . . Years later, I gave some thought to works of art as objective, living realities . . . The proof of that objective reality was that the reactions they evoked were identical, not random reactions. I could also predict the likely subjective reactions of people who were on the verge of coming into contact with the objective reality of a particular work . . . Because I could make those predictions, that meant that people's subjectivity was just as objective as others' objectivity was subjective. The worth of a particular work resided in the extent to which it remained manifestly identical to itself. The intersection of some work's reality with my subjectivity changed nothing: the worth of any given work was determined by its strength and the endurance that radiated it . . . At least that's how I wanted things to be, but I fear that now, today, any given work is no more than what we think about it – or want to think about it . . . and as a result, every work becomes insignificant, including my own . . . Back when I was going to visit Mrs. Komar and reading lots of books, I found it strange that I couldn't find a single writer anywhere who described the life of a human being from birth to death . . . as painstakingly as botanists might describe some variety of flower . . . from seed, to successive rings, to blossom and winter, when it fades . . . Nor was there a writer who said what the human race living on planet Earth was, the way biologists might say something comparable about birds, bees or frogs . . . I wanted to find everything in one writer . . . As a rule, foreign authors differed from Slovene ones in just one way: they knew how to describe the same world they all lived in better . . . For the most part, Slovene writers thought they were better than the world they inhabited. In fact, it's always the ones who know how to describe the world better who turn out to be the better writers, and that's why I read them. But I did so resentfully, because Slovene writers didn't give me any courage, and with sadness, because I couldn't grasp them...all of their earthly experience with nature and their faith in God, all their mythology... I felt both sad and envious, because I knew that was the only way I could have achieved some intimacy with the people around me...

It was high time for me to find some sort of work or employment...We were three months behind on our rent...we'd had to hide from the electric-bill collector several times...and we barely scraped together enough money for food. If I didn't find work, we were going to suffocate under all this revolting lava...Mother was getting steadily worse...all it took was for her to climb the stairs two or three times, and she'd be shaking so badly she'd have to lie down...she would lie motionless, her hair plastered across her nose, her face greasy and dripping with sweat. On top of that, there was the annual February onslaught of angina pectoris to deal with...as ever, it laid up both of them, both mother and Clairi...With the Herculean task that was facing me...if I gave it any thought...I would lose all momentum and just sit on the steps and light up a cigarette...None of the furriers had any work...And anyway, my teeth would start to chatter if a fur so much as got near me...I went from store to store asking if they could use an apprentice...the unheated shops gaped empty, their shelves bare with nothing in their display windows, while the salespeople, a handful of men and women in advanced old age, twiddled their thumbs under signs that read "Silks"…"Porcelain"…"Clothing"…as if they were in an air-raid shelter, passing the time until the all-clear was sounded up top…All one store had left was walking sticks, handsome canes with rubber tips…There were no jobs at any of the warehouses. On the top floor of a building in the passage connecting Tyrševa and Wolf Streets, there was a man who produced boxes…assembling them under a glass roof where it was terribly cold, and probably unbearably hot in the summer…I'll have something for you in April before Easter, the cardboard man said…I filled a suitcase with all our remaining furs and went from door to door alone, without Clairi…by this time, she would have had the same effect on people as a red cape has on a bull… I followed all the well-worn paths…to Mirje, the turreted buildings around the courthouse…Sure, people were ready to trade for their old clothes, a ripped cardigan…they were like Fate, always trying to trick me…so my sole gratification came from beating them to the punch and shaking my head at the old ladies and sturdy housewives the minute they started trying to offer me their worn-out stuff…Here and there, in spite of the doors and windows closed to prevent any smells from escaping…I caught the aroma of food…of sauces and even rich desserts, a sort of caramelized smell…wherever the smell was the strongest, nobody ever came to the door…You had to be as wily as an Indian, as persistent as a cat if you wanted to see them stuffing their mouths…in wartime, all you really needed to know was your adversary's allegiance and numbers, and you already knew what you were dealing with…

· 346

At last, I got a kind of apprenticeship with a furrier whose shop faced onto the Ljubljanica...three afternoons a week after school, including Saturdays, with a promise of 160 lire per month...That wasn't even enough for a two-month subscription to the newspaper, but it was at least a straw onto which mother could grasp when she was most worried about our survival...for me it meant that all my effort to achieve my ideal was in vain and that I would never be able to climb any higher...I was worried what was going to become of me in the future...I wasn't just in other people's way, but in my own...I conceded the almost universal opinion that I was an idiot...Experience had taught me that I wasn't much use...that I had nothing but deplorable tendencies...That I was a failure...That I didn't deserve mother's sacrifices...that I had no sense of honor...The furrier was a blond, bald man and his wife a big, ruddy-cheeked lady...Their workshop was ideally equipped, in contrast with Vati's...they had a wardrobe practically as big as a shipping container for winter storage, two of the big, blocky fur sewing machines made in Leipzig...all of their furs systematically sorted...bundles of handsome titmouse pelts hanging like little pine trees by the door...even the premises were respectable and well-lit...Except that the owner wasn't half the expert and master furrier that Vati was...I could tell that from the way he cut, sewed, stretched and stitched the hides...as if these weren't rare and valuable furs but pattern tracing paper or maybe just burlap...He wouldn't let me do any of the work...not even soak, stretch or pin up the furs...When I showed him the method of tanning hides using your fingers that Vati had taught me, he said that was ancient history, even though he had stacks and stacks of hides piling up, raw from lack of tannin...I would scrub down the workroom and showroom, sweep the sidewalk out front, clean out the wardrobes and display windows, chop wood, haul up coal, dump out ashes...I knew that everything I was doing was ineffectual and pointless...that I would have to give up all this useless activity...that it would be a lot better if I could become a soldier.

Then, soon after New Year's, who entered our workshop but Julijan! Dressed in a uniform and helmet, with a rifle, a folding shovel and gas mask..."*Schau, wer gekommen ist*,"* said mother, confused...That was a surprise!...He had come from his outpost near Mokronog...a modest base that housed three platoons. They were feeding him well, and in his leather kit bag, he had brought me a third of an army loaf to try, which was more than considerate of him...Had he seen any action? I asked him right off the bat..."I've only fired from a distance, just enough to clear out the barrel," he said. He stood his rifle in a corner and sat down in a wicker chair...He had a mustache...which was barely noticeable, but still...For now, all they did was drill and have target practice, he said...Had he seen any partisans?...Yeah, from a distance, through binoculars and when he flew on reconnaissance...What were they doing? Were they fighting? They don't engage, at least he had no evidence that they did...they bided their time more than they moved...Most of all, they threw parties and dances...The bishop's secretary was also with them...lately he'd

*Look who's here.

been photographed drunk in the arms of some partisan women...
the Home Guard had come into possession of the photo... He had it
with him... and showed it to me... In it, a handsome man wearing not
a priest's cassock but a uniform was shown from the waist up, with
a big smile on his face and on either side one arm wrapped around
a woman... on whose bushy hair was perched that low garrison cap
with the five-pointed star containing the hammer and sickle... They'd
been photographed on a nice day out in the sun... the man could have
been anyone... A priest who's vowed celibacy, with women? said Clairi,
shocked, because she'd understood what we were talking about...
Yes, but what's so unusual about that? Julijan shrugged, red-faced.
The communists also sleep, men and women mixed together... And
the officers and enlisted men don't eat from the same mess kettle
at the front, the way the Germans and Home Guards do, but separately... When they moved out of the forest, the officers' secretaries
and mistresses drove their wagons, while the ordinary soldiers had
to go on foot... a buddy of his from the base had seen it with his
own eyes... The partisan soldiers had even composed a song that
they sang, which went something like this: "With young blood, the
blood of partisans, a new land surges forth..." But hadn't they always
claimed that they were all equal? Propaganda! Didn't they always say
here that the Home Guards were fighting for faith, home and nation,
even though there were plenty of rotters in their ranks too... I looked
at him closely for signs that he'd changed... and he had, quite a bit,
he'd become more serious and a lot less impulsive than he'd been
before... He had to go... He'd only come to Ljubljana to deliver some

message to headquarters...He got up...I walked with him to the train station...Again there were leaflets strewn all around...on the walls lining the Ljubljanica, Tito's head had been stenciled in red paint... nobody bothered to scrub anything off anymore...in places, a black hand had been painted too...Who was the Black Hand, actually...? I asked him. Those were undercover Home Guards who executed the partisans and their collaborators. There was even a former partisan commander working for the Black Hand...but that was a long story, Julijan said...that commander wasn't a communist but a believer, and the Reds had tried several times to liquidate him and his followers where they were holed up in the forest...finally, he got so fed up that he fled, then he and some of his followers started killing communists... It was said that they sent each of their victims a sheet of paper with a black hand drawn on it, to let them know they were going to be killed some night soon...that was similar to what the French partisans did by sending little coffins to German collaborators whom they'd marked for death, as Jens had told me...That evening, I thought to myself that if I were to put a sheet of paper with a black hand printed on it outside the door of this or that person whom I didn't like, they'd probably die of sheer fright...

In the days when I was working for the furrier, I didn't see much of Lado Pšeničnik...and hadn't, in fact, since the previous December, ever since that performance...Mr. Becele had decided that our study group would perform a play for the children of St. Mary's pre-school and give them presents afterwards...every child would get one cookie, one orange, one rosary...The play was about two robbers who stole a painting of St. Nicholas in a gold frame from a church and planned to sell it to a pawnbroker...Because the painting was heavy, the robbers paused to rest somewhere, at some crossroads in a forest. But barely had they fallen asleep than the painting came to life...and then the real St. Nicholas stepped out of the gold frame and punished both good-for-nothings by turning them into little demons...After that last scene, we were supposed to present the gifts to the children in the auditorium, accompanied by both demons and various angels... Mr. Becele had decided to cast Tinček and me as the robbers, while Pšeničnik tried out for the role of St. Nicholas come to life, who was going to appear in bishop's regalia, with his shepherd's crook and book with a golden apple on the cover...I was assigned to create the big painting of St. Nicholas. Mr. Becele, who had been trained as a painter, didn't have time. I got paper and paints. Pšeničnik came to pose for me, so that the image in the painting would be exactly the same size as him and bear a reasonable resemblance...He brought with him a suitcase containing a chasuble and bishop's stole, as well as a staff. He stood in the middle of our workroom, as radiant as a real archbishop, while I drew on the paper spread out on the floor. Over the following days, as I filled in the design of the chasuble, which was quite complicated...he came by several times to criticize this or that...I wished so much I could just drive him away...he never did anything, he just gave instructions...and if I did try to say something to him, he would pretend that he hadn't heard...a trait I observed many years later in so-called political functionaries...whether they were being exposed or convicted of the most egregious crimes, they wouldn't react at all, as though the matters being revealed had no connection to them…if there was a thunderstorm, they could at least flinch at the lightning…Mother and Clairi thought highly of him…"*Ein geborener Manager*," Clairi enthused. "*Er kennt sich aus…so muß man es im Leben machen.*"* We rehearsed the play on the little stage of St. Mary's preschool…Tinček and I had to show how heavy the painting was in its gold frame, which was the hardest part because in fact it was made out of near-weightless paper…we had to gasp, swear within bounds, and fall convincingly when we got to the crossroads… and when the lights went out, we had to get the painting off the stage fast, so that St. Nicholas come to life could replace it…then we had to lie back down on our assigned marks, and when we woke up and St. Nicholas punished us, we had to run terrified backstage…where we put on masks with horns, tied on our tails, grabbed our cats of nine tails and went back on stage as devils…This was the first time I got to perform on a real stage, one with a curtain and stage lights…Gisela also came for the performance…and I realized how incredibly hard it is to pretend to be asleep amid strangers, while at the same time peaking out to see if the audience believes you…The whole audience laughed so uproariously, with their mouths open so wide that they looked like they were about to gobble us up…oh, how different it was when Gisela and I put on performances at home…here I was consumed with doubt…I realized what a wild, cannibalistic tribe a theater audience actually is…After that, Pšeničnik and I didn't see

---

*He's a born manager. He's got the knack…that's how you have to do things in life.

each other until our medical exams in the clinic at school... In the meantime, Budapest had fallen to the Russians, it was March, and the Americans were already in the Rhineland near Cologne... the last military postcard from Jens, dated May 1, came from the ruins of Remagen in Germany... The medical commission determined that because I was undernourished I would get my main meal each day from the clinic's kitchen... the kitchen and dining room were in the basement... there were some eighty school kids and university students from all over town who went there... all of us stick figures, skin and bones, whom you could see right through without any X-rays... I don't know how Pšeničnik managed to get himself assigned to us skeletons, when he already had his meals taken care of. After classes, the two of us went to the clinic together... all they had on their menu was mashed turnips, carrots, now and then potatoes, and once a week a cutlet of some ground meat or a tiny bit of pastry... I would take the pastry and meat cutlet home for Gisela and mother... Each time I'd wait for all the others to clear out of the dining room... as if by some error of fate, here and there on the tables there might be some bit of half-eaten bread that I could scoop into my bag to take home...

In those days, if you looked at a map of Europe, your stomach would turn... the Anglo-Americans had covered nearly all the dry land like leaves and grass... Flying fortresses had bombarded Tokyo for ten days in a row... with nothing but incendiary bombs, tumbling as they fell through the powerful winds... which also buffeted burning objects... even whole wooden buildings... up and down the streets... tongues of flame three hundred feet high would race after the people fleeing for air, so they could breathe...but then the fire would slam them onto the ground like playthings...leaving 97,000 people dead. The flying fortresses started crossing the skies over Ljubljana again too...Their escort planes, Mosquitos, dove bravely, shamelessly farther and farther down, until...*boom*! came the retort from somewhere close by...*boom*! once again, farther off. A bomb had fallen on Mirje! One bomb! The shock wave threw me back from the open window into the workroom...Now things had probably reached the point where we were up next...Everyone was downstairs in the cellar... mother, Gisela, Clairi, both of the Hirols, Mr. Praček, the café owner, the judge's family, the market vendor, Ana and her fiancé, who was a traffic cop...if a bomb dropped on our building, we were going to wind up with the strangest, most motley company for a day at the cemetery!...But we probably didn't talk much about the flying fortresses, even though they kept stubbornly flying over the city...Down there I heard people telling each other the most improbable things...loudest of all was Hirol! He always knew everything! Like everyone from down south in the Balkans...pampered, lazy, with excess imagination... he just made stuff up...down to every last detail, and such details, as though he were sitting in one of the B-17s and had Eisenhower next to him, whispering everything in his ear, confidentially, just between the two of them...

In mid-March, the Home Guard discovered yet another mass grave...On Congress Square...between the Ursuline convent and the shoe store, in the place where they sold Christmas trees in December and rings for tree stands...there were coffins set out...thirty or forty plain coffins made of unvarnished boards...peasants, their wives and children, whom the partisans had killed..."Victims of the communist marauders" was written on cardboard, and a guard wearing a surgical mask over his mouth and nose kept watch...They were all from Lower Carniola...poorly dressed...some of them in rubber boots that didn't disintegrate as fast as their feet...most of them just in footwraps... some had their throats cut, and in some of these cases the faces were still red, as though they were in the flush of health...the heads of others were twisted and facing the side boards, as though their necks had been broken...their wrists had been tied together with rusty barbed wire...there were little boys and girls dressed in night shirts that looked like altar boys' surplices...they looked straight up at the statue on top of the plague column in front of the church...some of them were already little more than sand and dirt up to the neck... others had partially decomposed faces that made them look like tattered cobwebs...The partisans must have really gotten busy while the whole village was asleep...I wasn't afraid, I wasn't disgusted...I just knew I could have been one of them...that tomorrow it could just as easily be me and my family lying like gravel in coffins like these, lids on or lids off...Fortunately we hadn't suffered any real violence so far in this war.

At school, we were required to attend anti-communist lectures. They had begun at the end of the previous school year and continued this year. We marked the subject in our schedules with the abbreviation ACL...We even had some older boys in the higher forms who came to school dressed in Home Guard uniforms. The Guard allowed them to keep going to school so they wouldn't fall behind a year…Nobody knew for sure if they were real soldiers or fake ones…Perhaps they were traitors, partisan spies or White provocateurs?…They would argue with each other and the rest of us about what they had or hadn't seen…we school kids didn't have the slightest idea what was going on…not the slightest!…we had avoided the very worst slaughter, the mass hangings, the decapitations of small children!…they kept repeating things like that as they occupied the hallways, the stairs, the basement and restrooms during air raids… they would go to the men's room three, four, whole squads at a time. The students would make fun of them…the first form students would make sounds like bombs, *boom*! and airplanes, *bzzz*!…that was the full extent of their repertory…*boom*! and *bzzz*!…the young soldiers got angry…go ahead and laugh! you bunch of shirkers and weaklings! just wait until some Red Mongol shows you the tree he's going to hang you from…

Our lecturer for ACL was the same one as the previous year. Nobody knew what his name was. That was a secret…He was cut from some entirely different cloth than our Home Guard cocks of the walk. Even though he was a young person and of very short stature…with a pale, round face and always dressed in the same cheap, brown suit… he made a stern, impersonal impression, without the least trace of leniency. The teachers would go out of their way to avoid him…even our math teacher Mr. Fink, who was brave, would describe a wide arc around him if they met in the hall…Ours wasn't the only school where the young teacher lectured on his subject, there were five others. He would come to our school from one of them, sometimes even running to avoid being late. He was courageous, and that was something we valued. He wasn't afraid of fights or assassination attempts in any of the overfilled classrooms of the high schools where he taught...Nor did he carry a pistol. And even though nobody really believed what he taught us, because ultimately it was all just propaganda, each of us was fully convinced of his personal courage...and some were even offended by the disdain he showed toward us all...

He began with the theoretical origins of communism...he showed us portraits of Karl Marx and Friedrich Engels...it was a bit of a shock to find out they were Germans, and it made you wonder if maybe everything in the world came from there...Then he spoke about the revolution and communism in Russia...he told us that, in order to subjugate the Russians and other nations, the communists had woven a vast network of spies...to the point where children even spied on their parents at home and denounced them to the authorities...and vice versa, that parents would report their barely adult daughters and sons to the Soviet authorities for questioning communism...In this way, Russia had managed to destroy the family and jail or kill anyone who thought differently or believed in God...We listened to him attentively...He spoke persuasively...reading authentic reports...excerpts from Russian books and novels...showing us who had written them and when...This, he said, is how a bloody revolution unfolded...through mass murder on a scale never before seen, except in the times of Ivan the Terrible and the Mongol conquest...the first concentration camps in the world were the death camps of Siberia and the remote islands of the Arctic Sea...Those who remained "free" had to join forced labor brigades building hydro-electric dams and railroads... and the lecturer read us a passage from a Soviet book called *The Volga Flows to the Caspian Sea*...where the peasants had all their land, forests and livestock taken away...and were forced into big government estates called *kolkhozes*, where they had to work as day laborers under their communist overseers...earning barely enough to feed their families...Despite Russia's size and fertility, the Red barbarians had brought the country to the verge of destruction...its harvests, which had once been enormous and fed half the world, were now so paltry that they barely survived on them and were forced to import meat and grain from America and Canada...Their industry, their factories produced substandard machinery that began falling apart the minute it came off the line...and they threw away huge sums of money on various research projects that subsequently turned out to be hoaxes or childish fantasies...considering that they had such vast material and human resources available to them, you had to wonder why nothing succeeded. The answer was simple: it was because...to be perfectly frank...they were slow, because they'd lost all touch with reality, because they despised work and, finally, because they appointed people to the most important positions whose chief qualification was that they had a membership card in the Communist Party...But the biggest sums of money that the Russian communists wrested from their subjects were squandered on the lavish lifestyles of their spies and agents around the world who were assigned to foment revolution...including our communists, the ones who had lived with foreign passports in various countries before the war and in luxury villas at home, without ever having to work for their daily bread…and they were spending this war, too, like vacationers on some scouting trip in the forest… well protected, which was apparently what they meant by securing the vanguard…while their naive, misguided followers had to contend with the largest mechanized army in the world…Communism led to apathy in every sphere of life…under no circumstances could we Slovenes afford the Russian approach: we had too little territory and too few people, and if the communists…who weren't nationalists, but internationalists…were going to keep massacring their people, and they would, we would be decimated into a tiny tribe…and vanish like the American Indians…We couldn't allow them to seize our homes, our land, our faith, our nationhood…The Home Guards had dedicated their modest force to preventing this from ever happening… They were barely more than a handful of men…Not only were their forces barely worth mentioning, they were poorly equipped…Just one example: while the Italians and Germans took cover or let loose with their anti-aircraft guns during air raids…they stayed out in the open, armed only with rifles…they didn't even have a single tank… It was a silly example, he admitted. But it was true…And yet that handful of legionnaires was also the core of a future Slovene national army…There wasn't a student in class, it seemed, who completely believed or disbelieved what he said…The truth was as plain as day, or it could be dragged in kicking and screaming…but one way or the other…it had been dragged into class by someone with confidence, who was courageous, bold, practically like a kamikaze... Now that we'd covered the material, our ACL lecturer said, each of us was to write a composition with the title "The Dangers of Communism" for a grade. We were not supposed to put our names on our compositions, he said as he handed out the sheets of paper, because the bandits had their spies everywhere and could hardly wait to take out their opponents and anyone who differed with them... Nobody knew what to write, including me... I suppose I could have described any event from the war... but I didn't trust any of them... nothing was so pure that you could believe in it unconditionally... everything was a dirty game, for show, propaganda... you had to be filled with enthusiasm for it to blind you, and then you could betray yourself... I knew that there was just something beyond all the human comedies and calculations: God... there was no abolishing God. God was behind everything... behind molecules when you broke them down into atoms, behind atoms when you split them into sub-atomic particles... he was even in fragments, in dust, in an explosion, he was Spirit... You couldn't kill the soul or do away with the inner life. That was the first thing, and as first thing it would remain... the source of all evil and good... The lecturer collected our sheets of paper, and the next time he came, he said that the best composition had dealt with God as the principal force standing behind the universe and life on earth... I could feel myself blush, and I didn't even need to turn around to face the others, because everyone knew who had written that...

Around that time, Clairi got a letter from the wife of that merchant who had a grocery store in the round building near the railroad crossing. She was a high-strung lady who sometimes came over to see us and always seemed so distracted that she neither saw nor heard anything around her...She wrote that she'd come into some furs and wanted to have them made into a coat. She could pay either in cash or in foodstuffs, whichever Clairi preferred, and would appreciate it if Clairi would stop by sometime soon...Clairi was on pins and needles. She had never before sewn a complete fur piece from start to finish...Vati had always guided her work and handled the trickiest parts himself. I went with her...because there was something else that was eating at her, not just the coat. *"Paß auf,"* she said, *"die Leute, zu denen wir gehen... ich meine, der Kaufmann...der ist ein Verräter..."** A traitor? Who did he betray? Clairi gave me a sour smile..."*Er war einmal bei den Partisanen... er hat die Kommunisten verraten, eine ganze Einheit."*** A traitor...that was the lowest of the low...whether they worked for one side or the other. As we approached the round, pink building near the barriers, I remembered that August five years before when the merchant's son Oto and I had chased each other amid the pillars surrounding the house, and how whenever he wanted, he went inside the store and, right in front of the saleswomen, stuffed candies from the tall jars into his pockets. I also remembered the living room with the paintings up above and the merchant himself, then still a pale, serious young man...Now a metal shutter had been lowered over the storefront, and there was a guard out in front of the house, a plain-clothes policeman...making

*Be careful. The people we're going to see...I mean the merchant...is a traitor.

**He used to be with the partisans...he betrayed the communists, a whole unit of them.

sure that no bandits could get into the house and kill the owner?...The policeman came toward us, when the lady appeared at a window and nervously screeched, "Let them through!" We climbed up the snail-like winding staircase, which was now badly beaten up, and entered the big, bare room...previously their living room!...that had just a couch and one painting on the wall. The lady of the house was nervous, haggard, mere skin and bones...when she smiled, she showed big teeth that looked like fangs...Her husband wasn't home, he was at work... his secret job? or as a merchant with the quartermaster corps?...the store had been closed for several months now...out the window, I could see a second plain-clothes policeman on their property who was keeping an eye on their house from behind..."Would you like to see Oto?" the lady smiled at me. "You played with him once, didn't you?...He's not here now...he's in a boarding school in Germany... you'll have to make do with his brother Robert." Robert, a little squirt, was sitting on the couch. "Čiči!" he said, tapping the cushion beside him. The lady and Clairi were examining the furs on a round table in the middle of the room..."You want to see something?" Robert asked me. I was embarrassed...and nodded. "It's right there behind the picture," he said, pointing to the oil painting over his head. He got up on the couch, still in his shoes. "Come on up...don't bother taking your shoes off!" he said. I took them off anyway, so as not to make a mess of the couch. "Look," he said. With an ease that amazed me, since he was barely six, he removed the painting in its gold frame and leaned it against the couch...There was a rectangular hole in the wall...he pressed a button or trigger...and *zzzip!* suddenly a little door opened up…in the cavity behind I saw a stash of firearms…two machine guns…pistols…three or four Italian red devils…boxes of ammunition…enough armaments for a whole squad…"Hm, why have you got this stuff?" I asked. "That's my dad's," he said. "If the bandits break into our house, he and I are gonna shoot 'em all dead…." Instead of the weaponry, I looked at him: he was a cute kid, his hair cut in a flat top, big eyes and very pale…and at that point my memory runs out…no matter how much I've tried anytime since then to excavate events after the sofa, I've never been able to get beyond the boy's face which fascinated me so much…

It was the end of March…The Russians and the Americans were not just in Germany, they had even surrounded Vienna…the pictures in the newspapers showed the inhabitants setting up barricades all over town…the Matica Theater was showing a color movie called *Golden Prague* with the famous Marika Rökk singing the lead role…I reread my papers…the one about my first love…the one about Vati's death…I kept them in a box under my bed…In the former, I had meant to describe the kissing and coupling under the arch of the old Roman house…but I couldn't get it to do what I wanted…I felt that I couldn't use the usual words, because they only meant what they were…but fancy words meant both too much and nothing… Similarly, Vati's death hadn't turned out as I'd expected…I had expected that a description of his death would automatically yield what was important and real…but it hadn't! At a meeting of our study group, Pšeničnik told me that a new magazine for young and beginning writers called *Slovene Youth* was going to be published. Anyone who felt they had something worthwhile was supposed to deliver their work to the editor-in-chief, Dr. Tine Debeljak, at the magazine's office, which was on the floor above the *Slovene* printing press... I made a clean copy of that last night when Vati died and gave it to the doorman sitting in the barred gatehouse at the entrance to the press... At the beginning of April, I got a letter... the first mail addressed expressly to me in my life... telling me to come to the editor's office... All of Old Square clattered to the clomp of wooden-soled shoes... only that sort of footwear, whether low cut or high ankled, was available for ration coupons at stores... there was barely enough cow and pig leather to cover the uppers... the soles were made of linden wood and were hard and inflexible... only high-ankled shoes occasionally had leather hinges for the soft part of the foot... In some dark, cavernous space dominated by balconies and columns, somebody showed me to a carved door, behind which the editor worked. I knocked... "Come in!"... I opened the door and saw inside the same Dr. Debeljak from the pictures... with his white, bald head and thick glasses, and next to him a priest... Fran Saleški Finžgar, the greatest living writer after our greatest living poet Oton Župančič... I couldn't even stammer. Somehow I managed to mumble my name, then stayed in the doorway, in case I needed to run. Dr. Debeljak first raised his head, then a hand. "Your sketch is going to be published in our first issue. And we're going to pay you for it. Congratulations..." There were also some features in a refined, pale face closely observing me: that was F. S. Finžgar... I had no idea how I got out of that cavernous space back onto the street, for I only really came to when I was running under the arcade of the marketplace... I ran, no matter that my inflexible shoe soles were squeezing and digging into my flesh, so I could get home as soon as possible and tell them the news…The piece really did get published…they sent me a copy of the magazine with a gracious letter from the editor inviting me to come pay a visit…a typewritten letter on letterhead stationery, with an official stamp…The magazine had a pinkish, almost transparent cover… reminiscent of a soap wrapper, which was a result of the war…and it had a vignette showing a young fellow and his girl dancing, dressed in Upper Carniolan folk costumes, which I had always loathed, ever since my first school processions and Falcon assemblies…Somewhere toward the end of the issue was my story, starting at the bottom of one page and continuing for the whole following page…The first letter of its first word was presented as an ornamented initial…between the feet of the "K" there was a drawing of an exhausted old man with a pauper's stick…in classical style, as in our readers, except that it had only a superficial connection to my story…The next day a review came out in the newspaper. "A fine sketch contributed by…" That was the first time I ever saw my name in the newspaper…not counting the ads we placed about Vati's workshop…everyone started flocking around me…Clairi said I needed to clip out the review and mount it on cardboard. On the day of the death of U.S. President Roosevelt, whom the newspapers had portrayed as an "American gangster and inciter of war," I set out to visit Dr. Tine Debeljak at his editorial office…He was very gracious when I arrived…he had me sit on a chair next to a tin vase with a sunflower that stood on the window sill, beyond which you could see the Dragon Bridge…He asked me where I was from…

I did a poor job of answering… He had published a book by the poet France Balantič titled *Ablaze in Horror's Fire*. He had also written a study about him. He was an expert on style. I told him that I'd read poems from that collection and that I liked them a lot… more than anything published till then. And that was the truth. He had interesting things to say about the Home Guard poet. "Life isn't always sordid," he said. "Now and then, of course…" In certain circumstances that really was true, and I conceded as much… People who don't endure any evil… prison, misfortune… see life as a cesspool and hate everything. But people who have undergone a fair amount of evil don't hate anyone. They live and let live… On the other hand, plenty of people who enjoy freedom and wealth are hard and embittered, full of hatred and envy, impatient, grim… Probably because they haven't served their time yet. As I said goodbye, Dr. Debeljak handed me a voucher for the honorarium and asked me to bring by more of my work… directly to his apartment… He lived in the building next to St. Joseph's Church… I was glad to have met him. In those times, it wasn't easy to come across a kind soul!… The cashier was in the building of the provincial seat… the same place where Bug, his mother and I had cleaned up the bank archives in the basement… And who was sitting in the cashier's office, but… Šešek's father, that fat, old, red-faced walrus of a man who sat on the veranda pasting coupons onto sheets of paper for the grocers… Without recognizing me, he gave me a grim smile and, the minute I handed him the voucher, told the young assistant seated next to him to pay me my money… I got 360 lire! I thought it must be a mistake… but no, no! "It's yours," the old man muttered begrudgingly. It was almost half-a-month's pay. With that much money, we could pay the three months' back rent we owed and the electric bill, and buy some cracklings and beans on the black market...

By mid-April...which was sunny and hot...the Russians had broken through to Vienna...and a week later were on the outskirts of Berlin...A photo in the newspaper showed Hitler on his birthday in the courtyard of his bunker, which was underneath the Reich Chancellery...looking drawn and pale in his leather coat with the collar turned up...he was handing out iron crosses to members of the Hitler Youth for defending Berlin ...they were just boys my age...some of them even younger...they were fighting the Russians from building to building, apartment to apartment, which reminded me of Stalingrad...The whole town was jittery...it felt to me like people on the street were constantly losing their minds...Mother was all confused, continually talking to herself...she wasn't sleeping at all..."*Wenn ich bedenke, daß es einmal Frieden gegeben hat,*"* she said..."*Das ist doch gar nicht so lange her, Mama,*"** Clairi replied..."*Jahrhunderte, Clairi! Jahrhunderte...*"*** "*Richtig, Mama! Jahrhunderte!*"****...Hirol had once again taken to eyeing us in the stairway, by the faucet between our apartments...wherever...brazenly! with his intentions stenciled across his forehead!...all that was missing was a club in his raised

*To think that there once was a time when we were at peace.

**That's not all that long ago, mother.

***It's been centuries, Clairi, centuries.

****You're right, mother. It's been centuries.

hand…He would be the first to come after us…and had a particular glint in his eye for Clairi, who was easy prey…it didn't take much to get her reacting in fear to everything, and all that did was stoke the flames even more…including the ones in the furthermost recesses of his heart…Mother's repertory always consisted of the same questions. *"Die Leute im Haus?"** What did Clairi think of them? *"Ich weiß noch nicht,"*** …she answered…*"Und der Hirol?"*** …*"Zweideutig… sehr zweideutig…"**** "Los, Bubi,"* Clairi said to me one day, *"gehen wir zur Rosa Weinberg!…"***** Rosa Weinberg was a Jewish woman from Czechoslovakia. Her husband was in a concentration camp. She lived alone with her two children in a building across from the rectory of St. Peter's Church. She made money by knitting and tending two pigs in the landlord's courtyard for eventual sale, although she herself never touched pork. Clairi and she were sort of semi-friends…She often came over to our house to visit…seeking shelter. When in September 1943 the Germans tried to deport her to a concentration camp, mother, as a German expatriate, petitioned the regional authorities to allow her to stay…considering that she had two small children whose only support she was, that she was a model parent who had never engaged in politics, that she could vouch for her as her long-time friend…She got

*What about the people in our building?

**I don't know yet.

***And what about Hirol?

****Uncertain, very uncertain.

*****Come on, Bubi, let's go visit Rosa Weinberg.

to stay. Rosa Weinberg was a short, fat, red-haired woman who always wore pants…In this war there were lots of far more agreeable people than her dying every five minutes…She got on my nerves, because she was constantly gabbing. Whenever we went to visit her, she was always piddling around with her black market rags…wearing pants, so that when she bent over, she had an enormous rear end. Rosa gave off an intense body odor…something not uncommon among redheads. Redheads have the same fate as animals…harsh and unfortunate, it pervades their skin…But it did arouse lust…She often related her past experiences with men to my sister out loud…and even now, new adventures kept taking place…and yet, as I understood it, she still found it a challenge to make contact with them…Once, when she was over at our house and it started to pour, I walked her home all the way to the rectory, carrying the only umbrella we could afford…She kept pressing up against me more than she needed, since it really was quite a wide umbrella…and I could feel whole layers of flesh through her coat…One gesture was all it would have taken from me, if I'd had any courage…She knew only the most basic Slovene, so she spoke to people either in Czech or German…*"Für eine gute Tat muß man sich bedanken,"** she said when we parted, kissing me on the cheek. *"Küß mich!"*** she said, and I did…She had one room and a little kitchen… there was a framed photograph of her husband on the wall…he was a willowy, scholarly type, a schoolteacher…smiling through his big

---

*A person ought to show thanks for a good deed.

**Kiss me.

eyeglass frames, with a hank of hair that the wind had tossed over one lens...I couldn't look at that picture of the innocent, absent-minded teacher without a sense of anger and compassion...Her children... two little boys dressed in overalls...were again something else completely next to their mother...they were inseparable from me and, while she and Clairi were gossiping, would spend the whole length of our visits climbing all over me. I drew them pictures...made puppets for them...a movie theater out of corks and sticks...Now, as we reached her house, both pigs started to raise a whole ruckus in their pen...from hunger? fear?...they oinked as though there were a hundred of them...Clairi assumed that, aside from her contacts with men, Rosa also had contacts with the partisans...The question just jumped right out of her, "Hast du auch an uns gedacht?..."* "Ja... ja..."** Rosa blurted back. "Na und?...Na und?..."*** She didn't even raise her head out of the pen...I turned away...this was too much... to ask somebody for help, foist your own bag of rocks off on them, it wasn't dignified, even if it was your best friend, don't ever ask them for anything!...even if they're willing!...think it over a hundred times before you accept any help..."Das genügt nicht, nur an uns zu denken,"**** Clairi said. Where did she find these wells of shamelessness?...

*Have you thought about what will happen to us?

**Yes...yes!

***And?... And?

****It isn't enough just to think about us.

"Es geht darum, daß du an uns denkst, bevor es dicke Luft gibt..." This
was the height of bad manners and abasement...*"Ja, ja, ja,"* Rosa, that
red-headed mound of flesh, kept answering without turning away from
the pen. "Clairi!" I shouted. *"Gehen wir...es ist Zeit...."* *"Ich kann
doch etwas von ihr verlangen,"* she shrieked, as though Rosa wasn't
standing right there. No, she could not, she dare not demand anything
in exchange for mother's kindness...all that did was invalidate the
act itself...far better to just beg for mercy...I wanted to tell her to
have some dignity..."*Gut!*" Clairi gave in at last. *"Mach, was du willst,
Rosa!"*...Rosa didn't say boo, or goodbye...she just stayed where
she was, looking indifferently into the pen. *"Ich glaube, daß es Schluß ist
mit der Freundschaft...Aus mit dem Du – und – Du,"* Clairi whined
once we were out on the street. *"Mit einer aufgewärmten Platte ist es
immer Schluß, hat schon der Vati gesagt...."*

One Italian city after the other kept falling into Anglo-American
hands...Bologna, Ferrara, Modena, Verona, Genoa...and then Milan,
where Mussolini still ruled...On the day before the May 1st holiday,
a photo appeared in the *Slovene*...showing the Duce strung up by his

---

*What matters is that you think of us before the feathers start to fly.

**Clairi! Let's go...it's time.

***But I have a right to expect something of her.

****Fine! Do whatever you want, Rosa.

*****I'd say it's all over with that friendship. That's the last time I address her with "Du."

******Vati always said you know it's all over when they serve you warmed leftovers.

feet, upside down from the pole of a filling station, his shirttails flopping down over his face…"In Milan, the Red rabble have heinously murdered the leader of the Italian people…" On Hrenova Street, as I was rushing to school, I ran into an SA gendarme…he had abruptly stepped out of the entryway of the Todt organization…"*Wo hast du die Augen, Lümmel?*"* And *wham!* went his fat hand over my mouth, causing everything around me to shake. He was a little tipsy, the high-strung moron!…Mother couldn't sleep nights…she kept calling out to us, as ever…put her hand on our foreheads, as though feeling our temperature…kept shuffling back and forth…sat down on a chair by the window…"*Sag mal, Mama, erinnerst du dich an die Bohoričstraße?*"** I asked her. She searched through her memory, "*Nein, Bubi! Nein!…*"*** "*Und an Nove Jarše?…und an Frau Gmeiner?…*"**** "*Warte mal! Warte mal, ein bißchen…*"***** "*Die Frau Gmeiner im neuen Haus! Sie hatte zwei Söhne!…*"****** "*Ja, richtig, Bubi…du hast recht! Frau Gmeiner! Ja…*"******* In the afternoons, I copied out stories I'd written and then gone through and edited with Mrs. Komar, so I could deliver them to Dr. Tine Debeljak's house…On May 1st, the newspaper had a black

---

*Look where you're going, oaf!

**Say, Mother, do you remember Bohorič Street?

***No, Bubi, I don't.

****How about Nove Jarše? And Mrs. Gmeiner?

*****Wait. Just a second, maybe a little…

******Mrs. Gmeiner who lived in the new house. She had two sons.

*******Yes, that's right, Bubi, you're right: Mrs. Gmeiner. Yes.

frame printed around it: "The Führer died while fighting to his last breath against Bolshevism..." The leader had designated Admiral Karl Dönitz, former commander of Germany's submarine fleet, as his successor. This was truly the end...and on May 2nd, Berlin fell to the Red Army...The people...What were the people like out on the streets? Buoyant, fast-moving, crowds blocking practically the entire street...every single person in that crowd, I imagined, could have some important task to fulfill...but which of them wasn't worth a cent?...

That was followed by yet another surprise...In Ljubljana, in the Tabor district, a new Slovene government was established in secret... All the most important politicians and members of the national council were assembled beneath the Yugoslav flag and a portrait of King Petar II to swear their allegiance to the Kingdom, the new government and the Anglo-American allies...Atop the castle tower, the national flag bearing the royal coat of arms and crown was unfurled...something I hadn't seen since 1941...Even the Home Guards covered the blue eagle on their sleeves with the Yugoslav tricolor...Julijan came tromping up to our attic...also wearing the tricolor of the erstwhile kingdom on his sleeve..."Now we're going to have to defend Ljubljana against the communists, until the Anglo-American forces under Field Marshall Alexander take Trieste and advance eastward," he said. "What a reversal of fortune!"...He and I went outside...there were a lot of people out...and what did I see? in the display window of the philately shop, the whole backdrop was covered with Allied flags...the English Union Jack with its blue and white cross against a field of red and the striped American flag with its white stars on a blue field...all handmade using different colored paper. "Now it's all going to be different from the way things have been up to now," Julijan said excitedly. I looked at him...his blond hair had grown darker, and there were deep hollows in his cheeks...I wanted to walk him back to his family's house in Prule, but when we got to St. Jacob's Bridge and I looked up at the tower, the flag with the royal coat of arms was gone..."Look, the flag's gone," I pointed out to him, worried. "Do you suppose the flagpole broke?" he asked. No, it hadn't...we waited five minutes, a quarter of an hour, without taking our eyes off the tower...not even a head appeared over the battlements..."I've got to run up there," Julijan said. "Find out what's happened..." And carrying all the gear he'd arrived with, his gas mask, rifle and kit bag, he set off at a sprint up the most gravelly path up the hill...That evening we learned... the Germans had caught the new government in Tabor right after the oath...they were on the verge of taking them prisoner...but the lot of them, including Bishop Rožman, managed to escape from the Falcon Assembly Hall through some basement windows...The next morning, the Home Guards were back to wearing just the blue eagle armbands on their sleeves...

Ba-doom! Ba-dang!...the thundering came from up above us, on castle hill, causing the whole hillside to shake...the partisans had to be getting close to the city...were they on Krim? or Golovec?... The Germans and Home Guard replied with artillery fire from their emplacements...serving them up the biggest caliber they had!...The cannons were like magnificent sheep dogs that were nevertheless helpless to protect their flock...At any instant, you expected giant shell casings to come tumbling down the hillside or rolling down from Upper Square and crashing into the streetcar stop...at any instant, I expected the ammo dump in the castle to explode toward all points of the compass, taking us with it...When the machine guns joined in, you could hear through their rattle as pine cones dropped onto the hollow forest floor..."*Der Himmel ist ganz rosa...hast du's gesehen?...eine neue Farbe,*"* mother said..."*Das sind die Explosionen zwischen den Wolken...*"** Clairi answered. "*Die Mauern zittern, mehr als gestern...die Erde auch,*"*** mother said...*Ba-doom!*...an echoing explosion came rolling in...from the marshlands...from Rakovnik? "*Alles das ist noch gar nicht zu Ende...*"**** "*Natürlich ist es nicht zu Ende!*"***** mother laughed strangely, so that her whole body shook..."*Plemplem? nicht plemplem?*"****** Clairi whispered to me..."*Überlege mal, Clairi, was wir alles schon erlebt haben...von Guček...Die Frau Guček! die alte Schlampe! der Hamm! die Bohoritschstraße! und der Herr Perme mit den Zinsen! die Hammans Kanzlei, das Gespenst von Hitler! und die Deutschen bei uns im Gerbergäsli, die das Ladenschild mit dem Namen Kovačič zersprengt haben!*

*The sky is all pink...did you see it?... a whole new color.

**Those are the detonations up in the clouds...

***The walls are shaking, more than yesterday...the ground, too.

****This is all far from over.

*****Of course it's not over.

******Cuckoo? Or not cuckoo?

1914!...soll ich rekapitulieren?..."* "*Nein, Mama!...das ermüdet dich nur, weiter nichts...rekapituliere nichts!...*"** "*Sie haben mich alle verpfiffen!...denunziert! Deutsche! Schweizer! Serben! und alle Atascheen vom jugoslawischen Konsulat...Mich, Vati, euch...*"*** "*Du wirst dich noch krank machen, laß sie doch, sie sind alle schon gestorben!...*"**** "*Meinst du das wirklich?...*"***** "*Ich bin sicher!...*"****** "*Ach, dann ist es gut! ich werde mich ausruhen.*"******* Clairi and I saw her back into bed so she could sleep...I headed to school...there was no agitation out on the street...except for a minor incident outside the grocery store...the leader of a Home Guard patrol...that little blond student with the white-rimmed glasses who had made such an impression on me two years before, at the time Italy capitulated...the way he guffawed and slapped his thighs in glee watching the young storekeeper

*Consider all the things we've been through, Clairi...from Guček...Mrs. Guček! That old bag! Hamm! Bohorič Street! And Mr. Perme with his interest! The Hamman's office, the ghost of Hitler! And the Germans who were our neighbors in the Gerbergasli, who tore down and trampled our shop sign with the name Kovačič on it! In 1914!... shall I go through it for you again?

**No, mother, that will only exhaust you, nothing more...don't go on.

***They all denounced me! Germans, Swiss, Serbs! And the attachés at the Yugoslav consulate...Me, Vati, you kids...

****You're only going to make yourself sick, let them go, they're all long dead.

*****Do you really think so?

******I'm sure of it.

*******Well, then that's that. I can go rest.

throw his wife Katarina out of the house... was now shouting and trying to kick some housewife who had evidently dared to say something to him and was trying to get herself and her broad, baglike rear out of range of his boots... In the course of the day, the bombardments subsided... After lunch at the clinic, Pšeničnik and I headed up toward St. Joseph's to stop by Dr. Tine Debeljak's house... I was bringing him three short stories... "Christmas Eve in Basel"... "August Holiday"... "On a Rhine Steamer"... These were my experiences... they included lots of nature descriptions... The way the snow fell onto the monuments and fountains in Basel... the look of the lawns full of daisies and flowering chestnuts outside the Lange Erlen Zoo... the glasses and glasses of lemonade on the cruise boat when mother and I rode it between both banks of the Rhine under the big bridges toward St. Alban's, and the way mother, who was wearing a white veil with black spots, clutched onto my arm and beseeched me, mortified, "Talk to me so that the sailors stop looking at me that way..." I had also drawn some illustrations... decorative initials for each of the stories that included more credible drawings, so that the editors wouldn't be tempted to replace them with unsuitable clichés... Just wait until I became a writer! It seemed like it was a matter of barely a few years... a few gray, inflated bumps resembling zeppelin ballonets that I would be able to climb over with ease... separating me from the day when I'd write my first book... A supremely precise book, because precision alone was the source of all real beauty... When Lado and I reached the Public Kitchen, Pšeničnik suddenly said, "I'm not going with you to Debeljak's," and without a word of farewell turned off onto

Strossmayer Street and headed downhill, toward the pawnbroker's... I was left standing there, as though I'd just had cold water thrown in my face. "Why not, Lado?" I called after him... He just waved me off without even bothering to turn around. Hm! So I continued on my way alone. At the Children's Home, all the ground-floor and upper-story windows were open, with mattresses hanging out of them, airing... Were they whitewashing the walls, or what?... I felt attached to that gray building and would have been happy to catch a glimpse of Sister Rafaela or at least Kajetana... All you need to know of people is their kindness and restraint... the way it is at the beginning... you shouldn't go probing beyond that, because that's when all sorts of rifts start opening up...

At the house on Zrinjski Street where Dr. Debeljak lived, everything was turned inside out... there were suitcases and crates placed in the garden and on the sidewalk... the lights were on in the middle of the day... A few people... some lady and a few boys showed me the way from the foyer... were those his wife and children? I entered a round room with books up to the ceiling and a huge desk... The library... nothing but books everywhere, even stacked up on the floor and the chairs... Dr. Tine Debeljak, wearing a short-sleeved shirt, was getting ready to leave... carrying books and packing them into boxes and crates... the telephone was constantly ringing... regarding some car that was going to wait for him at such and such a place. A bulb in its yellow lampshade cast a faint light from the ceiling, and the curtains were drawn... "How can you see a thing, Dr. Debeljak?" I said. "Why don't you open the curtains and windows?..." He was putting away some books that kept tipping over at the edge of his huge desk. "If I open them, I could be seen and shot…" he said…"Let's sit down for a minute." He sat down and adjusted his thick, black-rimmed glasses…"I'm leaving, I'm going away," he said. "I want you to have a good life…" "I've brought you three short stories to read," I said…"I can't take them now. Bring them by when we come back." He offered me his hand when we got to the door…it was dripping with sweat. "Take care of yourself!…of your soul." I went outside…and I never saw him again…it wasn't until twenty years ago that I heard for the first time that he was living somewhere in Argentina…I sensed he was fleeing, and I knew how hard it was to have to emigrate…He was a kind person, and the way he behaved was infused with a warmth from inside. Something like that fortifies you, it lifts you up and gives you the same sort of feeling that a beautiful work of art does…the world becomes your gift again, with or without the fire in which everything goes to blazes…Decency, that's it…that's the sort of atmosphere I'd like to live in…but it's so rare that we ought to set down a milestone for every day when it's granted to us…

It was cloudy outside, despite the fact that it was May…and there was some agitation…I had the impression that inside the houses along the Ljubljanica…in the Red House…people were whispering out loud, as though they were speaking through tubes…the voices sounded unclear, yet they had an odd sort of logic…But there was nobody in the courtyards, even though you could hear voices there, as though people were talking out in front of the house, on the embankment. But then, back out on the street there wasn't a soul, or at least nobody was talking. Had I started to hear things? Was my head no longer quite right, like mother's? I held my hands over my ears... the voices went away...and when I dropped my hands, they started in again...a sort of *mur-mur-mur-mur-mur*...Were the people in the houses getting ready for something...were they issuing commands? weapons?...

There were only a few people around the Prešeren Monument... suddenly, from the direction of the post office, I heard...*clickety! clack! clickety! clack!*...it was a hay wagon!...and there were three German soldiers...with no ammuntion belts or weapons...pulling it!...one by the tongue, two pushing from behind...on the otherwise empty wagon, they were transporting nothing more than their backpacks!... like three young fanatics, they rattled their wagon at a trot across St. Mary's Square...and then across the Triple Bridge...Yet another debacle! It was only at these times that you realized that everything that had endured until now was suddenly, like lightning, history...I watched the Germans recede, until they vanished behind the old regional offices...When I turned back around, next to the steps leading down to the men's public toilet under the Triple Bridge I noticed a bag leaned up against the bridge railing...a bag filled with little yellow gunpowder tabs...exactly like the ones that were strewn all over the place in the garrison courtyard during the looting of the quartermaster barracks in 1941!...People used them then to light bonfires so they could see better as they selected and loaded their loot. And here I'd run across them again! Can you imagine? Such kitschy coincidences are possible only in real life and in dreams...Now I knew that the war really was over.

I immediately picked up the bag...it didn't appear to be anyone's...
you could have a lot of fun with those little gunpowder tabs...If you
shook them out and lit one end of a long line of them...you got regular Fu Manchu dominos!...Gisela would sure have fun with that!...
I hurried down the embankment toward home...when suddenly,
out of the Kolmans' entryway...Firant barged out. Just what I needed!..."Hey, hey!" he hollered..."Where you goin'?" he said, planting
his feet in my way and studying me with those deep-set eyes beneath his
round forehead...Oh, he knew perfectly well how I felt...but he was a
regular devil!...the vilest thoughts would shoot through his brain in
an instant, like gossip between salesladies at the market. "What's that
you've got?"..."Gunpowder tabs." I took out two or three packages...
each of which had five tabs bound together with a rubber band...and
gave them to him. "Thanks!..." I asked him what was new...A patrol
from Old Square had shot some guy in the leg...That was low down!
"Aw, it won't be for much longer, a few hours at most...and then they'll
get their comeuppance!...and your people, too!..." He was right, we
were marked persons...there was no point in my hanging out with him
any longer, it would only rile him up that much more...I gave him two
more packages from out of the bag. "*Heil! Heil!*" he said...I made my
way quickly through so-called Carpenters' Lane..."*Heil, Bubi! Heil!*"
he kept shouting after me...It was true, he was filled with hatred up
to the brim! and that SA gendarme, too! and the merchant's little kid,
Robert! and Rosa Weinberg! and Dr. Debeljak!...not to mention the
four-eyes from the patrol! all of them...Firant...after Hirol, he'd be
the first person demanding that they line all four of us up against a

wall…he wouldn't rest until he saw me dead…I hid the bag in the entryway, so as not to upset my folks…But when I got upstairs, they were already beside themselves…*"Wo warst du die ganze Zeit! Was ist passiert?"* * Clairi burst out angrily, while Gisela threw herself around my neck…They'd spent the whole afternoon pacing the workroom, waiting for me and wondering where I was…what had happened to me…It was only six p.m. and the day was still bright…but the streets were silent and empty, as if extinct…Clairi was horrified…*"Die Mama ist ganz plemplem! Sie singt den ganzen Nachmittag schon…'Morgenrot, Morgenrot, leuchtet mir zum frühen Tod'…Bubi, jetzt müssen wir Wasser holen für die Nacht, bevor es dunkel wird, sonst wird der Hirol gottweisswas noch anstellen…"* ** So I went to fetch water…*"Und jetzt noch alle ins Kloset. Und dann sperren wir ab!…"* *** In the bedroom, mother woke up from the noise…She stood on the bed and made signs in front of her face with her hands, which gave us a good scare…*"Setz dich, Mama! Du gehst mir auf die Nerven!"* **** Clairi said…*"Du und nur du hast mir ein Schrecken eingejagt!"* *****…mother said…*"Heute nacht wird etwas passieren,"* Clairi

*Where have you been all this time? What happened?

**Mother is completely off her rocker, she's been singing all afternoon…"Break of day, break of day, light me on my final way"…Bubi, we've got to fetch water for overnight now, before it gets dark, or else who knows what Hirol is going to do to us.

***Now everybody make one last trip to the toilet, and then we'll lock the door.

****Sit down, mother. You're making me nervous.

*****You and nobody else but you scared the daylights out of me.

said. *"Wir müssen die Komode vor die Tür schieben..."* * *"Aber zuerst gehe ich mit der Mama noch hinunter..."* ** When she brought mother back from the toilet, Clairi said, *"Jetzt aber die Komode..."* *** She and I shoved the dresser up against the door...it almost came apart...as the floor of the workroom tugged against its spherical feet...*"Es ist am besten, wenn wir uns heute Nacht nicht ausziehen,"* Clairi said. *"Nur die Schuhe..."* **** Mother was humming in the bedroom.

"*Drüben am Wiesenrand hocken zwei Dohlen,*
Sterb' ich in Feindesland, fall' ich in Polen..." *****

"Mama, du fasselst wieder," ****** Clairi called out to her. *"Laß sie doch,"* ******* I said. Mother went on singing. It was my favorite song in German, one that had always moved me. *"Mama, hör auf!"* ******** Clairi said, crying..."*Laß sie dabei...es ist besser, wenn sie etwas tut oder singt..."* ********* I said. Those same droning voices were audible all through the night...

---

*Something's going to happen tonight. We need to push the dresser up against the door.

**But first I'll make one last trip downstairs with mother.

***Now let's move that dresser.

****It's best if we don't take our clothes off tonight. Only our shoes.

*****At the edge of the meadow, two jackdaws are crowing / If I should fall to the foe, if I perish in Poland.

******Mother, you're being strange again.

*******Leave her alone.

********Mother, stop!

*********Let her be. It's better if she has something to do or sing.

mur-mur-mur-mur...on the other side of the wall in the place where the dresser normally stood, beyond which you could always hear everything that was happening outside...I was impatient and could barely wait until morning. Mother kept singing on and off...Things always come easier if you shift into a different role...

December 1983